Praise for

The Coldest Winter Ever

"Souljah, an Emile Zola of the hip-hop generation, has written a naturalist novel of a world without redemption. Her story, like the cultures it exposes, is an unflinching eye at the truth."

—Walter Mosley

"Souljah adds a new voice to the most marginalized of the marginalized."

—*Black Issues Book Review*

"[C]ompelling . . . tugs at the emotions."

—*Chicago Sun-Times*

"I think she is an important voice in American literature, and I find her work spiritually rewarding and powerful."

—Jada Pinkett Smith

"[E]ngaging . . . a fast, fun read."

—*The Plain Dealer* (Cleveland, OH)

"This is a wild tale . . . a vivid portrait of a girl you'd rather have as a friend than an enemy."

—*Seventeen*

"Real and raw. . . . If a rap song could be a novel, it might resemble [this] book."

—*Booklist*

"This is a ghetto fairy tale with a surprise ending. . . . There's a lesson to be learned from *The Coldest Winter Ever*."

—*The Tennessean*

"[A] tour de force."

—*Kirkus Reviews*

THE
COLDEST
WINTER
EVER

THE
COLDEST
WINTER
EVER

A NOVEL

SISTER
SOULJAH

EMILY BESTLER BOOKS

ATRIA

New York   London   Toronto   Sydney   New Delhi

EMILY
BESTLER
BOOKS

ATRIA

An Imprint of Simon & Schuster, Inc.
1230 Avenue of the Americas
New York, NY 10020

This book is a work of fiction. Names, characters, places, and incidents either are products of the author's imagination or are used fictitiously. Any resemblance to actual events or locales or persons, living or dead, is entirely coincidental.

First Emily Bestler Books / Atria Paperback edition September 2005

EMILY BESTLER BOOKS/ATRIA PAPERBACK and colophon are registered trademarks of Simon & Schuster, Inc.

For information about special discounts for bulk purchases, please contact Simon & Schuster Special Sales at 1-866-506-1949 or business@simonandschuster.com

Printed and bound by CPI Group (UK) Ltd, Croydon, CR0 4YY

47

ISBN 978-0-7434-9938-5
ISBN 978-0-7432-7010-6 (pbk)
ISBN 978-1-4391-1997-6 (ebook)

DEDICATION

There is no such thing as love anymore,
the kind that is so strong
that you can feel it in your bones.
You know we used to feel that emotion
when we looked into the faces of our mother,
father, sisters, brothers, family and friends.

There is no such thing as love anymore.
At least not the deep satisfying kind
that sits on your heart and influences every
decision and action we take throughout each day.

There is no reason to celebrate anymore.
Just empty actions and empty reactions,
calculated gestures and financial arrangements.
There is no such thing as love anymore . . .

This novel is dedicated to the era in which we live.
The era in which love, loyalty, truth, honor and respect died.
Where humility and appreciation are nonexistent.
Where families are divided and God reviled,
The era.
The Coldest Winter Ever.

By Sister Souljah

THANK YOU

Serving Mother God and Father God, first, always
and forever.

Loyalty, respect, love and strength to my husband
and son.

A very special thanks to Tracy Sherrod.

Thanks for your professional services:
Judith Curr, Emily Bestler, Paolo Pepe.

THE
COLDEST
WINTER
EVER

1

I never liked Sister Souljah, straight up. She the type of female I'd like to cut in the face with my razor. Before I get heated just talking about her, let me make it clear who I am and where I stand. Don't go jumping to any conclusions either. All of y'all are too quick to jump to her defense without knowing what somebody up close and personal thinks. When it comes right down to it, those are the ones who really count, the people who was there, who seen it all. Hell, you can't smell nobody's breath through a camera. You almost can't even see their pimples. So you know that TV shit ain't real. Don't run ahead of me. Let me take my time and tell my story.

Brooklyn-born I don't have no sob stories for you about rats and roaches and pissy-pew hallways. I came busting out of my momma's big coochie on January 28, 1977, during one of New York's worst snowstorms. So my mother named me Winter. My father, Ricky Santiaga, was so proud of his new baby girl that he had a limo waiting to pick my moms up from the hospital. The same night I got home my pops gave me a diamond ring set in 24-karat gold. My moms said that my fingers were too small and soft to even hold a ring in place, but he insisted that he had a guy who would have it adjusted just right. It was important for me to know I deserved the best, no slum jewelry, cheap shoes, or knock-off designer stuff, only the real thing.

We lived in the projects but we were cool with that. We weren't wanting for a damn thing. I had three aunts, four uncles, and a whole slew of cousins. As far as we were concerned it was live for all of us to be chilling in the same building, or at least the next building over. We never had to worry about getting into fights because around our way we had reputation. Plus it was plain and simple common sense. If you put your hands on anybody in the family you would get jumped by the next oldest person in our family, and so on and so on. Sooner than later we didn't even have to say a word. Everybody understood that our family had the neighborhood locked down, it wasn't worth the trouble.

Our apartment in the projects was dipped. We had royal red carpets on the floors, top-of-the-line furniture, a fully loaded entertainment center, equipment, and all that good stuff. I loved my pops with a passion. He was the smoothest nigga in the world. When he came into a room he made a difference. His cologne came around the corner introducing him before you could even see him. He spoke softly, with deep seriousness. He was light-skinned, tall, with curly black hair and a fine thin mustache to match. He was medium build, definitely in shape. The thing that stood out about him was his style. His clothes were crisp-expensive. He never wore the same shirt twice. He could do it like that 'cause he was smart. He never used the drugs he sold. He collected his money on time and made examples of any fool who tried to cheat him. He had a saying: One copper penny, one finger.

All the ladies loved him but he wasn't what I would call a ladies' man. He never had no girlfriend, at least no female ever called the house trying to front on my moms. I can't recall any incidents involving other women, accusations or any uncomfortableness. He was a family man. Everybody in the whole world knew my moms was his wife, his one and only, his soft spot even. Moms and Pops had been young lovers and, unlike a whole lot of niggas, they stayed together. She was fourteen when she had me. Folks said she looked great during pregnancy and would switch her ass around the neighborhood flowing easy, like water. She would wear her fine Italian leather stiletto heels even in her seventh month. Moms had everything by the way of clothes and anything else you could think of. Her mahogany skin was smooth as a Hershey's chocolate bar. When she went anywhere she was well coordinated. If she had on a zebra skin hat, she'd sport the zebra skin pants and would have a zebra skin pattern on all ten nails. She'd even have the Victoria's Secret zebra pattern panties and camisole. What separated her from every other woman any of us knew was she just had so much class. While the others were putting their imitation leather and zebra skins on layaway, piece by piece, Momma wouldn't be caught dead without her shit perfectly arranged. By the time hoes sported their outfits all their shit was played out, straight out of style. When it came to shopping Momma had no mercy and that's the way Santiaga liked it. His woman was supposed to be the showstopper. Momma didn't work 'cause beauty, she said, was a full-time occupation that left no room for anything else. She'd sit at her vanity table for three hours making sure she positioned each extra long lash on just right. She'd argue with anyone who said she wasn't born with those lashes that framed her big, wide brown eyes that were gorgeous with or without falsies. She made it clear to me that beautiful women are supposed to be taken care of. She would whisper in my ear, "I'm just a bad bitch!"

Now a bad bitch is a woman who handles her business without making it seem like business. Only dumb girls let love get them delirious to the point where they let things that really count go undone. For example, you see a good-looking nigga walking down the avenue, you get excited. You get wet just thinking about him. You step to him, size him up, and you think, *Looks good.* You slide you eyes down to his zipper, check for the print. Inside you scream, *Yes, it's all there!* But then you realize he's not wearing a watch, ain't carrying no car keys, no jewels, and he's sporting last month's sneakers. He's broke as hell. A bad bitch realizes that she has two options: (1) She can take him home and get her groove on just to enjoy the sex and don't get emotionally involved because he can't afford her; or (2) She can walk away and leave his broke ass standing right there. Having a relationship is out. Getting emotionally involved is out. Taking him seriously is out. If a bad bitch is extra slick she can keep this guy on the side for the good sex. He then becomes a commercial to the money man who is the main program. The money man is the guy who knows how to provide, knows how to bring home the goodness and bless his woman with everything she wants. Now the money man might not be ringing any bells sexually, but if he has ends—if his pockets are heavy—a bad bitch will moan like this nigga is the original Casanova. When he's sexing her, she'll shake, pant, and cry out like he's creating orgasms as strong as ocean waves. Now Moms must have been a bad bitch because she had it both ways. She had the money man with the good looks, loyalty, and I know Pops was laying it down in the bedroom.

Moms got her hair done once every three days. The shop we went to, 'cause she always took me, was for the high rollers' girls. These were the few women in the neighborhood who are able to hook the big money fish. They all went to this shop to get their hair done, nails did, and, more importantly, to show off and update on shit going on. Earline's was where we could get our hair done while we collected information on the side.

By the time I was seven I understood the rules perfectly. Keep the family's business quiet. Most things were better left unsaid. Even though this was the high rollers' hair shop, we were clear that motherfuckers were jealous of us. My Pops's operation was steadily building. As a young guy he started off as a lookout but was so sharp that now he has organized his own thing. He has his own workers and whatnot. People knew he was headed to being the next Big Willie by his style. He was respected for his product, which was never watered down, always a fair cut for your money. So me and my moms would catch those jealous glances, but we threw those shits right back. Our attitude toward other females was: "Hey, your man works for my Pops, now bow down to the family who puts food on the table for you and yours."

Santiaga was the number one businessman in our area by the time I was thirteen, running thangs. Although he taught me never to sweat the small stuff, it seemed like every move he made he thought about carefully. I would hear his key unlocking the first door into our apartment. Then the men he was with, his workers, they would stand in the limited space between the first door and the heavy metal second door that actually led into our place, and talk. After they handled their matters you would hear the first door open, then slam again. Pops would lock it and then unlock the second door to come inside. Whatever pressure he felt, whatever weight or business he had was left in between those two doors because when he came inside he brought his sexy smile, excited eyes, and power along with him.

He would show us all love. He would have whatever any of us had asked him for in his pocket no matter how small the request, down to a Snickers bar. If any of us had a problem of any kind, we could ask him and he'd make the answer so simple that I'd wonder how I couldn't of figured it out myself.

If something was on his mind, he'd go in the back to a private room he had Woody the carpenter build and pull out his chessboard. Funny thing was, he wouldn't play with anybody, just against himself. When I'd ask him why, he'd say, "That's how I stay on top baby. I look at life from every position. I play from every side. You gotta know what each man on the board is thinking down to the littlest motherfucker like the pawn."

Now Daddy would explain that other players are quick to sacrifice or ignore the pawn, but he was too smart for that. "The pawns are my soldiers," he would say. "If I surround myself with strong soldiers, give them all a stake in the game, then they keep the hood strong and tight." He would look into my eyes as if to ask do I understand. I didn't want him to know that I dig him so much that I'd listen to him for as long as he wanted to talk, but I didn't give a fuck about a game of chess. He would break down how around our way there were always some young kids tryna "spread their wings" and test his operation. He said they mostly stupid though 'cause no smart guy is gonna try to kick in the door of the big man unless he got an extra tight, professional, strong, and ruthless crew. But every now and then some dumb-ass young kid who had seen too many *Scarface*-type movies will try to overtake what can only kill him. "He loses," Santiaga said, knocking the black king over on the chessboard. "He loses because he never understood the game."

The up-and-coming dealers on the block was Santiaga's number two problem. I was his number one. He loved me like crazy but was getting nervous about the way men, young and old, was checking for me. It was amazing how in one year, from age twelve to thirteen, my titties sprouted. I even had the ass to match. I don't know who was more excited, the men or me. I was walking around poking my stuff out in any direction that looked good to me. But anybody who stared my way for more than a few seconds was in danger of catching a critical beat down. Pops had already made an example of at least two niggas around my way. Santiaga sliced this one dude from his left ear to his right ear. We call that kind of cut a "hospital run." But this guy never got to go to the hospital. Santiaga let his blood gush out until Doc got to our apartment. Now Doc ain't really no doctor, he just had some medical training in the army. Santiaga calls him when he don't need the police and hospital buttin' around in his business. Well when Doc got finished with dude his cut just bubbled up all the way across his face. Everybody in the neighborhood started calling him Bubbles for that ugly scar. Bubbles's crime was looking at me with lust in his eyes while he was supposed to be installing the safe in our apartment. Now Bubbles was a walking billboard that no one is allowed to fuck with Santiaga's daughter. After that we got the second metal door installed in our apartment and none of Daddy's "workers" were ever allowed past that door again.

Now Moms thought Santiaga's ways was overboard. She told him she was just gonna get me some birth control pills and let me go, 'cause "When a woman wants to get fucked, she gets fucked. She gets fucked whether it's in a car or a closet."

Suggestions like this just got Santiaga more crazy. He made it clear to Moms, "Winter is not a woman yet. None of these lowlifes are gonna make a trick outta my flesh and blood." Pops would pull me to the side, grab my shoulders with his strong hands and firm grip, stare into my eyes, and tell me slowly, "Only a hardworking man, a sharp thinker who doesn't hesitate to do what he gotta do, to get you what you need to have, deserves you."

He repeated that lesson often. I would think to myself, *Hmm, only Poppa fits that description.* Now I loved Poppa but I hated the way he cock-blocked. Every teenage girl wants to cut loose and get close to the fire, but I was like a pot of boiling milk with the lid on. You know that's ready to explode and slide down the side of the pan.

So my peeps kept me busy by giving me things to do all the time. I had to watch my baby sisters Mercedes and Lexus, the twins. They was a real pain in the ass at eight months old. Then I had to look out for my other little sister Porsche, who was four. She wasn't half bad since she didn't shit all over all the time. Sometimes the three of them kids together got on my nerves so bad they almost made me want to go to school. But my policy was to go to school just enough so the authorities wouldn't kick me out. If I had a new outfit to show off or some new jewels I knew I'd get sweated for, fine, but I wasn't gonna report to school every day like it was some type of job when they weren't even paying me for it. School was like a hustle. Teachers wanted me to come to school so they could get paid to control me. What do I get out of the deal? Enough said, I just wasn't having it.

As busy as they kept me, there was Midnight. I guess he got that name because midnight was about the only thing blacker than him. He was one of my father's workers. He was real serious like my father. He always looked like he was thinking deep thoughts and had a lot on his mind. I figured maybe he had a plan to take over the world. I liked that because he would need to own the world to win me. He never smiled. He didn't joke around like other niggas in our age group. He did his pickups and deliveries like clockwork. My father once referred to him as a strong young lieutenant. Santiaga liked him because he said he never tried to test or flex. He knew Santiaga was the boss and he was comfortable and cool with that. Midnight never attempted to skim, pay late, or run games, like some guys did when they first started out.

I liked Midnight for other reasons too. In the summertime he wore white when he played basketball. His mother, or whoever washed his clothes, must have been more handy than them happy homemakers on the TV commercials 'cause his shit was crisp. But what really got me was that black skin. It was smooth and perfect. It laid on top of his bone structure tight like Saran Wrap. His arms were cut. I could tell he lifted weights. But he wasn't all big and swollen like those little-dick assholes in the magazines. He was tall, yet medium-sized, and perfect. His muscles were defined, his veins stuck out, emphasizing his strengths. His neck was slim and strong. He would come to the park only on Sundays. I know because I was clocking him like that. He would be wearing a new sweat suit everytime. He held his money in a gold money clip. He would take the money clip, with the money neatly stacked, out of his sweat pants pocket. He'd take off his pants, stripping down to the basketball shorts he had on underneath. His powerful legs were as cut as his upper body. For this I gave him mad respect. I can't tell you how many guys I've seen with strong upper bodies and legs like a chicken. He would put that money clip on the inside of his basketball shorts and play ball. My eyes would move in and out of his structure. I couldn't wait to put my lips against his skin and maybe even suck his collarbone or something. To make the package complete, Midnight's kicks were always new and clean.

Now Midnight never paid me no mind. I wasn't worried about it though, 'cause one thing I learned from my mother is a bad bitch gets what she wants if she works her shit right. Pops also taught me something useful about patience. He said sometimes a victory is sweeter when it takes a long time to carry out the plan, and you catch the person completely off guard. What I was up against was the fact that Midnight worked for my pops. So, even if he had ever considered me, he probably ruled me out. He was *five* years older than me. So, he might have also considered me jailbait. The worst thing about it was that I couldn't tell either way. You know how they say a person's face is a dead giveaway? Well Midnight was the opposite. His face seems serious all the time. His reactions just didn't show up. Even when he plays ball, he didn't talk trash like the other niggas. He didn't even react when they try to mess with him. He just seemed focused on the basket, made his moves, scored his jumpers, and didn't even smile when he won. At first, to get his attention I did the regular things like rocking my skirts extra mini, shortening my already short shorts, sporting halter tops and cute little metallic bras. As I got sexier, he went from looking at me almost never to never looking at me at all. While in his presence, or at least when I was in the same park he was in watching him play ball, I would try to get his attention by acting mad. I'd suck my teeth, roll my eyes at him, still nothing. So I decided to make him a long-shot project.

Meanwhile I had my own fun stuff going on. I would let niggas take me to the movies, or should I say I went to the movies with my girl-friends and met niggas there, not wanting to ruffle Santiaga's feathers by bringing a "worthless nigga" home. Sometimes we would just chill at my girl Natalie's apartment. Her moms was never home so we had free run of the place.

Getting my first sugar daddy was no problem. His name was Ster-ling. I met him in lower Manhattan at a grocery market when I ran in to get some Chap Stick on a fickle autumn morning. I guess my style just overwhelmed him 'cause instead of reaching into the cash register and giving me my damn change his eyes were sliding in between my breasts like he wished he could be one of my gold chains. I recognized him immediately as a sucker, somebody I could take for all he had. All his thoughts showed on his face. It was clear that I had his full attention as I gave him a blast of ghetto attitude. I put my hands on my hips, say-ing, "My money or your life?" He looked startled, stopped staring, and counted out my change. I laughed.

"Do you need your receipt?" he asked with his enthusiastic corny ass trying to prolong the conversation.

"If that's all you have to offer," I said with a serious look sprinkled with sexiness. He gave me my money, and cleared his throat, turned from the register with his cheap white dress shirt and two-dollar tie, and followed me as I walked toward the door. I guess he had it like that. He could walk away from the register because he was the store manager.

"So what's your name?" he asked, looking like he thought he could actually make some progress with me.

"Winter," I said, rolling my eyes with disinterest.

"You live around here?"

"Brooklyn baby!! No doubt."

The rest is history. He got paid every two weeks and so did I. He worked at the store and I worked on him. I had him buying me shit he couldn't afford. We ate at places he never knew existed. Whatever little money he took home in pay, I took my 25 percent like I was his freakin' agent or something. It worked out smooth, him living in Manhattan out of Santiaga's eyesight. Besides, the little piece of cash he provided meant a new outfit, an extra gold bangle to my collection, whatever—like mom says, you can never have too much.

Santiaga shook up what was supposed to be my sweet sixteenth with shocking news. We were all around the table. My chocolate Baskin-Robbins ice-cream cake was bombarded with small nuts and sixteen carefully placed maraschino cherries. Daddy handed me a long slim box, the kind I like because it almost always means jewelry. I tore off the gold wrapping paper and smiled wildly as I lifted my new diamond tennis bracelet off of the clean white cotton. My mother's mouth hung open as she inspected my diamonds from across the table. Even though she knew better, she was confirming that they were white, clear, and sparkled like diamonds, not cubic zirconias.

As I put the bracelet on, Santiaga handed me a birthday card. This was unusual because we weren't big on cards and poetry and shit like that in my family. As I fumbled with the catch on my bracelet, my mom opened the card, suspecting I guess that there must be some birthday money in it or something. She probably figured that if I got cash in addition to this bracelet Santiaga had gone overboard again, and would need a talking to later on. As she opened the card two Polaroid snapshots fell out and onto the table. She picked it up, twisted up her face with curiosity and said, "Baby, what is this?"

"It's our new house in Long Island," Daddy said coolly with pride and confidence. "I wanted to surprise everybody and I figured today was as good as any day. We're moving! First class baby! Only the best, top shelf for the ladies in my life." I was feeling crazy. The gold candles on my cake melted away and so did my dreams under the pressure of the flickering fire.

All I knew was the projects. It was where my friends, family, and all my great adventures were. I knew these streets like I knew the curves of my own body. I was like the princess of these alleyways, back staircases, and whatnot. What was the point of moving? Santiaga always said you gotta live where business is to avoid a hostile takeover. He said that a man gotta carry a powerful presence in his neighborhood so the small-timers didn't start itching with takeover fever. Now it was like we was cutting out. So I did something that I normally would not do. I questioned Santiaga.

"Why? What's the point? Why are we about to do something that you said we would never do?"

Santiaga simply said, "Baby girl, things is on a new level. It was cool to rest my head here in the past. But my business is bigger and better than ever. I can't let them get too familiar with the routine. I gotta switch up, keep 'em guessing." Me, Momma, and Porsche were all seated stiff and silent. The babies didn't know what the fuck was going on. Surprise swirled around, strangling us. He continued, "Everyone can't handle my success. Eventually some fool will snap out of order and try to bring it to me by hurting one of my girls." His long finger pointed at us. His eyes locked into each of our eyes individually. He was making good sense but I was still vexed. I figured, *yeah sounds good and all but I'm not down with the idea of running from a fight.* It's just straight up not Santiaga style.

Santiaga picked up on my expression quickly and said, "Now you know I don't run from no war. I'll take on anybody who wants to bring it to me! But what I'm not having is nobody fucking with my ladies. If they want war, let it be man to man, and only the men." It seemed like Santiaga knew something he wasn't telling us. He was dead serious and I knew that his statements were coming from somewhere. "This place," he added, holding up the picture, his finger pointing out the mansion, "this is a safe place. Man, wait till you see it. Shit, is laid out so nice it's like heaven."

The rules for our move out of Brooklyn were clear and nonnegotiable. Don't talk about it. We knew no matter how silent we were, there would still be chatter. My mother's brothers and sisters, and their husbands and boyfriends, who all worked for Poppa, would definitely have something to say. That didn't matter, Santiaga said, "I'll take care of everything. Just don't add to it."

In my last few days everything was moving like in a slow-motion film. Shit that stank, stank more. Anything sweet seemed even sweeter. I spent all my extra time with my girls. We were mad tight, many of us born and raised in this same spot. Take me and Natalie for instance, we did everything together. We even got our cherries busted together and lied to each other about how good the first time felt, when the truth was those big dicks ripped our tight little twelve-year-old tunnels apart. We fought over whose date was finer, even though Jamal and Jacob were twins! But I knew Jamal was cuter 'cause he had a fine black mole on his right cheek and that shit was sexy. Natalie said Jamal was the one who made my titties grow, 'cause after me and him started "getting down" I went from flat-chested to all eyes on me!

When my girl Toshi had beef with these chicks from around the corner, me, Nat, Zakia, Simone, Monique, Reese, all of us took off our jewels, greased up our faces, braided down our hair, and had our razors under our tongues ready to go to war. Before blows could be thrown or razors spitted out the big doofy girl from the other crew, who was s'pose to scare us, shouted out, "Yo, that's Santiaga's daughter. You crazy, I ain't fucking with her." Then the chicks we was supposed to be fighting started fighting each other 'cause some of them wanted to fight and some of them didn't. So we started running toward them. We charged thoses bitches and they flew. We ran till we got tired and cracked up laughing at how stupid they were. I know one thing, they never fucked with Toshi again.

We blew trees together then got so hungry we ate four family-size bags of nacho cheese Doritos and watched our girl Asia, the only chubby one in our crew, throw up from the bellyache. Hell, we went from patent leather shoes at five-year-old birthday parties, to match-ing tomboy outfits and brawls, to fighting over whose titties were bigger.

Chanté, who was older than us, taught us all the sexual positions. She let us watch while she got down with boys when her mother was at work. She liked the idea of being our "teacher." She even taught us how to suck a dick.

We had our first beef patties and coco bread, bun'n cheese and ginger beer together 'cause our girl Carmen was from Jamaica and used to take us to the spot where the dreds chilled out. She taught us how to dance like the Jamaican winders by moving our bodies slow and sexy like caterpillars. But none of us took fashion tips from her 'cause her gear was out of this world.

There wasn't nothing that we hadn't been through, including going to the funeral for Nique whose mother pushed her off the roof after she found out her man had been fucking her daughter. I was gonna miss BK, the music, the vibe, the hot dogs, and mostly the streets. It didn't matter what no one said, Brooklyn is the shit, number one in my heart.

No one was supposed to know we were leaving. But on our last day

there, Natalie, who had a way of finding out all and any dirt on anybody, said to me out of the blue, "I'm tryna get my mother to get our
long distance turned back on so I can make long-distance calls." When
we parted, she said, "Stay real, don't switch up on us, bitch."

We left in the evening. The whole thing was casual like we were
going out to dinner or some shit like that. We didn't take nothing with
us 'cause Santiaga said we didn't need it.

2

Oohs and aahs were the only sounds anybody could hear as my three little sisters were completely won over by the drive through the fancy big-money Long Island neighborhoods. As my dad's Lexus zoomed up the winding tree-lined driveway, the clean snow dropped onto the car windows, adding to their amazement.

The way I figured it they were young so they were quick to betray Brooklyn. The huge doors to our new home looked more expensive than our entire old apartment. The warmth in the house invited us in, yet and still Santiaga lit the fireplace. More like a museum, there was enough space in this joint to fit seven or so families. It was so wide we could even park our cars indoors if we wanted. The floors were made of white marble, huge three foot by three foot squares, to hell with tiles and linoleum. Momma sprawled out on top of the white mink rug that Poppa had laid out in front of the fireplace. The way she sunk into that fur and the way her eyes were twice their normal size made me know we were here to stay. The icing for Momma was when Santiaga said, "It's all for you to decorate any way that you like."

For an entire month we went through catalogs and magazines, mail-ordered shit, and received deliveries that Santiaga arranged. Santiaga was so live that he had a guy who could make whatever he wanted to happen, happen. Designers, carpenters, locksmiths, tailors, you name it, they came when he called. They gave him respect, tried to keep their eyes from roaming around Santiaga's home. You could see them shaken by Poppa's power. Although I wanted to be in Brooklyn, I could see that this is the way a man like Santiaga is supposed to live. What we considered to be high quality before wasn't nothing compared to now. But those slim corridors in the Brooklyn projects—where the smell of fried chicken collided with the smell of codfish and ackee, then got drowned out by the smell of liquor—still had my name on it.

The silence in the Long Island mansion was killing me. You

couldn't just open the window, yell downstairs, and find out what's jumping off later that night. The reality was that for the most part, in this area where we lived, nothing jumped off, period! The whole idea of next-door neighbors was dead. Forget borrowing a cup of sugar, a few cigarettes, or whatever. You'd have to walk what seemed like a mile just to get to the next house. Even then you wouldn't be tryna borrow shit from them 'cause, hell, you don't know them from jack and they don't know you. Your ass is black, they old and white and the bottom line around these parts is you're just expected to have your own shit and not borrow anything anyway. Now I don't want to lie to you, there were some blacks in the neighborhood but they asses was so uptight. I figured if I asked them a question they'd want me to pay for the answer.

When I registered at the new school I knew that I would be spending even less time there than I had at my other school. There was just nothing live about it. Plus it's bullshit moving anywhere when you're already a teenager. By this time everybody is all paired off, grouped up, friendships cemented. You'll look like an ass tryna link up with some-body's clique when you don't even know nobody in the whole circle. So I decided why fake it when it's not even worth it.

Now every girl needs company. Trying to figure out how to meet a young nigga out here was like a fucking brainteaser. It wasn't like people was walking outside on the streets like in Brooklyn. Here I could put on a Chanel suit, stand on the corner, and meet nothing but the wind and maybe even get a ticket for loitering. I had my driver's license now but it didn't matter. We had one car, the Lexus, and it was Santiaga's. He promised Mom she was next in line to get her car. I was sure that after her car came mine, but who knew how long that was gonna take. Santiaga had to hook everything up just right so as not to bring too much attention on himself with too many big purchases.

After a while, me and my moms were going stir crazy. But we were the only ones disappointed. My little sister's room was so big it was like a separate apartment. Even the twins were having a ball because they had plenty of space to tear up in. At the rate they were moving, we joked that our part-time housekeeper, a little Spanish woman named Magdalena, would be quitting any minute now.

"What good is all of this, baby, if I can't show it off? I need my family to share in what you have given us." Momma's words were never ignored by Poppa. Once she lured him into the bedroom she would get what she wanted. Soon Santiaga agreed to allow Mommy to throw regular Saturday night parties. Invitations were limited to carefully selected friends and family. Santiaga spared them no luxury. They ate like pigs, drank the liquor from our bar, and powdered their noses with the cane available in candy dishes usually reserved for jelly beans. They partied every weekend and stayed at our house so late that some of them were at our breakfast table on Sunday morning. These parties excited my mother and added the necessary spice to our new boring Long Island life. She got to show off her house, furniture, and all that good shit. If certain people were skeptical about giving us props before, they had to now 'cause our shit was official. Nobody from our neighborhood could lie and say that they had what we had. From the way their eyes popped open when they first came to the house, we could tell they had never been in nobody's house that compared to ours.

These parties did nothing for me though. Point blank, I wasn't invited. Even though I was sixteen, Santiaga couldn't get it through his head that I was growing up. Inside I think he figured if he treated me like a little girl I'd remain one. Somehow he thought he treated me better than any man claiming to love me would. So, that should be enough for me. But it wasn't enough.

So I learned to work around Santiaga's ways. First I found the bus stop. That may sound simple but believe me it took real detective work. It was about a mile and a half from our house. I took the bus to the mall. That's when I realized where everybody in Long Island is, at the mall! I cased the place just to see what stores they had up there. They passed my quality test. Coach store, yes, Versace yes, and of course Ralph Lauren, and Joan and David shoes. My heart rushed as I shopped. I spotted a few cuties, but not exactly my type of men. They had the blank sort of look in their face, not aggressive enough the way I liked 'em. Trust me, though, they didn't have to look no particular way to eat my pussy, and right about now that's exactly how I wanted to relieve my tension. So I sipped a chocolate malt, bought myself a designer T-shirt, hooked it up the way I wanted it, and smiled quietly to myself.

Saturday morning I prepared to fulfill my baby-sitting obligations. I dressed the twins in their matching Hilfiger jumpers and crisp new kicks. I did their hair up nice in some grown-up styles. I had on my tight brown suede pants. My brown suede jacket, brown leather shoes, and my Versace sunglasses. I put on my new custom-made designer T-shirt. I snatched up their little hands and headed to the mall, where I was sure there would be something exciting for each of us to get into.

By the end of the day, the twins had managed to rearrange their hairdos and decorate their jumpers with spilled hot cocoa. I could not believe that I didn't meet the man I pictured so carefully in my mind, my tension-reliever. Instead I was approached by one guy who walked up to me with his doofy ass asking me about my T-shirt. I rolled my eyes and made a face at him like he smelled like shit or something. He got the point and strolled away. Later on, going home on the bus I thought maybe the guys around here are not used to bold women like me. Maybe they were into manners, prissy bitches, and shit like that. Maybe my T-shirt, which read THESE ARE NOT MY FUCKING KIDS!, was too spicy for their precious eyes and ears. There was no doubt in my mind that I would have to find my way back to Brooklyn on a regular basis to keep my sanity.

3

"Daddy," I said softly, trying to lean on my innocent baby doll look. "I want to get my hair done at Earline's next Friday."

Sensing some type of plot, Santiaga asked, "Why would you go all the way to Brooklyn to get your hair done? Can't you go somewhere around here?"

"Come on, Daddy," I pleaded. "They don't know how to hook my 'do up out here. Earline be having my shit—excuse me, my hair looking correct!"

"There's plenty of black hairdressers out here. Go to Wyandanch. That's a forty-five minute ride. It just doesn't make sense for my baby to be riding a bunch of trains and buses just to get to Brooklyn."

"Bus! Train! Trust me Daddy, I wasn't talking 'bout riding either. I'm straight up hitting on you for a ride when you drive in on Friday," I said, laughing and begging at the same time.

"Winter, you know I don't mix business and pleasure. I do my runs solo. I don't want you to deal with that or knowing more than what you need to know. It's not smart. And I never been a stupid man. Just lay low for awhile. Your mother will have her car in a couple of weeks. Then you and her can go ripping around to take care of all that girly shit.

"Anyway," he said, with his cool face and half a smile, "there ain't a female in the state who looks better than Winter even without Earline's help." Even in my disappointed moment a compliment felt good, and worked, as it did every time. I accepted Santiaga's rationale and went back to my room to reshuffle my deck and think of another angle to get me into Brooklyn.

Days later I called Sterling, my old sugar daddy, out of the blue. After racking my brain for a plan to get into Brooklyn I realized he was the only sucker I knew who would get such a kick out of seeing me that he would drive all the way out here to get me. The price of the whole arrangement was that I'd have to tolerate him, act like I gave a damn about him when I didn't. I'd have to think of quick answers to all his wimpy bitching questions about where I had been, why I cut out on him like I did, why I never called and blah, blah, blah, blah, blah. Then I'd have to find a clever way to ditch him 'cause I definitely wasn't spending my Friday night with him. I'd have to be firm so he wouldn't start that damn whining. I'd also have to be sweet so if I had to use him again as my taxi driver from time to time, he would cooperate. The worst thing that might happen is I might have to end up giving him some pussy just to keep him in line or a quick blow job while he was driving. I wasn't sweating it, though. I had done it with him before and I could easily do it again, especially to get the hell out of Long Island.

Soon as Santiaga's Lex ripped out of the driveway Friday afternoon, I saw Sterling pull up in his little LeCar with the broken fender. I swallowed hard and got ready to pretend it was a limo. When I told my moms I was going to Earline's she wanted to come, too. I explained that she should not come because I was spending the night at Aunt Laurie's and would not be able to get her a ride back after she finished at Earline's. She screwed up her face as though she had a problem with me spending the night at her own sister's house. I quickly added that I would be back first thing Saturday morning to watch the kids. She let go of her anger and I jetted.

Adrenaline was pumping inside Earline's. I was like a junkie getting a fix as I got filled in on the what-haps around the way. The girls dropped the regular shit on me like who bumpin' who, who's pregnant, who's paid, who's not and why. Who's locked down, how long, and who's due to come home. Now Natalie was giving me the elbow, her discreet way of telling me to look toward the door without looking like I was looking toward the door. "There go Tasia," she said out of the corner of her mouth.

"Yeah. And?" I asked, waiting for the 411 on her.

"She's fucking with your man, Midnight."

The information hit me right in my chest. She was talking about my future husband.

"She's big on him, too! Especially since he got that new Acura with the rims." My heart dropped for three full seconds. It took one second for me to check Tasia out. My eyes zoomed in on her ears, humph cheap 10-karat gold earrings. Then her clothes. She was chillin' a little bit, strictly hip-hop style. She had big taste-me titties, a small flat belly, and a round ass. She was brown skin with chinky eyes. *Regular bitch!* I thought to myself. The rack that she pulled those clothes off of had one thousand pairs of the same shit, which means at any party four or five girls would have it on. There was nothing unique about her or even the way she hooked up her gear. It wouldn't be hard for me to move her right on out. But damn, it was the Long Island distance that was killing me. A second later my mind focused on what I really wanted to hear. Midnight had a new Acura! The one I would be riding in, the one he needed to have to sport a bitch like me.

After my hair was butter, I left with Natalie to go check my Aunt Laurie. I needed to at least show my face in her apartment and hang out for an hour or so. I knew my moms would call to check on me. I'd be out partying but at least Aunt Laurie would be able to verify that she had seen me and that I would be back there to spend the night like I told my mother I would. We had plans to go to Big Moe's, the local bar and dance set that be banging on Friday nights for the young crowd. There was never no problem about Big Moe or his bouncers getting in your business and checking IDs and shit like that.

I can't begin to tell you how my heart was racing just from being in the Brooklyn air again. Cars were positioned bumper to bumper for all three blocks surrounding Moe's club. Car and Jeep speakers were up, each one playing their own jam. Sound systems were fighting to outblast each other. A little bit of hip-hop collided with a little bit of reggae, rockers, and even slow jams. I was on foot, rolling fifteen deep straight Brooklyn style with fifteen razor-ready girls who all had each other's back. When we got in the club I put my plan into action. I didn't have long to work because Long Island was looming in the back of my mind like a threat. Midnight was standing on the right side of the club where the lights were low. He was kickin' it with about five other niggas. I caught the side of his serious face, his muscular jaw working. I laughed to myself thinking, *only this nigga would conduct business in a place where everybody else is trying to get their groove on.* I gave my girl Natalie the pinch and our whole crew started walking toward Midnight and his boys. We rushed his crew, bumping into all of them, rubbing our titties against them, using the excuse that the club was crowded. Of course it only took a second before my girls had his boys distracted. I stepped up, licking my lips real slowly, and said rough and sexy-like, "What's up Midnight, haven't seen you in a while."

I said this line with sensual power. I said it like he and I had been intimate in the past and I missed him and needed to get back with him as soon as possible. I was standing so close to him that one more inch and I could have slid my tongue down his throat. He looked at me unaffected, completely unmoved and nonemotional. My emotions were wilding. My nipples were up and the muscles in my pussy were beating like a heart.

"What do you want?" he finally said. Now I was pissed. I knew my perfume had to be working. I dabbed it on extra so when I got up close my scent would suck him in. Hell, I had on 18-karat gold earrings and 1-karat diamond studs, much more than that two-dollar, 10-karat hoe I heard he had been kicking it with had. I didn't want to go off. The bottom line was I wanted him, so I'd have to play it cool, make sure I pull him in just right.

I said sweetly, "What do I want?" I touched his hand with mine, looked him dead in the eye, "Oh, I want it all."

He pulled his hand back like I had a disease and slowly and coldly spit back at me, "Well, that makes you like all these bitches in here, now, doesn't it?"

Rage ripped through my chest as it became clear that I wasn't even a consideration of his. Hell, he acted like I wasn't even a woman. My mind automatically flipped to Santiaga, who I know would have ripped out Midnight's tongue for even talking to me like that.

Then, like a gypsy, Midnight, reading my thoughts, said, "What, gonna tell Daddy? I'm my own man." He turned and walked away.

I felt so played I didn't even want to turn around toward my girls. I'd have to tell my whole crew that I got dissed like I was a piece of shit. I just tightened up, put on my Brooklyn 'tude, grabbed the next nigga standing close to me, and started to dance. I was gonna move with fury, let Midnight know what he was missing. I handed my Coach bag to my girl and started shaking my ass all the way to Alabama, using this dumb fuck dancing in front of me like a prop as I tried to catch Midnight's attention again. My body was shaking and sweating as anger and desire fought it out. Yes desire, 'cause I was definitely turned on. The lighting situation made it hard for me to catch Midnight's eyes. At the point that my body wanted to collapse from exhaustion I saw Midnight looking in my direction and heading my way. Smiling to myself, I thought, *I know I'm a bad bitch.*

I knew he would come back.

As he got closer I realized he was signaling to his man who was standing behind me. He snatched him up and they left the club.

Later that night our crew was walking back to the PJs. I was feeling down but looking unaffected. We were joking, bugging, talking about people, when a spanking new, jet black, gleaming Acura with rims pulled up alongside us. We all stopped to look at what I calculated was a fifty-thousand-dollar car with forty-five hundred dollars in rims. The automatic window on the passenger side dropped down. Midnight was behind the wheel doing what he does best, looking good. I wasn't gonna play the sucker role and assume he stopped for me. I had done that already tonight. So I stood in the pack with my girls. He must of known he could of called any one of us over to him and not one of us would of stopped to consider the others. All of us were probably doing the same thing, imagining ourselves in the passenger seat of that car, which just increased in value as I checked the soft white leather interior and wood paneling.

"Winter!!" he called my name with a roughness that made me want to just hop on his dick and go buck. "Get in."

I don't remember walking to the car or nothing. I felt like I was just transformed or teleported right into the seat like I was on *Star Trek* or something. I turned to the side. The automatic window was up. Midnight was pulling his finger off the control button. I saw twenty-eight eyeballs glued to the side of my window, staring in my face. They was my girls but they were jealous. All I could think was, *yeah that's right. What did you expect? Or have you forgotten? I'm the queen of this ghetto!* As the window closed I could hear Natalie's voice saying, "Are you staying at my house or Aunt Laurie's?" I didn't respond, just thought to myself, hopefully neither. As we rode my confidence grew slowly. I decided he was just tryna flip the script on me, play hard to get. It didn't matter though, he came back for me. I had made an impression on him. I had sweated him and now he was sweating me.

The air in the car was crisp and clean-smelling. The stereo was so fly it sounded like the band was playing the music live in the backseat. He wasn't saying nothing but that was alright, I was used to his strange silence. It didn't make me mad. It made me want him more. I knew our lovemaking would be good just based on his mysteriousness. I opened my Coach bag and pulled out my little mirror. He wasn't paying me no mind. I tilted the mirror to the side angle so I could look at his face without him realizing that I was looking. He was black alright, beautiful. His long thin nose and big thick lips mounted his white teeth—white like those T-shirts he wore in the summertime.

Suddenly, it seemed, the music was abruptly interrupted by the loud and aggravating voice of Sister Souljah on the radio. I leaned up and reached for the button to change the station, when Midnight intercepted my hand, saying, "Don't touch my shit." I sucked my teeth, rolled my eyes, and sat stiff while Souljah went on to talk about some black struggle. *Humph,* I thought, *if there is some kind of struggle going on, she must be the only one in it. Everybody I know is chilling, just tryna enjoy life.* She, on the other hand, with these Friday and Saturday night comments, busting up the radio hip-hop flavor mix, is the only one who is always uptight. I had every reason to take it personal. She started talking about how young black drug dealers are the strong black men in the community, but need to change their line of business because it's destroying the community. As far as I am concerned Souljah is just somebody who likes to hear herself talk. She obviously didn't know the time because the drug dealers don't destroy nothing. If there weren't people on line to buy the product, then there would be no business. No drug dealer I know ever forced anybody, not one person, to take drugs. People do it voluntarily. They do it by choice. The niggas I know who sell drugs be tryna help the stupid crackheads. They be telling them to slow down and asking them are they sure they want to sell their last whatever just to get that hit. I even know a dealer who told this pregnant girl he wouldn't sell her no more crack until after she had the baby. She just took her dumb ass to somebody else and got the crack anyway. Then, when she had the baby boy, she tried to sell him, too. Now whose fault is that? People do what they want to. Maybe that's the problem. Maybe Souljah just wants people to do what she wants them to do.

"Why you even listening to this bullshit?" I asked Midnight.

"What the hell do you know?" he snapped back in his low and cool voice. This is when I noticed we were on the Long Island Expressway.

"Where are you taking me?"

"Home, little girl," he responded. "Your father paged me and asked me to bring you home."

"I thought you was your own man."

"For a hundred-fifty dollars, I'll run an errand. It's business. I pick you up, drop you off, collect my dough, and I'm out."

The one-hundred-fifty-dollar transaction was as smooth and nonincidental as a messenger service dropping off a package. After handing Midnight the money and closing the door, my father walked silently through the living room and into his den. The room was dark. He sat down, leaned back in his chair. The moonlight through the blinds lit up half of his serious face.

"Winter," he said softly.

"Yes Daddy?" I said.

"What made you think you could spend the night in Brooklyn?"

"I asked Mommy. I wanted to see my friends. Natalie and me were supposed to . . ."

"I guess you're not understanding."

"Not understanding what?" I asked, checking my tone to ensure that I was not sounding disrespectful, something Santiaga doesn't tolerate.

"Who you are. Who I am. Who we are." He said each word with precision. He was starting to sound like some type of philosopher or something to me. This whole thing wasn't making any type of sense. "You're my daughter. You just can't wander off and go anywhere, unprotected."

"Anywhere!" I said, upset. "I went home. I went to Brooklyn. I went to the only place I know. Where my peoples is at. Where everybody knows me. Those are my streets, Daddy!"

"Do you think those streets love you? Those streets don't love you. They don't even know you. You could walk those streets one thousand nights and one thousand days and they wouldn't even know your name. The street don't love nobody." It was crazy. His words were making me feel uneasy and I couldn't connect. I didn't like the feeling. I was used to feeling relaxed and in control.

"So what are you saying, Daddy? Are you saying that I can't go home anymore?"

"No!" he said quickly. "I'm not saying that."

" 'Cause Daddy, I'm not hiding from anybody or scared of anything. You taught me that."

"It's not about hiding. It's about being smart. I taught you that too. What makes you special, Winter?" he asked like it was the fifty-thousand-dollar *Jeopardy!* question or some shit like that. I ran the question through my head and drew a blank. "What makes you special is me . . . Santiaga! Your father. Your protection! You had full run of our projects when I lived there 'cause I was holding things down, making everything alright. My eyes saw everything. So everything was cool. Now this is home. This is where I rest my head. If I'm here and you are over there, I can't see you. If I can't see you, I can't protect you. When you're unprotected you're wide open. Anything could happen."

"But Aunt Laurie saw me. She knew I was there. Uncle Stevie was there just like usual."

"Look at my face Winter, and never forget what I tell you. Santiaga loves you. Your mother loves you. Don't confuse it. That's all you can depend on."

"Yes Daddy," I responded softly and turned to go to my room. There was no doubt in my mind that it was time to spark an L.

Luckily I had copped a nickel bag earlier in Brooklyn. I went to the linen closet and grabbed a couple of towels. I closed my door, pulled out my pack of incense. My mind shouted, *Hell no, the incense is a dead giveaway!* I went to my bedroom window, opened it, and decided I'd let the breeze in to whisk the smoke out. Sitting down on the bed, I pulled off my shoes. I opened my shirt, unsnapped my bra to let my titties breathe. I slipped on my slippers, walked to my dresser draw, stuck my hand underneath my folded blouses, and pulled out my philly blunt. I cracked it open, took the tobacco out, flushed it down the toilet. I put the weed in, wrapped it, licked it, and stuck it under my nose as a teaser to my appetite. Yes, I needed to relieve my tension. I'm backed up sexually, stuck in the suburbs, and my dream lover is a mummy.

Just as I went to position the towel to jam up the space in the door my moms knocked and without hesitation pushed open the door gently. I got up, threw the towel on the bed to cover up the blunt I had laying there.

"Hey Mommy," I said, trying to act casual. I checked her face. You could always tell when Santiaga was upset because it showed on my mother's face.

"Your father really went off when I told him you were spending the night in Brooklyn."

"Yeah, we talked," I said, hoping to avoid two speeches in one night.

"I tried to get him to loosen up but you know how that goes," she admitted.

"Ooh, that's a fly design you got," I said, checking her freshly sculpted, painted, and immaculate nails. "Where did you get that done?"

"A little shop about fifteen minutes away. Santiaga took me."

"What else did you get? Don't be holding out on me. I know you got something else."

"Ah, just a little dress for me to rock tonight at my party," she said.

"Yeah," I replied disinterested.

"I know, that's how I'm starting to feel about the parties, too. I just need to get my whip so I can get in, out, and around."

"When do you think you'll get it?"

"If I have it my way, and I always do, I'll get it next weekend." She smiled confidently.

"Yeah, but the way Santiaga was talking, even after you get it, we ain't allowed in Brooklyn! Now you know that's crazy."

"He's just protective and sometimes he overdoes it. But, girl, we can sneak!" she said, smiling. Her mahogany skin was glowing in my dimmed light. Mommy was pretty alright. A definite advantage to having babies at a young age. You get to chill with your moms like she's your sister or something. Fuck all those old stiff bastards complaining about teenage pregnancy, this and that. Me and my moms could party together. Nobody would ever know that she was my moms. I got some shit in my closet that looks better on her than it does on me. I know some niggas from around my way in Brooklyn who'd rather fuck her than me. Now they'd never admit it. It would be suicidal. Santiaga would . . . Oh yeah! Just the thought of Daddy snapped me back into reality.

"Sneak to Brooklyn," I laughed. "Santiaga runs Brooklyn. There's no sneaking in and out of his territory! Hell, he beeped Midnight at a club and had him bring me home, embarrassed the shit out of me. How did he know I was there?"

"Well, you know Big Moe got to answer to Santiaga," Moms said, being vague. "Speaking of Midnight, I'll bet you liked riding in his car," she smiled knowingly.

"What?" I played it off. She laid back on my bed, rolled over, and started tickling me like I was a little girl or something. Hitting all of my secret spots, I cracked up with laughter.

"Midnight's cool," I said matter-of-factly.

"Don't front on me little hooker," she said, like she was really one of my girlfriends. "I see the way you look at him."

"When?" I asked.

"When? Okay when you were thirteen, when you were fourteen, when you were fifteen, when you were sixteen," she laughed. "He's a good catch, though. A good man, loyal, paid, strong."

"He don't like me, though," I said, admitting something I would never tell one of my girlfriends.

"It's not that," she said. "Midnight just likes life. Santiaga would squeeze the life out of him."

"I wish that were the truth! No, I'm saying I wish it was that he was just scared of Santiaga. I'm saying that he straight up don't like me at all, period, as a woman! He talks cold, says very little. He didn't even try to be nice to me on the way home."

"Trust me, there is no way he don't like my baby. You're young, fine. You got everything a girl could want, pretty hair, beautiful eyes, clothing, jewels. It's got to be Santiaga standing in the way."

"So when do you think Santiaga will stop standing in my way?"

"Who knows," she said, exasperated.

My mother got up and headed toward the door. As she stepped out of my room she leaned her head back in and smiled, "And don't light that joint in the house. That will really make Santiaga snap."

Damn, I thought to myself. It seems like the both of them know everything. But nobody was gonna stop me from getting my buzz on. I crawled outside of my window, sat on my little slanted side of the roof and puffed my lah in the spring breeze and moonlight. After the feeling of "no worries" came over me, I leaned back, closed my eyes, and drifted into the night . . .

We were all seated in the family room. Santiaga was playing chess against himself. My mother was flipping through her hundreds of album covers, her collection. My sisters were all glued to the television watching the cartoon network. I was reclining in a chair, redoing one

of my fingernails, when the doorbell rang. Santiaga answered. When
the door opened, he stood face-to-face with Midnight.

Midnight looked Santiaga dead in the eye and said, "We need to
talk." Santiaga led him into the den. I jumped off the reclining chair
and tiptoed to the den door, plastering my ear against the side of the
wall. Midnight told Santiaga slowly and respectfully, "I know you love
your daughter, and so do I." Santiaga's face first held a look of surprise,
then grew vexed. He remained cool. As he leaned forward about to
speak, Midnight quickly went on.

"I know what I need to do as a man. I've been working on it for a
long time and now I'm ready. I wanted you to be sure that I'm for real,
that my love for your daughter is for real." Midnight reached into his
inside pocket and pulled out an elegant black velvet ring box. He
cracked it open and the 2-karat diamond sparkled. My nosy eyes
beamed in on the stone. "I want to marry Winter," Midnight said
firmly. "I'll surround her with the finest things in life, like she
deserves, like you always have. My finances are solid, stashed away,
ready. Maybe we'll buy a house up here. Live next door to you."

Santiaga smiled at the idea of keeping me within arm's reach. My
insides screamed. *Hell no! Not here!* My heart interrupted and said *OK,
anywhere, you fine ass, paid motherfucker!* Santiaga said, "Winter is
young."

"Yes," Midnight said sternly. "Young and beautiful. Like your wife
was when you two married." Santiaga checked Midnight's face to make
sure that Midnight meant no ill by his comment. Then Midnight took
control.

"I respect you as a man, Santiaga. I always have. I value your business and have served you well. But I'm my own man and this is what I
want. So what do you say, what's up?"

Santiaga embraced Midnight. As Midnight's face pressed against
Santiaga's shoulder he looked at me and said with that masculine
authority that made me hot, "Pack your stuff, Shorty. It's me and you
from here on out."

Excited, but not wanting to appear desperate, I threw my hand on
my hip and said, "Let's see what you have there." Midnight opened the
box and took out the ring. As he placed it on my finger . . .

The phone rang, jerking me out of my sleep, ruining my dream. If
only it could have rung after the love scene.

I snatched the telephone as my sleepy eyes checked the digital on my dresser. "Six o'clock in the fucking morning. What do you want?" It was Natalie. She laughed, "My long distance is working! Hey-ey wake up, hooker! So what happened? Where did you go? Did you get it? How was it? Was it small? Was it big?" She fired questions like bullets.

My mind was still sleepy. I needed enough energy to get my lies straight 'cause I was definitely about to tell some lies. "We went out for a late night/early morning breakfast."

"Where?" she demanded.

"He took me to one of those big fancy diners out in Queens. He had steak and eggs with potatoes. I had the shrimp and fries."

"Shrimp and fries! That's not breakfast food."

"Girl you know I don't eat breakfast!"

"Anyway," Natalie screamed. "Get to the good part." Before I could even start talking, she was filling in the blanks for herself.

"Oh, my God. Wait until Tasia finds out about this. It's on now!" Now Natalie bringing that hoe Tasia's name up only gave me fuel.

"After breakfast me and Midnight got back in the car. He took me to one of those lookout spots by the river. He started kissing me. Girl, his lips were so big and warm. He started rubbing my titties with those big-ass strong hands. Girl, I thought I was gonna explode. He started taking off my shirt and that's when I went Brooklyn on his ass!"

"What?!" she screamed. "What happened?"

"I told the nigga: 'Look, don't try to play me out. If I'ma take off my clothes, you gonna take off yours, too. You want to see my body? Oh well it's all here. But, I want to see your body, too!' "

"No you didn't!"

"Yes! I did," I said.

"So what happened?"

"He took off his shirt and said, 'Now, you take off yours.' So I did. He took off his pants and said, 'Now you take off yours.' So I did."

"Oh shit!" Natalie was going ballistic. "Then what?"

"He took off his draws and said, 'Now take off yours.'"

"Did you?"

"I damn sure did! Girl, I looked at his big-ass black balls laying against that soft white leather car seat and that was it. We got busy!"

"Was anybody looking?"

"Hell no! I don't know! We weren't worrying about that. After that wild sex we just chilled butt naked. Him in his seat butt naked. Me in my seat butt naked puffing lah!"

"Get out of here. You lying!" Natalie screamed.

"Uh-uh girl, that's for real. I made sure my sweat sunk into the car leather just to let every other bitch know *I was there.* The next bitch that gets into that car is gonna smell me all over!" We both laughed.

4

The next weekend came so swiftly. It was twelve noon when I woke up. It was my mother's voice. She was going off about how she was not spending one more day caught up in the house.

Where was her fucking car? She wanted to know. "Today is the day! Today is the day my fucking Benz is supposed to be parked outside of my bedroom window with a big red ribbon on it. Where is it?" she demanded. The tone of my mother's voice was rare. I could hardly say I ever remember it being this rough. All I could think is here go two Concord jets about to have a head-on collision.

My three little sisters came running into my room, stuffing their little bodies under the covers with me. I expected to hear Santiaga yell back but he didn't. Instead my mother just continued blowing her cool and doing something she told me not to do. She was making it clear who the boss was. A real woman was not supposed to do that. A bad bitch controlled without the man ever knowing that he was being dominated. A bad bitch was so slick that she made him think he was calling the shots while she planted the seeds and was the owner of all his thoughts. Not today. My moms told Santiaga she didn't want to hear no shit. He was going out with her today, her birthday, to buy that car. She was leaving with him, she instructed. After his business was transacted, Santiaga was to buy that car she had been holding her breath for. She wasn't interested in no other presents no matter what they were. Through the walls I could hear the bass in Santiaga's voice, but not his exact words. The next loud sound I heard was the door slamming. From the silence, I knew that both of them were gone. As my mother had said last week, she always had her way.

Saturday evening the stars fell down, six minutes after six. Six hours after their argument. I remember it clearly. That was the time the phone rang. "Winter, get the kids ready, I'm coming to pick you up." I didn't recognize the slow, steady voice.

"What? Who is this?"

"This is Midnight. Listen, your father asked me to pick all of you up and bring you out here."

"Oh, you're becoming a regular little taxi driver, huh?"

"This is serious," he said. "I'll be there in two hours." Click! Damn, should I beep Santiaga? This had never happened before. Then I thought to myself, Midnight can be trusted. I got the three little girls ready and two hours later we waited anxiously at the door.

My eight-year-old sister wanted to fight me for the front seat of Midnight's Acura. I told her to take her little ass in the back with the twins. I wondered what would make her think she could ride in the front seat with my man. Hell, she probably already had a crush on him. Little girls start getting horny at a younger age every year.

"Where we going?" I asked. My heart was filled with all kinds of feelings.

"We have to rush. Just get in. I'll tell you when we get there. It's not for little girls to know."

Midnight tried to fill up the empty space with the radio. Other than the music, we rode in complete silence while one of my sisters tried to peel the last bits of sticky paper off her Now and Later candies in the back. *Oh God!* I thought to myself, *I hope she don't suck the candy and leave it stuck to the side of the seat like she normally does.* I imagined Midnight pulling over and throwing all of us out on the expressway for messing up his leather interior. I laughed to myself.

Just then the aggravating voice of Sister Souljah leaped out of the radio and started choking me: "The Ancient African elders believed that what you sow, you reap. If you do something positive, something positive will come back to you. If you consciously do negative things, then negativity will rule your life." I sucked my teeth and thought, *Why don't that bitch just move to Africa?* She's always talking some African mumbo jumbo. Somebody should stick a bone in her nose and a plate in her lip, maybe then she'd feel at home and shut the fuck up. I made myself laugh, thinking, *Them damn Africans must of been some fucked up niggas. If they believed doing something positive caused positive things to happen why are their asses all fucked up bald-headed, naked, starving, stinking, and the whole nine. They must of been doing some foul shit!! Hell, that bitch don't know, she just be talking to talk.*

When we got to downtown Brooklyn, I asked Midnight where he was headed. He was turning right, our old neighborhood was to the left.

"I said I would tell you," he said. Minutes later Midnight pulled over, put on his emergency blinkers, and ask me to get out. Puzzled, I got out. He came around to my side. He didn't let the girls get out.

I said, "I know we ain't leaving them in the car."

"Come here, I got to tell you something." He put his arm around me and looked me dead in the eyes, "Your mother is in the hospital. She's been shot."

My whole mind went blank. It was like someone took an eraser, the type they clean the blackboard with in school, and just wiped everything out. One second later my mouth was screaming. My mind was blank. My body was cold. Midnight's arms were around me, hugging me, embracing me, and trying to hide my face and tears from the girls. They had their faces glued to the window, saying something like, "Oooh, Winter's kissing Midnight. We gonna tell Mommy." My body was stiff, my mind wouldn't think. I felt out of control. What do I do? What do I do now?

"Is she okay? Is she gonna . . . Is she gonna . . ." Midnight held me tighter, firmer, almost as if to demand with his body that I get it together.

"She was shot in the face. I don't know how she is. Santiaga is upstairs with her now. I'll watch your sisters. You go upstairs and check on the situation with her now. Vega will take you up on the elevator," he said, nodding in the direction of one of Daddy's men stationed in the main lobby door of the hospital.

"You come with me?" I begged him.

"No, this is my position. We don't want the little ones to know nothing yet."

Upstairs Santiaga looked like a madman. His face was dark with sadness. When he looked at me, I could swear that I saw tears, something I could honestly say I never seen in his eyes before. He hugged me hard, strong, and warm. As he laid his head on top of my head, his voice whispered, "I'm sorry. I fucked up. I fucked up. I fucked up."

"What happened, Daddy? Is she okay?"

"She's going to be alright. They're operating on her now," he said flatly. "I should have just gotten her the car," he muttered. "I shouldn't of hesitated."

"What happened?" I repeated.

"I never should've let her ride with me today. I knew better than that. What a stupid mistake. What a stupid fucking mistake. Them motherfuckers is gonna feel it. Violation." He grabbed my face with both hands. "They'll take care of your mother," he said, using his eyes to point out his men stationed in the waiting room. "You take the children and stay with Midnight."

"Where are you going, Daddy? Can I see Ma?" My words hit his back. He walked out the door.

The doctors, nurses, attendants—hell, it took the entire hospital it seemed like to hold me back. I wanted to see my mother. They kept telling me, "She's on the operating table. She'll be in intensive care later. Contamination, infection, blah, blah, blah." Pizzaz and Driguez, two more of Daddy's workers, were standing near the operating room doors. They was tryna look casual but it's hard for two big black niggas from the streets to look casual in a hospital. It ain't like somebody was gonna mistake them for doctors or nothing.

My mind started to clear up as I sat and sat and sat. It dawned on me to call Natalie. If something went down around our way she would definitely know a little about it. Natalie's voice was apologetic, she said sorry so many times you'd think she pulled the trigger. I didn't have to say nothing. Natalie just rambled on. "I know it was them niggas from the C building on the other side. They been tryna blow up around our way for some time now. On the low they've been shaking niggas down, looting, and terrorizing everybody. They got their little operation going on but, damn, to blast Santiaga's woman in the face. That's some raw unnecessary shit! The way I figure it, there are enough crackheads around here for everybody to get money. But they'll learn. They young boys anyway. They'll catch it. Santiaga will set them straight. It's gonna be a blood storm in Brooklyn tonight!" She acted excited, like she was watching a heavyweight fight at Madison Square Garden or something.

"Where you at?" Natalie questioned.

"The hospital," I mumbled back.

"Where are the kids, with the housekeeper?"

"Nah, they downstairs with Midnight."

"Midnight! What's he doing there?" she intruded, then continued on. "Oh it's *like that* now, huh. Oh, that's your man now'n shit?" I hung up.

Driguez motioned to me to come toward him. Discreetly he leans toward me, saying, "I'm taking you downstairs now. You won't be able to see your mother until tomorrow. Midnight is waiting downstairs in the front. You'll leave with him."

"What exactly happened?" I asked. I got no response.

"Drop the kids off at Aunt Laurie's house," I told Midnight from the passenger seat. "I want to go check on some stuff." He looked at me with complete defiance, told me that he already had the plans from Santiaga and I should just sit back and do as I'm told. "Just let me make one stop then," I said, figuring I needed to be on my Brooklyn block where the shit was jumping off at. I needed to be with my girls ready to do whatever we had to do.

"That's the problem with all you women," Midnight said dryly, like he was forty years old instead of twenty-two. "Nobody can tell y'all shit. You never want to listen. Never want to follow instructions. Then when shit goes down, all the fuck you can do is cry."

We crossed the state line into New Jersey. Midnight pulled into the Marriott Hotel parking lot. As many times as I had thought about me and Midnight's hot bodies all twisted up on some crisp clean cold new white hotel sheets, I never imagined that we would be here under these circumstances.

"We're gonna stay here tonight," he said. A big smile spread across my lips. "No, this is serious," he spit, as though my delight was somehow illegal. "I'll check in for all of us. Most likely nobody will ask, but if they do, we're one family renting a suite, last name Cooper."

"Cooper, is that your last name?" I asked.

"See," he said. "You don't even know my name. Remember that." *Humph*, I thought to myself, *is that supposed to be some kind of fucking answer or something?*

The suite was immaculate, top-of-the-line. I couldn't of asked for more if I was on a honeymoon. There was one king-sized bed and a living room with a couch with a pull-out bed inside. Each room had its own television. The bathroom was huge marble down and looked brand new. I stepped in there, took a deep breath and figured maybe after the kids went to sleep we could room-service some Cristal and sip it while we took a bubble bath together in the Jacuzzi. I needed something to relieve all my pressure and why not get with the man I always wanted.

"You four can take this bed," Midnight said, pointing to the bedroom. "I'll sleep in the living room. We'll be here for the next three days, so get comfortable, and chill. You three, don't make a mess," he said with a certain joking tenderness that must be reserved only for children.

"Three days!" I hollered with my hand on my hips. "Can I talk to you a minute, please?" I pointed toward the living room. He rejected my order, turned the television to the Disney Channel for my sleepy sisters and then came into the living room at his own pace.

"What is this shit about three days? I have one dress with me, the one I'm wearing. The three little bears have no clothes and already have spilled shit all over themselves. My mother's in the hospital. I want to see her. I need to know what's going on. I'm not down with this *Mission Impossible* shit. And, as for that shit you were talking in the car about women crying when shit breaks down, that's bullshit! I'm a fighter. I've held heat before and I know how to use it. I can cut a bitch with my razor so fast and so clean she wouldn't even know what happened until she bled to death. The problem with you, Midnight, is you think you know every goddamn thing. What you're not understanding is that I can help. I can be your right-hand man. Just let me know what's up, what's going on?"

Nothing moved except Midnight's jawbone, something Mama said was a definite sign of a man's anger. He reached in his back pocket, pulled out a stack of bills. "First thing in the morning I'll take you out to get some clothes. Don't worry. I realize you're a high maintenance bitch. Gotta keep you up in the style you're accustomed to. How many fighters do you know find themselves in the middle of the goddamn war and all the fuck they think about is fashion and the clothes on their back. Hell no, you won't ever be my right-hand man."

I was impressed with the big stack of bills and excited about going shopping. I wondered if this was his money or if Santiaga had given it to him and he knew all along that he had orders to take me shopping. Maybe it was a little bit of both. Maybe he was using his own money, but knew Santiaga would pay him back.

"Okay, one last question," I pushed, knowing I was aggravating him yet enjoying the attention. "What clothes are we going to wear out to go shopping in the morning when all of our stuff is dirty? . . . Never mind. I know—the laundry service."

As I pushed 8 to call down to the laundry room he put his finger on the phone, disconnecting my call. With a muscular hand on my shoulder, he said sarcastically, "Think like you come from the projects. Take your clothes off and wash them in the sink. Hang 'em up by the heater to dry. You know how to wash clothes, don't you? The laundry service is closed now. It's almost midnight."

After stripping the three bears and tossing their clothes in the sink, I put them under the sheets and blankets. I talked to them about the things we were going to do tomorrow and assured them that everything was okay. They knocked out to sleep one by one like clockwork. I slipped off my dress and stood checking myself out in the bathroom mirror. Thank God I listened to Mamma's advice about always have nice clean sexy underwear. If I was a tackhead, I could of got caught out here with some beat-up drawers on my ass, with a shit stain and a big old hole in 'em. Just the thought cracked me up. I peeled off my panties, undid my bra, and put them in the sink. I stepped in the shower and let the warm water turn hotter, steaming my whole body from the tension of my crazy day.

My mind was downloading slowly. What about Momma? What would her face look like now? Would she have to get plastic surgery? Would her face be temporarily disfigured? What would Santiaga think about her face? Of course he would make sure she would get the best medical treatment and everything. How long would she stay in the hospital? Oh, my God. Would I become a professional baby-sitter, getting stuck with my little sisters? Santiaga would definitely have to hire the housekeeper full time instead of part time to help watch the kids. What about Midnight? What was his beef with the world? Or was it that he just liked pissing on my world? For once Mamma was wrong. She told me that Midnight wanted me. She told me that only his fear of Santiaga stood in the way. But that was not what I saw in his eyes, fear. He never seemed fearful of anything or anyone. He just straight seems disinterested in me. Now he and I were forced together for three days, like being stuck on a deserted island. If I was the last woman on earth, would Midnight turn me down? What the hell could he be thinking?

Stepping out of the shower, I grabbed two towels, wrapped one around my wet hair and the other around my body. I swerved into the living room where Midnight had positioned himself in front of the TV. His dress shirt was open. Underneath he was wearing one of those crisp white undershirts. I could see his gun on his waist, half-tucked in his pants. My eyes slid down his legs, I could see another gun he held near his ankle. The blackness, the guns, his muscle structure, that white shirt, those white teeth, and his unfiltered anger was so seductive I had to try again to get with him. "Do you want me to wash your clothes? I'm getting good at it now."

"No that's okay," he said, without even taking so much as a look at me. I stepped over and into the chair opposite him.

"I'm tired," I said, stretching my arms slowly above my head.

"Go to bed then," he answered cruelly, as if he didn't want to be bothered. I picked up my legs and placed them on the arm of my chair. I was now going to become the freshly showered, hair-wrapped, body-wrapped-in-a-towel Ivory girl. I started playing games with my legs, repositioning them, opening them slowly, closing them slowly. I was making it possible for him to see the hairs on my pussy, if he only wanted to. When I got excited enough, my juices would start to flow, releasing the scent of a willing pussy, definitely something he wouldn't be able to fight.

"Are you a homosexual, Midnight? 'Cause if you are, that's cool. To each his own and all that good shit."

He laughed a rare laugh and, without turning around, he said, "Go to bed little girl."

"Little girl! Do these look like little girl titties to you?" I stood up and released the towel, dropping it to the floor. I wanted him to see my 34Ds so he could take back his insult. I wanted him to see my whole body. He stayed stiff like a mummy, unaffected by my nakedness—and I mean I was butt naked, standing in the middle of a hotel suite which was designed for fucking.

Midnight leaned up, grabbed the remote, and started surfing channels.

"I'll see you in the morning," he said finally, like a father would. I sucked my teeth, picked up my towel, and returned to the bathroom.

I washed, rinsed, and twisted the clothes as if they were the source of my anger, laying each piece out to dry separately, some by the heater, some on the shower curtain. I tiptoed into the bedroom, not wanting to wake my sisters. I grabbed one of the pillows from the bed and sat my bare ass in the comfortable chair next to the bedroom window, where I slept.

In the morning, I used the hotel blow-dryer, conveniently situated on the bathroom wall, to finish drying the damp clothes. I slid into my dress, hating the idea of repeating yesterday's fashion. Without a proper cleaning, the clothes were stiff and rough like cardboard. Brushing my hair into a French bun, I heard Midnight talking. I pushed open the door connecting to the living room. He abruptly ended a conversation he had been having on his cell phone.

"What's up?" I asked.

"Your mother is out of surgery. She's still in intensive care but she's gonna be alright. Montenegro and Farrara are at the hospital now looking after her."

"Yeah right!" I mumbled. "The first people I'm sure she'll want to see when she opens her eyes has to be the bodyguards." I rolled my eyes. "C'mon, drive me over to the hospital. I want to see my mother."

"Nah!" Midnight responded coolly. "Your father said you should relax. We'll get the kids ready and all go shopping. They should like that. They can run around a little."

"Santiaga called? You knew I wanted to talk to him. Why didn't you call me to the phone?" I screamed.

"Take it easy, Winter."

I don't know how it happened, but just then I lost control. "Is it that you don't hear me or am I speaking French, motherfucker? I want to see my mother. I want to talk to my father."

I turned quick and grabbed the hotel phone so I could beep Santiaga. Midnight grabbed my wrist, causing me to drop the phone. I spun around wildly, asking, "What the fuck is up with you?" He didn't answer. I pushed him. As I swung on him he used his strong body to restrain me. Stuck in his grip, I cursed him. "Get the car ready, nigga! I'm going to the hospital." Instead of slapping the shit out of me, he hugged me even tighter. Feeling his warm body close against mine, my resistance stopped and I found myself crying into his shoulder. Over his shoulder, I saw two of my little sisters staring at us. "What's up with you two?" the eight-year-old asked.

Midnight turned my body and face away from the girls and whispered in my ear. "It's alright Shorty, I knew you would break down sooner or later. But, you gotta hold it together or your sisters' gonna start bugging, too."

When I saw my own tears fall onto my hands I got mad at myself for crying. It was not like me. But I liked the feeling of being up tight on Midnight. I liked the way he was holding me. I even liked the way he was treating me right at this moment. So I pushed it. I took a genuine situation and was about to make it work for me, cry some more, get even closer for a little longer. But then three of my sisters tried to muscle their way into my act. One by one they started crying, too. Midnight released my body, looked around the room at the four weeping willows and got a look on his face that indicated he couldn't stand the pressure. He put his hand in his pocket and pulled out a stack of cash. "Alright, whoever showers and gets dressed first gets fifty dollars." Their tears turned to excitement as they shot into the bathroom to box each other out for the dough. The money was like smelling salts; it revived everyone.

Midnight turned toward me, "Yo Shorty-tough, two more days, that's it. Then you'll be back home. Try to stay cool, you know?" I couldn't answer. I was straight in love with this nigga. I was replaying my new nickname, "Shorty-tough."

Trying to break the spell, Midnight waved a stack of cash back and forth in front of my eyes. "Yo, you must be an impostor. Where's Winter? Nobody has to ask her twice to go shopping," he said, flashing a rare smile.

I laughed, grabbed my jacket and said in a sexy way, "I'm ready."

At the mall the war of wills kicked in. I had one side of the hanger with the miniskirt I wanted to purchase while Midnight's tight grip held the other side. My sisters ran in and out of the aisles under the clothes racks, while me and Midnight argued. With one hand on my hip, I clenched my teeth and spit, "I've worn skirts like this before. It's my choice. Don't act like you never seen me rock a mini before." How and why did Midnight think he could tell me what I can and cannot wear? Now I'm saying, maybe if he was giving me some dick, making me feel good and relaxed, I might have considered his ideas.

"You check this out, Shorty. I'm responsible for you right now. Whatever you did before is your business. For these two days you gonna wear something decent. Come on, put this shit back." He grabbed my hand and led me out of the boutique while my sisters traveled close behind. His touching my hand shot a sensation between my legs and through my body. Now I wanted that miniskirt. I had others like it. But him grabbing me in the rough style made me want him even more. It seemed now that he cared, I was breaking through his ice-cold ways and it was worth temporarily losing control.

He led me upstairs into Bloomingdale's. "Now wait here." He

moved around the clothes racks with the rhythm of a leopard on a hunt. He held up an Eileen Fisher pantsuit. "Alright, this is banging. This is something I would pick for my sister to wear. Let's go get some shoes," he said.

Now the pantsuit was fly I'll admit. The material was high quality and all that good shit. But Midnight's comment had reduced me to the level of his sister.

"Is this something you would want Tasia to wear?"

"Who?"

"Tasia! Tasia! Your girl! 'Cause I don't give a fuck what you would want your sister to wear. I want to know what you would want your girl Tasia to wear."

"Tasia is not my girl," he denied. I rolled my eyes.

"That's not what I heard."

"Fuck what you heard. You and them silly bitches you be with. They don't know me. They just chickens, a bunch of chickens who ain't got shit to do except run they mouths."

I placed both hands on my hips. "So are you saying you weren't fucking Tasia?"

"Is that what you want me to do to you?" he asked. "Fuck you then talk about it with some other hoe?" I weighed his words, thinking, *Is this like some type of trick question or something?* Yes, I did want him to fuck me. Hadn't I made that clear? No, I didn't want him to talk about me with some other hoe. I want him for myself. Was he calling me a hoe?

"Fuck it, wear what you want to wear," he said, frustrated.

I got all the things he liked for me. We picked up some clothes for the kids. We ended up in F.A.O. Schwarz toy store. Midnight wanted to find me some games for the girls to play with to minimize their missing Mommy and Daddy, and most of all to stop them from asking too many questions. The more fun they had, he figured, the less questions they would ask. When we were finished, we had so much shit it looked like a late Christmas. We had so much fun we had forgotten about lunch and had worked up quite an appetite for dinner. It was clear to me that Midnight was in control for now. So I didn't even ask where we were going to eat or try to give directions. I just sat back and waited for him to take us to the spot of his choice.

We went to the North American Lobster Company somewhere in Jersey City. I felt nothing but delight. The tables were big and round.

Each one had a beautiful candle centerpiece with sexual flicking flames. The male customers wore white shirts and ties, placing their business jackets carefully on the back of their chairs. The women quietly talked to their mates, their faces soft and expressive. One hundred percent class. There was no doubt that Midnight was as smooth as Santiaga. He was made just for me. He lifted Mercedes and Lexy into their chairs, pulled the chair out for Porsche.

"Do you have any kids, Midnight?" Silence. "Answer the question," I insisted.

"You ever seen me with a kid?" he asked, now aggravated.

"That's not the point. A lot of niggas got kids everywhere but you never see them."

"Yeah well, I'm not a lot of niggas! If I had a kid everybody would know."

I felt easy again. "How old are you, anyway?" I asked, already knowing the answer.

"You starting to sound like the police."

"Not hardly," I said, smiling real sexy-like.

"I'm twenty-two."

Without missing a beat and without being asked I responded, "I'm eighteen in three weeks."

He looked at me serious like: "Lying sure comes easy to you. You don't have to take a breath, blink, twitch, nothing. The lies just roll straight off your tongue."

"How old do you think I am?" I asked Midnight.

Porsche jumped in, "She's sixteen. She'll be seventeen in January." I pinched her leg under the table.

Back in the hotel room, we played Go Fish, Pitty-pat, I Declare War, Old Maid, Candy Land, Trouble, and Sorry before the three little ones passed out. Everything was less tense than yesterday evening and for me this meant an opportunity. Before I could organize my approach, however, Midnight grabbed the remote and clicked on CNN News. I got up and stood in front of the television. He had entertained the kids, it was time for him to entertain me. He got an instant look of disgust on his face.

"Why don't you do something with yourself," asked Midnight, annoyed.

I glanced up toward the mirror to check my appearance. I looked good to me. So I asked, "Something like what?"

"I don't know. What do you do? What are you into?" My mind drew a blank. "So what's up Shorty, what's the answer?"

I smiled, liking the fact that he was playing with me.

"The answer to what?" I asked. He shook his head, as though I was frustrating him or something. "What? Is there something you want to hear, something I'm supposed to say? What?"

"I asked you a question. What are you into? What do you like to do?" My mind started clicking.

"I like to enjoy myself," I said with much attitude. "What do you know about that Midnight? I like to feel good, relax, get high, fuck, dance, shake my ass, shop. I like to be turned on and I love to turn another motherfucker on."

"What do you read?" he asked. "What's the name of the last book you read?"

"I like movies, I like chillin' with my girls. Matter of fact, if I wasn't stuck here with you I'd have plenty of good shit to get into."

"What you gonna be when you grow up, Winter?"

"Whatever. Maybe I'll get a job like yours," I said, cutting back at him and letting him know me and him are the same kind of people.

"I got plans," he said, going back into himself. Midnight went over to his leather bag, unzipped it, and said, "Here, pick out a book or tape. Do something with yourself. Just stay out of my way."

The Art of War, The Wretched of the Earth, The Judas Factor were a few of the books Midnight had in his case. They didn't look interesting to me and I wasn't gonna read some shit I didn't like just to get his attention. I went for the tapes. He had Sade, Al B. Sure, Stephanie Mills, En Vogue, and Blackstreet. Mainly the old cool-out shit. I snatched up his Walkman. The wire for the headphones was twisted in between Midnight's wallet flap. When I pulled the Walkman wire, the wallet flipped opened. With my back to him, I went through his stuff. He had a picture of a dark-skinned older woman. She looked about thirty-something. She had dark eyes and was wearing a scarf. The next window was a picture of a girl. She seemed about fourteen years old, with a cute little face and big innocent eyes. I figured it must be his sister. She seemed way too young to be his girlfriend. She was dark just like him. Also inside the wallet was a piece of paper folded twice over. It was old and worn. I opened it carefully trying not to make noise. It was a flyer advertising a Sister Souljah speaking event. Covering most of the page was a picture of her. The voice from the radio and the face on the picture didn't match. I had pictured her to look like a man, rough hands and veins popping out of her neck. In the picture she looked normal, young, with a decent face. She looked like a regular uptown Harlem girl. You know in the picture she had her mouth wide open. On the bottom of the page was an event address: Brooklyn Friendship Baptist Church, on Herkimer Street. I quickly folded it up and slid it back into the wallet. I laid the wallet back into his overnight bag and went back to my room, closing the connecting door. Taking one of the pillows from the bed, I set up the corner chair for myself once again. I turned on an old Al B. Sure jam and drifted out to: "All I do is think about you night and day." I can't say that I remember my entire dream that night. But I do remember a vision of me and Midnight's children. There were three of them. The oldest was a nappy-headed, rugged-looking boy, my son. Rough the way I like 'em. The girls had good hair like me, they were the color of hot caramel with diamond earrings. All of them were styling in complementary colors, Pelle Pelle jumpers with some kicks so fly they ain't even been invented yet!

When I pushed the door open the next morning, Midnight was stretched out on the floor doing push-ups in his undershirt and under shorts. He was breathing and sweating. My eyes raced across his body.

"I'll drive you home at about ten tonight," he said. Inhale exhale. "Everything's straight. Santiaga will be there. We just need to find something to do with the girls today. You know, to keep their attention."

At the count of one hundred and fifty, he dropped and rolled over on his back. He curled up his fist in his undershirt, exposing the solid six pack in his stomach.

"What you think we can get the shorties into today?" he asked. I didn't respond. "Winter, what up? You in there." I smiled. He looked into my eyes and smiled. "You always looking for trouble, some shit you can't handle."

Midnight delivered us home at 10 P.M. sharp. My handsome father was standing in the doorway waiting. His white linen suit gleamed in the light from the moon. His big hands rested in his pockets. He embraced Midnight as if he was family. He held my younger sisters in his arms one by one and gave me the warmest, securest hug back into my safe home. The house was extra clean. The music, an old

Earth, Wind and Fire album, played softly in the background. Santiago took Midnight into the den. Midnight came out a short while later, offering a general good night without so much as a glance in my direction. Santiaga sent my sisters off to bed with the idea that Mommy was away, as if on a trip, and would be home next weekend with candy and presents for everyone.

Daddy followed me to my bedroom. I knew to be quiet. Santiaga looked more peaceful than he did on the day of the shooting incident. I switched on the lamp on my vanity table, and the added light revealed a strange scar on the right side of my father's head. There was a maroon-colored dent hidden close to the right side of his hairline. The scar just made him more masculine than ever, just tough, sexy, unstoppable.

"Alright Daddy, just fill me in. Whatever you need me to do. I'm down for you. You just let me know the plan!" He smiled. "How's Mommy?" I asked.

"Your mother's OK. She's a soldier. She'll be home by the end of the week. Now, she'll have bandages. She'll have to take it easy for a while. But we'll all help make it easier for her. You know how conceited she is," he added, half-joking, "so don't act like anything's wrong with her face. She will have to have some type of treatment after a couple of weeks. I got something to make her forget the whole thing." He signaled me to follow him. He led me down the hallway to the back window. "Take a look." My mouth dropped open when I saw the big red set S-600 v12 Mercedes-Benz with a thick red bow and ribbons everywhere.

"Oh shit," I mumbled. My mind started working up a new wardrobe. If you gonna sport a ride like this, you gotta be dressed to kill. Me and Mommy would have to go shopping immediately. Santiaga was still talking but I couldn't hear him anymore. I kept seeing the expression on Natalie's and Simone's faces when I came to Brooklyn pushing not a 190 baby Benz, not a 280, but an S-600 v12. Would my mother let me drive it? Or would she only think of herself? Would she make me wait until Santiaga bought me a car? Or would she kick it with me like sisters would?

Wait a minute. She was sick. Maybe she'd need me to drive around and do errands for her. Maybe she'd be a passenger for about a year or so. OK, I thought. Maybe she'd let me drive her around, but she wouldn't let me chill in the car with Natalie 'n them. It would defeat the purpose of having a red Benz if you couldn't flash it for your girls, ride around flexing. You know how many niggas would be on my bra strap after they saw me behind the wheel? Mad niggas! I'd be making them beg me, do shit they wouldn't ordinarily do. Kiss my ass. Suck my toes. I started cracking up.

Santiaga looked at me like I was bugging. I straightened my face. "Now, I've known a lot of cats who been shot before. Shot all over the body, the leg, the chest, the stomach, but every dude I know been shot in the head, never been the same no more. That's the shit that worries me. That's the shit that makes me want to kick my own ass for letting this happen. Winter, where's your head at? I'm talking to you. If me and you are on point, everything else will fall in place. Here's what I need from you. Stay out of Brooklyn, until I tell you it's OK."

"What!" I said.

"Now, listen to you," he said. "Ten minutes ago you were saying just tell me the plan, I'm down for you Santiaga. Now you're ready to betray me."

"No Santiaga, never betrayal. Betrayal is for suckers. That's what you taught me. I'll do what you want. I'll stay out of Brooklyn until you tell me otherwise."

"And less talking is better. A *whole lot less talking*. You know how we do. The less you know, the better off we all are. And don't get too comfortable just because we're out here in the suburbs. Play your hand close to your chest like you're still in the ghetto. Trust no one and answer no questions. Don't give anybody our phone number who doesn't already have it. Now don't get paranoid. Just don't get sloppy."

A long pause fell. I broke the silence. "You know when Midnight called the night of the incident and said he was coming to get us, I didn't know whether I should have beeped you to confirm what was going on or just go along with what he was telling me to do. I figured everything was cool with him 'cause it always been."

"It's good that you thought twice about it," Santiaga said. "But Midnight's clean. He's as loyal as a blood-born son. I never had a problem out of him. I couldn't have left him with my girls if I didn't think I could trust him with my money and my life. Why, everything went OK, didn't it?"

"No, it went fine. He was a real gentleman," I stated firmly, so as not to cause no problem between the two men I love. "Where did you meet Midnight?"

"He was just a kid who had a brush with the law. You know how they do. Don't want to give a kid a second chance. They force a man into a position where he can't survive, can't make no money. But when I first saw him, I knew he would be a good worker. He just had it in his eyes. Plus he didn't have no family. A cat like that is gonna be loyal. He needed to be able to take care of himself."

"What happened to his family?"

"I haven't seen you this interested in nothing. What's all the questions about?"

"You know Daddy, I'm growing up. Look at me. I'll be seventeen soon." Santiaga watched me spin from left to right.

"Yeah, you are growing up. I been thinking about that a lot lately." He put his head down into his hand as though this topic was too heavy for him.

"What about it?" I asked.

"Do you know what I want for you? I want you to settle down. Meet a *nice guy*. One of those budding doctors or lawyers or engineers."

"You talking crazy, Daddy."

"No, seriously, Winter. My life from the outside is all good. But believe me, whether it's actually all good or bad, right or wrong, there's no letting up. No time to relax and just enjoy life. It's right when you think you've made enough big moves, now you can take that deep breath, that's when the next guy gets you. He'll figure he caught you sleeping, call you a tired old fool and move on you. Nobody wants to be all the time with one eye looking over your shoulder and one eye at the door. You, Winter, you deserve better. You deserve to relax, kick back, have the easy and finer things in life. No stress. One of these big-headed doctors, lawyers, engineer boys around this neighborhood can give you that. A man in Midnight's line of work can't."

5

When Momma was wheeled into the house the following week, it didn't matter that Santiaga had coached us on how to act and what to say. By this time he had told my younger sisters that Momma fell down and had a little accident where she cut her face. But no rehearsal could have prepared them for what they saw. Anybody who knew Momma could only be thinking one thing: Damn! Who was that? She looks bad! Me and Magdalena tried to smile and make light of the situation. But that look of shock and horror that came over the kids' faces when they saw her could not be erased by any joke. Momma was thinner than usual. The area around her mouth was twisted and disfigured. She still had a piece of bandage covering a small part of her face. There was only one thing I was sure of. I *would* be driving the big Benz.

Later that evening, while Santiaga was out, I pushed my mother's door open and quietly walked in. "What's up, Momma. How you feeling?" She was responding but her words were slurred. She sounded like an old-style wax record with the needle dragging on it. "OK, Momma, don't talk," I said, holding my hand up and smiling wide to make her feel comfortable. "I got a lot to say. Let me just fill you in. Nordstrom's has the perfect all-leather red Adrienne Vittadini suit for you. I even spotted some red driving gloves that go with it real nice. You hurry up and get better 'cause we gonna be cruising!" She gave me a sigh, then a half-smile. I knew that meant I was making her feel good. Hell, this was Momma. I knew what made her feel good!

"The housekeeper is here full time now. We been taking care of everything. The girls missed you so much, they're real happy you're home. Oh and Santiaga, he's like a puppy without his woman. You gotta hurry up and get better 'cause he needs you." Just then with the mention of Santiaga's name, one tear rolled out of Momma's left eye. "Don't worry, Momma. If there's anything you need, I'll get it for you.

We gonna get it together." I leaned over and gave her a kiss on her forehead, then whispered in her ear, "We bad bitches, remember? Bad bitches don't die." Again she cried instead of smiling. I tried to remain cool. "Girl, Santiaga's gonna get you the best of everything, no doubt. Your face gonna look even better than it did before the accident." At Momma's gesture, I handed her the pen and pad from her night table. She scribbled a note to me, which read: *Stay out of Brooklyn.*

Overcoming boredom was my new project in life. I had spoken with my girls from Brooklyn, but I ended those conversations as soon as the questions started flowing. Usually the questions started flowing immediately. Of course nothing but a Mack truck could stop Natalie's mouth from yapping. She volunteered the information that some serious shit had gone down around our way and some peeps turned up missing. Which really meant nothing to me except nosy niggas around the way ain't see certain people for awhile, but for all they know niggas could be down South visiting relatives or some shit like that.

"The block is hot." That's how Natalie put it, which meant that the 5-0 was everywhere. That shit didn't scare me 'cause we always had plenty of cops around our way in Brooklyn. Sometimes they were on the scene of the crime and looked the other way 'cause they had a piece of the action.

The way I figured it everybody had to have a hustle to survive. The cops wasn't no threat as long as their cut was in it. As Santiaga said, "You gotta know how to spread the cheese around the table." Natalie also filled me in on the up-and-coming cuties who was buzzing around the way and the goings-on. She had seen Midnight only once in passing. He didn't say shit to her. He never did and according to Natalie he just seemed to keep everything on the down low. He hadn't been to the club and Tasia been running round with little Nickel.

I wasn't going to tell her about the new Benz. But it was taking all I had for me to keep it a secret. Then Natalie remembered that my birthday was next week, on Friday. She said she wanted to big me up on my birthday, take me out, get some bubbly, and do our thing. The bonus was that Slick Kid, her man of the moment, was cool with Bullet. We could double-date and live it up at their expense. "Bullet?" I asked. "Little Bullet."

"Girl get up on it. Little Bullet is Bullet now and ain't nothing little about him." I thought about it for a second. I always thought Bullet was a little cutie, swift on his feet, a fast talker, and definitely had the hustle in him. He was a small-timer though. Not the type I'd ever consider to set up with or marry, but I could easily swing an episode with him. The puzzle was that I couldn't go to Brooklyn. I also couldn't mention that I wasn't allowed to go to Brooklyn.

I had been stalling and lying to Natalie about why I wasn't coming around the way. Security at our house was at an all-time high. The Saturday night parties were dead. Other than Magdalena, security, and the workers, we couldn't invite no houseguests. Now I needed to come up with a compromise, an alternative. This date was something I needed in order to connect with myself and my people. I really needed the attention. Mamma had been hogging all of it up lately. Santiaga been either having meetings in the den, out working the streets, or on the phone.

"Yeah, I'm down for the double date," I told Natalie. "I'll call you back to set up the details. But let Bullet know I'm all in."

Strategizing came easy to me. I got that from Daddy. I just laid the problem out like a chessboard and thought of different angles to come at it. The key was to be able to relax enough to see the whole situation in your head. If you got stressed out, Santiaga taught me, then you start making mistakes, overlooking critical shit. Now I wasn't a chess player myself, but everyday problems, I could decipher that shit.

Thoughts was running through me like a high-speed train. Stretched out on my bed, I came up with a brilliant plan. I say it was brilliant because it wasn't just a simple everyday plan. It was one that took everything and everybody and every possibility into consideration.

There was only one week left until my birthday. I started activating my plan that same afternoon. Mother was out of the confinement of her room and moving slowly throughout the house. Her mouth was still crooked and her face stiff and slightly swollen. She wouldn't go outside because of the embarrassment of her appearance. She was waiting for some type of operation to put her face back in order, but it was still too soon. The doctor said she had a few weeks of healing before her body could undergo another operation. I knew she was feeling bad. In fact, this was the first consideration in my plan.

"Momma, you're looking good today," I lied. "I can see where you're healing." I touched the left side of her face with two fingers. "Listen, let's go outside and head to the mall." She rolled her eyes at me. "No really, Mommy. I picked out some fly things for you. Since your face is looking better, you might as well get back on your feet. I know you like to be on top of things. You do want to look good for Santiaga and all." Momma smiled. It was funny, everything else could be fucked up but mention Santiaga and Mommy's whole world would light up. But still she protested; "I can't drive. It's not safe. I don't feel ready yet."

"Mommy, I can drive. I'll take you anywhere you want to go. Treat you like the queen you are. We can leave the kids with Magdalena. How about it?" I opened my arms wide to give her a hug.

She smiled. "I've been dying to get in my new car, but I didn't want to torture myself."

"Don't worry, Mommy. Just remember I know how you feel. We have both been trapped in this house too long. But today is our day and we might as well enjoy it." I helped Momma get dressed and ready. We picked out a full wig and tried to hide the left side of her face by letting the hair fall down in the front. I lent her my sharp leather hat. We went outside, cut the red ribbon, and both got high off the smell of the fresh leather interior.

Pushing a Benz was like being the president of the United States. It rode like a private jet. Even the potholes couldn't affect the smoothness of the ride. Everybody I passed on the road looked to see who was inside, yet the tinted windows shielded us like we were top-notch celebrities. Momma looked happy discovering more and more features in her car: the wood paneling, her engraved initials, the CD player, digital display, lighted mirrors, and so on. She relaxed. I knew I had accomplished step one, getting Momma used to the idea of me driving her car. I had to get her on my side so we could convince Santiaga that I needed to drive this car on my birthday.

Mommy and I got manicures and even pedicures at the mall. We even let this butch-like Swedish lady give us each a massage. We ended our day with a dinner.

"Wait until Santiaga sees your new outfits," I teased her. "He's gonna chase you all around the house."

"He won't have to run fast to catch me," she teased. "Winter, Santiaga told me that when I was in the hospital he had Midnight watching you and the girls. I didn't tell him I thought it was a stupid idea. We were already dealing with enough. But I wanted to check with you to see what happened. I know how you feel about Midnight."

I avoided her eyes. "Nothing happened, Momma, not a damn

thing. He was everything Santiaga wanted him to be. He walked a straight line. I guess I'm not as good as you, Moms. I can't get what I want from that man, he doesn't like me."

"He likes you," she snapped back. "He'd be crazy not to like you. You have everything any man could want." Momma had tears in her eyes again.

"It doesn't matter anyway. Santiaga said he doesn't want me with a man like Midnight, something about it being dangerous and unpredictable. I gotta tell you I was shocked to hear that, all of a sudden he started talking about I should marry some doctor, lawyer-type guy, not nobody like him. I guess it's because of what happened to you, Mommy. What do you think? If you had it to do again, Mommy, what would you do? Would you have married some engineer or doctor?"

Mommy cried, "Never, never. I love Santiaga more than I love my own life. The hell with other men. Santiaga is the *only man*. He takes care of me. He does everything a man supposed to do. He has given me everything. If I had to catch a bullet for him, so what. I'd rather they shot me than him. There'd be no sense in living without him." Her words fell on me like huge rocks. I was not used to this kind of talk. I was impressed by Momma's loyalty to Santiaga and I hoped one day me and Midnight would share the same kind of love.

"So you still think Midnight's a good catch for me?"

Momma sipped her Coke through the straw and said, "He's gorgeous, he is strong. He's a *young Santiaga*. It don't get no better than that. Let me work on Santiaga. By the time you're eighteen I could see him giving his OK. Hell, it's progress that he talked to you about men, period. That means he sees you're becoming a woman. He can't hold on to you forever."

I exhaled, rolled my eyes. "Eighteen! By that time I'll be so horny I'll die." We both laughed.

"You're young. Have fun. It's not like you gotta sit around waiting for Midnight. He'll come around."

"How's he gonna come around when he's in Brooklyn and I'm all the way out here?"

"I'll figure it out. We'll get him up to the house or something. We'll work on it. But you stay out of Brooklyn."

"Until when?"

"Until Santiaga says so."

The next day I strategically dropped bits of information about a party going on at Hofstra University, which is about an hour from our house. If I was going to meet college-educated men, like Santiaga suggested, I had to start going to some of these events.

By the end of the week I had buttered Momma up with compliments about her face. Now she was comfortable with lending me her car on my birthday and allowing me to go to the party at the university. However, I still had to get permission from Daddy to go out at night, even if it was my birthday. Convincing Santiaga was always a hard bridge to cross. He just had a natural suspicion about everything. One slight thing triggering his intuition would cause the whole thing to get shut down. I waited in the kitchen Monday night for him to come home.

"Santiaga, how you feeling?" I asked sweetly.

"I'm okay, baby girl. What you need?"

"Who said I needed something?"

"You're looking and sounding so innocent you gotta be guilty or something." He was talking in a joking way.

"I want to show you something, Daddy. Stay right there." I ran back to my bedroom and returned with my birthday outfit on a hanger. It was a black satin Chinese dress. I held my Joan and David shoes in the other hand. "In case you forgot, Friday is my birthday."

"Have I ever forgotten you on your birthday?" he asked, smiling.

"Listen, Poppa. So what I'm saying is Hofstra University is giving a sorority party on my birthday. I want to go. Mommy said I could drive her car and I plan to make friends like you said. The school is in Long Island and who knows I might even meet some bigheaded lawyer guy." I killed him with my smile. "So what do you say, Santiaga?"

"Who you going with?"

"I'm going with Vanessa," I said, to my own surprise. I had instantly conjured her up. "She doesn't have a car. So I'll pick her up. I met her at the mall, she lives about a half hour from here in Deer Park. She's gonna be a sophomore at Hofstra next year. She's studying to be a psychiatrist and . . ."

"OK, alright, don't fast-talk me. If your mother said you can use her car then fine. Be careful. And Winter, you are not to go to Brooklyn. Don't bullshit me. Don't give me no excuses. None of that. Stay out of Brooklyn. Be home by 3 A.M. Winter, if you meet some bigheaded lawyer guy, have him come here by the house before . . ."

"Before what?" I asked innocently.

"Before I have to break his neck for trying something stupid."

Thursday night I tied up the loose ends with Natalie. I played it cool but I was so excited it was hard to sleep. I turned on my radio, dimmed the light, and let Jodeci help my eyelids close.

When I woke up Friday morning, my sisters were all jumping up and down on my bed, smiling in my face, acting like they were having a sugar rush or something.

"What you doing in my room?" I asked.

"Happy Birthday!" the twins yelled.

Porsche rolled her eyes. "We thought you'd never get up."

"What's the hurry?"

"Daddy went out," the twins said.

"So?" I yelled at them.

"So he left a birthday present for you down in the living room and we are waiting for you to open it."

Sitting up, I laughed. "Why are y'all waiting for me to open *my* present?"

" 'Cause everybody knows you always get the flyest shit," Porsche said. "Meanwhile, I get a Mickey Mouse watch or Barbie dolls or something disgusting like that." My eight-year-old sister was going on twenty-two, always mad that she isn't me and always jocking what I have.

We invaded the living room and they held their breath while I opened another long slim box. It contained the matching diamond necklace to the diamond tennis bracelet I got one year ago. My sister sucked her teeth at my sparkling jewels. I was amazed at how clear each individual diamond was.

"See, that's what I'm talking about," Porsche said bitterly.

Later that afternoon I discreetly placed my Gucci overnight bag in the trunk of the Benz. By early evening I was all dressed up in my birthday outfit. My mother looked at my body filling out the black satin dress. Instead of complimenting me she cried. I thought to myself, *Damn, all she does lately is cry.* But tonight was my night. I pulled out the driveway cautiously, trying to keep my mother's confidence in my driving skills secure. I was sure she was watching through the window. When I was out of sight, I ripped down the road, headed for the highway. Santiaga said no Brooklyn and I will respect that. Natalie, Slick Kid, and Bullet were gonna meet me at the 42nd Street bus terminal in Manhattan. They had no idea I would be pushing a

Benz. The best part of my birthday was gonna be flashing the ride. I might even tell them Santiaga bought the Benz for *me* for my birthday.

On the way down I pulled into one of those all-service Amoco stations. I popped the trunk, grabbed my bag, jetted into the bathroom, and took off the ridiculous satin dress. My real outfit was red leather shorts that wore like a miniskirt, a red leather vest that accentuated my titties and fit tight around my small waistline. There was no use for a blouse. I threw my stockings in the wastebasket. My legs were shapely, big, and beautiful. There was no sense in hiding them. I had no scars or bruises. So what if it was cold. I wasn't walking. I was toasty in the red Benz.

I threw on my diamond necklace and my diamond tennis bracelet. My soft red leather jacket made it all perfect. With a piece of tissue, I wiped the foggy, gas station mirror. I could only clean a small area. The mirror was permanently dirty. I drew on my lipstick, checked my hair, and slipped my feet into my red leather Gucci shoes. I was good to go. Tonight was not the night for the bigheaded lawyer boys or engineers. Tonight was the night for raw Brooklyn-style fun and live niggas. In the trunk, I carefully stretched the black satin dress on top of the case, so it wouldn't wrinkle.

In the car, I pumped up the radio to stay alert during the long drive. I kept the car windows closed. I would creep up to the corner of 42nd and 8th, slowly lowering my window, then I would shout, "Surprise motherfuckers! Get on in!!" The scene played over and over in my head. The thought of the jealousy Natalie would feel thrilled me. I knew she would get over it quickly, though. That was my girl. She would be happy to ride shotgun in my whip.

On the radio, suddenly Sister Souljah started talking shit, her coarse voice overpowering the music. "The number one group of people dying from AIDS is young black women." I popped in a tape to shut her down before she started gettin' on my damn nerves.

I slowed the car to a creeping speed. Natalie, Slick Kid, and Bullet were chilling on the corner. Bullet was looking good. I could see his gold teeth shining. That shit got me hot. A mouth full of gold is sexy like a motherfucker. It just adds to the ruggedness, accentuating the attitude. Natalie was right, Bullet had filled out a little something. He had on black baggy jeans and some crisp Jordans. Slick was rocking a Pelle Pelle leather jacket, backpack, and jeans. Natalie had on an outfit I saw in Banana Republic the other day. Slick Kid turned around and caught sight of my Benz. He didn't know it was me but the car was so hot I had his full attention. His eyes popped out and he started checking the vehicle, sweating my rims, stepping up close. Natalie and Bullet followed. When they got up close to the glass, I lowered the window and said real sexy-like, "Y'all waiting for me?"

Natalie screamed, "No you didn't! Oh bitch no you didn't. Uh-huh uh-huh, I know this ain't your car. Don't even try it. What!" Bullet and Slick Kid immediately grabbed a guy on the street who shoots Polaroid pictures and flipped him a twenty-spot. They started posing on the hood, leaning against the car. I jumped out and we all posed together.

Bullet licked his lips, put his arm around my waist as he said, "Damn you look good." He opened his arms, and stepped back. "Let me look at you." I swung my ass around slowly. "Big pretty legs," he said, talking sexually like we were doing it already. He touched my legs with his finger, smiled and said, "No stockings. Nice." I smiled.

"I'm not walking. It's warm in the car. Get in!" We all got in. I checked Natalie's face in the rearview. There it was, that jealous look. Seconds later, just like I said, it was gone. She was whispering to Slick Kid, kissing and messing around.

"Hold on," Bullet said. "Where we going to the club on . . . Nah fuck that, let's go to a quiet spot. I don't want to have to bust nobody's ass tonight for tryna get mine's. I rather just chill with Winter. Let's shoot to the Marriott on 44th and Broadway." Right before we got there Slick Kid jumped out the car and picked up some Alizé and Absolut from the liquor store.

Slick went into the hotel with Natalie to check in. Me and Bullet sat in the car waiting.

"I ain't seen you in about a year or so," he said, looking into my eyes.

"Yeah, that's about right." I was playing shy.

"Where the hell you been?"

"Handling my business just like you, nigga. You never said nothing to me when I lived around the way."

"A nigga likes his life," he said, referring to Santiaga.

"Then why are you here?" I asked sharply.

" 'Cause times changed. A nigga grew up. Gotta a little weight on my own. Don't try to play with me, Winter. You wasn't checking on me either."

"Whatever. There's no sense in wasting time," I said. " 'Cause time I don't have a lot of. You look good to me. I hope I look good to you. I ain't had it in a long time and I'm ready to bring it together." I was looking him dead in his eye, letting him know I was serious. He leaned over and stuck his tongue in my mouth. He had a strong kiss. For a moment my head was gone. It seemed like I blacked out. I was kissing him with all the passion locked inside of me. It didn't really matter who he was. He was a warm body, a masculine body. He had flavor. He would get to feel all of me tonight because I needed it.

Natalie was knocking on the window and trying to see in at the same time. "Room 609 y'all. Come on up when you're ready. Glad to see we're getting along." She snickered and handed me the key. "We're in 610." Natalie headed back into the hotel. We pulled the car to the valet station and headed on up.

Bullet poured me a drink of Alizé mixed with Absolut. I sipped on it and felt relaxed. "Take off your shirt," I ordered. "Let me look at you."

He grinned. "Oh that's how you do it, huh? You like to be the boss." He pulled his shirt off. On his shoulder was a tattoo of a gun dispensing a bullet. The heat in me went up a notch. He walked over to turn the lights off.

"Oh no," I said, "I want to see everything. Turn 'em all on. We ain't got a damn thing to hide." I took off my jacket. I started to unbutton my vest, slipped it off and stood in front of him with my young 34Ds standing upright with extended nipples. I didn't have to say shit. He was all over me in an instant.

"Do what you feel," I said. I stepped into him and began licking his neck. He didn't taste salty and I liked that too, a clean body. I slid out of my shorts. They dropped to the floor. I began to undo his buckle and went for his zipper. When his pants fell to the floor his big penis stuck out of his boxers. I jumped on him, wrapped my legs around his waist and removed his shorts with my feet. Everything was physical the way I liked it. Watching his leg muscles go up and down, watching his ass move got me excited. I rode that dick like a professional jockey. All the energy in my body started running wild and high, then moved to the center and released. My body shook, then relaxed. I slid down his body onto the floor.

"Oh no you don't. Not until I get mine's." He mounted me on the floor doggy style and started giving it to me from the back. The chorus of his grunts and my moans turned me out. It was just a little freaky thing about me, the more I turned a nigga on, the more excited he got, the more excited and wild I would become. Two orgasms does the body good. We ended up in the Jacuzzi with Marriott bubble-bath bubbles foaming up everywhere. We had our drinks, puffed our weed, and was cool with the silence. Then loudmouth Natalie came busting up in the room through the connecting door with Slick Kid. "Where y'all at?"

Slick Kid laughed. "Baby, just follow your nose." Next thing I knew Slick Kid was in the bathroom where we were with his Sharp VL video camera rolling. He was cracking up and filming me and Bullet's cool-out session in the tub.

"Wait a minute," Natalie yelled. "Let me get in it, too. You don't mind, Winter, do you?" She pulled off her shirt and pants and hopped in the Jacuzzi with me and Bullet. Slick was laughing and taping us talking 'bout, "Ah Bullet, you a big willie. Now you got two girls." Bullet positioned himself between me and Nat to pose for the camera.

"Don't put your hands on my girl," Slick Kid joked and yelled.

Natalie loved it. "We're in the movies, y'all. Want to do any shout outs?"

"Oh yeah," I said, liquor talking. "I want to give a shout out to Simone, to Zakia, Asia, my girl Toshi, and all the live motherfuckers in Brooklyn BK to the fullest. I love all my peeps! Stay live y'all." Slick Kid wanted to get in the movies so he started filming himself with the camera.

"Attention niggas, this is Slick Kid. I just wanted to say the black man is God." Bullet cheered him on and added in his shout outs. We all laughed, drank, and puffed. We played cards, ordered movies and room service, buffalo wings, french fries, and lemonade. We had a good old Brooklyn-style good time.

At 2:30 A.M. I told them I had to roll. Bullet wanted me to stay but I told him I had to take care of some important shit and I'd pick it up with him later.

"What about breakfast? Time to make the doughnuts!" Slick Kid yelled. They decided to stay in the room till checkout since they paid for it. By this time Bullet confirmed that he still lived with his grandmother and he didn't have no ride home. I told him don't worry about it, I'd come pick him up some time in the Benzo and, as long as he kept it real with me, we could do it again!

My buzz was wearing off. This was a good thing because I was driving in the light rain of the late night/early morning, organizing my story about the college party. I had never been to one in my life. As far as I knew Santiaga had not either. Still I rehearsed it, knowing how clever Santiaga was.

When I pulled up into the driveway, Santiaga's Lex was not there. I was surprised since I was an hour and a half late and one hundred percent sure he'd be sitting in the kitchen with a mean old screw face ready to drill me. Luckily I realized that I was still wearing the red leather shorts. Panicked, I swung the car around to the back. I popped the trunk, grabbed my Gucci suitcase and unzipped it. I pulled out a fresh pair of stockings and picked up the satin dress. I was quiet about closing the trunk so as not to wake Mommy. I ran under the shed in the back of the house and started to peel off my little red outfit. My body was covered with goose bumps and shivering from the cold 4:30 A.M. air. When I took off my Gucci shoes, I realized I had left my Joan and Davids in the car. I clutched my car keys, tweaked the alarm off and tipped back to the trunk. I stuck the key in and swapped the shoes. By the time I got back under the shed my feet were covered with mud. I took off my panties to use them as a tissue to clean my feet. When I went to slip into my new stockings I pushed too hard and my big toe ripped through the bottom. The tear ran all the way up my leg.

I took a deep breath to calm me down. People who panicked made stupid mistakes, overlooked critical things, I reminded myself. OK so I'd put on the dress, no stockings, and I'd say they tore at the party. I started fumbling to put my hair back into place when I heard a noise from the side of the house. It sounded like cracking sticks under somebody's foot. I kicked the mud-covered panties under the bush and stuffed my little red outfit into the nearby garbage can.

"Come out of there whoever you are before I blow your fucking head off." The voice came from the side of the house. It sounded like my mother. I was trembling.

"Mommy," I called out. "Is that you?"

"Winter, are you OK?" She asked as though somebody had me bound and gagged.

"I'm fine, Mommy. I was just parking the car back here." She swayed around the corner with her flashlight and the little .22 gun Santiaga had given her for personal security.

"The light, take the light out of my face, Mommy, please," I said, not wanting her to see my panties in the bush. "Everything's OK." I went toward her, hugged her and walked her back around to the front of the house. "What happened to the lights in the backyard?" I asked.

"They broke 'em. They broke everything. Messed up all our stuff. They took the Lex. They took Santiaga. They tore up the house." Her words were going into my head in slow motion. My body froze like ice. Anger consumed me.

"Who took Santiaga?"

"The police. They came with papers talking about they charging him with this and that and the other thing. They searched through all of our belongings. They cut up my damn mattress. They scared the shit out of your sisters. They was crying and screaming."

"Where did they take him?"

"Central booking, the regular. They said they don't know where he'll end up. Just call the precinct, they said. He won't be arraigned until Monday since this is the weekend night."

"When did they come?"

"Santiaga got back right after you left here. He said he had a feeling that something wasn't right. I'm surprised you didn't see him on your way out. The cops pulled up here about a half-hour later, big Long Island white-boy, by-the-book cops. They came from everywhere without warning, up the driveway, out of the sky, the roof, the backyard. Before I knew it, they were inside the house, outside the house, all in everything like roaches. They arrested everybody, Santiaga, our security, everybody except me and the kids. I didn't know how to get to you, Winter. Eventually I beeped Midnight. It was about 10 P.M. I told him what happened and asked him to go out to that school to tell you to come back home. He called me back at about 11:45 P.M. talking 'bout you wasn't there. He looked all over."

My guilty eyes locked into my mother. Her eyes were bloodshot, her mouth twisted, her face stained with tears. We needed a strategy to get out of this confusion. "What did Santiaga say?"

"He was calm, cool. Of course they had his hands cuffed, locked tight in back of his body like he was some kind of criminal. He looked me dead in my eyes. All he said was sorry." Momma was hysterical or delirious or both. "I told Santiaga not to worry. I would come to get him out. Then one of them smart-ass cops, not the one in regular uniform, one of them feds or something, said it would be a long, long, long time before you'll see him anywhere besides behind bars.

"'That's what you think,' I told them bastards. 'That's what you think.' The next cop picked up your picture and was like woo wee that's a fine ass. That's when Santiaga started breaking. He said he would make it so that cop would never see his own kids again. The other cop started reading Santiaga his rights."

"Mommy, how many cops were there?"

"Inside or outside the house?"

"Both."

"About fifteen cops inside and twenty outside, in the back, everywhere." I sat down on the kitchen stool.

Daylight seemed to rush in. I made my mother take one of those sedatives the doctor prescribed for her facial pain. She had fallen asleep along with the kids. At 9 A.M. Magdalena arrived to work.

"What happened?" she asked with her Latino accent.

"Long story," I muttered. "Take your time cleaning this mess. We gotta straighten it up but it's no hurry." She had a look on her face as if she expected to be paid more money to repair the disaster.

"Don't worry, I'll take care of you at the end of the week," I told her. Money, money, I thought. Santiaga's gone. How will we get money? The upstairs safe popped into my head, the one situated behind my mother's clothing closet that I wasn't supposed to know about. I ran up the stairs. I pushed open my mother's door gently, not wanting to disturb her. She was there sitting on the bed smoking a cigarette, something I never ever saw her do.

"Looking for the safe?" she asked. "It's gone. It's empty. It's gone." She pointed to the closet where the safe door was open and empty. "Them bastards had warrants, papers, a whole bunch of shit. They said they been watching us for a long time."

"Other than the money, did they take anything else?"

"Other than the money," she said sarcastically. "OK, other than the hundred and fifty thousand dollars they stole from our safe, for *evidence* they said. Ha! *Evidence.* They're probably out shopping with that dough right now. They took the guns. They took plenty of guns."

"Coke?" I asked cautiously.

"None, Santiaga had just come back from his runs. Everything he had was already gone."

"How much money you got?" I was afraid to hear the answer.

"Seven hundred bucks, that's it," she said dryly.

I had nine hundred fifty dollars myself. That made a total of sixteen hundred fifty dollars, which, based on what we were used to spending, might as well have been seventeen dollars. Who could we call? My mind went blank. I sat on the floor in her room and my nerves numbed neutral. I had no feeling. The ringing of our telephone brought me back to reality. I picked it up. It was my mother's sister, Aunt Laurie, on the line.

"Where's Santiaga?" she demanded. Not having thought of what I would tell people, and when to tell them whatever I decided to tell them, I said nothing.

"Winter, stop playing, put Santiaga on the phone. These motherfuckers came and picked Stevie up outta here this morning and I need Santiaga to send somebody over to see what's happening and to bring some money so we can get him outta there."

"Santiaga's not here right now Aunt Laurie. Call back in a little while. Mommy don't feel well. Or I'll call you back. Sorry about what happened. I'll give Santiaga the message."

"Winter, these motherfuckers went crazy out here, arrested everybody. Tell your father somebody gotta come help us out down here."

By sundown it was apparent it was a total wipeout. One by one, women's voices filled with fear, rage, and hysteria, called demanding that Santiaga rescue their husbands, brothers, sons. They had all been bagged. I contacted Santiaga's lawyer Bob Goldstein. He was already on the case. He told me that right now there was nothing he could do but wait. He had phoned the precinct and verified Santiaga's presence. Now he awaited arraignment and placement. He was seeing what the bail looked like, what all the charges were, and what the evidence was like. He told me to come down to the office on Friday to handle matters and to bring my mother.

Magdalena did a hell of a job bringing the house back together again. I slid her a fifty-spot for the extra work. It killed me to let go of the cash, but I did it just to keep the peace with her. I'd need her to watch the kids. Magdalena grabbed the money real quick and held onto it real tight.

6

Monday morning we all was up early and dressed. There was no doubt that we would support Santiaga at his arraignment. We would show those motherfuckers that family sticks together. My mother put the girls in the back of her car and took the passenger seat. As I started to back the Benz up I saw flashing lights moving up our driveway. A cop on the loudspeaker said: "Turn off the ignition." I weighed my options. I wanted to floor the gas pedal, ram the police, and then pull out to go handle my business. But my little sisters were in the car, so I turned the ignition off.

"Get out of the car. Everyone step out of the car. Move away from the car." The police signaled the vehicle behind him. It was a police department tow truck. The officer walked up to my mother and handed her a piece of paper: "We are authorized to remove this vehicle, which is now government property."

"Uh-uh, motherfuckers! This is my car. How the hell you gonna come and take my car?" Angry tears shot out of my eyes. "You don't have the right to take people's shit." I went buck wild cursing them assholes out. I pushed the car door open, jumped out and started swinging my fists in the air.

"Ma'am, ma'am, ma'am, calm down, ma'am. Now listen. Here's how it works. We're going to take this car, right now, right here, today, this minute. We're authorized to do so. You go downtown. If you can verify the source of your income and prove that you personally purchased the vehicle, then you can get it back. We hold it for sixty days, if you can't prove it, we sell it at the auction. All merchandise purchased with illegal monies, by criminal activity, are subject to seizure."

Momma thumbed hysterically through the yellow pages trying to locate a cab that would come around our way. It took an hour to strike a deal with a somewhat local cabbie to drive us into the city. I paid a hundred dollars to get into the city. Money was going fast.

By the time we got to the court, we had missed Santiaga. I called the lawyer's office. His secretary said the lawyer must be on his way back to his office because he was there at the court to represent Santiaga earlier today. I hung up the phone without verbally acknowledging her words. It took damn near all day just to get back to our house on public transportation. Then we had to walk three miles to get from the train station to our "safety house."

Tears didn't have no place in this situation. *What would Santiaga do?* I asked myself. He would think, plan, and not panic. Alright, it seemed to me that we needed to have one big sale to get rid of all this shit in this house and get some money. I never liked it here anyway. We could move back into the city, get an apartment or something. I started pacing around the house randomly pricing things in my head. Who would we sell this stuff to? We didn't know nobody around here. We would straight up have to put an ad in the papers, hang up garage sale signs and directions to our house. Let these folk come pick over it and pay way less than they would normally pay in the store.

I found Mama in her room. She had busted open a new pack of cigarettes and was going at it. "What do you think about a sale?" I asked her. "We sell all this stuff in the house to generate some cash flow."

"I want to talk to your father," she said.

"Seriously, Momma, what do you say?"

"I want to see what your father says. Whatever he wants to do that's what I'll do."

"But Mommy we gotta make plans like Santiaga ain't here 'cause he's not."

"You tryna say he ain't coming back?" she asked like a crazy woman.

"No, I'm trying to say maybe if we put our heads together we can have some ideas ready for Santiaga. We can go see him tomorrow. I'll know by the morning time exactly where he is." The idea of seeing Santiaga delighted Mommy, who was starting to seem like an impostor to me.

"What we gonna do with the kids, they too much trouble to be tryna walk and travel back and forth with," she asked, worried about everything.

"Magdalena will watch them," I told her.

"Oh you think so. Lately, she been acting kind of funny," Momma said.

At nine o'clock the next morning I was on the phone line tryna locate Santiaga. I slid Magdalena an extra twenty dollars and told her to baby-sit while me and Mommy took care of some business. She looked like she thought about rolling her eyes at me. She put the extra money in her pocket. We found out which jail Santiaga was being held at. Then we went to find out the cost of bail so we could pull the money together somehow. The court clerk smirked when he punched in the case numbers for Santiaga on his computer.

With some strange look of pleasure he pronounced, "The judge has denied bail because of the extremity of the charges. He'll be sent out to Riker's Thursday. You can visit him there."

My mother's face saddened with disappointment. As we turned to walk away her tears started flowing.

When we got home, Magdalena complained about the phone ringing, ringing, ringing. We thanked her for her patience and sent her home for the evening. The good thing was that in two days we would be able to talk to Santiaga. He would help us decide how to move. My mind was still tryna put things together. I asked my mother whose name the house was in and if it was a monthly cost or was it paid for in full. She told me it was paid for 'cause that's how Santiaga does things, but she never saw the paperwork because it wasn't her concern.

This time when I picked up the telephone, it was Natalie. "Girl what's going on? It's like a ghost town over here in BK." *Everybody's getting locked up,* I thought to myself. Whoever heard of a person who just starts talking before she even says hello, before she's even sure if she's talking to the right person?

"Who got knocked?" I asked, playing it off. She rattled off a list of familiar names, Daddy's workers, bodyguards, and all of my uncles. Then she said, "I heard Midnight got picked up earlier tonight."

"Get the fuck out of here," I said, almost mumbling.

"Yep, Asia saw the cops cuffing him over in front of Moe's bar." I wondered if Natalie had heard about Santiaga and was she just waiting for me to say something. "Yeah, Bullet told me about Midnight, too," Natalie said.

"How's Bullet doing?" I asked.

"He's alright. His girl just had a baby. It's a boy, eight pounds, six ounces, big huh?"

"His girl! Natalie you didn't tell me he had a girl."

"Like you would've cared. Don't try to get new on me, Winter."

"That's not the point. I'm just saying you suppose to have my back. You suppose to let me know what's going on."

"Yeah, I'm supposed to fill you in like you be filling me in, right!" Natalie said, getting loud with me. I really didn't have time for Natalie's attention games so I told her I had to go.

"The policia," Magdalena said, peeking her head into my room without knocking on my bedroom door. "You motha is in the shower." I jumped up, threw on some pants and a shirt, and headed downstairs.

"Good morning, ma'am. We'd like to speak to Mrs. Santiaga please. We want to ask her some questions."

I put my hands on my hips and asked if they had a warrant. As soon as they said no I got ready to say Momma's not home. Then Mama came out of nowhere wrapped in a towel. Her hair was wet, her eyes wild, and her mouth twisted. "What is it now?" she asked.

"We want to ask you some questions."

"Do you have a warrant?"

"No, ma'am."

"Then get the fuck out of my house. I've had enough of you all for one week."

"Ma'am, we just wanted to ask you some questions about your husband. Under the RICO laws, you could also be charged if you were aware of or in any way connected to the distribution of narcotics. We would like you to cooperate with us. It will be better for you."

"Get the fuck out," she yelled. "Do you see a lawyer in here? How you gonna ask me some questions without my lawyer present. Do I look like a fool to you?"

"You're right. You're entitled to have a lawyer present," his partner chimed in. "But you know we could easily get a warrant under these circumstances, ma'am. Or you could just cooperate."

"Winter," Momma commanded, "close the damn door."

Momma was renewed on Thursday morning. She picked out her best outfit and was gonna take Santiaga by storm at Riker's Island. She asked me to help her with her makeup. I tried to make the best of the situation and put it on as nicely as I could. I brushed her hair back and used the same wig that worked for her the day we went shopping. Momma pulled out her perfume, the expensive shit that was thick like syrup. She dabbed it on in a small amount. When you have good stuff, she once told me, you don't have to pile it on. She looked fine, at least compared to the last few days when she let herself go in ways I had never seen before. She handed me the Visine. I dropped two drops in each of her eyes. I reminded her to take off her heels, put them in her pocketbook and wear flat shoes since we had to walk to the bus stop. She protested.

"We should take a cab to Riker's," she said.

"We should really save our money, 'cause we're running low," I warned.

"We'll save it some other day. Today we're going to see Santiaga."

"Yes, we have a warrant and we're gonna run you down for questioning," announced the same cops from yesterday. They arrived when me and Momma were leaving. As we opened the door to go see Daddy, we were confronted by the two cops.

"Am I under arrest?" my mother asked sarcastically.

"If that's what we need to have a civil conversation with you." Momma handed me her pocketbook. Unwilling to cooperate with the police, she stuck out her wrists as if to say "take me." The police read Mamma her rights, cuffed her, and put her in the car. Magdalena and the girls watched in horror from the kitchen. I stood there shocked and watched them take my mother away. On the way out the smart-ass cop's partner paused, turned around, and hollered to me standing in the doorway.

"By the way, how old are you?"

"Seventeen," my sister Porsche blurted out. "And where are you taking my mother?"

"How 'bout you, little girl? How old are you?"

"Eight," she said, snotty and proud.

Their lights flashed as they sped away.

I took out a twenty, handed it to Magdalena, collected my things, and made fast tracks in my Nikes headed to the bus stop.

Santiaga walked into the room accompanied by a corrections officer. His body was tight and his face serious. He still maintained his powerful presence. He had a way of looking good, even in those jail greens that hung on him like a leisure suit. I smiled when I saw him, he smiled back. "Where's your mother, downstairs?" he asked.

"No, she wasn't feeling good. She had to take two of those pills and they knocked her out cold. You know, only something *that* dramatic could keep her away." I had practiced this answer the whole trip to Riker's, no sense in adding to Santiaga's problems.

"And my girls?"

"They're fine. You know they miss you and all, but they're tough, they'll do alright."

"Maybe," he smiled. "Porsche has seven years in the projects under her belt, she's tough. Mercedes and Lexy, now they been sheltered. They're straight up suburban kids." I laughed but wanted to hurry on to the business.

"Daddy, tomorrow I'm going to see your lawyer. I'm gonna find out everything. What do you need me to tell him?"

"I been talking to him on the phone every chance I get," he said. "He'll want to talk money. He don't have to worry about that though. I got money."

"Daddy, they raided the safe at the house. They took a hundred and fifty grand." He held his hand up to keep me from talking.

"Just get ahold of Midnight. He got fifty dollars of mine." I was sure that this was a code for fifty thousand dollars. "He'll take care of everything. Just let him know I said it's that time."

"Daddy, someone said Midnight got picked up, too. I don't know if it's true. But that's what I heard." Daddy's eyebrows knitted together as if Midnight's arrest was somehow not what he had planned for.

After a short pause he said, "He'll be out soon. They got nothing on him. He's clean. I kept him that way. Just chill, and wait for him. He'll come through. He always does. Meanwhile tell Goldstein I said 'use the key.' That'll be a deposit on his fee."

"Daddy, Uncle Steve got picked up, and Harry, Van, and Ron."

"I know. I seen all them. Driguez, Pizzaz, they all in here. It's like being at home." He smiled, I'm sure more for my benefit than anything. "They just tryna shake my niggas up, scare somebody until they sing. You know what I mean. I'm alright Winter, don't worry about me. It's Momma you gotta look after. After that bullet, she's delicate. She don't know it, but she is."

"About the house, Santiaga, I think we should sell it. You know, so we'll have some money flow."

"I like your mind," he said. "Tell Goldstein. Tell him I said sell it. Winter, you gotta be tough. It's time. Remember everything I taught you. Keep your ears open. Follow the directions I gave you to the letter, and just play your hand close to your chest." We said that last line together. I had heard it so many times. I had never really thought about how important it was, but it was sinking in now.

"Tell your mother I want to see her one week from today on Thursday. Tell her I said pull herself together and get down here on Thursday in her best shit so I can show her off."

Magdalena had her stuff packed and at the door when I reached home. Her face was serious and fed up.

"What's up?"

"That's it." She rubbed her hands together. "Finished."

"What is it? You want more money?" I asked her. "I'll give you more money. I was gonna pay you on Friday. That's tomorrow, payday. Hell, I tipped you every day this week!"

"It's not the money Ms. Winter. But I do need my pay for up until today."

"Magdalena," I pleaded, "come on, girl, you know I need you. My father's gone. My mother's gone. It's just me and the kids. If you leave me, I won't have anybody to help me with the kids."

Magdalena busted out crying. "There is no kids."

Her words hit me one by one. Each word in slow motion. "No kids." I lost my composure. The tears burst out. "No kids?! What the fuck do you mean, Magdalena." I grabbed her shaking her shoulders uncontrollably. "Where are my sisters? What the fuck do you mean no kids? Huh? Huh? Huh?"

"The BCW people came and said they were sent by the police. They said they had to take the kids 'cause there is no adult in the house."

"What are you talking about, Magdalena? You're an adult!"

"But Ms. Winter I had to tell them I no responsible. I have to leave at 7 P.M. this evening. They had de papers from the gobernment. They took 'em. I'm sorry, I'm sorry," she cried. Then the horn honked, the signal from her son who picked her up every night in that raggedy 1970-something car.

As she held her hand out to be paid, I yelled, "You bitch! You couldn't cover for me, you couldn't just cover for me." My voice echoed in the middle of this huge empty house. "I ain't giving you shit," I screamed, throwing a vase at her as she rushed out the door.

Every step I took around the house sounded like it was magnified by a microphone. I could hear my own heart beating in my chest and in my ears. I started hearing shit I never heard before, noises and heating systems and water dripping. I was stranded without a ride, without a family member. I was out in the fucking woods.

Just then Sterling, my old sugar daddy, became the most important person in the world. I ran upstairs, pulled my jewelery box out, looked for his number and called him. I had to calm down first. The worst thing I could do was make Sterling think I needed him. Then he would try and turn the tables.

"Sterling, this is me, Winter. It's funny how you just came to mind. I was sitting here by the fire with my panties on, and I thought damn, I miss Sterling. Do you think you want to see me, 'cause I definitely want to see you."

"Winter," he said apologetically, "I have company right now." A tear dropped from my eyes. I cleared my throat to bring the strength back into my voice.

"Who's there with you?" He answered with silence. "Is she better than me Sterling? You know how good I can make you feel and I'm really needing you tonight, right now."

"OK," he said. "Give me a couple of hours. I'll pick you up at eleven." I packed my overnight bag. My money was running low, so I dropped my diamond bracelet, earrings, and necklace in my bag, too. If needed that was as good as money to me. I ran around the house turning on all the lights, TVs, and radios to convince myself I wasn't alone until my ride came.

If I fucked Sterling that night I didn't know it. It didn't matter. My mind was on vacation. Apparently Sterling was so stupid that just my sweet face was enough to make him do whatever I wanted. The next day I convinced him to let me drop him at work and use his car. I promised to pick him up later that night. The idea of him seeing me two nights in a row was enough bait for him.

I putt-putted in the LeCar back to the house in Long Island, hoping that my mother would be released and I could meet up with her. At some point she'd figure out she had to cooperate even if all she said was I don't know, I don't know, I don't know. Then they would release her. Hell, she was completely innocent. I hated to think of her in jail, especially with her being so fragile. Since when does spending your husband's money become a crime? If it were, more than half of all women in the whole county would be locked down. If she wasn't at the house by the time I got there, I'd swing by the precinct. The way I figured, they'd just try to shake her up. Try to get her to give evidence against Santiaga, which she would never do. I'd pick up my Moms. Then we would track down the girls.

The driveway to my house was blocked off. It wasn't a regular police car—you know, the kind with the siren—it was one of them cars like the D.T. drives, undercover. I pulled to the side of the road. I climbed the winding driveway leading up to our home.

"Excuse me, Officer, this is my house and—"

"This house and all the belongings inside are now the property of the federal government. No one is allowed on the property unless he is an agent of the federal government."

"Who are you?"

"The FBI," he said with authority and a puffed out chest.

"Explain this to me," I said, carefully. "How is it that you people can take people's property, steal their house, and not even allow a woman to get her clothes out or her baby sister's bottles?" I was going for sympathy. I had no wins running up against the glock.

"In America, miss, all material items purchased with illegal money made from illegal actions and transactions are subject to seizure. Now if you want something in there all you gotta do is bring some pay stubs from your job and prove you have a legitimate occupation. If those items inside the house are within the boundary of your earnings and you can prove it to the judge, you can get them back. You can pick up the necessary paperwork from the precinct or have your lawyer call us up and we'll send it to him."

I wanted to spit in his face but for now it wouldn't be smart. The only thing to do now was go straight to Santiaga's lawyer. Otherwise all these cocksuckers would give me this official talk and send me away empty-handed. I would get the lawyer involved on my mother's behalf as well. As the LeCar maxed out at sixty miles per hour, my mind calculated the value of everything in my bedroom—jewelry, clothes, shoes, electronics, TV, etcetera. *Hats off to the motherfucking police,* I thought to myself. They had the best hustle in town. They were the real criminals.

Goldstein's office was plush. The chairs were buttery leather, the walls walnut. The windows looked out onto the outlines of the city. I wasn't surprised. It was my father's style to be affiliated with the big-timers. I sat down in the big chair. It was reserved for clients and positioned directly in front of the attorney's chair. I kept thinking that this chair was the hot seat. It got you all impressed. Then just as you started to feel all comfortable, the lawyer would demand a minimum of ten grand just to peek at your case.

"So you are Santiaga's daughter, beautiful, beautiful?" He smiled like a gentleman. "Where is your mother? I thought I told you to bring your mother."

"She's locked up." His left eyebrow raised up. He reached to his desk and grabbed one of those legal pads and listened to my whole story. He didn't interrupt me once. Only the lines on his forehead answered. Every now and then he'd scribble on the pad.

"Well now, you've got about five different matters here. Your father, that's one. Your mother, that's two. Your sisters, that's three. You want me to look into the matter of your house, that's four. The cars, that's five. It's going to take a lot of manpower to get this job done."

I could feel him setting me up for the kill, fattening me up like a pig before the slaughter. He just wanted the bacon. "Right. Santiaga says, use the key." He repeated my message from Santiaga to himself. Then he muttered something like power of attorney. He found the paper he was looking for in the file. He smiled, told me he'd get to work on all these matters. He would use the key and let me know *what else* was needed. He asked for my phone number and address.

"Haven't you been listening? I have no address. I'll be drifting. I'll call you."

"By the way," he said as I was stepping out of the door, "how old are you?"

"Seventeen, why?"

"Because my best bet is that the Bureau of Child Welfare will be looking to pick you up as well."

"I can take care of myself."

"Yes, but according to the law, the state is your temporary guardian until you turn eighteen years old. You are a minor. Not to worry," he said smiling again, "we'll just need to get ahold of your mother to get around this mess. My office will be the meeting point. When I get your mother, I'll bring her here or at least you can check in periodically with one of my secretaries and they will be able to tell you where to meet her."

Between the money that I took out of my mother's pocketbook, plus my own cash, I had a total of $1,480, a diamond necklace, a diamond bracelet, diamond earrings, and the clothes on my back.

If there hadn't been a flashing pink sign that read DINER, when I walked out of Goldstein's office, I wouldn't've remembered to eat. I had been three days without thinking about food. I had a chance to eat but I kept trying to get my head to think of answers to all these situations. Soon as something clicked into place something else popped out of order. Making a plan was complicated. When would my moms get out? What fee would the lawyer charge? I couldn't come up with a good plan because I couldn't relax. I was cool on the outside, but inside I was in a state of panic. Normally I'd be plotting on a party. Now I was plotting on survival, something Santiaga always took care of for me. If nothing else was clear, the fact that I had to take care of myself was. The girls were little and cute. Somebody would give them shit for the time being. I, on the other hand, would have to get mines myself.

I wasn't sure if I could go back to Brooklyn yet either. I tried not to get paranoid and start thinking there was a hit on me or something crazy. Out of respect for Santiaga and my moms, I decided to wait. Besides, Brooklyn represented too many unanswered questions for now. Aunt Laurie would be vexed because we never called her back about Uncle Steve. By now she would've found out Santiaga got knocked too. Everybody would be expecting our family to roll out the dough, bankroll everybody's situation like normal. We were no longer in the position to get down like that 'cause money had to go toward our own problems, especially Santiaga's case. I wasn't about to put *myself* in the position of having to borrow shit from them either. I could see them tryna flip attitude on me something lovely. Bowing down was not something I do.

I knew I could always chill at Natalie's. Her moms wouldn't give a damn and probably wouldn't even know I was there. But the shit Natalie pulled with Bullet had me looking at her like she couldn't be trusted. Realistically Natalie was a lifeline. She had information. What I could do, I decided, was play her. Get to know what I needed to know. Tell her as little as possible and even throw her a curve ball now and then. I definitely wasn't gonna give her the pleasure of feeling like now me and her was on the same level. I would focus on the loochie, the cash, the loot, and just how I was going to make it.

I picked over my cheeseburger deluxe for an hour and a half before I came up with a plan. The impatient waitress tried to clear me out of the diner by exhaling real loud like I was taking up too much space for the amount of money I was spending. The key to getting back on top was Midnight. He had the fifty thousand dollars Santiaga told me about. Even though it was Santiaga's money and I didn't know how much of it he would need toward legal fees, there would be no harm in me getting my hands on the dough. I was not in jail so I might as well be useful. The smart thing to do would be to flip the cash. Invest it and double it at least. Then I could deliver the fifty grand to the lawyer and have a nice piece of change to set myself up as well.

I would use Sterling for as long as possible, at least until I got answers to the big questions about my mom, pop, and sisters. I couldn't see him minding. He seemed to enjoy being used. I'd just pretend that all of a sudden I realized he was the one for me. He'd stare at me with those big dumb eyes and be happy I had finally seen the light. Whatever chick he had there before I came last night, she'd just have to wait. Eventually she could have the man, I just wanted the pockets, the apartment, and access to his little putt-putt to handle my business.

Goldstein located Moms swiftly. He told me she was being charged with resisting arrest, insulting and assaulting a police officer. From his estimation those charges were just a means for them to hold her for questioning about Santiaga and his operation. He put in his notification of representation. The court was backed up and she wouldn't be arraigned until Monday morning. He said this was a good thing because he needed time to get to Santiaga's safety-deposit box at the bank to see the status of things so we could settle the financial matters. He told me he was 98 percent sure he could get the prosecutor to lessen the charges on Mom, drop them completely or at minimum get her out on her own recognizance since she had no previous charges. This way she wouldn't have to post bail. She'd just have to show up for her court date. He sternly told me to call him around three o'clock Monday.

Things were out of my hands. I had two hours before I had to pick Sterling up, so I went shopping. Nothing expensive, the Gap, Banana Republic, basic shit to get me through the weekend and the following week. Three hundred dollars was the budget I gave myself.

Why waste words on Sterling? Know that he was quick to dump the female friend he had over the other night. He was glad I decided to stay with him for the two weeks "my parents were out of town." He said he couldn't blame me for not wanting to stay in that big house alone and that he was happy I chose to spend my spare time with him.

Early Monday evening, Momma was released. She had on the same clothes she went in with. Overall she looked busted. Wig off, hair in bad need of Earline's, mouth permanently twisted, I guess. She went off about the feds seizing her leathers, furs, suedes, jewels, furniture, and house. She was enraged by the loss of her record collection, which she had carefully acquired over the past seventeen years. "Whoever heard of the legalized robbery they orchestrated?" she cried. "And whoever thinks they can steal my babies got to be crazy 'cause I'm going to get them first thing tomorrow when the Bureau of Child Welfare office opens. And Magdalena needs her ass kicked. She should of known better than to let some woman in the house who was not in our family. And let me see some motherfucker driving around in my red Benz, sporting my wears. They'll get their ass car-jacked right on the spot."

"Where are you going to live?" I asked Momma.

"Don't worry about me. What else can they do to me?" she asked. "They already shot me in my face. What they gonna do next," she started laughing like the Penguin on *Batman*.

"Are you going to stay with Aunt Laurie?"

"Yeah."

"She's gonna be pissed about Stevie and money and everything," I warned. She waved her hand in the air as if to say none of that mattered.

"After all I did for her. Santiaga gave that worthless husband of hers a job when nobody else would. She better recognize. She just better make room for me. Treat me like the queen I am and just help out till Santiaga gets home. He'll straighten all of this out." Speaking Santiaga's name put her in another frame of mind. I saw her eyes switch and her voice did too.

"I saw Santiaga," I said. "He's alright. He asked about you, of course. He wants you to come down to see him on Thursday. Dress your best he said. He wants to show you off." Mamma cried.

The twins were divided. "We don't like to do it, but all of our facilities are overburdened. We had a space for Mercedes Santiaga in Manhattan. The other one, Lexy, is in Brooklyn. Porsche Santiaga is in Queens. There will be no problems getting them ready for release, but we have to release them to a stable environment. As it stands, Ms. Santiaga, you are still under criminal investigation. You have no residence. The address you're listing here, your sister's apartment, is a section eight residency. This means it must meet federal regulations for living arrangements. Your sister already has three children in her apartment. There are only three bedrooms; therefore it would be a violation of federal codes for us to release three more children into this apartment, or even one for that matter. Your sister has one daughter and two sons. Under federal regulations, a male and female child cannot share a room together after they reach ten years of age. You stated your sister's sons are twelve and fifteen. We just can't do it. Do you have a relative who can speak up for the children who has extra rooms in a non–rent subsidy, federally regulated building or house?" All of our peeps were in the projects. So that question didn't deserve an answer.

"Look miss, I just want my children," my momma said. "Now I'm good for raising hell. But I'm tryna be nice, work with you here. I've been through a lot, I'm innocent. I'm not perfect, but I just need to have my babies with me. I'm not a drug addict, crackhead, or criminal. I just need to have my girls back today."

"You're presently unemployed," the lady said, as if we didn't know it. "The only option we can offer is the emergency assistance program. We can put you and your children up in a family shelter with a kitchenette so you can cook your own meals. We would allocate you food stamps and medical coverage for the children, but there's a waiting list for these type of facilities. There's no way we could release the children to you with no income and no apartment. To be honest with you, Mrs. Santiaga, there are also some more problems with this case. The girls are five years old, but they're not registered in kindergarten. Why? Did they attend private schooling?"

"No. If you check the birth date on my girls you'll see that they turned five after the deadline for kindergarten registration."

"Oh, I see, OK. Anyway, Mrs. Santiaga, we are willing in the meanwhile to place you in a women's shelter while you try to pull things together. Sometimes it's better to check into a shelter than to move into another problematic environment. The girls tell me, and our records show, that there is another child, one Winter Santiaga. Is that you?" she asked, eyebrow raised.

"No, I'm Rosie, a friend of the family," I lied.

"We'll need to know the whereabouts of the other child. Legally she is still a minor and we are responsible for her. We can place her in a group home with lenient rules and regulations since she is an older child. We can help her to complete her schooling. As long as she has no history of emotional problems, violent behavior, or educational dysfunctions she would not have to live in a restrictive or reformatory facility. When can you arrange to bring her in or provide us with an address so we can have her picked up?"

My mother glanced at the big-armed security police stationed in the corner of the room. She looked at me and said, "This is unbelievable." Thinking of the time she spent in jail, she said in a polite yet aggravated voice, "Can I have your business card, miss? I'll give you a call and let you know what I want to do."

"Give us a call soon. We need to locate Winter. Should I put you on the family shelter waiting list in the meanwhile?"

My mother lowered her eyes. "Yes. But I believe you'll be seeing me in court very soon. I need to get my girls back right away."

In Goldstein's office my mother went off. Goldstein had the confidence of a well-paid elderly gentleman. He let her rattle on and remained courteous.

"Let's separate the matters," he said calmly. "First of all, we're operating with a nut of fifty thousand dollars. This is what I retrieved from Santiaga's safety-deposit box. The real money is in his bank accounts. But his bank accounts are all frozen. His business records have all been siezed. None of that money will be accessible until after the case is closed. Depending upon the way things unfold, that may never be attainable. Given these circumstances that's a small nut. Deduct seventy-five hundred dollars for Ms. Santiaga's case."

"Seventy-five hundred dollars for what?" my mother screamed.

"For getting all of the charges against you dismissed, Ms. Santiaga. That wasn't easy. I had to really lean on the prosecutor in Long Island. You could be doing six months to a year and a half right now. I'd say your freedom is well worth your money. Wouldn't you agree?"

"But I didn't resist arrest. I didn't assault no officer. How could I have assaulted them when I was already handcuffed?"

"Be that as it may, I took care of everything. My fee is seventy-five hundred dollars. The case for your children will require a retainer of three thousand. That's a discount. Family court is a messy matter. It's time-consuming. If the matter drags out, then you'll receive my bill with the additional particulars. As far as Mr. Santiaga is concerned, I'll need a retainer of fifty thousand dollars just to get involved. This is a big, big, case. He's looking at years on top of years and possibly even life. A lot will depend on whether these cases get separated or not. There are several codefendants. Some of these cases can drag on and on. It's a little early to discuss, however, if we go into appeals we're looking at another major set of expenses. You need to be prepared for that. It all depends on how far Santiaga wants to take it."

"So what exactly is my father being charged with?" I interrupted. The lawyer surrendered one of the folders in Santiaga's file. There were ten sheets of green papers issued by the courts.

"The answer to my question," I said. "What is he charged with?"

"Everything. You name it. Santiaga is being accused of it, conspiracy, murder, weapons, money laundering, tax evasion . . ."

It was ridiculous to me. People don't understand Santiaga's world. It's business. Nobody kept a drug dealer's business in check but the dealer himself and the team he set up. There has to be punishment for those within the team who test too much and step out of line. There has to be punishment for outsiders who attack the business. Violations have to be responded to; otherwise the business don't flow correctly and people try to take advantage. They shouldn't be able to barge into our business and force their rules on us. Not when Santiaga knew his workers better than anybody from the outside. Everybody in this game understood what he was dealing with.

Nobody forced them into this business. They understood the risks. Besides, the drug dealers helped America to be rich. If it wasn't for us, who would buy the fly cars, butter leathers, and the jewelry? We put so much money into circulation. More than them little nickel-and-dime–paying taxpayers. We employed half the men in the ghetto. Nobody else gave them jobs. So why be a player hater?

It was sixty thousand five hundred dollars that had to go to the lawyer up front. Goldstein already had fifty thousand. Soon as I track Midnight I'd locate the loot and deliver the ten thousand five hundred to Goldstein. I'd have thirty-nine thousand five hundred to push around and double. Daddy said Midnight would be released. I'd offer him a partnership since he already knew the business. He'd go for it as long as he got his cut. Momma and Goldstein were closing out their talk. Momma was asking if she could arrange to see the girls at the places they were being held. Goldstein promised to look into the matter.

On the way out I asked Momma, "How was last night at Aunt Laurie's?"

"It's as cool as can be expected. She keeps asking if Santiaga had any money put away for a rainy day. She wants me to know that it's raining and she needs the cash."

"What did you tell her?"

"I didn't tell her shit. I just looked at her like this." Momma made a real ugly face and rolled her eyes into her head. I laughed. Momma was becoming a real comedian. "After I made this face she knew the deal. Don't ask me for shit!" Momma said.

I never mentioned to Momma that Santiaga told me about Midnight having some money set aside. I don't know why I didn't, I just didn't.

After repeatedly beeping Midnight, he finally answered my page:

"Who's this?" A shock wave shot through my body.

"Winter."

"What do you want?"

"Santiaga . . ."

"Where do you want me to meet you for dinner?" he asked strangely. "I'm in Manhattan. I can meet you on 34th and 8th tonight at eight. We can go any place you want from there."

When I hung up I began piecing together a cute little story to tell

Sterling so he wouldn't have a fit about me going out tonight without him. Then I picked up a new skirt suit to rock for dinner.

The cold air stung my face. The wind was whipping the pleats on my wool miniskirt, offering a free peep show to anybody who was looking. I was feeling a little more relaxed in the new suit, though. I knew my money was real tight, but this suit was an investment. If I could walk Midnight into my corner, we could regroup, create a new hustle, and land on our feet like cats.

Whatever Midnight decided to do *would* affect my father and even my own life. But I wasn't about to give him the impression that I was desperate. I wasn't stupid enough to go and try to get my hustle on without the input of a *real player.* Midnight knew the ins and outs. Plus he knew my father was loyal to him and he could duplicate Santiaga's style of running things. In fact Santiaga could somehow counsel him from the inside. Santiaga had stayed on top for so long that Midnight, in the few years of working for him, had to have learned the secrets to his business. I knew at first me and him would have to squash any beef we had in the past, even though I never understood what the problem was anyway. He acted like me wanting to get with him was a crime. As serious as things were now, I was sure he would see that me and him gotta work together otherwise some lowlifes were gonna be happy to watch us sink down to their level. I promised myself not to piss him off. I was gonna stick to business.

"Don't talk business over the phone." Midnight had rolled up to the curb and dashed open the window. He didn't even get out of the car. He didn't even say hello, peace, or what's up. "You called about the money, right? Well, I'll have it for you Monday morning. Where do you want me to drop it?"

"I thought we was going for dinner," I said nicely, bugging out on the way he was treating me.

"That was just something to say to keep you from running your mouth on the phone. There's a lot of brothers in jail today because they or some silly girlfriend don't know how to shut up over the phone. I knew what you wanted, I'll take care of it. Meet me Monday at 1:30 P.M. on the pier outside of Louie's restaurant at the South Street Seaport." He pressed a button and the window closed tight. As his wheels started to roll, I kicked his car with my foot.

"Wait a minute. Wait a fucking minute. Who the fuck do you think you are?" He hit the brakes, reversed, and the passenger window rolled down.

"Are you crazy? The last thing you want to do is make a scene."

"Well, I'm gonna make a movie if you don't show me some respect."

"Respect," he laughed. "What you know about that? I saw your naked ass on that videotape sipping champagne with Bullet. Who'da ever known that Santiaga's daughter was sipping bubbly with a nigga who's a worker for the other side! While your daddy was being raided by the feds you were having drinks butt naked with the enemy." His words pierced me like knives. I was tongue-tied. I had been part of a setup. My mind tried to reject any blame. I would never do anything to hurt Poppa. My chest was heated up. My mouth cranked up and said whatever came to mind.

"Yeah, I was with Bullet. So what! You gotta problem with that?"

"I spent the night in jail behind your stupid shit. That's right! Slick Kid brought the video to Big Moe's to celebrate how much of a fool some small-timer like him made of Santiaga's daughter. He showed the video on the bar TV at Moes! Our spot! Where we used to run shit. I'm chillin' in the back room doing what I'm s'pose to be doing, when Moe comes to the back to tell me what's going on. I come out to the bar area, blowing my cover. Here I'm the only nigga on the team who ain't got pinched by the feds. They ain't got nothing on me, but I gotta sit in the pen for two nights for beating the shit out of a little broke-ass nigga 'cause you *stupid bitch*. Back off my ride. I'll bring your money on Monday." He pulled off.

Furious wasn't enough to describe the intensity of my feeling. Below the anger my thoughts played dodge ball. I ran to the nearest telephone and gave Natalie a call. She picked up. Her usually bold voice was quieted by sleepiness.

"Yeah?"

"What's up with your man Slick Kid?"

"Oh, forget him. I'm not messing with him anymore. He's ridiculous."

"So you know that he's running around showing niggas my ass on the videotape."

"Don't take it personal. My ass is in the tape, too. Why sweat it? We in shape. Niggas can't lie and say they saw some cellulite or stretch marks or nothing like that. Our shit was tight. I should thank the fool. You know how much dick I got sweating me now? His ass was straight up tryna dis me and I flipped it on him, ha ha, now niggas checking for *me!*"

Natalie's calm ran against my fury. "So why you didn't tell me Bullet was down with them other niggas around the way?"

"Oh that. Bullet's cool. He's getting a little name for himself. He's pulling in the loot. It's just a money thing with him. He ain't got nothing personal against you or your family. He's cool peeps. He really like you. I mean for real for real."

"Yeah, with a wife and a newborn baby?!"

"What? Oh, I didn't tell you? Remember Patches from around our way? You know how all the boys in his family got that big hairy black stain on the side of they face that they be saying is a birthmark? Well Saria had that baby and it had a big-ass black hairy mole like Patches. Now Saria swearing up and down that it's still Bullet's baby, it's a miracle or something. Bullet's grandmother talking 'bout there's no way her fine-ass grandson gave birth to an ugly little something like that kid. Now Bullet's looking like a fool. He's all caught out there, filled Saria's house up with Toys "R" Us stuff for the kid 'n all that. He's standing in the waiting room with the cigars and champagne when Patches, Jr., slid right out. I overheard Saria talking to her girl Fatimah who be kicking it with Monica saying even though Patches is *ugly* he *can* eat a mean pussy! That's why Saria kept seeing him on the side. When she got pregnant, she just told Bullet it was his kid 'cause Patches is broke as hell. She *knew* Bullet was a good guy who would support the baby. Now I saw Bullet today. He said as soon as Saria heals, he's gonna go upside her head. He said he knew she was a hoe. He just want to be a man about it and represent for the baby that Saria swore up and down was his."

"Damn!" It was all I could say. Natalie had a way of mixing up and confusing any conversation.

"Oh, I seen your mother back around our way. She's like a whole 'nother person! I heard she was supposed to get some kind of surgery to fix her face."

"Yeah she'll be alright." I hated to think of my mother walking around all crazy like.

"Sorry about your father." I knew I needed to hang up. Natalie was just being a nosy-ass digging for more shit to talk about.

"Oh, Natalie, I gotta go. The cops over there about to throw a ticket on my Benz." I slammed down the phone.

A winter white outfit was gonna make me feel alright. The color white for me was like a new beginning. I was standing outside of Bloomingdale's at 10 A.M. Monday morning when the doors opened up. My meeting with Midnight would happen in a couple of hours. I hoped that time might have cooled Midnight down, making him more reasonable and receptive toward my business deal. My moms was definitely right. There had to be some love in Midnight's heart for me. He fought Slick Kid for me! What other reason would he have had to beat Slick's ass? He went to jail for me, defending my name.

My Nicole Miller dress was not that expensive. It was the shoes and the bag that sent the bill soaring. I took a chance at a new hairshop, at least it was new to me. Those girls from the Dominican Republic hooked my hair up lovely! It was a silky long wrap, Chinastyle, blunt cut.

At 1 P.M., the South Street Seaport was alive. Glasses were clinking, spoons, knives, and forks in action as the lunch crowd flowed in and out. The restaurant was in the open air. You could feel and smell the breeze coming off the East River. I fit right in with the well-paid executive lunch crowd, sporting my diamond necklace, bracelet, and earrings. When Midnight walked in the room, everything around him seemed to slow down. He had the presence and body of an NBA player. He was perfectly in control. The hostess led him to his seat and handed menus to both of us. The busboy filled our glasses.

"I told you to meet me on the pier outside of the restaurant. You have a hard time following directions."

"I was hungry so I stepped in." His bad mood was ruining my outlook.

"We got a problem," he said.

"We?" I said sarcastically.

"Listen, I don't have time to play games with you. The money is gone."

"What do you mean the money is gone? That's bullshit. No, that's more than bullshit. That's fucked up. You took the money for yourself. I was gonna share it with you. Santiaga said you was honest.

He is gone for two minutes and look how you do!" Midnight had his hands folded in front of him. His jawbone started flickering and his big thick lips curled under.

"If I was a different type of man I'd break your ass up right here in front of everybody. Now, hear this Shorty. Your father was like a father to me. He gave me a break. For five years I never sifted one penny from him. I could of easily, because I was close to him. But Santiaga paid me well for my services. I got my own loot." He grabbed the bottom of my face tightly, adding, "So don't ever use your pretty lips to destroy my reputation. It took me a long time to build it, and believe me I earned it."

"Well, what happened then? What happened to my father's money?" I asked desperately.

"May I take your order please?" the waitress asked.

"Give us a few more minutes," Midnight said. The waitress exhaled and left like we were gonna jerk her for her tip or something. "You don't need to know what happened. Less is better."

"Well what will I tell Santiaga?"

"I'll go and talk to Santiaga," he said.

"Well what am I supposed to do?" I asked, my voice was trembling. I was using all of the strength inside of me not to break down or maybe go crazy and start throwing steak knives around the room.

"Let me try to work something out. Give me until Friday. I'll try to do something for you."

The waitress returned. "I'm sorry," she said. "This is the lunchtime rush. We need you to order now or—"

Midnight stood up, placed a twenty-dollar bill on the table. "We'll be leaving."

When I called Momma she asked for the seven hundred dollars I had taken from her pocketbook. When I told her I was broke, she started cursing and yelling about needing money to go and see Santiaga. Not wanting to give her anything from the last five hundred dollars in my pocket, I tried to humor her but she wasn't going for it. I know how locked in on an idea she could get, so I promised I would go through my belongings at "Sterling's mother's house" and try to pull together some cash. "We could go and see Santiaga on Thursday because those were his instructions anyway."

"Those were his instructions to you! I am not a child. I'll go and see my husband anytime I want to and I say I am going today. You go get that cash together now. And meet me at Goldstein's office at three."

I hopped on the train and jetted back to Sterling's house. I had to take off my dress and switch my bag before I met Momma or else she'd be pissed that I spent her money on clothes. I took the tags and clothing receipts out of my white pocketbook and laid them to the side just in case I needed to return everything to get some extra cash. The idea was painful to me because I couldn't see anybody wearing that dress as good as me.

When I arrived at Goldstein's my mother was wearing a dress I had seen Aunt Laurie wear more than a few times. She had a long blonde wig that also belonged to Laurie but didn't match my mom's face at all. She put it on to cover the left side of her face. It did cover her scar, but the fashion trade-off was just not worth it. I gave her a kiss and she immediately turned and asked, "Did you get the money?"

"Yes, Momma. I have enough for both of us to go see Santiaga, eat some dinner, and for you to get back to Brooklyn."

"Good," she said. "Let's go."

"Don't you have to see Goldstein?"

"I already saw that crazy man. He's talking about I can go and see Porsche tomorrow but it will be a supervised visit. We can't leave the facility with her. These people tryna treat me like I did something wrong, like I'm some type of child molester or pervert or something."

They processed us at the jail, checked identification, made us take our shoes off and laughed at the hole in Momma's stocking right at the big toe. They patted us down, frisked us, and escorted us to a bus that took us to the prison waiting room. We signed in a big book, learned my father's prison number, were told never to forget it, and we sat. The room was filled with all kinds of women, all ages, and some children, mostly all dressed in what would be their bests with about fifty different perfumes, deodorants, and colognes hogging up the air. The carefully stationed guards stood in each corner doing nothing except making sure we did nothing. There was one big-mouth guard coming in from the corridor that led to where the prisoners are. He would come into the room yelling the last name of the prisoner, escort the visitor to the back, and signal when your time is up.

When he finally came in and called out "Santiaga," my mother got up. So did this young Puerto Rican woman holding a baby boy.

My mother went to the guard and asked, "Are you calling for Ricky Santiaga?"

The officer replied, "Yes, ma'am." But both women kept approaching. I was seated in the chair waiting for Momma to see him, then I would be next. I checked out the mix-up.

The Puerto Rican girl I guess was about twenty-two years old. She had long, jet black hair down to her ass. She was sporting a Donna Karan pantsuit, something to mention because that was the expensive line. Most people could only afford the DKNY line. She had a big diamond ring on the unmarried finger. Her son had on baby Jordans, a Guess jumper with a matching hat. He had a gold identification bracelet on his little wrist.

The officer held up his hand and said, "Sorry ladies, there is only one visitor at a time. Now who's gonna be first?"

I thought to myself, *That's how my son's gonna look, dipped and paid.*

My mother said, "I don't know which one of us you're talking to. I'm here to see my husband, Ricky Santiaga."

The Puerto Rican girl was proud but reserved. She said, "It's OK, officer, I'll wait."

My mother blew up, jumped in the girl's face, and said, "What do you mean you'll wait? I'm here to see Ricky Santiaga. Who are you here to see?"

"No, it's OK," the lady said, waving her hand so my mother would go away.

"What do you mean, it's OK?" My mother's face was angry and her twisted mouth was going nonstop. "Who are you going to see? Are you tryna say you're here to see my husband?" The lady stood there blank-faced and did not answer. "I said, who are you here to see?" my mother yelled.

The guard jumped in between the two. "Ma'am, it really doesn't matter. The lady said she'll wait. So you come along with me and leave her alone." The guard grabbed my mother's arm firmly and led her down the corridor for her visit with Santiaga.

My investigation started the minute I could no longer see my mother. I went to the sign-up book, telling the officer I wanted to make sure I put down the right number for my father. I checked the number me and my mother wrote, and ran my finger down the row of numbers until I saw Santiaga's number written again. I slid my finger across to the left side of the page to see the name of the visitor. It read Dulce Tristemente. I approached Ms. Dulce slowly, sat in the chair by her, and said "So, are you here to see Ricky Santiaga?"

She looked into my face nervously and said, "No!" But then I saw the baby bracelet. In big block letters it was engraved RICKY SANTIAGA JR.

"You lying bitch! You are here to see my father? You fucking whore. Don't you come here looking down on my mother like you better than somebody!"

"Look I didn't say anything to you so back the fuck off me."

Sweet little Dulce's five-foot-two petite frame turned into a roaring fire, the kind most of the Puerto Rican girls I know have. If she wanted to fight I was down for that. What I wasn't gonna do was let her post up and act all cute and snotty like she had one up and over on me. "We can take this right outside," I said, threatening her.

"No, we can do this right here," she said, handing her son to an elderly woman seated next to her. "What you gonna do, c'mon."

The guard from the right corner threw himself in between me and her. He smiled and said, "Ladies, this is a jail. What are you gonna do, kill each other *over some bum behind bars?*" Then Dulce and I both started screaming on him. His response was, "I'm gonna put both of you out if you don't shut up. Now you go sit on that side," he said, pointing. "You on the other side." Me and her exchanged stares. I wanted her to know I would catch her again and next time I would have my razor.

When I looked at that baby seated on her lap with the jet black curly hair, those big brown eyes, those clothes, and especially that bracelet, I knew it was my father's son. I wondered how much money Dulce got away with? I bet nobody raided her house. She probably got all kind of jewels and cash stashed away. Apparently she still had her clothes, too. There was no telling how much of our family wealth she was using up. I became enraged at the idea that he was taking better care of this little bastard than he was of *me, his firstborn.* Here I was scheming on survival when she was living a life of luxury. Why? Only because she gave Santiaga the son he always wanted.

When Momma came out from seeing Santiaga, she glanced at the baby boy and threw her head up in the air. Dulce stood up with the baby and I guess the old lady was the grandmother or something. They went and stood by one of the guards. Momma asked if I was going in to see my father 'cause I was just sitting there motionless, steaming.

"No, not hardly. Not today," I told her.

Momma straightened Aunt Laurie's dress. She pulled out a small mirror and checked her wig. She patted it insecurely. She shot one last look at Dulce. Then she ran her eyeballs up and down Dulce's clothes, grabbed my hand and said, "C'mon Winter."

On the bus ride home Momma explained that the whole thing was just a crazy mix-up. Santiaga told her that the entire jail was filled with Blacks and Latinos and a lot of inmates had the same last name. "It happens all the time," she told me. "Don't worry about a thing." I just listened, feeling sorry for my mother. For the first time in my life, I was mad as hell at Santiaga.

The next morning, I waited in Penn Station for my momma. We were set to see Porsche at the group home in Queens. So much had happened the day before that I hadn't had much time to think about my sister at all. I decided I could pick up some five-dollar stuffed animal for her. In Long Island she had a collection of stuffed animals that Santiaga brought for her from every and any place he ever went. At last count she had eighty-six stuffed animals. Santiaga even had special shelves designed for the animals to sit on. There were three levels that extended across four walls in all directions. Each stuffed animal was seated in an assigned seat Porsche gave them. She had a name for each one of them and knew them all by heart. Whenever the twins would sneak into her room to play with them Porsche would know because they could never put them back in the right order.

I picked up a Winnie the Pooh because Porsche always liked him. I checked for the price. The Winnie was more than ten dollars. I heard my mother's voice over my shoulder, "Yes. That's perfect for your sister."

"Yeah, I think she'll like it," I said without turning around. When I looked up, I dropped the bear. Momma was *completely bald, her entire head was shaven clean.* She had on a leather miniskirt from Aunt Laurie's tasteless wardrobe. Her top was a white Lerner's type of cheap collection blouse, imitation silk. On her feet were the *unforgivable* Payless buy-one-get-one-free ten-dollar shoes.

"Ma—what— Oh, oh my God. What did you do?"

"Don't make a big deal out of nothing," she said, playfully slapping my arm. "I just decided that this is who I am. You like it?" She stood in the middle of the store with her hands thrown up in the air like she was some type of fashion model. "Actually Winter, these short cuts are in style right now. Get up on it! Come on before we miss the train. Grab the other Winnie over there. That one's all dirty." She picked it up and placed it back on the closest shelf.

On the train ride to Queens Momma told me how I should move back to Brooklyn. Aunt B, her other sister, said I could stay with her, share a room with Bianca, my cousin. For the first time in my life the idea of going to Brooklyn struck me as the last thing that I wanted to do.

Porsche came out with an attitude. She had her arms folded across her chest like a grown woman. She rolled her eyes. "What is wrong with your head, Momma? Did they do that to you in jail? Did the police shave your head like that?"

"Baby. This is a high fashion decision straight off the pages of *Vogue.* Y'all are just late with the styles! Don't worry, y'all will catch up."

"So why am I locked up in here and Winter is out there with you, Momma?" Momma popped her eyeballs out at the supervisor who was there to monitor our visit, as if to say mind your own business. "What y'all looking at?" Intimidated by the bald-headed, twisted-mouth momma, the supervisor turned her head away slightly.

"First of all," Momma whispered, leaning over to Porsche. "This is not Winter. This is Rosie." Porsche's eyes widened.

"What?" she asked. Momma placed her four fingers over Porsche's mouth and winked while she whispered, "Sssh. Do you want them to take your sister away, too? Just play along. Call her Rosie."

The supervisor cleared her throat. "Excuse me Ms. Santiaga, please don't do that." My mother stood up, put her hand on her hip.

"All of you think you can boss me around. This is my baby and I am talking to her right now. How they treating you, baby?"

"The food sucks. There's no cable, no Sega Genesis. They won't give me the clothes I asked for out of the closet in my room at home. They won't give me my stuffed animals. Their beds are too small. My counselor's breath stinks. And, I'm bored to death. When can I come home with you?"

My mother clutched Porsche's shoulders. "Don't worry baby, Momma's coming to get you."

"What about Lexy and Mercedes? Will the twins come home with us, too?"

"Oh yeah," Momma said, but I know she was feeding Porsche a dream. "Everybody will be there and we're gonna have a big party, Mommy, and Daddy, and Winter, Lexy, Mercedes, and Porsche, one big happy family. We'll even have Big Bird, and Ernie and Bert."

Porsche flagged her hand at Momma, "I don't even watch them anymore." By the end of our visit the supervisor had to drag Porsche out of the room, kicking, biting, screaming, and crying. She wanted to leave with us. Momma jumped the supervisor and fought too. I jumped in 'cause that's the way it goes. We were thrown out when extra security arrived. The supervisor was all torn up.

On the train I tried to talk to Momma. I wanted to understand what was going on with her. She just seemed different to me. For the first time in my life I was even a little embarrassed by her. I caught myself on the train trying to look like I was alone, with no connection to the bald-headed weirdo in the next seat. I would stare straight ahead, then turn my legs slightly in the opposite direction so people wouldn't think we were sitting together. Momma kept talking to me anyway, making it clear that we were together.

"Seriously Momma. Why did you cut off your hair?" She started to make jokes and I grabbed her arm. "No seriously. Why did you cut off your hair?"

"I was just mad."

"Mad at who?"

"Well it started with Aunt Laurie. She knew I had been wearing the blond wig because it worked for me. She come talking about she wants to use the blonde wig because it goes with her tiger dress and she's going out to the bar tonight. Now she knows I don't have the money to go to Earline's right now and I'm damn sure not about to ask Earline no favors. I figure your aunt was tryna be cute by taking the wig away from me. Now she knows I'm not the type to go borrowing things in the first place. So I said, 'I'll fix her. I'll never ask her for no more of her wigs. I'll just cut all my hair off.'"

"But now everybody can see your scar and where they operated on you and everything."

"That's right," she said, smiling.

"But why?" I asked.

"Well, when I was in the mirror at first tryna style my own hair I realized I wasn't really gonna get no money for no plastic surgery, I might as well be proud. You can't get no respect in Brooklyn being all down on yourself. I was sitting in the living room looking at Aunt Laurie's old record albums. I saw that live hoe Grace Jones. It clicked in my mind. It's a sign. I ran in the bathroom and just cut it all off. Now I'm gonna rock it just like Grace. She don't care what nobody says and neither do I." For the rest of the ride, we sat in silence.

It was clear that I was gonna have to take my Nicole Miller dress back to the store. I just couldn't spend my last four hundred fifty dollars on a new outfit. I would return this one, get the money back and use it to purchase a new one. The upcoming meeting with Midnight was important to me. Everything had to be as perfect as I could make it. If he was successful in locating some of Daddy's money, I still had to break him down so he would at least talk real with me about what we were gonna do. He might reject my business arrangement at first but now that Santiaga was locked up, he'd have to make money too. Wouldn't he? He couldn't stay speechless and distant toward me forever.

I was so jumpy about our meeting the next night that Sterling kept asking, "What's up? What's wrong? What's the matter? It's like you're not even here or something."

I smiled sweetly, thinking to myself, *Hey idiot, I haven't been here since I got here.* I can't believe how dumb Sterling is. He sickened me. He wore tight briefs, not boxers. He left small clunks of toothpaste in the sink after he brushed and little droplets of piss on the toilet seat. What really did it for me, though, was the skid marks in his draws that he leaves visible 'cause he is too lazy to put the lid to the laundry pail back on. Worst of all he reminded me of the bad shape I was in myself being homeless and all. I hated him for it. Sterling only had about one hundred to one hundred and fifty dollars a week spare cash on hand after paying the bills. He really ought to have realized he couldn't buy no quality ass for that kind of money. Friday it would all be over for him. I would tell him my parents were back from vacation. I'd leave with my things in one of *his* suitcases. He'd call me later in Long Island. The phone would be disconnected. He would spend the rest of his life tryna figure out where I had disappeared to.

I'd have the money from Midnight and a little business going on. Hell, maybe Midnight would let me chill up in his spot until I could get my place situated.

I traded my Nicole Miller outfit easily for a Calvin Klein dress. Things went smooth. There was no sense in the store clerks arguing with a regular customer, even if they could detect that I'd already worn the dress. I had time to get my hair touched up as well as my nails. My hair was swept up into a French bun and my skin was perfect, smooth and clear. My ears held my diamond studs and I carefully put on my necklace and bracelet.

I tried to speculate on exactly how much money Midnight would come back with. I came up with an A budget and a B budget. The A budget was if he came with something around fifty thousand dollars. I would bring money to the lawyer for Santiaga even though I was still mad about Dulce. I would take a couple of thousand dollars for an apartment. If I was lucky, I'd find a place big enough so my moms could get my sisters back and we could all chill. The rest of the money would be for me and Midnight's investment. Now the B budget worked like this. If he came back with twenty thousand dollars, I'd pay the lawyer ten, invest seven and keep three for myself. When our investment paid off, then I would worry about everything and everybody else.

At 59th and 8th, I sat outside of Central Park near the statue and waited for Midnight to arrive. When I spotted his freshly washed black Acura with the gleaming rims coming around the circle, my heart jumped. He pulled up to the curb. "Get in."

"How you doing, Midnight?" I asked, really sultry and cool. I was gonna be more womanly and in control, I told myself.

"I'm cool," he said with little emotion.

"Well, what did you come up with?"

"Yeah," he said, "we can check out that museum. It's only a few blocks over."

"What?" I asked as I knitted my eyebrows together. He raised his hand to cut the conversation short.

I was wondering what was going down. I sat quietly. Glancing to the left, into the backseat I caught the glimpse of a suitcase strap. My body filled with panic when I saw Midnight's bags packed. So many different thoughts filled my head. The first one was: treachery. Midnight had all the money. All of it, I thought. All the money

Santiaga had, he had. Now he was gonna break me off a little piece, pretend the rest had been stolen and fly to Colombia or something to hide out.

Midnight must of been down with the other team all along. He sold Daddy out and that's why he was the only one who didn't get locked up. Now he was dipping out on not only Santiaga, but the other guys too. He had a plan so sweet that he has ended up with all their cash and both of the other teams got jerked.

When I turned sideways and looked at him, I thought he looked so sincere. A new thought came. He was gonna show me the money, all of it, in a yellow business-type envelope! No—a briefcase, a black briefcase! Then he was gonna say that he and I should go away for a while to regroup, organize ourselves, make some more dough, big money. We would send the money to the lawyer for Santiaga and give some to Momma, then we would leave. But then, why didn't he tell me last time I saw him to pack my bags?

"Get out and wait on those steps," Midnight said, interrupting my thoughts.

"Where are you going?" I was worried.

"I'm gonna pull the car around over there where I can park."

"What's up with the museum?" I questioned him after he'd parked the car.

"We not going in there," he said.

"So why did we come here then?"

"Come on. We'll sit down right over there." He pointed to a table with benches. When I got over there, I noticed nasty blotches of bird shit splattered around.

"Let's sit over there," I said directing him to another table with an umbrella surrounding it.

Midnight grabbed my arm tight. "I said sit down here, a little bird shit ain't gonna hurt you. I gotta be able to see my car."

I grabbed a little leftover newspaper off the round table to cover the shit on the bench. It took everything I had not to show how aggravated I was. With slight attitude I asked, "So what's up?"

"I don't talk in my car," Midnight whispered. "You never know who's listening in."

I laughed. Either he had lost his mind in the last four days or he was just telling a joke.

"Everything is fun and games for you, Winter, huh?"

I got serious then, too. I wasn't gonna let him make me feel like a child. "So what's all the luggage for? Are you going somewhere?"

"Yeah, I'm leaving."

"Going where?" I was horrified.

"That's my business. All you need to know is I'm outta here."

"No, that's not all I need to know," I said, standing up. "I need to know what the fuck is up? Santiaga said you had his money and it should be obvious by now that I need to have it."

"I talked to Santiaga," he said. "He knows what happened. The money is gone. Even the money he put aside for situations like this is gone. Somebody he trusted double crossed. The way I see it, he got raided by the street niggas *and* he got raided by the authorities. The authorities uncovered shit nobody but family should've known. Now niggas is turning state's evidence on Santiaga. The shit is bad, real bad."

"Well let me ask you something, Midnight. How come you get away smelling like you ain't had shit to do with nothing? How come everybody else is behind bars and you cruising around in your damn Acura like your shit don't stink?"

"Because I'm smart. I figured this day would come and I planned for it. Nothing good lasts too long. I never did no talking to anybody. I never kept no shit in my place. You can't be in this business yapping off at the mouth like a woman. Half the evidence they got on niggas is niggas telling on themselves over the phone and in their cars. The feds is listening in, clocking niggas, recording shit, straight up snooping. Niggas running around buying too much shit with no reasonable cover to explain where it came from, flashing, making a scene. Stupid shit. But a man can't tell another man what to do. You can't teach a man how to humble himself if he don't want to. Every man gotta do it his way. *I did it my way.* It worked out for me, that's it."

"You tryna say you a better man than my father?" I asked, tears running down my face.

"Nah, nothing like that," he said. "Your father's a smart man. I learned a lot from him. Sometimes a man as smart as your father can see everything and everybody else but he can't see himself. Your father was sharp but sometime, he let women influence him to make moves he knew he shouldn't make."

"Women? Are you referring to my mother?"

"For the most part," he said in such a cool way I wanted to kill him. Did Midnight know about Dulce all along? Had he met with Santiaga in Dulce's apartment the same way he met with Santiaga in my house? What other secrets was he keeping?

"Women," he said, as though he was an old man, "are emotional. That's why a man gotta be strong. Now emotional women have a way of pushing for what they want and not thinking about how things gonna end up."

"Sounds to me like you don't even like women."

He laughed. "I like women, but I like smart women. A smart man never chooses a dumb woman. All she can do is make demands, spend his money, and bring him down." Now he was stabbing me back. He thought I was gonna bring him down. Or maybe he thought Momma brought Santiaga down. Any way you look at it, it was a knife in my stomach, an insult, a dis. I had no time to dwell on the pain, so I pulled the knife out by saying, "What about me? What am I supposed to do? What did Santiaga say for me to do?"

"Santiaga said go back to Brooklyn, it's OK now."

"Go back to Brooklyn and do what? Live where?"

"Your Aunt B has a spot for you. Santiaga worked that out already." The idea of returning to Brooklyn with nothing seemed crazy to me.

"So what, Brooklyn's not good enough for you anymore?" he asked.

"Apparently it's not good enough for you, that's why you leaving right."

"Nah. I live simple. Brooklyn was alright for me. I'm leaving 'cause there's nothing to stay for. The feds would love to catch me slipping or pin some shit on me I didn't even do. They hate to be out-smarted. They ain't got nothing on me. My place was clean. No drugs. No jewels. No money, and they hate it. Rather than sit around waiting for them to cook something up—and them devils will cook something up—I'm out. I'm out like I was never even here. I did time already. The first time was the last time. Anybody try to take me down, we all going out, right there on the spot in a hail of gunfire. 'Cause I'm never going back to jail."

His words were clear. He said them with so much strength I couldn't even front like he was lying or something. But I still wanted to know about the money. Somehow it just didn't seem right that there was no money left. Where was he getting money from? How was he gonna make money? Where was he gonna stay? "How you gonna make your dough where you going?"

"I'm gonna be straight, Shorty. Don't worry about me. I got plans. I'm about to come into something. Listen," he said pulling a white envelope out of his pocket, "this is for you."

I looked at it. I knew it had money in it. I exhaled.

"Don't be stupid, Winter. Learn how to use that head of yours, otherwise you'll end up like everybody else." He said some other stuff but my mind drifted. How much was in the envelope? I wondered what would I use it for first? What step should I make next?

Midnight planted a kiss on my face and snatched away the object of my childhood crush with two little words, "Take care."

"Can I come with you?" The words dropped out of my mouth before I could stop them from embarrassing me.

"No."

"No? Why not? I'm not saying I have to be your girl. I'm just asking if I could roll with you. You might think I'm dumb but I'm not. I know a lot of shit. I understand. We can put whatever little money we got together and make something out of it. I am seventeen now you know. I'm not as young as you think."

"None of that has nothing to do with it," he said.

"Then what is it? What is it?" I asked over and over again. "Let me in on the big secret why you never wanted me. Why is the answer always no with you. Let me know why you would leave me in Brooklyn knowing what's happening with my family. Everybody's gonna find out and you just bouncing out like it's cool."

"I already told you. I gotta do what I gotta do. What happened to your family ain't no secret. Everybody already knows. You hiding from Natalie and all those silly bitches and they already know." He grabbed the leftover newspapers from the table beside us. He balled them in his fist and pushed them into my face. "Can't you read? Santiaga been in the newspaper every day. Page two, page three, page four. You see? That's what I'm talking about—dumb women! You don't even know what's going on around you. If it ain't on the front page you don't know it. But you know the name of every designer in Bloomingdale's. Hell no, you can't come with me. Your dumb ass ain't bringing me down, not me."

Midnight walked away. I stood on the steps crying mad. He drove right past me. I ripped open the envelope and couldn't believe I was flipping through tens, twenties and fifties. The grand total was three thousand dollars. Three thousand measly dollars. What the hell was I supposed to do with that? In the envelope was a business card turned backwards. Scrawled across the back of the card, in neat handwriting, it read: *I know you don't like her, but she can help you get your head together.* I flipped it to the front and Sister Souljah's name was on it with an address and phone number. I sucked my teeth and put the envelope in my pocketbook.

8

I walked until I saw a cute little coffee shop. I bought a newspaper from the stand and ducked inside. Inside I flipped to the section with apartments for rent. I took a jar of nail polish out of my pocketbook and splashed a red dot on all the listings I was gonna check out. I had already decided I wasn't going back to Brooklyn with everybody feeling sorry for me. I wasn't gonna give Natalie the pleasure of feeling like me and her were on the same level. I'd find a decent place to stay while I put my survival plan together.

I put the money for the tea and fries on the table plus a dollar tip. After walking halfway through the coffee shop door, I turned around, and grabbed my tip off the table, realizing I had to save my dough. I hit the pavement, heading for an available advertised apartment in Harlem.

The building was a brownstone, on a block of brownstones. This particular one was real nice and neat with a decorative iron gate on it and flowerpots on the left and right sides of the entrance. The landlady came to the door and peeked out the curtain. She was only about five-foot-two, real dark-skinned with a colorful scarf on her head, a dress, and house slippers. After opening the outside door, she stood behind the locked gate, looking me over from head to toe. She spoke with a thick West Indian accent, "Good afternoon chile, what can I do for you?"

"I'm interested in the apartment you have for rent." I was confident, I looked good, expensively dressed, with a fresh hairdo.

"Are you alone?" she asked, as if she couldn't tell I was standing on the step by myself.

"Yes I am," I replied, trying not to be snotty. She went into her front pocket on her multicolored dress, pulled out a small key, and unlocked the gate.

"What's your name?" she asked.

"Winter Shulman," I said proudly.

"Are you married?" she asked.

"No I'm not."

"Do you have any children?"

"No."

"Oh," she said, "because we have working people in this building and little babies are wonderful but they can be a loud disturbance in the middle of the night."

"No, I don't have any children," I reassured the suspicious little lady. "What floor is the apartment on?" I asked, trying to hurry her along.

"Oh, it's on the second floor. We'll go up in a minute. So how did you hear about the apartment?"

"I read about it in the paper," I said, wondering why she put an ad in the paper if it was supposed to be a secret.

"Oh," she said. "How old are you?" she asked, still digging.

"I'm twenty-two."

"Oh, are you a student?"

"Yes, I am," I lied. I figured that must be what she wanted to hear.

"Oh, that's nice. What are you studying?"

I paused, couldn't think of anything. I looked down at my shoes and quickly said, "Fashion."

"Oh, that's nice. Well you look good chile. I hear dem models make a good living. But that means you'll keep irregular hours?"

Not understanding her, I said, "What? I mean, excuse me?"

"Well like I said, people in this building, we're all working people so most of us are out during the day. So my husband and I turn the heat down during the day because nobody's here. Around 6 or 7 P.M. we turn it back on. It's a way to conserve and save money."

"Yes, but in a few months spring will be here," I told her.

"Oh, you are planning to be here in the fall, aren't you?" she asked in a threatening tone. "I don't rent by the week. This is not a hotel. If you want to live here you'll have to sign a lease agreement for a minimum of one year," she said. "Stay right here I'll be right back." She slid behind the closed door of her apartment and came back with a clipboard.

Who is she fooling? I thought to myself. What difference does it make if I sign a lease? When I'm ready to bounce, I bounce. What is she gonna do, call the rent police? There were twenty million people in New York.

"Come on," she said, signaling me to follow her up the stairs. She pulled out a large circular key ring with a whole bunch of keys on it. One bedroom apartment with a little kitchen, fully carpeted. The place looked like a Barbie doll was supposed to live in it, that's how cute and compact it was. For me it was perfect. I pictured maybe a leather love seat, a cable-ready big-screen TV, and a fancy designer phone. I pictured myself walking around the apartment barefoot with my pretty pedicure toes sinking into the thick carpet.

The living room was more than a little smaller than my bedroom on Long Island, but it was cool. I could definitely deal with it. "I'll take it," I said, smiling, looking at the lady, and grabbing my envelope with the cash. I began counting out the dough.

"First things first, chile," she said, looking at my cash suspiciously. This was the first time I had ever seen anybody turn their nose up at cash. "You'll have to fill out this application."

"Why?" I asked nicely. "I've already told you everything."

"I know," she said. "It's just the way we do things around here. I need this for my records." She handed me a form, asking for my name, address, place of employment, education . . . "You know I'm the president of the block association," she mentioned. "It's small. We're just getting started. Most of the responsible people on the block participate. But you know there are always those few . . . We're trying to clean the block up, get rid of the drugs, make it better for everybody. We're real careful because a lot of drug dealers have cash. They've got the money to spend. They send a pretty little thing like you in here. But you don't know anything about that filthy way of living." She smiled and added, "I can tell. Such a lovely face. Do you have a check?"

"No, I don't." I responded hesitantly.

"Oh. Here you must need a pen," she handed me a ballpoint, stood close over me and the application. I filled it out, making stuff up as I went along, figuring I'd play along with her inspection, get my new keys, close my door, and never speak to her again except on rent day. I was Winter Shulman, I attended Brooklyn College, I was twenty-three years old, I previously lived at 123 Green Street, etcetera, etcetera.

She looked over the application, glancing up at me after each section as if she thought I was stupid enough to tell on myself. I smiled politely.

"I thought you said you were twenty-two?" she quizzed.

"Oh yeah, I'm sorry. I just had a birthday. I haven't gotten used to being twenty-three yet." I laughed.

"Don't worry chile, the older you get the more birthdays you forget. I'm twenty-three, too." She laughed, getting a real kick out of herself. I pulled out my envelope, counted out six hundred fifty dollars, and handed it to her.

She cleared her throat, "You must have misunderstood. The total to pick up the keys and move in is nineteen hundred fifty dollars. One month's rent and two months' security."

"Security for what?"

"It's a normal procedure. It's just to cover anything you leave broken in the apartment, damage to the rug, if you fall on hard times, and miss a payment. Don't worry chile, it's fully refundable at the end of your lease. If everything is in order, you get your two months' security back in full. If you lose your keys, it's a hundred dollars because we have special locks and we'll have to have the whole lock removed and replaced."

There was no need to be nice anymore. There was no way I was giving her all the money I had left. She looked at my screwed up face. "Every decent landlord around here is gonna ask for the same thing."

"Sorry miss" I said, "you must be bugging. Didn't you hear me say I was a student?"

She shot me a mean look. "When I was a student I had two jobs. You have to work to make it in this country. That's how I got where I am now. I had to work to own this property. No kind of work was too good for me either. A dollar is a dollar is a dollar."

I handed her papers back and left. Sterling wasn't that bad, I thought. I'd just tell him a new story. Something bigger and better. I'd stay at his place for a while until I figured everything out.

Sterling's apartment was quiet from the outside, my key slid in the lock. Inside the door sat a suitcase. I pulled the case up onto the couch and opened it. My belongings were inside, carefully packed. I rummaged through my jeans, shirts, and dresses, checking to see if everything was there. The side pockets had my jewelry, and toiletries in a separate plastic bag. I laughed. Hmmm, too bad he wasn't as neat with his own stuff!

Sterling startled me when he came out of the back room. I hadn't realized anybody was home. On the way over, I had practiced for this moment. It was time to put my act into action. "How are you feeling, baby? You must've got home early?"

"You look nice," he said checking out my outfit, the same one that didn't work on Midnight.

"You like?" I playfully spun around.

"I always have," he said softly.

"So anyway Sterling, sit down. I'm gonna let you in on my idea." He walked over, hesitant and suspicious. "We been cool roommates for the past couple of weeks and—"

"And tonight you're leaving, right?" he interrupted in a voice that attempted to be authoritative. He started mouthing words but no sound was coming out. It was like he wanted me to read his lips or something. In a low, low voice, "Winter, I have company."

"Company," I said loudly, surprised. He put his long finger over his lips to sshh me.

"Remember when you called me to come and get you from Long Island? Remember I told you someone was here. Well, she's in the back room and I don't want no trouble Winter. You did say you were leaving tonight. It's been two weeks."

Sterling's eyes were concerned. Just looking at his weak ass made me sick to my stomach. But I had nowhere else to go. I remained coolheaded, or at least I tried to give that appearance. "Oh, there's no trouble Sterling, just get rid of her." I laughed. He didn't say a word. So I came up with a new suggestion. "OK, I'll just stay in the living room tonight but I think—"

A girl came out of the back room. She was overweight with a big chubby face like one of those church ladies you see singing in the choir on the cable channel on Sundays. She had on a long shapeless floral dress—I guess it was supposed to hide her fat. I was sure Sterling wasn't about to replace me with this cow. "Sterling," the woman said in a tone that sounded more like a mother's than a lover's. "You said five minutes."

"Oh. Winter, this is Judy."

We both looked at each other but neither of us spoke. She came out and sat on a chair facing me. I could tell Sterling was uncomfortable with the silence. He kept playing with his fingers.

"So you live in Long Island?" Judy asked dryly.

"Yeah."

"They have some really nice houses out there. The traffic must be really bad on a Friday night."

"Yeah," I rolled my eyes at Sterling.

"I packed your things up for you," announced Judy. "You have some real nice taste."

"Yeah," I said, realizing the only way I could stay was to humiliate myself completely.

"So where do you plan on going to college next year? Sterling told me you were seventeen. You must have started thinking about it seriously."

"Not really," I said matter-of-factly; thinking to myself I hate these stuck-up college-type bitches. They think they too cute to get down and have a Brooklyn-style fight to keep they man. They want to do a lot of smart talking like they somehow better than somebody or at least they be thinking they can prove that they are.

"I had no choice except to go to college. My parents made that clear," she added, as though I had asked her a question. She seemed fully prepared to have a conversation with herself. "What do your parents do, I mean for a living? They must be well off not to be stressed about whether or not you should go to college."

Sterling interrupted, "Winter, I'll help you carry your things downstairs."

"But I don't have a ride," I begged. "Sterling, aren't you going to drive me home?"

Judy cut in. "No, sorry, our movie starts at 8:05 P.M. Sterling already called your dad before you even got here. Your dad's gonna pick you up downstairs at 7:30 P.M."

What kind of game was this *two*-dollar nigga tryna run on me? And what in hell made this fat-ass girl think she was running things?

"So is your mother or your father Sterling's mother's sister or brother?"

"What is this, a goddamn interview?" I said, losing my cool.

She scooted over to Sterling's side. "Sterling, I'm sorry. I didn't mean to aggravate your cousin. It was just small talk." Then she turned to me. "I'm sorry. I just thought it was nice that your parents trusted Sterling to baby-sit. Your families must be really close. I'm telling you, I missed him so much for the past couple of weeks, I thought I would die. I will say, I was jealous at first, you know when Sterling told me you were coming over for two whole weeks. Jealous of you getting all of his time and attention. I can see that he was right. You *are* just a kid. He was just helping out and everything worked out perfectly.

"Come on, I'll walk downstairs with you guys."

She walked over to the closet, grabbed my jacket, and said, "This is yours, right? I left it out when I was packing your belongings. I thought it might get cooler at night. Here, don't forget it."

We went downstairs, dead silent in the elevator. In the lobby, Sterling handed me an envelope.

"Call me and let me know you got home safe." I grabbed what I knew was some small sum of money, sucked my teeth, and walked away with his suitcase and everything I owned inside. I don't know why I didn't go off, I don't know. I just didn't have anything left inside to go off with. The whole thing was so unexpected.

If I would've beat up the girl what would've happened? If anybody was predictable it was Sterling. But not this time. Sterling couldn't control me, so he picked this motherly girl to fill my shoes. She's probably been around him for years hoping and praying for an engagement ring, but if you asked me it wouldn't last. It was obvious her pussy is no good, otherwise he wouldn't have lied to her to be with me in the first place.

At the train station, I broke down and called Natalie. There was only one place to go, a place I used to love—Brooklyn. When Natalie answered, she was all hyped up and happy to hear from me. "Where you been, girl? We all waiting to see you! Where you been hiding at? Why you treating us like we ain't family? What took you so long to call?" For about three seconds I felt bad for not calling her. Maybe it was really all good in Brooklyn. Maybe I had been bugging out, making things worse than they really were. I told her I was on my way to my Aunt B's apartment. I would be there around ten o'clock that night. "Good. Let's hang out. Meet at my apartment at eleven. We'll go to the club."

"Why didn't you call first?" That's all Aunt B had to say when she opened the apartment door. I was thrown off 'cause Midnight, Momma, and Santiaga made it seem like Aunt B was gonna be happy to see me or something. She had an aggravated look on her face. She pointed for me to go straight to my cousin Bianca's bedroom. Yelling down the hallway, she reminded me to use the bed on the left side of the room. "Remember to leave Bianca's stuff just like she left it, 'cause she don't like nobody fooling with her stuff." As I passed the small kitchen to get to the bedroom, I saw a long set of male legs inside. There's the problem, she has company, a man-friend, and I busted up her groove. I could dig it. I put my suitcase down, went in the bathroom, freshened up, and headed to Natalie's.

When I banged on Natalie's door, my girl Simone answered with a big-ass smile on her face and a little pregnant belly. My girl Toshi screamed out, "Surprise, bitch." All my girls were there—Asia, Zakia, Natalie, with Hennessy and passion Alizé in hand and Ls laying on the table just like old times. I felt real good. In a few minutes I was sure I was gonna feel even better.

I thought as I sparked up my second joint, this is what made life worth living, good friends, free weed, and lots of laughs. Simone filled me in on the oohs and aahs of pregnancy. "Not as bad as people tried to make it sound," she said. Her and Little Biz broke up. "No real bitch need a nigga to survive anymore. Plus the next nigga's bound to be coming around the corner any day." I told her I heard it wasn't cool to drink liquor when you were pregnant. "As fucked up as the world is today, the baby will need some Thug passion just to be able to roll with the punches." We cracked up. Simone couldn't take it no more and laughed so hard she accidentally pissed on herself. I laughed until my stomach ached while Natalie sprayed enough air freshener in the living room to choke us all.

Zakia, Monique, Reese, and Toshi had a game of Spades going. I checked Toshi cheating as usual. She had them tricks down pat. She'd have you talking about the juiciest shit while her hands were switching shit around. Meanwhile she would use those eyes to signal to her partner. She even had coded songs to sing that Reese understood 'cause she was always her partner in Spades. For what she had going they should have been getting paid or in Vegas or Atlantic City with the big-timers.

Fun didn't break up until about five o'clock in the morning. Natalie's mom came home. I could see that she had her own high going on, but something about her being in the apartment just changed the mood. One by one, people started breaking out. I nudged Simone, who was passed out on the couch. "Come on, girl, let's walk over to our building together."

"Good looking out," Simone muttered.

Outside night glided into early morning. Blue-gray skies framed what was the quietest time in the projects. At six-fifteen the sun snuck up and mugged the moon. Partygoers were inside their apartments passed out in their clothes. There was nobody outside except the crazy-ass crackheads. I was surprised to see my mother in the lobby of my aunt's building, bald-headed and thinner than I last saw her. She smiled when she saw me, laughed for no reason at all, and started explaining that she heard I was here in the neighborhood. She was just out checking on me. She knew how Aunt B could be sometime. I could tell she had her buzz on too. I didn't believe for one minute that she was down in the lobby checking on me at this time in the damn morning. I rode the elevator with her and Simone. Simone got off on the third floor, me on the fifth. As the elevator door was closing, Momma was huddled in the corner rubbing her arms like she was freezing. As the doors closed on her bizarre face, she was saying something like, "You look good, Winter." I was glad that door shut so fast 'cause I definitely could not return the compliment.

I woke up that afternoon to Aunt B wanting a loan. Since I wasn't crazy, and Aunt B's husband was locked up with my father, I knew that if I gave her any money I'd never get it back. If I gave her money today, she'd start to expect it from me. Eventually she would start to demand it from me. After a while she might even try to collect rent for the bed and six feet of space on my side of the room. She was flat broke like all of my aunts are now. Their *houses* didn't get raided and ransacked *like ours,* though. Their belongings didn't get repossessed and seized only to be auctioned off somewhere for pennies. They still had clothes, jewelry, stereo equipment, and all that good shit.

"Nah," I replied.

"C'mon girl," she pushed. "Just lend me a twenty spot. I'm expecting some money on this Wednesday. I'll give it right back."

"Seriously, though," I said with a straight face, "I don't got it. I need a loan myself." I went over to my Coach bag and emptied my stuff onto the bed. "See. Nothing." I didn't keep my money in my bag 'cause that's what people expect. I left it pinned to my bra, a trick my mother once showed me a long time ago.

Aunt B sucked her teeth, "Alright," then disappeared from the room. She's stupid, I thought to myself. She should've got some loot from that long-legged nigga she had in the kitchen last night. Pussy should never be free.

Simone called asking if I wanted to go shopping. "There's a big concert tonight and we should both get outfits and go find us some cuties." I agreed.

In the stores, my blood was rushing at all the new clothes. New styles seem to come in everyday and the stuff I bought weeks, even days ago didn't excite me anymore. I teased Simone about looking for an outfit that would hide her pregnant belly. She denied it, saying men loved pregnant pussy and if she wanted to she'd sport a halter top and let her belly hang out! We laughed as we imagined how crazy that would look. Meanwhile Simone picked out a whole bunch of outfits.

"Damn, I gotta pee again." This was like Simone's third time peeing in one hour. Not to mention she stopped at McDonald's to use the bathroom on the way here. Meanwhile, I found the perfect outfit with shoes to match. It killed me to pay the grand total of five hundred dollars, although it was a savings from my usual sprees. Simone finally came out the bathroom. The cashier handed me my change. "How much," Simone asked as if she was financing me.

"No big deal," I said as if I had a Swiss bank account or something. "You wanna check Nordstrom's? They usually have all the flavor designer shit. They even got a fat lady department," I kidded her.

"Nah, I got everything I need," Simone said. "Just chill."

At Simone's apartment, everything became clear. In her big Coach bag, Simone had every outfit she'd picked up and admired at the store. She even had one of those machines that removes the metal alarms from the clothes. She also had accessories, belts, costume jewelry. She had shit I didn't even see her pick up. In her closet, she had more shit, some with the tags still on 'em. She had two and three of the same items in different sizes. Straight up, Simone was a professional booster. The pregnancy, she said, has increased her take. She made more money now 'cause she could walk out with more layers of clothes on her body and not look suspicious. "You look shocked," she said.

"Nah. I'm not shocked. I'm mad as hell that you stood there and let me drop five hundred bills when I could've got all my shit for free."

Simone exhaled. "Yeah, you was always paid like dat Winter. Don't worry, you can take that shit back and I'll pick it up for you later."

"I'm wearing this outfit tonight."

"We'll just return it Monday. We can do that but you gotta watch it. They'll ask to see your ID and if your name pops up on the computer as returning too much shit, next thing you know they'll be knocking at your door with a badge. You gotta watch these stores, they be updating their tricks everyday. I'm on top of it, though. I know all the tricks."

"How many tickets you got to the show?"

"Four," Simone said. "It was supposed to be me, Natalie, Toshi, and Zakia. But Natalie's going with Will. So you can have her ticket."

"Who's Will?" I asked.

"This nigga from Fort Greene. He's a player. He got a custom-made yellow Land Rover, rimmed out. You should see it, it's phat. Natalie gon be acting up. Nobody gonna be able to say shit to her tonight. That nigga bought the whole box seat section for the show. He began lacing her lovely with all the butters every since they hooked up."

How the fuck was we getting to the show? I wondered to myself. Am *I* supposed to take a train, or walk, or hop out a yellow cab while Natalie was styling in a Rover?

Uh-uh. There had to be a better way. "You got a phone book Simone?"

"What?"

"A Yellow Pages. Let's rent a limo."

"Alright, let's do it."

Brooklyn's finest, Uptown and the Boogie Down filled the concert hall. As usual, the show outside the theater was the biggest. Females in spring leathers, patent leathers, plastic, lace, cellophane shorts, skirts, the works. Enough gold on necks, arms, and teeth to fill Fort Knox. Players was rocking fresh Nike, Fila, Armani, Versace, Kani, Mecca, and all the flavors. Hip-hop vibes hogged the airwaves and we filed in looking every person up and down and side to side, checking for authenticity. It was a car show, a hair show, a fashion show, and a hoe show all rolled up into one. Each male and female in the audience was as important as any star on the stage.

At showtime, the crowd went wild as the biggest names in hip-hop blew up the stage. The huge speakers blasted out the hottest jams, and the crowd rocked to one rhythm. The MC had the niggas chanting "Make money money" while the ladies overpowered them with our "take money money, take money money!" Natalie was up in the box seats with the kid Will whose hands were holding all kinds of shine—jewels and other signs of big cash flow.

Everything was cool until I saw her standing up, clapping, with a sky blue thirty-five-hundred-dollar Chanel skirt-suit on. This bitch pops out of nowhere with some wears that was strictly my style and overreaching for her. In all the noise, a silence surrounded my head. My body shook with anger at Santiaga and Mom. I also thought of Midnight *leaving me* when that could have easily been us in those box seats, profiling. Now what was I supposed to do while Natalie was pretending to be me? I leaned over close to Simone's ear, "Do you see Natalie?"

"Yeah, everybody see Natalie up there!"

"That suit she got on is banging," I painfully admitted.

"The security at the Chanel store is too tight or else *I'd* have that suit on! I told you, that nigga Will is shot out on Nat." I had only been living in Long Island for one year. Was shit actually moving so fast that Natalie had become large? "Since when did Natalie become a high roller?" I asked.

"Girl, you don't know the half. Ever since she made that little video movie with you, she been like a little star around our way."

"What little movie?"

"Don't front, Winter. That video with you and Bullet and her and Slick Kid. In one part she was sucking Slick Kid's dick real nasty-like. Now niggas is sweating her like she Vanessa Del Rio or something." Natalie waved to us when she spotted us looking up in her direction. She was all excited. She signaled us to meet her afterwards. Simone smiled, nodded yeah, and turned to me, "Yeah, she's a little bigheaded but she alright."

The last performers came on, ripping shit down. I moved with the crowd but I was still boiling inside. The MC came on to close the show, then shouted, "A special thanks to Sister Souljah for putting this show together, all proceeds going to her children's program." Sister Souljah came out the side of the stage wearing some shit she mixed and matched from the Macy's clearance rack. People clapped for her. How is this bitch supposed to help the community when she don't even know how to rock her shit? I checked her arm, no Rolex, not even a Timex, nothing. No weight on her neck, nothing. Her hairdo was phat but that don't mean nothing when you don't know how to accessorize. Besides she could use a few sit-ups for her belly. Humph, Midnight got some nerve. I sure wasn't asking her for shit.

"What's up, girl?" Natalie was smiling ear to ear as we all crammed in to the concert hall lobby. "Winter, I called you this afternoon to ask you if you wanted to chill up top with us but you was gone already. So come on, girl," she said, clutching Will's arm. "Roll with us to the diner." She elbowed me and whispered, "It's on Will. You want to ride with us?"

"Nah, we got a ride," Simone jumped in.

"What you pushing, Winter?" Natalie asked.

"We pushing a limo, a driver, champagne, the whole nine."

"Alright cool. Tell the driver to follow us. We'll meet over there and eat before we head up to the after party." Now Natalie was giving directions!

There was something sexy about Will. I didn't know exactly what it was. Maybe it was the 1-karat diamond stud in his ear. Or maybe it was just me wanting dick, being stressed out, and ready to get fucked no questions asked. It could be the fact I didn't like him being with Natalie. He made her act different, like she was better than somebody else or something. If all she had to do to get that Chanel suit was suck his dick good, *I could've gotten a whole wardrobe.*

Brooklyn heads jammed into Junior's restaurant. I was checking niggas I ain't seen in a long while. People had different ways of dealing with me but nobody tried to front on me like I fell off or something because, father or no father, I was wearing this Isaac Mizrahi dress like nobody could. My hair was hooked and my face looking fresh and sensual. We all stuffed into a booth and ordered all kinds of things. Natalie talked loud as usual. "It's on me, y'all. Order what you want," Natalie said loudly.

Will acted like he was the Lion King surrounded by all us women. He was quiet. He paid and profiled for all niggas who only had the pleasure of having one woman's attention for that night. We was laced, all of us, a crew of girls dipped in the finest shit, ordering shit we knew we weren't gonna eat, and just talking, joking, and having a good time.

The money in my bra was sticking me in my right tittie. I headed to the bathroom to adjust it. Afterwards I glanced in the mirror and threw on some more lipstick. I licked my finger to lay down a piece of my hair that was about to get unruly. As I was coming out of the bathroom, Will was standing at the pay phone. The thing that ran through my mind was, what's up with him using the pay phone? I had already noticed him carrying a Motorola Startac cellular. I threw my right leg out to push right on by him.

"Santiaga's daughter right?" he asked, even though he already knew the answer—everybody did.

"Yeah, what about it?" I asked defensively.

"Nah, nah, I got a lot of respect for him. I see life is *still* treating you good." His eyes were concentrating on mine, like he was tryna hypnotize me or something.

"I take care of myself," I responded, letting him know there was no reason to feel sorry for me.

"Yeah, I can see that. What you need to do is let me take care of you." I flagged my right arm to show him no, I'm not interested. "C'mon girl. Just give me your phone number. I know you're with it. It's all in your eyes."

"Listen man. I don't even get down like that. Natalie's my girl—"

"And you would look better in that Chanel suit than she does. Just give me the word. I'll tear that shit right off her ass and put it on yours."

I thought about it for a few seconds. I'd be a liar if I said it wasn't a good offer. He smiled slyly, flashing his gold teeth, chewing real sexy like on his bubble gum.

"C'mon. Give up the number. I'll drop her ass at home, swing around and pick you up. Then we can talk, get to know each other for the rest of the night." My nipples hardened. They started sticking out of my tight dress. He saw them too, licked his lips, and smiled some more.

I opened my Coach bag to get a pen. He pulled his pen out quicker. He scribbled on a book of matches as I recited, 555 . . . when Natalie appeared in the doorway. She looked at him.

"Why you using the pay phone?" she asked, just to have something to say. When he did not answer, she looked at me with my bag open. Then looked at him with his pen in his hand and said, "You little sneaky bitch. You fucking low-down sneaky bitch."

"Wait a minute, Natalie. He asked me—"

"He asked you what? What did you ask her?" She spun around to Will.

"Baby, I didn't ask her shit. She needed a pen. I had to make a call. I didn't want it traced to my cellular so I used the pay phone. I was giving her the pen and that's it. C'm here. Why you so suspicious all the time?" He pulled her and gave her a big bear hug to calm her down. As she buried her face in his wide chest, he looked over her shoulder at me for the last four digits. I silently mouthed 4728. Still embracing her, he mouthed, "I'll call you."

Back around the table, none of the girls at the table knew what happened but everybody could feel that things had tensed up. Our food had arrived and Natalie wasn't saying or eating nothing. She was all back on Will's dick, but looking at me like I was a murderer or something. Finally Natalie blurted out to me, "Nice dress."

Toshi said, "Yeah, that shit is banging."

"Did Simone pick that up for you?" Natalie added in a sarcastic voice. Simone cut her eyes at Natalie then looked at me for a sign of what was going on. My teeth were locked with anger.

"Nah, she bought that today," Simone said. "I wish I would of picked it up for her because half that dough she spent on it would be in my pocket right now." Everybody except me and Natalie laughed at Simone's unending one woman comedy show.

"Yeah, your little suit is nice, too," I responded in a snotty voice. "It's just *my style.*"

"Yeah, I picked it up for fifty dollars at the auction the FBI did at your house in Long Island, along with some other fancy shit."

I lunged across the table for Natalie's neck. Zakia jumped in between, tryna separate us with her arms as Simone held me back. Toshi held Natalie and Zakia told Will to step back.

"You sneaky bitch," Natalie yelled. "You *always* thought it was *all about you.* Nobody could have shit but you! Here I am being a friend and you stabbing me in my fucking back. Here the whole block talking about your crazy-ass crackhead, bald-headed mother and your *broke,* homeless ass. I'm taking up for *you* and *you* tryna cut my throat. Don't think you ain't gonna take no ass-whipping for that. Later for Will. This is about me and you."

"You ain't nothing but a low-class hoe Natalie. You been biting my style *forever* 'cause you don't have no style. And for the last time, *your man came to me.* If your shit was *all that,* he wouldn't be sniffing up and around my ass. So get it together."

"I'ma fuck you up, Winter. Don't let me catch your ass in the hallway or anywhere. I'ma fuck you up."

"Yeah, yeah, yeah. Y'all coming?" I asked, getting up from the table to leave. All of them was looking back and forth to see what each one was gonna do. Simone hopped in the limo with me, the others stayed with Natalie.

"If I wasn't pregnant," Simone said, "I'd have your back. But I gotta look out for this one here," pointing to the belly. Me and Simone stayed up drinking the rest of the night. I stumbled into Aunt B's at 5 A.M. and fell asleep in my clothes.

By 5 P.M. Sunday evening I woke up with a headache, peeled off my clothes and stepped into the hot shower. My mind flashed back on the past twenty-four hours and my tears mixed with the shower water. The idea of my personal business being yelled out at Junior's restaurant had me shaking still.

Will called at six. "So what's up? You ready? I'm coming to get you."

"Stop playing. You didn't even check for me last night when your girl was going off on me."

"Don't pay that no mind. If I would have stepped in, she would have only got more dramatic. The way I handled it was to let her blow off some steam until she tired out."

"Ooh really," I said, nonchalant-like.

"Come down at seven. I'll pick you up. I'll be driving my green Q45, not the Rover."

"Alright, meet me in the back of the B building." I knew I was living dangerously, but I wasn't worried. What Natalie didn't understand was that I needed Will for business purposes. She was way too dumb to relate to the ideas and business plans I had put together. She had crossed the line when she tried to play me out in public. I was about to build an empire so I didn't have to be concerned with lowlifes like Natalie and her off-the-wall comments.

Outside, the car was dark green and crisp. Mint-green custom upholstered leather seats with dark green piping. The rugs were mint green, too. I slid my shoes off as I entered the car, afraid to get even a lint ball on his interior. "Pretty feet, Winter. So how about the bottoms?"

"What?"

"The bottom of your feet. Are they soft like silk or hard and crusty like sandpaper?"

"Don't compare me to the second-rate women you're used to."

"Second rate, huh?" he repeats quietly without sounding the least bit insulted.

"Yeah, the ones with ashy ankles and elbows. The ones with the hard feet and the chipped nail polish. That's what you're used to," I laughed. "And the ripped panties and dingy bras with the wire popping out and the stinking hairy underarms and—"

"I got you, Winter . . . I get the point."

"Good. Don't insult me and I won't insult you. Where are we going?"

"I want to check the new Bruce Willis flick."

"Oh," I responded, uninterested.

"Why, what do you wanna do?"

"I want to talk."

"Damn. Why do women always want to talk? I just met you. What do we have to talk about?"

"Something that's important to me—business."

He laughed. "Ha, 'business.' What kind of business?"

"You know what kind of business."

"Oh," he said, then paused. "You don't want to talk about that. That's a man's game. Business is a rough sport, like football or worse. You don't want to get into that."

"I been around it all my life. I know what I'm dealing with. Right now I'm in a tight spot. I need to make some dough, fast money. I know you can relate to that."

"You know how I know you ain't ready for this conversation? Because you don't even know me and you talking about some shit you can't trust nobody in."

"I already thought about that but the deal is I gotta start somewhere. Panicking about who to trust and who not to trust ain't getting me nowhere. I'm ready to take a gamble. The way I see it, whoever gambles with me, gambles too. We both have something to lose."

"Yeah, but I ain't the person. This ain't the angle I came in on. I asked for your number because I think you're a classy chick. I wanted to spend some time with you. Shoot the shit, catch a movie. Now you trying to muscle in on something else. I can't do business with you, Winter. I play hardball, the major leagues."

"Alright, look at it from another angle. Think of me as an investor. I give you my money to invest in your trade, you give me the return on my money."

"What if you give me your money and I don't give you back nothing? See? This business is like a chess game. You gotta think of every possible move any and every player in the game can make. To every move you gotta have a smart reaction. You don't have no crew holding you down, then where's the threat? What's gonna prevent any nigga from jerking you, robbing you, killing you? Santiaga's gone, his whole crew is gone. It was good while it lasted. That's why I'ma pile up my dough and get out before it's too late." My face dropped. Will saw my sadness. "Alright, how much you working with."

"I got twenty-five hundred dollars," I said proudly. Will laughed and laughed and laughed. "What's so fucking funny?"

"I don't even deal in those small sums of money. The way you were talking I was thinking you was about to negotiate a major deal. You talking about you working a corner hand to hand competing with the other sellers who been out there and got a flow going with they customers. You talking about sparking a beef over turf just based on them niggas being down with the new and you being a reminder of the old."

"Well then, *you* put me on. I'll be down with your crew. Train me and all that good shit. Put me on." Will looked like he was thinking about it as we pulled into the drive-in.

"You know there's a lot of ways to make money Winter, not only one way."

"Yeah, like what?"

Will smiled. I shot him a fuck-you-I-ain't-no-two-dollar-hoe look. "I ain't tricking, working no dirty alleys and shit like that."

"I would never put Santiaga's daughter on the hoe-stroll. You too good for that kind of work."

"So what you offering?"

"Just stick with me, Winter. You want some popcorn?"

"No," I said, frustrated.

Will came back with everything *size large*. Large drink, large popcorn, large nachos. As I sat there watching him crunching on his popcorn, I wondered, *What is Will really into? Who is he?* Did he have any value or purpose to me or was I just wasting my time? He obviously didn't want to do business with me. He must've only wanted the pussy. I tried to take a good look at him again, but it was too dark. I could only get a glimpse when a blue or yellow or red light flickered off the screen into the car. He looked alright as far as I could remember. But he didn't give me that uncontrollable feeling that I felt when I was in the car with Midnight. He had all the right stuff and I'd give him some pussy to get it from him, but only if I could be sure I was gonna get exactly what I wanted. I seen plenty a niggas who will flash their jewels, cars, and gear, run through pussy and leave the girl with rug burns on her back and nothing else. I needed cash, training, a solid team, and a real man to look out for me in every way. So I started to fuck with his head. "Let me ask you something, Will."

"What?"

"You supposed to be a great businessman right?"

"No doubt," he said confidently.

"You watch how your money moves, look out for people tryna pinch the stash, don't want to make moves with no small-timer with small money."

"Yeah? What you tryna get at," he asked slightly aggravated.

"So why does a man who works so hard for the dough drop three Gs on a bitch like Natalie for a Chanel suit."

"Damn, that suit really got you heated, huh," he joked.

"No seriously, it's no secret that Natalie fucks around with anybody. You supposed to be a man who watches the company he keeps and look who you end up in box seats with."

Will was aggravated. "Look, you want to get raw with me, I'ma get raw with you. I'ma talk to you like you one of my boys, now. Natalie sucks my dick like no other hoe ever sucked my dick."

"Yeah, but you could've got your dick sucked on 42nd Street."

"No, not like that. There's an art to sucking a dick. Natalie got that shit locked down. She gets the whole dick in her mouth and still finds room for my nuts. When I bust in her mouth, she swallows like it's pancake syrup. Hell, she earned that three-thousand-dollar suit." He laughed. "One of my boys from Fort Greene was just saying Natalie's fucking around with this other kid he know around your way. I told my boy if she's sucking *his* dick like she be sucking mine, I know why he's risking his life fucking one of my hoes. But as long as she's sucking *my dick* like she does she can get whatever she wants."

"So what did you want my number for?"

"Just 'cause a chick can suck your dick good don't mean she can be your girl. I figured that shit out."

"Oh, so you saying that—"

"I'm saying that you Santiaga's daughter, you're beautiful, young, top-of-the-line. A nigga don't have to teach you how to act. You naturally classy, now that's different."

"Oh, so you tryna make yourself look good by making Winter Santiaga your girl. But then you're gonna let Natalie suck your dick on the side *while* you blessing *her* with clothes 'n cash."

"First off, I didn't say nothing about giving her cash. I give her *things* she wants. And if you asking me to cut her off you must be saying you gonna do me better than she do, so I wouldn't have no reason to fuck with her again." Will rubbed his balls with his left hand until his thick erect dick was sticking out of his pants.

"Oh, now you actually got the nerve to ask me to suck your dick?"

Will started laughing. "Listen girl, you just don't know. Some niggas smoke weed, some niggas hooked on cane, some on the pussy. My pleasure is having my joint done right. If I ain't gotta *girl* the minute I want her, I make one of them crackhead niggas suck my joint. Man them niggas is so turned out on that crack that they'll get on their knees and suck my dick just like a bitch for a hit of the pipe." He laughed. "Men got stronger jaws. That shit feels even better."

The movie screen turned black. Will's lips were moving. He was talking but I couldn't hear no more sound. That was it. If there was a feeling in my body for Will, it was dead. I told myself if I could calm myself down, maybe I could still have Will as a possible business partner somewhere down the road. The bottom line was, I was sitting next to a man who thought it was okay to let another man suck his dick. Somehow Will figured that only the crackhead is the homosexual. Will saw himself as "all man," the powerful dealer. Just to keep it real with y'all, I can't take no man seriously who I gotta guess about sexually. I can't be seduced or excited by questionable masculinity. I need to know that my man is rugged and rough to the bone. I would never have to worry about Midnight saying or doing this. If a crackhead even suggested oral sex as a trade-off for cash, Midnight would've put a bullet in his head. What Santiaga might have done in that situation is unmentionable.

I bobbed and weaved like a boxer for the rest of our date. I knew I had to play my cards carefully not to burn a potential bridge. At the same time I refused to end the night with my face buried in Will's lap.

Tomorrow I would consult with my father about my financial options. My anger toward him was slowly wearing down. I felt backed into a corner. The truth of the matter was I needed some good advice from Daddy, a man who had always loved me. The pain of it all was trying to talk through a thick glass or having to speak through a small vent or having to talk on some dirty old phone surveilled by the police. There would be no kind of privacy. I would have to pick over each and every word. I hated the idea of not being able to touch my father, having to watch him move in calculated steps because his hands and feet were chained together. And what would I say to him about my mother? What had Daddy already heard? Who would he blame? Wasn't my mother's condition his fault? Wasn't it the incident with Dulce that pushed Momma over the edge in the first place? How much did Dulce cost Daddy? Did she have money hidden that belonged to Santiaga? Tomorrow I would get answers from him, to all of my questions. I crawled into bed and noticed my cousin Bianca was back and fast asleep in our small room.

"I saw you get out of his car. When I catch you bitch, your ass is grass." That was my 5 A.M. wake-up call from Natalie. She couldn't rattle me, though. She's so petite that I didn't even think of her as a fighter. I thought to myself shit definitely had changed a whole lot. 'Cause there was a time when she wouldn't even dream of threatening me, much less following through and putting her hands on me. She was the gossip operator in our neighborhood. Therefore, she knew my situation. She knew my family wasn't tight like it used to be. The only worry I had now was when and how Natalie would attack. Would she jump out of a dark corner with a razor on the steps where the light is always broken? Or would she pay one of the local crackheads to do some ill shit to me? I'd have to stay alert.

At six, seven, eight, nine, and ten o'clock the phone rang. Each time, the person calling hung up. I knew it was Natalie. By 8 A.M. my aunt was screaming about the crank phone calls. She paced the hallways talking about there are three grown women living in this apartment and whenever this kind of shit happens it means somebody is sleeping with somebody else's man! I didn't answer. Bianca looked at me and rolled her eyes as if to agree that her mother was bugging and to go back to sleep.

Out of frustration I got up and headed for the shower. The steam surrounded my naked body and heated water drops slid down my breasts. *It's time to leave here,* I said to myself. So I asked myself, *and go where?* I came up with no response, but I knew I needed to leave fast. *Where is Midnight now?* I wondered. I imagined him in a villa in Spain sipping a tequila sunrise. Tequila, was that a Spanish or Mexican drink? Oh, what was the difference? Or maybe Midnight was disguised somewhere in a shack in Alabama. Nah, he was too smooth for that. He was sitting in the back room of an elegant club in Chicago— one that he owned. He dressed up every night, blending in with the darkness but still wearing sunglasses. He raked in mad dough, but ran the *real* operation out the back room of the club. He was saving up enough dough to come and rescue me from this bullshit. He'd take me to the nightclub, bring me on the stage where the spotlight would fall on me. I'd be wearing a silver designer dress that was so top-notch it wouldn't even have a name. A dress especially prepared for me. No other dress like it in the world. I'd have on silver shoes imported from Italy and handcrafted stockings with designer garter belts. Midnight would say, "Ladies 'n gentlemen, I present to you my wife, the new hostess of my club Winter Storm." The crowd would cheer and I would graciously accept my new role as the top hostess/madame in town. In the shower, I made myself laugh and laugh and laugh . . .

"Don't you hear me knocking?" My aunt's voice sliced through the sound of the showering water.

"Yeah Aunt B?"

"Somebody's here to see you."

I grabbed back the shower curtain saying, "Oh Aunt B I forgot to tell you, I mean I forgot to ask you, if Natalie comes by or calls, just tell her that I left already."

"Why?" she asked suspiciously. "I thought that was your girl?"

"No she is . . . I just don't feel like being bothered with her today 'cause I got a lot on my mind."

"Oh," Aunt B said, "you must be thinking about that stretch limo you was riding around in Saturday night or maybe you're thinking about Natalie's man. What's his name again? Bianca!" my aunt yelled to her daughter. "What's Natalie's boyfriend's name?"

Bianca didn't answer.

I stood there speechless and naked and getting cold as the air blew in and the steam moved out of the open door.

My aunt stepped out of the doorway. "I ain't that damn old. I know what goes on around here, especially in my own house."

"Aunt B," I said, "who's at the door?"

She stuck her head back in and said, "You'll see, get dressed."

Patting myself dry, I dashed to the bedroom. Bianca was up and out of her bed. I thought damn, where did she go that quick? I went in my suitcase, pulled out my jeans and a shirt. As I reached for the bra I had laying on top of my suitcase under the folded dress I took off last night, I immediately saw that my safety pin was not there. I ran my hand along the lining of the bra. The pins were gone. My twenty-five hundred dollars was gone. A sense of emergency overcame my body. *Don't panic,* I mumbled to myself. I unfolded my dress, shook it out to see if my money had somehow gotten tangled up in there. Nothing. I picked up my panty hose, shook 'em. I threw open the top of my suitcase and started running my hand along the side pockets, searching for the cash. I looked in places I knew I had never and would never have put the money. Sweat broke out on my forehead, mixing with water beads from the shower.

Aunt B stuck her head into the bedroom door, shook her head with disapproval, and said, "What a mess. Please don't keep company waiting." She cleared her throat. "Are you looking for something?"

I opened my mouth to speak, then immediately closed it. "Nah."
She walked away. I got it, I caught it. She had been in my things. My
aunt had stolen my money. She thought it was even steven because she
didn't have no money and she figured I got more money where this
comes from, 'cause I must be holding out on her. This bitch took my
life savings. I screamed out loud, no words, just sounds. I stood butt
naked in anguish.

My aunt came back to the bedroom door with her hands on her
hips, followed by an older white woman. She was peering into the
bedroom at me like she was trying to see as much as she could as
quickly as she could. My aunt turned to her and said, "Good luck
with her. She's a mess, she don't want to listen to nobody. She always
want it her way. And she's a nonstop liar. Winter, this is Ms.
Griswaldi. She's from BCW."

"Nice to meet you, Winter. We've been looking all over for you.
I'm just glad I got the call about your new address this morning. Come,
get dressed. Let's go."

"I'm not going anywhere with you."

Ms. Griswaldi leaned toward me. "I'm sorry this is the way you
feel, Winter. In fact, I'm sorry for everything that has happened to
you up until this point. For now and for the next 330 days, you are
officially a ward of the state. We are your legal guardians. Please come
along with us. The marshal will escort us." I glanced down the hall
and saw a man in a uniform.

"Wait a minute, hold on. Aunt B, can I talk to you for a second?"
Aunt B looked at Ms. Griswaldi as though she all of a sudden needed
permission from her to have a conversation in her own apartment.
Ms. Griswaldi looked at her watch and said, "You have five minutes.
We're on a tight schedule. You're not the only pickup we have to do
this afternoon. Please pack all the belongings that you plan to bring
along with you."

I grabbed Aunt B's hand, said excuse me a minute, and closed the
door. "Come on Aunt B, *we family*. Did you actually turn me in? Did you
call the fucking authorities on me? Is shit that bad? Damn, I would have
gave you some goddamn money." Tears of anger filled my eyes.

"Don't be stupid, Winter. You think I'ma call some authorities
into my crib. That nosy lady been snooping all around my house. You
think I want some more police, and heat in my place. You're just a
dumb ass, Winter. *You* don't run shit around here. You better check

yourself. That stupid bitch Natalie probably called the authorities on you. Now this white lady know all our business. She know I got too many people living in this apartment to be on Section 8. She know Alvin's locked up. She know your mother's on drugs. *She's looking at my arms checking for tracks.* She's staring in my face like I'm supposed to confess to some shit. I just want her to get the fuck outta here before she start writing my ass up. So pack your shit up n'go. To be so damn smart, you sure are stupid. I don't need no trouble."

"What about my money, though? That's all the money I have to my name."

My aunt looked me dead in the eye and said, "What money?" She stuck her two hands in her pants pockets pulling the pockets inside out. There was nothing in those pockets but lint. "I don't have any money. And as far as I know, you didn't have any money either."

Aunt B gave me the evil sarcastic I-told-you-so grin. My mind snapped. All I know is I had my two hands around her neck choking her. She was gagging for air. I wasn't going for her no-money-in-my-pockets act. I ripped off her shirt. She fought back, but she couldn't fight me—well she could, but she wouldn't win. I snatched her bra off. The money wasn't hidden there. Ms. Griswaldi and the marshal entered the room. The marshal restrained me. Ms. Griswaldi picked Aunt B up off the floor and tried to help her reassemble herself.

My aunt stepped back from Ms. Griswaldi's assistance. With only her pants left on her body and a busted lip, she snatched a big piece of her shirt off of the floor to cover her titties. "You see," she said to Ms. Griswaldi, breathing in and out real hard, "Winter is violent and spoiled. You'll need to lock her ass up. She can't be trusted. All I can say is, I opened my place to her and she turned on me. She'll turn on you, too."

I understood how she was tryna set me up. I just mumbled, "You junky bitch," and packed up my shit to go.

10

The House of Success was a group home for teenage girls aged thirteen to eighteen. Don't ask me how or why they picked that name. As far as I was concerned it was a joke like everything else. This building was set up like a house. Somehow somebody thought they would take a whole bunch of anonymous females, put 'em in a building set up like a house and have them pretend they was like family. There were four girls in each big room. There were about ten big rooms. There were two kitchens and one big-ass living room that doubled as the recreation room. There were offices where the people in charge did whatever they were pretending to do. Across from the offices were a set of small rooms that some counselors and personnel slept in when they did the overnight shift.

This was minimum security where a girl had to follow certain rules and would somehow be rewarded with "little freedoms." As Ms. Griswaldi put it, "For the next thirty days you will be evaluated. If you are not deemed to be violent or suffering from a learning disorder or illness you will be treated like a young adult with adult responsibilities." So the deal was I had to be on lockup, meaning I couldn't leave, or come and go as I please. I had to stay within the facility for thirty days while they decided if I was ready for the world.

I wasn't scared. Santiaga raised me to be strong. I'll admit I had all those fucked-up scenes in my head from the movies like some squad of butch women dragging me out of my bed, fucking me up in the bathroom, and shoving a broomstick up my pussy. But I would fight anybody I had to before I would let them get me down. They'd have to kill me before I'd let some chicks eat my pussy or make me lick theirs. All that shit was dead.

The House of Success wasn't like the movies, though. In the room I was assigned to, I met all kinds. First, there was this girl from Haiti. The only thing I could say about her was that she was the greasiest person I ever saw. She had a dogged-out, uneven, jheri curl with all the grease activator and gel that comes with it. She had the jheri curl grease colliding with the Vaseline on her face. She had greasy lotions for her hands and feet, and in general always looked wet. Her name was Claudette. There was no worse nightmare than the clothes she wore. It looked like she picked a year from the past, let's say 1975, and decided all her clothes would be from that time. To make it worse, she just said fuck the color scheme. I'll wear a purple shirt with green gauchos with a yellow hat with a big pink flower on it and I'll top this shit off with some wooden platform open-toed shoes so I can show off my big maroon bunion. Needless to say, Claudette mostly stayed to herself. The only time I seen her chilling with the other girls in the house was when they chipped in and bought her a cheap Walkman for her birthday. She was ridiculously happy. They claimed the only reason they bought it was because Claudette played some old fucked up Christian radio station with gospel music and a loud whacky screaming preacher on the AM dial. They couldn't take hearing it no more so they got her the radio with the headphones.

Lashay was a trip. She was kind of chubby with a big cute face. She was one of those girls who decided that she didn't care if her body was a size 16. She was still gonna wear size 11 clothing. She had big hips, a big booty, and a waist that was small compared to the rest of her butt. You couldn't tell her she was fat, though. The way she figured it, if the hips are forty-eight inches and the waist thirty-six and the titties forty, that's a perfect hourglass shape!!! She wore halter tops when it obviously should have been a crime. She wore Daisy Duke shorts, and shoes with laid-to-the-side heels that were begging for forgiveness with every step she took. Her thing was "the boys" who, if you let her tell it, *all* were in love with *her.* She had damn near every issue of *Word Up!* magazine with all her favorite pictures of rap stars glued to the wall in a raggedy collage. She was the show-off type. It was more like she was a comedian to me 'cause how you gonna show off in busted shoes and clothes you bought from some Indian at a candy stand in the train station?

Rashida was into her own little world. She was pretty, but it didn't count. She never made it work for her. She wore her hair back in a ponytail all the time, every day. She had no flavor about cuts, wraps, twists, nothing—no style. She had a cute little figure, but kept it covered up like it was on punishment or something. She had the nerve to, in this day and time, wear dingy no-name kicks on her feet. You know the ones they sell in the supermarket for four dollars. She didn't decorate her side of the room at all. If you looked over there it was plain, period. She was extra clean and tidy. All she did was read. She didn't even watch television unless it was the gloomy-ass news.

Noni was the girl whose bed I got. She was transferred to another room. The girls said Noni smoked cigarettes like a smokestack even though there was no smoking allowed. She had taken a roll of string, made a line and a curtain around her bed out of a sheet. It didn't matter, they said, 'cause the smoke kept stinking up the room anyway. They said she had a nervous problem, was molested by her stepdad and beaten by her mother. Smoking made her feel good and she would kick any ass who tried to take her cigarettes or report her. They said the counselors who did the overnight just let her keep smoking 'cause it was easier to be Noni's friend than her enemy. As a consequence, other girls just followed her lead and lit up, too. When one girl in the other room turned eighteen she was released and had to go and make it on her own. When her bed got free they put Noni in there 'cause there were three more smokers in that room. I got her bed and ended up with Claudette, Lashay, and Rashida.

My first week was crazy. They took me into the office for an interview with my newly assigned social worker. Her name was Kathy Johnson. As soon as I got in the room, I peeped her. She had her hair pulled back in a neat sweep. Her perm needed a serious touch-up. I could see she tried hard to lay the naps down with some gel that was turning white and flaking. She did her own nails, but believe me she was the type who was too lazy to take off the old layer of polish, so she just piled the new layer on top so it didn't lay smooth on her nails. On her feet were some pleather knockoffs. The kind that when you flipped them over, had a stamp on the bottom that read "man-made uppers." Her pantsuit was JCPenney's or Sears, definitely polyester or rayon.

"Come in, Winter. Have a seat," she said, like I needed her help. She pushed the manila file open and flipped through some papers. I checked her left hand. No engagement ring, no wedding ring, nothing. On the wall she had some kind of degree from Fordham University.

"Winter, where do you go to school?" she asked.

"I use to go to Half Hollow High in Long Island."

"Then what happened?" she asked.

I sucked my teeth and said, "What's the sense in having all those papers in the folder about me if you gonna ask me what you already know?"

"OK, Winter. Did you drop out, did you reregister at another school after Long Island, and how do you plan to finish your education? These are the type of things I need to find out from you."

I gave her answers, short ones. No sense in getting all involved when she was a walking, talking example of what education amounted to. What was I supposed to do? Struggle to be like her? Pay some big school big, big money so I could get a little job in some little place making an iddy biddy bit of cash. What do I get? To hang a stupid-ass degree up in my little office where I don't make enough dough to get a regular manicure, pedicure, or perm. I should be interviewing her, asking her what's *her* problem.

She asked me about my sisters, who, for the most part, I had put out of my mind. She asked me about my mother and father and every nosy thing she could nose around in, at which time I gave her any answer that popped in my head. She asked me could I read and write. I told her, "Of course, and I can talk too."

After two hours I was leaving her office. I asked how do I get money in here? As she explained it, I got sixty dollars a week. The institution got eight hundred per month, per child. The sixty dollars a week represented my spending money after the institution paid its expenses.

"What expenses?" I asked.

"We take care of everything else you would need, Winter. We purchase the food, clothes, shelter, etcetera."

"You mean to tell me you bought those clothes all them girls is wearing?"

"No, not exactly. There's a voucher system. Your social worker, that's me," she said proudly, "will accompany you once every two months or three months to get what you need."

"You're gonna help *me* shop?" I repeated and laughed.

Ms. Johnson said, "You know, if you don't follow the rules in here you forfeit all of your privileges. That includes nights out, weekend passes, and your weekly stipend."

"Stipend?" I asked.

"Your money. You know, Winter, you're one of the older girls

around here. Most of the sixteen- and seventeen-year-olds get after-
school jobs. You're not going to be here long. I suggest you focus on
making specific plans for your future. I'm here to help you in any way
I can."

After a box lunch, I saw the institutional psychiatrist. She was a
nut. She asked me all kinds of questions about my mother and father.
Did my father touch me, did I ever want to have sex with him, did
my mother ever beat me. No matter how many times I told her ass no
she would put the question another way but still be asking me the
same shit. She asked me dumb things like how did I feel when they
took my sisters away. She might as well of asked me is a burning
building hot! She asked me about my relationship with my friends
and men. I looked at her like, lady, do you really think me and your
old ass is gonna sit here and have girl talk? To entertain myself, I
started making things up—I break out in a rash when I'm in the
room with more than two people. I'm a virgin and would like to be
one until I'm thirty. I masturbate to the sound of the washing
machine—I was cracking myself up. She was sitting there with a long
yellow pad actually trying to come up with an explanation for all the
gobbledygook I was giving her.

More tests. Reading and math. If they found out anything, it's
that I can read, write, and count. As Santiaga would say, everything
else is just extra unnecessary. I met with the birth control lady who
really wanted to get personal. I wouldn't tell her nothing, but I did
take sample foam sponges and those free condoms even though there
were no men in the house. I figured when they loosen up on me I can
have them just in case.

At night most of the girls were gone. They got evening passes,
which allowed you to leave until 11 P.M. Some had jobs to go to,
others had free time. If you came in after 11 P.M. and missed curfew,
you forfeited your passes for the rest of the week. If you were late
three times in thirty days, you permanently lost your evening
"opportunities." I was stuck inside with the girls on punishment, the
newcomers who had to be evaluated like me, and the uniformed
ladies who guarded the door, registering girls in and out.

Laying on my bed, I put together a list of things I needed. Top of
my list was a lock. I needed to lock up my suitcase before somebody
pulled one of Aunt B's capers and tried to lift some of my clothes. I
had already decided if anybody put their hands on my stuff we'd go

head up. After I got my list together, I sat and thought. The challenge for me now would be making something out of nothing. How to make money when I had no money to start with.

Then I was hit by a brilliant idea. I jumped up from my cot and walked into the bedroom across the hall. "Noni, let me borrow a dollar. I need to make a couple of calls."

"When am I gonna get it back?"

"Friday."

"Alright, I'll lend you one dollar, one time. If Friday comes and I don't see you or my dollar, your credit is dead and don't ask me for shit no more."

"Cool," I responded, got four quarters, and waited on this chick Jinja to get off the pay phone.

"Simone. What's up girl, I got a deal for you. You got any money?"

"Yeah, I got a little something. Heard you were in some trouble."

"Nah, I ain't in no trouble, at least nothing I can't handle. Listen, I got a list of shit I want you to pick up for me. It will run you about two hundred."

Simone laughed. "It ain't going to cost me nothing."

"All the better," I said. I read the list, told her to pack everything in a box. "I'll call you back Friday morning. You'll meet my girl, give the box to her. I'll pay you for the stuff on Sunday night."

I figured there were forty girls in here including me. Every one of us had sixty dollars a week, at least. Some had jobs. That meant altogether the girls in the House of Success took in a minimum of twenty-four hundred per week. There was no way I was gonna be standing around in some polyester McDonald's suit saying May I help you, sir? Would you like a Coke with your fries? I would set up shop in here and provide everybody with what they needed. I would even help them to *understand* what they needed. I was locked in for three more weeks. That was three Fridays, which meant at best there was a maximum intake of seventy-two hundred. All I need is five thousand for myself. When I got my evening "privileges," I'd invest my money in the streets, triple it at least, and get my own place, loot, and life. I might as well have Simone for a partner 'cause she understood business and wasn't a gossip like Natalie. She was gonna have a baby soon and would need my help as well. We'd get paid together.

I spent every day up until Friday getting to know the girls in the house. It wasn't hard. Everyday I would get up, do my hair in a different fly style and rock my clothes like I was going out on a real special date. Only thing was, I really wasn't going anywhere and everybody knew it. The girls watched me and asked me how I did my hair in a certain style, how I manicured my own hands, pedicured my own toes, and where I got my clothes and shoes from. I gave them answers. After a while they started asking questions about me, who am I, my background.

Eventually they started telling me about their lives. They liked my stories better, though, 'cause theirs were mostly hard-luck stories. I told them about the big birthday party Santiaga gave me on my fifth birthday. It was in the ballroom at a local hotel. Santiaga filled the room up with five hundred balloons, a hundred for every year I had been alive. All the little kids from the block came. I got my first party dress, the kind you wouldn't want to be caught dead in when you're thirteen but are delighted with when you're five. I had Gucci patent leather loafers and white lace stockings. We took family photos together and Santiaga gave me a charm bracelet with a 24-karat gold elephant. Every year until I was twelve he gave me a new gold animal. When I turn thirteen, I turned the charm bracelet into a necklace. I didn't wear it because by that time I had even better stuff, but I treasured it. Of course they asked where all my stuff was and I lied and told them in storage until my parents worked out their situation.

I found out which girls had jobs and which didn't. Who had extra money and what kind of taste they had. All the while I was talking, my mind was organizing what kind of stuff I could sell, what type of services I could perform, what type of prices I could charge, and how much I could expect to accumulate over the first couple of weeks. Friday, when Lashay was leaving on a weekend pass, I told her to meet Simone in the local pizza shop to pick up the box she was delivering to me.

First thing I did was pull out my lock and chain for my suitcase that I had been guarding with my life since my arrival. I put all of my new stuff inside and locked and chained it up. I organized the magazines I had asked for on my desk and I officially opened up shop. My first customer, the person I volunteered to be my best customer, was Claudette. I figured if I could fix her up, make her pay for it, she'd be a good example of what my work was worth. I also found out that

Claudette never spent her money. She was seventeen years old, worked on weekdays, and sent a hundred and fifty dollars a month to that whacky preacher she listened to. She stashed the rest.

"Claudette, you gotta boyfriend?"

"No," she said shyly.

"Oh, I guess you can't have a boyfriend because you're a Christian."

"No, I *can* have a boyfriend. There are just some things we can do, some things we can't."

"So what happens," I asked her. "You meet a nice guy and he finds out you aren't gonna give him none so he breaks out."

"No, we don't even get that far. I like a guy. He doesn't like me, that's it."

"I know what you need."

"What do I need, Winter? I am sure that you know. You seem to know so much."

"If I show you what you need, and give you what you need, it's gonna cost you."

"Oh no," she said. "I don't want to spend any money."

"But after I hook you up you will meet any man you want to meet. Your whole life will change. You give money to your preacher right?"

"Oh yes, this is different."

"But he doesn't do anything for you."

"You don't know that. He makes me feel good, better everyday."

"But I can make you feel better than he can and once I show you, you can do it for yourself. Alright let's make a deal. I'll fix you up. If you like what you see, you pay me. If you don't, you don't owe me nothing."

I handed her a stack of magazines, told her to flip through and tell me who she wanted to look like. I talked Claudette's ear off, got her hyped up on change. When I had her settling in the chair ready for a new cut, I could've cried with laughter. The only thing I knew about cutting hair was what a good haircut was supposed to look like when it was done and whatever I had peeped from Earline's. What made me calm though was there was no way for me to fuck up Claudette's hair any more than it already was. So I started cutting until she was damn near bald.

The way I figured it she needed to start all over again. I gave her finger waves. If I say so myself, it looked fly. I gave her a facial, unclogged all the Vaseline and that cheap one-dollar drugstore makeup she wore. I busted out my nail kit, gave her tips, a French manicure and pedicure. I made her take off that red skirt with tube socks and sandals and told her that, because I liked her, I would let her take a quick look in my suitcase. I unlocked and unchained it carefully to make her fully understand that she was about to enjoy a special privilege. From now on, I told her, she could order her clothes from me. "Let's just take it slow," I told her.

She selected one of my designer dresses. When she glanced in the mirror, saw the French manicure, fingerwaves, natural face with quality MAC lipstick, and the Donna Karan dress, she smiled at herself, turned to the left side, right side, front and back.

From what I could tell she was stuck in a state of shock.

"Now try these on," I said. I took my shoes out of the shoe box I kept them packed in. They were one size too small for her but she got the concept.

"Now Claudette," I said, holding her face between my hands, making her look me dead in the eye, "I have to take my dress and shoes back, but look at yourself and know that you can look like this if you let me help you. Your life will change."

"How much?" Claudette asked.

"For the face, hair, nails, and feet?"

"Yeah, and the dress."

"Oh, you can't afford this dress, it's mine. But I can show you something just as nice. I'll show you my catalog later tonight. You pick 'n pay and we'll be in business."

"How do you know I can't afford the dress?" Claudette asked with a funny accent.

"Even if you could, which I doubt, you can't have it. It's a designer exclusive," I lied just to gas her up. "They only made a few of these, but you can get something almost as nice. Let me work on finding the right thing for you." I charged her sixty dollars. She paid me. I watched as she got an extra switch in her walk. For another sixty, I convinced her to buy a pair of my jeans and a blouse, shit I got from the Banana Republic. I talked to her about toning down her colors. All in all I made a permanent customer. That was week two in the House of Success and I already had a hundred and twenty dollars plus my sixty-dollar stipend. Once Claudette spread the word—not

through talking because she was kind of shy, but just by being different from the fresh-off-the-boat girl she used to be—I was gonna rake
in the dough.

Things took off quickly. I had what everybody needed *at better
prices than they could get it themselves.* Everybody was happy. I organized all the fashions from the magazines into a catalog, put numbers
on the items and the whole shit. I let the people in the house order
their clothes from me. I let Simone boost them and sell them to me
for a small price. I resold them to the girls at less than half of what the
store would charge. Lashay was my unsuspecting runner, which put
money in her pocket. She got to meet Simone, pick the stuff up for
me, deliver it to me, and drop off whatever I wanted. I had cut-rate
cartons of cigarettes for Noni, wholesale candy for Lashay, clothes,
hairdos, fingernails, pedicures, and fashion tips for whoever needed it.
I had beer and joints at the right time on the down down low.
Depending on what was going on with Simone, I had things as big as
cellular phones and CD players available. At the end of twenty-one
days, I had two thousand five hundred dollars in my pocket and I had
never left my room.

Kathy Johnson, my social worker, recommended I finish school. I
disagreed and told her to make arrangements for me to drop out. To
keep things cool, I agreed to take my GED exam so I could get that
bullshit equivalency. I even agreed to look for a job, which I wasn't
really gonna do. The other girls in the house put me up on the scam.
All I had to do was fill out a form weekly saying I looked for a job and
where I looked for the job. I could get real company names and
addresses from the want ads, complete the form, turn it in, and qualify
as having looked for work. Work that as far as I was concerned I
would never find because I already had a more profitable hustle going.
Ms. Johnson threatened to sign me up for all kinds of technical and
business schools like I would want to be some kind of refrigerator
repairman or some crazy shit like that.

The psychiatrist recommended me to attend weekly psychiatric
sessions, labeled me some kind of sociopath or something like that
because I told her all those kooky stories that she was "educated"
enough or should I say dumb enough to believe. She recommended
that once I got my privileges, I should go visit my little sisters and that
the whole family go to counseling. I had a better plan. I believe you

see people when you have something to say and something to offer
and I was still working on it. What was the sense in seeing my sisters
when I couldn't do shit for them. They'd start talking about they
wanna come with me. What would I do then, move them from one
shelter to another shelter for teenage girls! People always seemed to
have stupid suggestions.

On my first free day, I hooked up with Simone. We had talked
regularly on the phone, but only about business because time was limited. There was only one phone on my floor and everyone wanted to
use it. No sense in hogging the phone and pissing off my customers.
Simone seemed real happy to actually see me. We met at a pizza spot.
She updated me on Brooklyn, said Natalie and Will were still together.
Natalie hated me and had told all my personal business to everyone.
My moms had sunk to an all-time low, had been seen wearing a full-
body catsuit, you know the tight two-dollar legging with the bodysuit
attached with no panties underneath. Her head was still bald, face still
twisted, and body still on crack. Of course Simone didn't word it that
way, but let's cut through the bullshit. I'm smart. Word on the street
was Santiaga ain't never getting out. Aunt B was screwing for money.
My whole family had individual hustles going on and in general shit
was tight. On the side Simone added that she had fixed up the room
in her apartment for the baby. She had a new crib, blankets, toys, the
works. Everything was pink. I told her it was dumb 'cause what if the
baby was a boy? She had a sonogram, she said, and was sure it was a
girl, so everything was in perfect order. She said she was seven months
pregnant now, and getting tired all the time. She wanted me to know
that she had put some money aside for the baby and she would need
to slow down for the eighth and ninth month. Now I was no dummy
so I caught the signal. My plans had to kick in as soon as possible. If
she was gonna slow down that would affect the chain of cash flow we
had going. Let's face it. She was a booster. I wasn't. She had the know-
how and the connect. I didn't. To tell the truth I wasn't even interested
in being a booster as long as I could make what Simone was already
deep into work for me.

"Simone, I want to make an investment."

"What kind of investment?"

"Crack."

"That ain't my area Winter, you know that. You know I have a
weed connect but it's out in Brooklyn back around the way."

"No, fuck that. I need a closer connect up here. Weed is cool, but crack is better money. Once them baseheads get going they completely loyal customers. I need to at least triple my money so I can make moves."

"I got a guy I can talk to, a cousin uptown. He's real tight with his shit though, he might not even have a conversation with me. He be acting like he don't be doing what he doing when everybody know what he be doing. Winter, I don't know about getting into that shit. When you get caught you do time, hard time." She hesitated, lowered her eyes, "Look what happened to your father."

Right, I thought, that's who I should be talking to, my father. And no matter what Simone said, my father got at least *twenty years of good high living* out of the business. Nobody could argue with that. That's power. To be able to set up your own empire in your neighborhood, or even somebody else's neighborhood for that matter. To buy cars, Jeeps, trucks. To sport the flyest shit made by top designers everyday. To be able to buy property, mansions, and still have apartments on the side. To be able to shit on people before they get a chance to shit on you. That's power. Who could argue with that? A regular nigga worked all week for change to get to work plus a beer to forget about how hard he worked. My pops was a major player for a long time. With the benefit of his knowledge I could make the world kiss my ass, but better than he did 'cause he could now teach me about the mistakes. Let's compare it, ten years of good living and twenty years of high living versus sixty years of scraping to get by. Enough said.

I told Simone, "Listen, work on that connect for me. Try'n set me up a meeting. Here's a list of what I need for the house. Let's meet here Friday night at nine. I'll pick it up."

"What about Lashay?" Simone asked.

"Who?" I responded, my mind drifting to Santiaga. "Oh, I don't need her anymore. I can get my evening passes now. I can be out till 11 P.M."

"So what's she gonna do?"

"Whatever she was doing before I got there." I gave Simone a hug and broke out.

On the bus ride to the jail I organized a clever way to key Santiaga into what I was saying without exposing my hand to guards or phone surveillance. As Santiaga had taught me, hold your cards close to your chest. Also, I wouldn't bring up the Dulce issue because that might cause him or even me to get mad and then I might end up leaving the jail without the information I needed. I would say yes, I saw Porsche, Mercedes, and Lexy. How were they doing? Fine. Getting big growing up, and going to school. What could I say about Mama? Well, it was unusual but I didn't have an answer up until the time I arrived at Riker's, went through checks and searches and the whole process. I still had no answer. Up until the time for me to sign in the book I sat nervously biting my lip about Momma, a woman who, despite everything, I know Daddy loved so much.

The guard said have a seat. I preferred to stand. Somehow I thought I could think better standing up so I went to the corner of the room and paced back and forth, back and forth.

When the guard returned he said, "Sorry Ms. Santiaga, Ricky Santiaga does not want to see anyone today."

"What? Did you tell him it was me? Did you tell him it was his daughter, Winter Santiaga?"

"Yes, I did. I gave him the same name you gave me."

"What do you mean he doesn't want to see me? What did he say? How did he say it?"

"He didn't say anything. I told him you were here. He shook his head no. He doesn't have to come out. A prisoner has the right to refuse a visit."

Tears welled up and splashed out my eyes. The guard said, "Listen, if you write your name and address on a piece of paper I can give it to him. Maybe he'll write." As I jotted down my name, address, and phone number, I put on the bottom of the ripped piece of paper, Daddy please call me right away. I need you badly. Winter.

At the House of Success everyone asked me what's wrong. I looked at their faces and thought to myself, *You're not in my damn family. Don't try to act like you are.* I shut them out and didn't respond. I went to my bed, took off my shoes, and balled up under the cover in my clothes and slept. I slept through the rest of the afternoon, evening, and the night. I slept through the next morning, the next afternoon, and next evening again. Girls came and went. Can I buy a stogie? Do you have any more perm cream? What time can I get my hair done? Where did you put the catalog? My response was nothing.

On the third bedridden morning Ms. Johnson the social worker came. "If there's a problem, Winter, we can talk about it. We can work it out." I just stared at her face, then rolled over and balled up again.

By noontime the psychiatrist came and insisted that I needed a session. "Pent-up aggression wouldn't solve anything," she said. I had better eat some food or at least drink some water. I said nothing. By one o'clock security came, poked me with a nightstick and said I had to get dressed and go to the psychiatric office immediately. The rock-face lady-man with the big arms made it clear that if I didn't move my ass she would move me. I got up and went through the motions of preparing to go.

Rashida was seated on her bed. She watched me with tears in her eyes. As the guard waited outside the door, Rashida came to me and said, "Alright Winter, you don't have to say anything. I can understand it. But whatever happened to you, I been there before. It's a real bad place to be but I been there. It almost make you wonder if being dead isn't better. But let me just say this. Once I took a bottle of pills 'cause I wanted to die. I figured I die, no more pain right? Wrong," she said, answering herself. "I ended up on the operating table with the doctors pumping my stomach. A lot of pain. When I got better, there was still pain. So I tried it again. I slashed my wrist with a knife. I figured, surefire way to die, right? And when I die no more pain, right? Wrong. When I woke up I was in a hospital room with tubes everywhere and stitches in my wrist. When the anesthesia wore off there was pain for weeks later. I still had a cast, painkillers, and pain. Soon as the pills wore off there was more pain. Even when I got better, there was pain. Pain's a part of life. That's my point, pain is part of life. When it's your time to go, you go. If it's not your time, you don't go. Until then make the best of it. If you find God, the good in yourself, you can take most of the pain away and then the few times you get pain you can just surrender to Allah and the pain will go away."

I couldn't connect to what she was saying. The security yelled in and said, "C'mon Santiaga, the doctor is waiting." I got up.

Rashida said, "Listen, tonight I'm going to see Sister Souljah speak. She's a real beautiful sister who has helped me to understand myself a little more and get it together. If you want to come I'll take you, my treat."

"Your treat! It cost money!? What the hell you giving her money for?" My face was vexed and Rashida was intimidated by my sudden change and instant anger. "I could see if you were gonna see a show," I went on. "Then at least you get what you pay for. You going to listen to somebody talk shit. Souljah gets paid. You get nothing, stupid ass!"

Rashida looked shocked at the dramatic change in my personality. "I guess I am a stupid ass for tryna help you!" Rashida exclaimed.

As she left the room, probably just to get away from me, I shouted, "Do me a favor."

"Oh, now you need a favor."

"Ask Sister Souljah if she knows somebody named Midnight."

My session with the psychiatrist revived me. Not because of anything she did, because of what I did and said. The story I told her just made me laugh inside and that helped to take away some of the depression I felt. I told her I had a best friend named Natalie and ever since childhood we had been connected. We were so connected that when she cried, I cried, when she was sick, I was sick. When she was happy, I was happy. Even when we were separated I could still feel Natalie's emotions and she could feel mine. Natalie had made one of her other friends angry by telling some of her personal business, so the girl beat Natalie unconscious. The reason I was stuck in bed for three days was because I was unconscious like Natalie. After the story, she asked me a thousand questions, all of which I answered. I can't repeat my answers because I made them up as I went along and forgot them just the same.

That day I decided I would think of everyone in my family as dead. This made everything easy. It would be me against the world. Simone would be important to me because she was my business connect. I had learned that there was no point in getting personal. It was just a waste of time. As Santiaga would say—I mean, everybody knows—time is money and money is time.

Simone was on point as usual. She delivered my things, I gave her the loot.

"What's wrong with you, Winter?" she asked, as though I was different than normal.

"Nothing. Just going over the numbers in my head. What's up with that connect?"

"It's not gonna happen. Forget it, Winter. He don't want to get mixed up with no trouble. He got vexed just for me mentioning his business. I told him I could trust you, that you were in for self but he said that was hard to believe."

"Damn!" I said, frustrated.

"Any other options?" she asked.

"I got a couple of ideas in my head. Let me work on 'em. Alright Simone. So what else is up?"

"I'm debating on whether to go to the show tomorrow night or not."

I laughed at her. "Yah belly kind of out there," I said, looking at her belly.

"No, crazy, that's not it. I figure if I'm gonna go to a show I ought to be able to stay awake. This sleeping shit is getting out of control."

"Who's performing?"

"Wu-Tang."

"Let's do it," I said.

"What you gonna wear?" she asked.

"Hey, Saks Fifth Avenue got this dusty pink suede dress with a matching jacket, banging. Pick it up for me. I already got the shoes. I was tryna wait for you to get them, but there was only one pair left in my size and I didn't want anybody else to buy them. If you can cop the dress and the jacket, I'll give you $350 for it. That's a little more than half of the price."

"You got it, Winter. Let's meet at your spot about nine. How we rolling?" Simone asked.

"Limo, like usual," I said with a half-smile.

"Alright big-timer," she agreed.

When I got back to the house, I apologized to everyone for buggin' out for the past few days. I told them my mother was hospitalized and very sick. It got me depressed because the doctors said she might not pull through. I saw her today and thank God she was gonna be alright. They all accepted my apology. I gave them discounts on shit they needed for the weekend. After the discount we were all cool again. None of these girls would hold a grudge because they'd had their good days and their bad days, too.

One by one, girls were leaving on weekend passes. I hung around because Friday night was a money night for me. If I had a good take, I would have a total of twenty-eight hundred dollars saved.

Rashida came in and threw shade on me. For business purposes, I immediately apologized to her. The truth of the matter is Rashida was one of maybe two girls in the House of Success who never bought anything from me. She didn't borrow money, didn't ask for shit. However, in business, I know that if a bad feeling spreads about the saleswoman or the product, it can infect others. So I was being scientific about it. Rashida accepted my apology, but not in a way that made me believe things were cool between us. She was cautious. But I'd rally her back to a good position, find out something she liked and provide it to her.

On Saturday morning I went out to the stores. There was really no need for me to shop anymore 'cause Simone could get what I wanted. But nothing could replace the whole idea of the store along with the thrill of being there. I kept my finger on the fashion nerve by always being in and out of the top stores. This made Simone's job easy because I could tell her what I wanted, which store to lift it from, down to the exact section and sometimes the exact rack. I liked to keep up with cosmetics, although I didn't need anything besides a little lipstick. My skin was smooth, my eyelashes were already dark and long. Some of the girls I sold shit to had uneven skin, some had blotches, and some straight up had scars, razor cuts they wanted to hide. My being up on the skin remedies, new cosmetic colors, styles, and exclusive shit they could never have known existed, meant they would have to keep coming back to me. I had packaged my advice, products, and styles like a secret potion that they could only purchase from me.

While I was out, I saw a cute pink suede hat that I wanted. It would go so perfect with the dress, jacket, and shoes. I was gonna get Simone to pick it up for me, although I was tempted to buy it myself just in case. Sometimes Simone was slow to answer her beeps. You couldn't blame her because she was usually in the middle of *picking something up*.

Later I wandered into a pawnshop just to price what I could get for my diamond tennis bracelet, necklace, and earrings in an emergency situation. I found out the shop owners were not only thieves but perverts who made it clear that they weren't above fucking me in the back room of the shop. Four hundred dollars was what they offered for a bracelet that cost my father a few thousand. The only good thing was if I got desperate and needed the money I could pick up the four hundred dollars and buy the jewels back later.

I saw a phat nail design in this Chinese lady's shop so I went in and got my hands redone. She was overcharging. When I asked her the price she could tell from the look in my eyes that she was about fifty dollars over the normal nail-design fee. But she was smart. I never seen the same nail designs she was pushing anywhere, so I told myself, *Hey, she's a businesswoman, I'm a businesswoman. Motherfuckers gotta respect that.* I got a fly design and easily calculated a way to pass this personal expense on to my loyal customers at the house.

11

Saturday evening the House of Success was like a ghost town. Besides the security staff, no one was there except Rashida. She was lying on her bed, reading her book, of course.

"What's up, girl?" I asked Rashida, trying to get things between me and her back to normal by striking up a little conversation.

"A letter came for you," she said dryly. "It's on your bed."

Winter—

This letter is to the most beautiful daughter any man could ever have. I couldn't see you the other day. I was concentrating on things that needed to be done. But the real shit is I needed a shave and a haircut. I didn't want you to think your pops was falling off (smile).

Listen, don't worry about me, you know I'm holding it down. I'm a fighter and so are you. I raised you to be on top. I got to admit, I wish the rest of the family was strong like the two of us. A lot of them been breaking down under the pressure, slipping. I thought I could depend on certain family members to take care of some small but important things, now I know that I can't. Now there's a lesson for you Winter. When you're making the dough it's all love. The click is tight and the family's 'bout it. When your dough is low, you ain't shit. Niggas forget what you done for them, what they owe you.

I need a small favor, Winter. If you can do it, good. If you can't, don't worry over it. Get in touch with Midnight, I need something taken care of that I can't trust anybody else to do. Tell him to drop me a line or pay me a visit.

Poppa Santiaga

Two tears came rolling down without my permission.

"Is everything okay?" Rashida asked. "Is your mom alright?"

"Everything's cool," I said, quickly clearing the tears from my face.

"Why do you always do that?" Rashida asked.

"Do what?"

"Act like you're so cool, like you're in control of every little thing. Why can't you just admit when something isn't alright so somebody could help you?"

"You bugging! These are happy tears; I'm fine. But since we're on the topic of things people do that we hate, why do you always wear that damned ponytail? Why don't you try to live a little? Let your hair down."

"Depends on what you consider living, Winter."

"Oh, I guess you're not like everybody else," I said smartly.

"I try not to be."

So I pushed it. "Do you have a man, Rashida?"

"Nope."

"Probably because of that damned ponytail," I laughed.

"Listen," Rashida said, like she lost her mind and was about to get loud. "I'm not Claudette. I know who I am and all that. I'm not just looking for a man, I'm not ready yet. When I'm finished working on myself then I'll bother with that." Ignoring her explanations, I asked and stated at the same time.

"So you like girls, huh? It's cool, I don't judge nobody."

"You're crazy, Winter! I didn't say nothing about liking girls. I'm just taking my time. I'm only sixteen."

"Are you still a virgin, Rashida?"

"You're not?" she shot back at me.

"Yeah I am . . . *Hell* no," I said, as I busted out laughing. "I been fucking since I was twelve years old. I started late. How about you?"

"Well, you could say I'm a virgin because I never had sex voluntarily. I just never had those kinds of feelings for a man. I guess you could say I just find it hard to trust any guys. So I'm waiting to meet a brother who won't mind just taking everything nice and slow."

"Good luck!" I said, with a doubtful voice. I wasn't gonna get all personal with her. "Hey, do you want to go to a concert with me tonight?" I asked.

"Who's performing?"

"Wu-Tang and Death Squad. You know, hip-hop."

"Nah, I'll pass," Rashida said unenthusiastically.

"You might as well come. If not, you'd be the only one left on this floor," I warned her.

"It's OK. It took me awhile, but now I'm okay with being alone. Besides, security is here."

By 10:20 P.M., I figured out that Simone wasn't showing up. I wasn't mad at her, but I wasn't rolling to the concert alone either. No doubt her big ass was either somewhere eating or sleeping. Finally I got Rashida to loosen up enough to try on my Adrienne Vittadini dress. She spun around, looking at herself in the mirror.

"You see, this is what I'm talking about. This kind of dress gets a girl in trouble. Trouble is what I don't need. I tried it on. Are you satisfied? Now you can have it back."

Rashida looked so good in my dress I was happy to take it back from her.

When the lights went out I lay awake in my bed thinking about Santiaga's letter. I know I said I was going to act like he was dead. Now things were different. I understood why he refused my visit last time. He didn't have anything to give to me. He felt he couldn't do nothing for me. I believed him when he said he didn't want me to see him 'cause he didn't have it all together that day. What he didn't know was that he would forever be my hero, regardless of the small stuff. Before, I was crushed, devastated even. Now I realized that me and him were just alike. We were both born to win. And, when we were not winning, it was OK 'cause we were busy planning to win.

Next time I see Simone I would remember to ask her to sniff around and see if anyone in the Brooklyn neighborhood had heard from or seen Midnight. If anybody knew of his whereabouts, if anything had been said or even whispered, Natalie would know it. It would be hard to get Simone to ask Natalie about him because since me and her started hanging out Simone made it clear that Natalie gets on her nerves. Plus Natalie would know that Simone was asking about Midnight for me. You know she wasn't tryna help me out. But I was sure if anybody would know, Natalie would. If Natalie knew, somebody else around the way knew, 'cause Natalie can't ever keep her mouth shut!

It had been months since Midnight had left me. Santiaga's letter brought him back to the centerfold of my thoughts. It had been weeks since I had laid there in the dark imagining his fine body on top of me. No doubt I still had mad love for him. If what Daddy wanted would lead me to being able to see Midnight again, then locating him could make both me and Daddy happy at the same time. My thoughts were interrupted by Rashida's voice. I thought she had fallen asleep.

"Remember when you asked me to ask Souljah if she knew somebody named Midnight? Well I did. And, I think the reason you don't like Sister Souljah is because of a man."

"What?" I responded, with my ears at attention. "I told you I don't even know her."

"Yeah, but you know this guy Midnight. From the look on Souljah's face when I asked her if she knew Midnight, she knew him well. You know, like in a man-woman way." I felt the heat in my body rising. I sat stiff in the dark waiting for Rashida to continue on her own. But she didn't.

"What did she tell you?" I asked, trying to sound half interested.

"Oh, now you're interested in what Souljah has to say!" Rashida said with a chuckle. I could tell she thought she had the upper hand on me. So I played cool.

"No, I'm just saying, Rashida, did Souljah tell you that Midnight was her man or something?"

"Don't try to play it off, Winter. I can hear it in your voice. You're in love with this guy and Sister Souljah is *his* girl so you don't like her. You're jealous!"

Needing to stab her back because she was tryna score points on me I said, "What would Sister Souljah be doing with a drug dealer as a boyfriend?" Rashida became quiet. So I continued. "Wouldn't that make Souljah a fake, dating a drug dealer?"

"Is Midnight a drug dealer?" Rashida asked, as if she didn't hear what I said.

"Is Midnight Souljah's man?" I pushed, waiting on an answer.

Rashida, in a less confident tone now, added, "Well Souljah didn't say Midnight was her man. She just had a look on her face when I mentioned his name, like there was some love there. You know she had one of those smiles you see in the movies, like Diana Ross had for Billie Dee Williams, or Jada Pinkett had for Allen Payne, or like Nia Long had for Larenz Tate in *Love Jones*. You know what I mean."

I pictured Rashida's dumb ass sitting in the dark trying to duplicate the smile. I decided right then and there that she's a crazy bitch who definitely can't be trusted to be my middleman in any negotiation. I'd squeeze her for as much as I could get out of her. Then I'd cut her ass off.

"So what else did Souljah say?"

"Well," Rashida said reluctantly. "She got curious about how I knew Midnight. I told her I didn't know him but have a friend who does."

"What did she say then?"

"She said she had spoken to Midnight recently and he was doing much better."

"What else?"

"That's it."

My mind was listening for each little detail. What did Souljah mean Midnight was *doing much better*. Was he sick or something? Rashida, still trying to put two and two together for herself said, "So, am I right? Are you in love with Midnight? Is he a drug dealer?"

"No," I said to Rashida, "I'm just like you. I don't love nobody. Midnight is my first cousin. We grew up together. He moved away and I haven't heard from him. My mother practically raised him. I need him to get in touch with my mom right away, just in case anything happens with her illness, you know?" Rashida became quiet. "He's not a drug dealer. I just said that to shake you up a little. You should never just follow somebody the way you follow Souljah. Just think how disappointed you would have been if she turned out to be a hypocrite."

"True," Rashida mumbled, "but she's not a hypocrite. She's for the people. She's helped me a lot personally just being able to talk to her, to know she's actually listening and really loves me means a whole lot."

"Do you really believe she *loves* you?"

"I'm just saying . . ." Rashida backtracked. "She cares about how my life turns out, how my story ends, that's more than I can say about a bunch of people. Even people in my own family."

"Whatever, Rashida," I said shortly, dismissing her.

"I really wish you would come to meet Souljah or join her woman-hood class or something."

"Not hardly," I shot back.

Early Sunday morning I called Simone. I didn't get no answer. Maybe she decided to give somebody some of that pregnant pussy. I couldn't be mad at that. Simone had worked hard for her baby. She deserved a good fuck. I laughed just thinking about what type of posi-tion a dude would have to twist her up into just to get close to her stuff. I bounced out to the stores for the rest of the day. I had ideas that needed to be taken care of.

When I got back to the house late in the afternoon, seconds after I arrived, Lashay called me to the phone. I stepped into the corridor to pick it up.

"Winter! Are you sitting down?" Simone's voice asked.

"What," I laughed, "are you having triplets or something?"

"I got knocked."

"What?"

"I'm *locked down.* I been here all weekend long. I'm cold, I'm hungry, and I'm dying to get the fuck out."

"What happened?"

"What happened? That stupid-ass pink dress happened, that's what. That shit was so fly they had security guards just to watch *it!* Anyway, I need fifteen hundred dollars to make bail."

"Fifteen hundred dollars," I repeated. "Why so much? What ever happened to ROR [released on your own recognizance]?"

"Yeah well, they seen me down here more than a couple of times before. So the crab-ass judge tryna lock me down for a year. If these motherfuckers try to take my baby, they gonna have to upgrade my charges to murder!"

"Alright, Simone, who do you want me to see about the money? Who do I need to talk to?"

"Stop fucking around, Winter. This shit ain't funny. Just put the loot up and we'll make it back as soon as I walk out this dump."

"What about your money? Where were you keeping that stashed?"

"You mean the *baby's money?* I can't touch it, Winter. It's for the baby. Come on, just do me this one solid. I'll hit you right back soon as you bail me out. *You know how we do!*"

"Can't you get it from your moms or anybody else?"

"Winter, that's a dumb-ass question. You know the runnings. I can't get shit that I don't make for myself."

"So why can't you use the baby's money to get yourself out? Then you could make the baby's money back."

"Damn, Winter! Because anything could happen with the baby. The way these motherfuckers got me stressed the shit could drop out right now. Winter, listen, I might have to use the baby's money for a lawyer anyhow. They sent some legal aid guy with a nervous twitch and a nasty skin problem. He's already talking about plead guilty and shit like that. This motherfucker was kicking it in the hallway with the prosecutor like they old buddies 'n shit. There's something about this time that got me worried." Simone's voice sounded serious. "Winter, I can't have my baby in here, word up. It's dirty, it's cold, it's wet. They'll take her from me. Just come on down. I'm good for it. You know I'm good for it. I'm in the pen downtown."

That's one thing I hate about friends, I thought. Now how you gonna game a gamer? How does Simone think she's gonna trick a trickster? She purposely made that story up about the pink dress having got her arrested. Now I'm supposed to feel guilty about the situation and spend my hard-earned cash to get her ass out. How do I know that's what really happened? Sure, she helped me to make dough in the past, but not really when you think about it. She brought the products, but I *paid* her for the products. It was all fair and square. It wasn't her doing me a favor, it was a business deal straight up. She would have never done business with me if *she* wasn't getting *her* cut out of it. I was the one who had to take the time to get along with all of those crazy stupid-ass females in the House of Success. I was the one who had to convince them one by one to give me their money. Them hair products and *all* that shit wouldn't mean nothing if I didn't have the flavor to freak the styles the right way. Besides, who was she fooling, talking about the money she saved is for *the baby.* Hell, the money I saved is for something too! She acts like that baby is supposed to mean everything to everybody, when the truth is it only means something to her! She probably ain't even got no dough saved. She did something stupid with her money. Now she wants me to do something stupid with mine. Now I'm calculating this scene. She already told me she was planning to slow up with her boosting. Which is just one way of saying she don't want to do it no more. Now I'm supposed to give my cash to her. She'll pay me back, she says. But I can see it already. I'll bail her out. She'll get scared that the judge is really gonna put her ass away. Then she'll give me some lame-ass excuse, like she's too tired to boost. She keeps falling asleep. She needs to lay low until after she has her baby, just to be on the safe side. When the kid comes out, she'll be talking about how the baby changed her outlook and she don't wanna get back into trouble. The bottom line is, I get beat for my dough. Every way I turn this around I lose. I thought about it a second. If I leave my partner in the cold that makes me "the bitch." But, I'd rather be a bitch with money in my hand, a sure thing. Like Santiaga said: When you got dough everybody's cool with you. When your dough is low nobody knows your name.

I'd have to get my own hustle on now. After shopping today I only got twenty-five hundred to my name. I'd make it work to my advantage. I ain't giving Simone shit. I laid my finger on the receiver, the call disconnected. Simone called back one more time. In exchange for two cigarettes the security guard told Simone, "Winter ain't here."

By Tuesday night I was in deep concentration. I had spent my day putting a package together for Santiaga. It had everything I could think of him needing inside. I had dipped in my stash to get him some Salvatore Ferragamo shoes. I bought him a crisp, white Versace dress shirt, the kind he liked. The slacks I purchased from Barney's. I bought him a carton of cigarettes and a carton of cigars for bargaining. I placed two hundred fifty dollars in an envelope to drop in his commissary. All this with a bottle of Issey Miyake cologne would set him up lovely on the inside. A lot of people think a prisoner can't style. They think all he can rock is a jail jumpsuit. But prisoners who ain't suckers, who got family who ain't been convicted yet, can chill in the best clothes. Now if a man holds position, he can keep the shit he owns 'cause niggas know better than to try to rob him for it. Santiaga wouldn't have problems like this. After thinking about it, I knew it was important for me to get this package up to him. I needed to show that Santiaga got family on the outside checking for him.

There would be no surprises on my next visit. I set my mind up so that if Daddy refused to see me, I could handle it. 'Cause after I put the money in his commissary and dropped off the package it would only be a short time before he would welcome me in or at least drop me a new line.

Cattle on the bus was the way we rode to Riker's Island. I caught the bus in Queens with sixty other women and children. Chemical warfare is the only way to describe what happens when cheap perfume, body splash, body spray, underarm deodorant, curl activator, hair spray, and pissy Pampers collide. I chose to stand up after I almost sat down in a seat with some red Juicy Juice drink spilled in it. My white sharkskin skirt would have been ruined. Lucky for some kid and her mother I didn't make that mistake. 'Cause in addition to overcrowding, there would have been some ass-whipping on that bus. From the bus to the Riker's Island waiting room, the air went from stank to stale. With all those bodies in one area . . . Let's say, niggas draw heat.

I wasn't there in the waiting room ten seconds before some armed corrections officer picked me out of the huge waiting-room crowd of women. He was over six feet tall with a chest of steel. The funniest thing about him was he still rocked a box-style haircut and that style had been played out for more than a little while. He walked stiff, like he had a pole up his ass, like a lot of cops walk. He had a confident smile on, like he was ziggy or something. Both of his hands rested by his gun, which was on his waist with all that other shit cops wear around their waists.

He said, "Now, let me guess which one of these losers you're here to see." I rolled my eyes, and shifted my body position away from him. "I can't understand it," he said, speaking in a low voice so others couldn't peep his conversation. "I see it everyday. Y'all get all dressed up to see these animals who can't do nothing for you. You ride one train, two trains, a bus to see these fools. You can't touch them. They can't touch you. A brother with a good job and benefits can't get a play? So how 'bout it, cinnamon?" he asked, with his arms extended. "Pass me your number. I'll call you as soon as I get off. I'll take you to lunch, dinner, breakfast . . ." he suggested. "Wherever you want to go." I wanted to scream on this asshole, but he had a gun.

So instead, I said, "No, that's alright, ain't nothing happening."

"You got kids?" he asked.

"No, I ain't got no goddamn kids," I responded immediately. "I'm here to see my father, not my man."

"Oh, so where your man at? If I was your man, I'd be sitting right there next to you." I didn't say nothing. Alright then he pushed.

"I'll give you my number. Maybe you'll think about what I said and give me a call sometime." He handed me a business card.

"I doubt it," I said, crashing his ego down to the floor.

"Who are you here to see?" he asked with authority, as if this was now some type of police matter. His eyes searched the package on my lap. "Ricky Santiaga," he said, reading the words printed on the box I brought for Daddy. "Well now, you're about four days too late." I shifted my weight back in his direction and peered into his eyes with hatred.

"What are you talking about?" I demanded.

"That dude Santiaga killed two prisoners in here four nights ago. He's out of here. We bused him out and up north." I didn't like the idea of this c.o. playing head games with me. If I would've given him my phone number, would he still be making all this shit up? "Oh, you don't believe me," he chuckled. "Go wait in line. Go get searched. Go through the metal detectors. They gonna tell you the same thing when you get up there. They might say Santiaga 'allegedly' killed two prisoners. Either way they say it, he's not here."

"How do I find out where he is?" I asked, now desperate.

"In a few days he'll probably write you. He can read and write, can't he?" he asked and actually waited for a response. "Well you can't take nothing for granted around here." I got up quick.

"He'll write. It's not like he has anything better to do," the guard shouted. With my back now to the c.o., I moved swiftly toward the exit door. The last words I heard him say were: "Call me. I can make you feel better."

Yeah, I thought to myself. What a difference between the way men treated me before Santiaga got knocked, and the way they speak to me now. Like Santiaga would say, They feeling themselves, thought it was time to spread their wings. I know what happened behind those bars at Riker's, some kind of disrespect. Somebody tried to test my father. So, he was forced to set an example. He let everybody know. Don't fuck with Santiaga. The penalty is death, baby, ghetto style. I took a deep breath. There was no sense feeling bad. My father is all man. This is what I loved best about him.

Next stop the liquor store and a pint of Hennessy to mellow me out. I slid into the movie theater in Queens and bought a ticket. What show? Any show. I just wanted to be where nobody would bother me, see me, or ask for none of my drink. It was just me, my brown paper bag, and two watermelon sticks to take away the liquor smell on my breath.

Lights on, then off again. I stayed to see what I didn't see, twice. One skinny white boy with an elevator suit came over and shined the flashlight in my face. But after the light landed on my face, hair, skirt, and brand new Joan & David heels, he took the light off me 'cause I surely wasn't a homeless bum. Besides, I had a stub.

From dark to dark, the inside of the theater into the night I was calm. I bought a nickel bag from a dred I ran into in the street. I'd rather give him my business than my body, which is what he wanted when he first approached me. Niggas always think when they see a girl walking alone in the street they can slide up in her. But I decide when I'm getting fucked or not, even when I'm drunk.

My body jerked back, forward, and sideways as the silver train jetted through the underground. The lights blinked on and off, bugging me out as my mind tried to move faster than the train wheels. The crazies on the train were more animated than ever. One old chick with four pounds of bottom lip and no top lip at all sat across from me muttering, "That's a lie, that's a lie, y'all know that's a motherfucking lie." I busted out laughing 'cause everything in my eyes at the moment was magnified. People had the nerve to look at me like I was nuts or something.

The weed had me hungry so I slid Daddy's package, which seemed to be getting heavier and heavier, into a locker at Penn Station, Manhattan, on 34th Street. For fifty cents I locked everything up and dropped the key into my pocketbook. Now I was free to get dinner. I treated myself to Steak 'n Brew restaurant. I sat in the dim light by myself eating my food.

"Do you mind if I give you the check now, miss?" the hurried waitress asked. "It's ten-fifteen and my shift ended at ten, I'm sorry."

"Don't worry about it." I paid the bill. A couple more bites of my steak, well done, and I realized what the waitress had said. It's ten-fifteen, it's ten-fifteen, it's ten-fifteen. Curfew is at eleven. I ran to the bathroom, peed, and straightened myself out. Then I caught the local downtown to 14th Street. I still had to walk to the East Side.

I puffed my last L as the light wind moved in and out of my legs walking toward the House of Success. Ten minutes to curfew. I didn't want to hear shit about them revoking my upcoming weekend privileges. My two-inch heels clicked on the sidewalk, making music. My theme music. I didn't know if anyone else could hear it, but it sounded real loud to me.

When I turned the corner onto the block I felt nervous out of nowhere as if something wasn't cool. The lower-Manhattan block turned into a haunted museum. The skinny little trees appeared to be armed enemies. I was seeing all types of shit like snipers on the roof and vipers crawling on the ground. I hated this little block that was tucked away like a fake suburb. I mean, on a normal block in New York there are lights and people, plenty of people. Bodegas and niggas sitting on milk crates playing cards or shooting c-low or sipping brew. But this little street was full of shit, pretending to be something other than it was.

Halfway down the block in the front entrance of my building, the

outline of a body stepped forward like in an old Hitchcock flick.
Energy shot through my body. My mind shook my high to the left,
then shook it to the right. My eyes focused in on the shadow cast by
the dull light. An alarm within me sounded. Oh shit, it's Simone!
Damn, had she peeped me? Did she think she could hide her pregnant
ass by standing behind the tall thin wall at the top of the stoop? What
did she plan to do in her condition? *Fuck her!* I said to myself. She
can't do nothing. In a flash, maybe half a second, she jumped off the
stoop like an overweight acrobat. And, out of the right and left side of
the stoop shot four wild mommas in black Reebok sneakers, black
jeans, and bright yellow hoodies, charging toward me like killer bees.
Brooklyn, the only females bold enough to wear some bright shit in
the middle of the night when they was supposed to be on the down
low. I folded my pocketbook like it was a brown paper bag. Outnum-
bered one to five, and unsure whether one of them was a big woman
or a man, I turned on my heels and ran like my Joan & David's were
Air Jordans.

"Go back, Simone, go back, Simone," one of them kept shouting,
but Simone kept coming like a clunky pickup truck talking 'bout,
"I'm gon' git a piece of this trick bitch's ass."

"Get back, Simone!" But like a mad bull she kept coming. The
short one was gaining on me, but my slim yet muscular thighs were
dodging them other fools. I was working that miniskirt. As I damn
near flew around the corner, I looked back right in time to see Simone
bust her ass falling flat on her face.

I dashed down the subway steps. Two of the killer bees kept coming. I assumed the other two went to help Simone. When I tried to
jump over the last five steps, my feet landed instead on the bottom
step. I had lost my balance. I had lost one shoe. With only one shoe
on I heard them on my heels. I saw the train doors about to close and
shot unevenly through the doors. As soon as I turned around to see if
I shook 'em, the doors shut tight. Whatever they were screaming on
the other side of the closed glass and metal front door didn't matter
'cause it was drowned out by the departing screech of the train. But
their middle fingers, I could read that.

Relieved, I fell into the small space between a fat lady and a young
guy with headphones on. With one shoe on and my blouse buttons
popped open, my titties heaved in and out, in and out, from heavy
breathing. I gasped for air. When I looked up I saw half of all the

other passengers' eyes on me. I sucked my teeth, loud, began button-
ing my blouse, and spit, "What the fuck everybody looking at?"

At the first stop I got off and switched to the uptown train line. I
was sure them Brooklyn femmes weren't going that way. I plunged my
hand into my Coach bag to take inventory. My box cutter was still
there. I ran my fingers over the handle, thinking, *that's right. Simone
was smart enough to get her little crew 'cause she knew one on one she had
no wins. Even if there had been only two of them I would of fought. But
five? Who knows if they had burners on them?*

I felt for the yellow envelope that I keep taped to the bottom of my
Coach bag. I hated ruining the leather inside the bag with the tape, but
ever since Aunt B stuck me for my loot, I never left my money and jewels anywhere, no time. And my bag never leaves my side, never.

OK, think, think, think. What's the plan? Simone and them ain't
gonna wait for me at the House of Success forever. So I could ride for
awhile and wait them out. No, I'll get off at the next stop and get to a
pay phone. I'll call the house and find out what's up. Rashida or one of
them would fill me in.

Now should I leave one shoe on? Or should I walk barefoot on the
filthy subway platform? How long would it be before I could run into
a vendor who could sell me a pair of socks? What would be a bigger
spectacle, a female with one shoe on or a well-dressed female with no
shoes? This is New York so I said fuck it.

"You blew curfew, Santiaga." The House of Success bitch security
guard's voice was blaring through the phone.

"I know, I know."

"I'm gonna have to write you up," she said, taking her job seriously.

"I got a carton of Newports that say you don't have to say nothing."

"Make it two. Now what do you want?"

"Let me speak to Rashida."

"Rashida's asleep."

"Well wake her up," I told her.

"She's in the shower."

"I thought you said she was asleep."

"Whatever. Do you want to speak to Lashay?"

"What's going on, girl?" I asked Lashay, hoping that if she knew
something she would volunteer to tell me.

"Nothing," she said in a calm voice.

"Has anybody called for me?"

"You should've asked security, you know they take all the messages. Anyway, I saw your girl Simone a few hours ago."

"What did she say?"

"You know, the regular. She said give her a call she needs to talk to you about something."

"Anything else?"

"Nah, nothing."

"Listen Lashay, my moms is sick again. It looks like I'm gonna sleep over in the hospital with her tonight. Could you do me a favor?"

"Yeah anything, just hit me off like old times." Lashay laughed, but I knew she was serious. I didn't mind putting a few bucks in her palms for a favor.

"In my room taped to the inside railing of my bed there is a key. Use it to unlock my trunk." I further explained that she should pack some selected dresses, pants, blouses, and two pairs of my shoes, one flats, one heels.

"All that! Damn, where are you going?"

"I'm going to the hospital to stay with my moms. She needs me. Besides, you know me with the clothes. Even if I'm just going for one night I need to have choices," I told her. Lashay laughed. "Meet me tomorrow at twelve noon at Penn Station, downstairs under the schedule board's digital display."

"Tomorrow, twelve noon, Penn Station, under the schedule display," she repeated.

"And make sure you lock my trunk up and bring me the key."

"Got it," she said.

Lashay had a damn good question, where am I going? But in the interest of not being predictable, I wasn't going back to the House of Success tonight. From the subway platform, I walked upstairs at the 96th Street station. I had decided to keep the one shoe I had on my left foot. After a minute of looking around I realized the only types of stores that were open were restaurants, delis, and vegetable stands. Eight minutes later, my dirty, black foot got a splinter or a piece of glass or something in it. It was the first time my own body ever grossed me out. Finally I came upon a twenty-four hour pharmacy. They didn't have no shoes for sale, but I was able to buy some hairy, pink bedroom slippers, cotton balls, alcohol, and sewing needles.

I found a chair outside of a café to sit on. As soon as I opened the cotton balls and took the top off the alcohol, a waiter came out.

"May I take your order?" he asked.

"Nothing for me," I responded.

"Well, there is a drink-and-entrée minimum to occupy these out-door tables and chairs."

"I'm not hungry. This'll only take a minute."

The waiter looked suspiciously on my side of the table, saw my foot and said, "Oh no, miss, you won't be allowed to do that here."

"OK, then I'll have a cheeseburger deluxe and a Coke."

"I'll have to ask you to leave now, or I'll go and get the manager."

So I walked around aimlessly until I discovered the wide open deserted steps of the Museum of Natural History. With only the midnight moonlight and a dull glare from a streetlamp, I sat wiping my foot with the alcohol and cotton balls. I successfully removed the splinter with the sewing needle. The pink slippers were definitely not the bomb. But there are two of them and they matched. Besides, it would only be a ten-hour fashion statement. The stores would open and then I could get some proper shoes.

Whether or not to check into a hotel was running through my mind. After shopping for Daddy, I only had sixteen hundred and fifty dollars. Not having a clear plan was stressing me so I decided to save my dough until I was sure what my next move would be.

I walked for blocks and blocks, just tryna keep it moving. In a city like New York, sitting still could make you anybody's target. The McDonald's I lucked up on closed out at 3 A.M. So I took the fifteen dollars' worth of magazines I just purchased from a newsstand and moved next door to the doughnut shop. I ordered two glazed doughnuts and coffee just to keep the cashier from saying I couldn't sit at the counter. I opened my hip-hop fanzine and began to read the articles about my favorite hip-hop stars. *Look at these rap chicks in the magazine,* I thought to myself. If I could rhyme, I could get paid out the ass. Some of these rap girls had loot and still couldn't figure out where to get their weaves put in right. I cracked up.

Just then some dude wearing the finest blue metallic suit the thrift shop had to offer sat in the chair next to me.

"Hey sweetheart," he said, flashing a smile with so much plaque on his teeth it looked like a yeast infection. "What can I do for you?" he asked. I pushed my face into my magazine, ignoring him. "Are you a ballerina sweetheart?"

"What!!" I said so loud, I put him on blast.

"Calm down, sweetie . . . I just wanna talk to you for a minute. I'm saying 'cause you look like a ballerina to me with those long sexy legs. Now me, I'm a manager. I'm always looking for new talent." He laid a dirty business card on the counter which read Girlz Galore Management.

"No, I'm not no damned ballerina," I said, picking up my stuff. "Do I look like a fucking ballerina. Do you know any ghetto girl ballerinas?"

Checking my hostility he said, "Now come on now. Don't get uptight. I'm just tryna do some business with ya. Ballerina's just a fancy way of saying 'dancer.' "

"Well I can dance," I said, moving down two chairs, separating him from me, "but I ain't no dancer."

"Now don't go turning up your nose little girl. A good dancer can bring in about three to five hundred a night."

"Doing what?" I asked with interest.

"Why, dancing . . ." he said, with another nasty smile. I looked at his whole entire face, that fucked-up suit and the black dirt caked up under his long nails.

I jumped up, threw one hand on my hip and said, "Yeah right, dancing, sucking a little dick, taking it up the ass a few times, and a bunch of shit like that, huh?" The man who spoke with a lowered voice left as quickly as he came.

By 5 A.M. a fat lady wearing a cheap greasy apron nudged me.

"There's no sleeping in here." She pointed to the sign on the wall that said No Loitering, No Barefoot.

"It don't say no sleeping," I said.

"Well you ain't buying nothing, so you are loitering." I pointed to the glazed doughnuts and the cold cup of coffee left on the counter two seats over. She twisted up her mouth and said, "That was here when I started my shift." I stood up to get my pocketbook that I was sitting on. I pulled out fifty cents and said, "I'll take a glazed doughnut." She spun on her dirty plastic work shoes with attitude, handed me the doughnut in tissue paper. I looked up at the clock, thinking, I only have one hour until sunlight. If I have to buy one doughnut every ten minutes, I would.

I strained to think at 8 A.M. The sun was well up, but I was so exhausted I couldn't put anything in order in my head. The only thing I had decided for definite was, after Lashay brought my clothes I would check into a hotel, sleep, shower, and figure it all out. The fact that Simone—well not really Simone, but her crew—knew where to find me, put me on the defensive. I didn't like that arrangement. I should be the one coming up with the surprises.

The Koreans, who are always open the earliest and the latest, sold me a hat and a pair of sunglasses. Total cost: seven dollars. They were disposable. There was no way I was gonna walk out in the morning rush where professional people wore suits, dresses, and trench coats, with bedroom slippers on my feet. At least I wouldn't walk without first shielding my eyes with the sunglasses and the hat to add to my disguise and a sense of mystery.

Anyway, by 10 A.M. I would be standing outside of Macy's on 34th Street. I'd get some new shoes, maybe a moderately priced dress, then I'd toss this depressing disguise. Why should I go shopping when Lashay was going to bring my clothes? Because I wouldn't give her the pleasure of seeing me down and out. Besides looking tired, she would never know what happened to me last night. I wouldn't be caught dead in this getup by anybody who knows me.

Macy's bathroom was a welcome relief. It definitely beat the filthy, claustrophobic closet bathroom in the doughnut shop. The couch, comfortable chairs, clean counters, soap dispensers, and toilettes were just what I needed. I had already begun to smell my underarms. I slid straight out of my soiled panties. I threw them in the garbage can. I washed myself with the rough paper towels. I splashed my face with water to wake up. A sprinkle of water in my hair, I swept it up in a bun. I took a deep breath and said, "This will have to do."

My keen eyes were ready to find the best quality walking shoe at a reasonable price. As I picked through some of the sale items on the table, I looked up briefly only to notice an elderly white man watching me. Every time I would look back to see if he was still there, he'd be staring right back at me. He was careful to stay about four feet away from me when I was walking. When the entire scene became too aggravating for me, I turned around quickly to startle him, throwing my hands up in the air then on my waist.

I said firmly, "Yes, can I help you?"

At first he tried to have a blank look on his face. Then he stepped to me and said in a repulsively mild and courteous tone, "Do you mind if I take a look in your bag?"

"You're damn right I mind," I snapped, my natural reaction.

He held his right hand up, holding a security badge.

"Listen, miss, here are your options. You can cooperate with *me,* or I can get the police involved."

"Police, for what?"

"Miss, please calm yourself down. Lower your voice, you're alarming the customers."

"I am a customer."

He looked me over, head to toe. His eyes landed on my pink slippers, then back on my face. I'm thinking my shit don't match, but that ain't no crime.

"Come with me, miss." He walked me into a back room, one you wouldn't notice if you were just an ordinary customer like me, I thought.

"Sit down," he ordered. I sat in the chair right next to a silver two-way mirror. I could look out and see the customers, but I knew they couldn't see me. "Now I would like you to volunteer for me to look in your bag."

"Why?" I asked. "I didn't do shit."

"I saw you when you were at our front door early this morning, at 9:45 A.M., to be exact. You were wearing a black knit hat, black sunglasses, and pink bedroom slippers. You walked around the first floor for about ten minutes, looking at and touching the merchandise. You took the escalator to the third floor clutching your bag, then entered the ladies' rest room on the west side of the building. You were in the bathroom for approximately thirty minutes. When you exited, you were no longer wearing the hat or the sunglasses. Now, because of your suspicious behavior, I need to be sure that everything in your bag belongs to you."

Sucking my teeth like a fast car hitting its brakes, I opened my bag. I had a feeling this military asshole was willing to take this foolishness all the way. Besides, I hadn't stolen anything.

He said, "May I take a look at the bag?" He turned it over emptying its contents onto the blotter on the desk. His wrinkled face, with the bulging eyeballs, looked over everything. He knew he was wrong, but he was determined to be right. First thing he grabbed was my box cutter. "How old are you, young lady?"

"Twenty-one," I said, with no hesitation.

He opened my wallet, glanced over my business cards then discovered my House of Success ID. Looking from the ID, then into my eyes, the ID, then into my eyes again, he said, "You're seventeen, not twenty-one. You know it's illegal for anyone to sell a box cutter to a minor in New York."

"Listen," I said curtly. "You accused me of stealing. As you can see, I didn't take anything that belongs to your store." Busting a small sweat, I told him I just wanted my bag back. Luckily, this idiot did not even see the envelope taped to the bottom of the bag. This is why I cooperated with him. I didn't want him to call the police. Then I'd have to explain where I got sixteen hundred in cash and my diamond jewelry from. No doubt, even if I offered the police a great explanation, they would have wanted to drive me to the House of Success, where I didn't want to go. No telling what would've happened when the counselors and authorities found out how much dough I had without having a job.

On his signal I picked up each and every item belonging to me and put it back in the bag. With an impatient face, while tapping my foot, I asked, "Can you please let me go now?"

"One minute," he ordered, "raise up your arms." He ran his two hands from the top of my shoulders down to my wrists.

"C'mon, this is ridiculous. You can tell there's nothing in my blouse. It's tight. All of my clothes are tight."

"I can still get the police," he threatened. "They can get a warrant and search you . . . *thoroughly.* I can make you sit and wait for them to get here."

This bastard, whose hands couldn't stop shaking, ran over the center of my back, right down along my spine. Facing me, he then ran his two hands from my shoulder blades right over each of my titties, cupping them a bit. Infuriated, I saw nothing but images of the cops cuffing Momma, stealing Daddy's stuff, impounding Momma's car. If I could tolerate him for a few minutes, I would be home-free. "Take off your skirt."

"What?"

"Take off your skirt."

"See now, you're bugging. I ain't taking off my skirt. What do you think I have, a pair of high heels hidden in my panties?"

"I've seen all types of things happen before, miss. I'm just doing my job." I looked down at this man's little hard dick poking through his pants.

"I think you're doing a little more than your job." Just then a lady security officer, short and fat with cat woman glasses, opened the door with her key.

"Hey, what ya got in here, Izzy?" she asked, like Izzy was her best pal.

"Nothing," I answered for Izzy. I gave him a threatening look, letting him know I'd blow the whistle on his little perverted party. "We're finished, right?"

"Yes, everything seems to be in order," he said. I brushed by the lady security officer and walked out swiftly and kept going until I got out on the street. The clock said 11:15 A.M. I'd run to meet Lashay. Fuck it. I don't owe her any explanations about my appearance anyway.

As I placed the plate and pizza crust into the garbage can, my eye caught a glimpse of Rashida coming up the subway stairs and into the mall in Penn Station. She didn't see me standing there.

She kept looking over her shoulder nervously. She'd run in and out of every little indoor store in the huge waiting area. Wondering what she was doing, but not wanting to see her, I stepped three steps back into the pizza store and glanced outward from my discreet position. That's when she did it. Like a woman having a nervous breakdown, she went directly under the huge digital train schedule display on the ceiling and shouted with both hands on her head.

"Winter, Winter, Winter. If you hear me please, please—"

Stunned, I came. I rushed over so she could shut up. When she saw me coming toward her she got excited, like I was Ed McMahon delivering a Publishers Clearinghouse multimillion-dollar-sweepstakes check.

Without talking, she grabbed my hand and jerked it, pulling me toward the staircase that led to the uptown train. When I resisted, she said, "Winter, seriously, we got to get out of here." I saw the terror in her face. I followed, knowing she ain't the slick type.

"Simone is going to kill you, well maybe not kill you—Well maybe not kill you, but hurt you real bad. She has a gun. You must of did something terrible to her."

"How do you know this?"

"Everybody knows. Last night Lashay said that Simone said that you was a double-crossing bitch. Lashay was with Simone yesterday from eight to ten. When Lashay came inside she told everybody that you was gonna get popped. She said you deserved it 'cause you had double-crossed her too, and cut her out of some money. They was waiting for you. Lashay said Simone had a crew of girls outside the House of Success. Everybody thought you'd be in before curfew. I was praying you didn't come. I told them the whole thing was between Simone and Winter and it was stupid for anyone else to get involved. I told them, 'Y'all don't even know Winter's side of the story.' "

"Then what happened?"

"They locked me in our room and kept their bodies against the door so I couldn't get out. They locked me in there till, like eleven thirty."

"Then what?"

"I don't know. Nobody wouldn't tell me shit."

"So how did you know I was here?"

"Last night, after everybody thought I was sleeping, Lashay came in our room. They was looking for something 'cause they were all over your bed. Next thing I know, Lashay had opened your trunk. They was picking and choosing who wanted what and Lashay was giving your stuff out. From what I could see, they took everything, down to the barrettes and the face cream. Even the security guard was tryna get something out of the deal. But none of the clothes could fit her. So she stole those cartons of cigarettes you had in the pouch on the side."

"But how did you know I was gonna be in Penn Station at twelve?"

" 'Cause when Mrs. Porter came in this morning about nine, she asked the girls if they knew where you were. She wanted to know if you came in last night. Everybody started looking nervous and guilty. So Mrs. Porter stepped to me. Before I could open my mouth, Lashay blurted out that your moms was in the hospital and you slept over with her. Lashay said she would see you at twelve noon at Penn Station because you needed some clothes and she was gonna bring them to you. Now Lashay was getting calls all night, going back and forth to the security desk, so I knew she was up to no good. I didn't know if you had spoken to her or even if you would be here or not. But I took a chance, I didn't want to see nothing bad happen to you."

Rashida hugged me and my body stiffened. It was time to figure everything out.

"Come on." Rashida grabbed my hand and guided me swiftly through the train station like I was in kindergarten or something.

"What's the deal?" I asked. "Where we headed?"

"To a friend's house, Winter. Someone who can help you out."

"I don't need no help," I told her. "I just need a couple of minutes to think." By the time we got off at the stop she wanted, it struck me, dropped into my head out of nowhere. Without saying a word I turned around and began to walk back onto the subway platform in the opposite direction of Rashida.

"Winter, please," she begged me. "I just want to help."

"Oh no, you tryna take me to Souljah's house like I'm some kind of charity case. A homeless runaway or something. You can forget it, girl. I ain't gonna do it."

"Winter, seriously though. Do you have somewhere else to go?" I didn't answer. I didn't like her self-appointed mother role. "You already live in a girls' home. You already don't have no family."

"I got family bitch, you bugging. I got mad family, you don't know the half."

"If you got family, Winter, so much family, why don't you live with them? Where are they? You can't come back to the House of Success. It wouldn't be safe. And you don't have to live at Souljah's. Just chill for a few days while we figure out what to do next."

"We!" I screamed, throwing my hands up in the air. "Now all of a sudden it's *we."*

"Fuck you, Winter!" Rashida screamed back at me. "That's it. I try to do the right thing and look at you. You don't even realize when somebody's tryna help your ass." As Rashida cried, I laughed. My laughing threw her off. She stopped crying. "What's so funny?" she asked.

"You don't even know how to curse right. You sound funny. You don't curse." She got back at ease and led the way.

"Her house is right up there. Just do me one favor, check it out before you just flat out say no."

12

Two big cemented roaring lions sat on opposite sides of the cement steps leading to the place. The door was made of solid thick glass, framed by maple wood with all kinds of carvings. Behind the solid glass was a black designer gate, an expensive and fancy way to say "keep the hell out." The building was one of Harlem's Sugar Hill brownstones with five floors. What really caught my eye was the money-green Mercedes Benz illegally parked in front. A little black, ugly girl answered the huge door. It was so wide and heavy that it opened slowly.

"How are you, Rashida," the miniature lady asked. Once inside the door we were faced with another door, lighter in weight, that the girl swung right open. Parquet floors with color designs. I caught my breath and reminded myself that months ago I lived in a place three times phatter than this, so no need to get excited. While the troll interrogated, "Rashida, did you let Souljah know you were coming today?" I checked the next spacious room behind two more opened wooden doors, which revealed a winding staircase leading to the second floor.

Now, art, I don't follow that shit, but there was enough paintings on the wall. Of what? Don't ask me. African titties everywhere and wooden mask carvings. There were big pictures with big frames. The kind I hated, that were supposed to be a portrait of a person. To me the person was painted to seem alive, but almost always looked dead.

"No, I didn't tell Souljah I was coming, but I know it's not a problem because she told me if I ever needed . . ." The short girl disappeared into the darkened huge room before Rashida could even finish. From what I could hear she was talking on the phone for three seconds. She came back out and said, "You can go on up, Rashida."

It was like walking through a museum. There were huge ivory

tusks that had to be straight off an elephant, carefully placed in a sitting room with huge windows. Chess pieces, marble tables, statues, heavyweight curtains, and plants everywhere. The plants were like decorations as the designer or whoever hooked this place up had them draped over each window and outlining the walls up at the top near the ceilings, then cascading down to the floor.

On the third floor were doors closed tightly as though something top secret was done in there. Each corridor on every floor was elegant with marble stools for sitting and plant holders with more plants.

By the time I reached the top floor, I calculated twenty-seven hours since I had slept. My heart was racing out of the normal rhythm. Now, what was bugged about the fifth floor was it was huge and clean, with tall windows and beautiful wooden floors like the rest of the house. But it was as if the designer decorated the whole place, got to the fifth floor and just quit.

"This is it," Rashida said. "There is where Souljah is." She knocked lightly on the half-open door and pushed her way in like she lived there. "You can sit there." She directed me to a basic wooden chair near a small table. Rashida exited the room where I was seated. She walked through a small kitchen, the fourth one I had seen in this house, and into another room. I watched everything as Rashida began to talk to someone who was concealed behind the half-open door.

"Souljah, I have a sister out here who's a good friend of mine." And that's all I heard because Rashida stepped into the room and closed the door. She probably purposely lowered her voice so I couldn't hear her begging. She better not be begging.

The room I was waiting in was like a library. There were two wide and towering sets of bookcases that went from the floor to the ceiling. There must have been at least a thousand books on those shelves, big, small, every color, old, new, hard, and soft. Some of the books had papers hanging out of them. One shelf had magazines and newspapers only. The windows in this room had no curtains even though the people in the brownstones across the street could look right in. How did I know, because that's what I was doing, standing in the window looking in their house. But their windows had curtains.

The kitchen was clean, but nothing was in it. Curiosity made me open the refrigerator just enough to look in. Water, salsa, and ginger ale. That's it.

I heard a slight movement and closed the refrigerator door real quick. Souljah was taller than I thought, about five-foot-six. She had big brown eyes, long lashes, and chubby-type cheeks. Her hair was shining like it just got done. It was a flat twist style, kind of original. She was a typical uptown girl: big ass, wide hips, and, nope, not a flat belly. She still needed to do those sit-ups. Nothing to say about her clothes: blue jeans, white shirt, and, wait a minute, a pair of skips. Nondescript sneakers, skips, like she was from one of the Long Island flea-market towns. *No she didn't,* I thought to myself.

The thing that stood out most about her were those eyes. She was staring right into me. She didn't try to hide it or even look away when I looked at her. I wasn't gonna stare back at her 'cause what was all this about anyway. She walked over toward me. As far as I'm concerned, she was standing way too close in my face. You know people need personal space. You're not supposed to tell them that. They're just supposed to know.

First thing she said after long, uncomfortable moments of saying nothing, was, "You are so pretty." I turned my head to look behind me. But I knew she was talking to me. What was I supposed to say in response to that? "Where are you from?" she asked.

"Long Island." It just dropped out of my mouth. Less is better. I wasn't gonna tell her all my business. There is no telling what Rashida had already told her, but I would fix that.

"No, I meant what country?"

"What?" I said, thinking to myself, *What the hell is she talking about? We all come from right motherfucking here.*

"No, I was thinking maybe your family is from Panama or Trinidad, or one of the Islands maybe?"

I gave her a one-word response, "Nah." Then I continued to push for what I wanted. "Rashida said that you know my cousin, Midnight . . ."

"Yeah." She answered with one word.

"Listen," I said, "I don't know what Rashida has told you. She doesn't know me very well." Rashida rolled, then cut, her eyes at me.

"Anyway, you know how family moves around a lot. I grew up with Midnight. After he was about sixteen, we just lost track of one another. My mom doesn't have long to live. I'd like Midnight to see her before she dies. He would hate himself if she died without him being able to say a few words. We were close like that. Well, anyway, Rashida mentioned that you know my cousin. She said you'd probably be able to give me his phone number or address."

"I'm sorry to hear about your moms. Midnight calls me every now and then," she said casually, "like maybe once a month. But I don't call him or have his number."

"How about an address?" I pushed.

"No, not even that," she said, smiling politely. "Rashida said you need a place to stay?" she asked, still looking into my eyes. But my dad taught me how to have a poker face, so I put one on.

"No, not really," I answered her. Rashida exhaled, threw her hand up and said, "Winter!"

"Winter," Souljah repeated. "That's a different kind of name."

"See, that's what I was telling you. My friends call me Sasha, but Rashida wouldn't know that."

"So Sasha, you're not having any trouble like Rashida said?" Souljah asked, her eyes leaving my eyes and landing on my bedroom slippers.

"It ain't nothin'. Just some jealous girls at the place where I stay. They don't matter though, 'cause in two months I'll be eighteen and then I can get my own place."

After a pause, Souljah said, "The only problem is that in New York, beef between young sisters living in the same space can end up so many different ways. It could be a small thing. Or it could be murder. Jealousy is a dangerous emotion. Jealous people are usually so intensely dissatisfied with themselves that they have a burning desire to destroy anyone who has something they want, but feel they can't have. You can stay here if you want. You don't look like the type to stay too long. But since you are family with Midnight, I don't mind letting you stay until he calls. Then you two can hook up and take it from there."

I liked the way she put it. So I agreed to stay. Rashida just said things all wrong all the time. She acted like she had one of those red flashing ambulance lights right over her head. She was always too eager.

We went to the bedroom where I would stay. The place was real plain. But there was a big mirror and two comfortable-looking beds. "My sister, Lauren, stays in that bed," Souljah said, pointing to the right side of the room. "Watch out for her. She's a trickster. She should be home now. But she's not, whatever." Those were the last words I heard because I lay on the available bed in my clothes and twenty-seven hours of sleeplessness kicked in.

Around midnight, my eyes reopened. For three brief seconds I tried to figure out where I was. It was the pink slippers on my feet that shook my memory into place. The quiet argument going on outside of my door got my blood going and I listened in.

"I thought I told you if you were gonna go out and stay out overnight, you should call me."

"I didn't know I was gonna stay out," the unfamiliar voice shot back.

"How does someone not know they're going to stay out for two nights in a row? Now you explain that."

"I don't really want to explain nothing. I just want to get some sleep."

"What you need to do is have some respect."

"You're not my mother, you're my sister."

"It doesn't matter that I'm not your mother. I'm your sister, I'm the oldest and I take care of you. That's enough reason for you to give me your respect." Then she sucked her teeth.

The door to the bedroom swung open, I jumped to sit up. She clicked the light on. I could tell she was surprised to see someone in her room by the look on her face. She closed the door back immediately.

"Who's that in my room? Or should I even bother to ask."

"Her name is Sasha. She'll be staying for awhile."

"Well, what's the deal?" she asked.

"What deal?" Souljah responded.

"The 411," I heard her sister say.

"Nothing, she's cool," I heard Souljah say. "She's Midnight's cousin."

"Ooooh ooooh ooooh," the sister said, while I sat there wondering what all that meant.

Tall and slim, the sister who was named Lauren looked like a brown China doll. She was the model-looking type of girl. I couldn't call her a fashion model 'cause she had no fashion. She had nice hair, but with too much gel in it. She had cheap shoes—which I figured runs in her family—knock-off earrings, and a little Joyce Leslie–Sears–Lerner's type of outfit. I always said it don't mean shit if you don't know what to do with it. She came and introduced herself. Her eyes bounced around the room while she talked. I guess she was checking to see if I messed with any of her shit.

"So what are you in for?" Lauren asked.

"What?"

"What's your problem. Everybody who stays with Souljah got some kind of problem. That's the only kind of people she likes."

"Then what's your problem," I asked her.

"My problem is that I'm related. And, of course, my problem is like everyone else's problem, 'cash flow.' I work for Souljah answering the phone, when I'm here."

A soft knock at the door and then a push. "Sasha," Souljah said, "my sister Lauren can tell you the house rules. She knows them, even though sometimes she doesn't follow them. Tomorrow we can arrange to pick up your clothes."

"No, that's alright. I'm gonna go shopping for some things tomorrow."

"Oh, you do have money?" Souljah asked.

"A little something," I said, smiling. *Yeah, that's right, I ain't no charity case. I got my own loot,* I was thinking to myself.

A loud bell chimed throughout the house.

"Could you get that?" Souljah asked, calling from the bathroom across the hall from our room. The shower was running. "Lauren, can you get the door for me?" she asked again.

"Are you going out?" Lauren yelled back into the bathroom.

"Yeah," Souljah said. I watched as Lauren lay down on her bed.

"Sasha, can you get the door please? I'm tired." I knew her type. Everything was a test. I'd play her little game for a minute.

When I got downstairs finally, I pulled back the curtain on the lightweight door. I couldn't see the face 'cause the porch light was off. But the streetlight off to the side lit up the red Range Rover double-parked on the side of the money-green Benz. The rims on this Rover were so hot I wanted to fuck the truck.

"Are you gonna let me in or what." Now I stood face to face with GS, one of the top hip-hop artists in the music industry. With one 2-karat diamond in his ear, my mouth hung open. Now, there's not much shit that could surprise me, but right now I was stuck guarding the entrance to the door. Shocked, I could not move. I had seen all of the top artists in concert, even GS. Nobody could of convinced me that we would ever be standing one on one in the same house.

"Souljah here?" The Guess jeans and fresh-out-the-Nike-box kicks looked good, but meant very little once I peeped the gold Rolex with the diamond bezel face.

Now, honey just stepped over me like I was a roach. Or maybe he confused me with the maid. I watched his six-foot frame as it disappeared up the stairs. With my mouth wide open and my hands on my waist, you might have seen steam coming out of my ears had you been there.

I checked how I just got played out in an expensive, but two-day dirty outfit and slippers. They knew who was at the door and they didn't even warn me. Hell, everybody know how much first impressions mean. I didn't even take a minute to brush my hair.

It was right then that I realized how vexed I was that the bitches in the House of Success had raided my trunk. I was so happy that I had escaped with my loot and jewels that I wasn't focused on the clothes. But now I stood there calculating the costs. Leaning against the second door, I outlined the shopping I would have to do in my head.

It was obvious that there's money in this house, I thought to myself. I wasn't sure how I would get a piece of Souljah's hustle. I was *sure* that I would. I knew she had to be some kind of con artist. Where did she get the money for this house, the Benz, and all that? Bigger question: Why would GS go out with someone like her, a girl who rocks skips and just wasn't . . . just wasn't fly? The answer must be because he hasn't weighed his options. Someone like Souljah had access. She must have used those charity concerts to get in good with the stars. Well now *I* have access. Staying here wouldn't be as bad as I thought. But like Souljah said, I wouldn't be here long.

I passed the happy couple on their way downstairs. She said "Peace." I mumbled something back. Then I had to double right back and lock the door as they left.

"So are you ready to hear the house rules?" Lauren asked, laying on the bed smoking a cigarette.

"Yeah, give it to me," I said unenthusiastically.

"First rule is no smoking." She started to laugh. "Souljah's allergic to cigarettes. Plus she hates them. So I do it when she leaves, with the window open as you can see. She won't be back for a few hours. I'll spray this stuff," she said, squirting cherry-aroma household spray. "Now when she gets back she'll still ask me if I was smoking a cigarette even though our bedroom door is closed, the window open, and I sprayed this shit. Second rule is you can never stay in this house when no one else is home. You'll either have to go out and do your own thing, come with me, or leave out with Souljah. Oh, and you can't have a key. Those are Doc's rules."

"Who's Doc?"

"She's the doctor who owns this house. She runs her medical practice on the first floor. You probably didn't notice it because her office has a separate lobby and a separate entrance. She has a lot of expensive stuff, equipment and all that. So she's real strict about the key situation. I have one," she said, shaking her small set of keys. "Next rule. You can't bring nobody to this house. The only strangers who are allowed in are the patients who come in the side door and Souljah's students on Thursday and Sunday nights. Now the men's group meets on Thursday nights. It's for men only. We can't even stay back here in our room."

"What about Souljah, where does she go?"

"She's the teacher. She stays with the men. The women's group is Sunday night. Souljah will want you to attend the womanhood meetings."

I couldn't help but roll my eyes. Lauren was calm. She just said, "Yeah, I know, right. Well she won't force you into a meeting. But she expects anyone she's dealing with to at least give it a try. They ain't that bad. I go just for the laughs. As far as food goes, this is the deal. I don't cook. Blimpie's is right on the corner, pizza, McDonald's, and there's this good Jamaican spot on the avenue. Souljah cooks good, but she's always on a diet. When there's food here you can eat it. Souljah will share almost everything. Other than that, just expect her to try to get your life together whether you like it or want to or not. Don't try to stop her. It's in her blood.

"Now the benefits is the reason I bother at all. Souljah's VIP, she gets invited to everything, concerts, parties, dinners—she knows everybody. The thing is, unless she has a special reason she really doesn't go. So we get to use the invites and meet everybody who's anybody."

"Like GS?" I had to throw it in.

"Yeah, he's a fine ass, ain't he."

"That was him at the door," I said, hoping she would throw in some more information since she had already been so helpful.

"Yeah, I figured it was him," Lauren said casually. "Them two is weird." I started laughing. Somehow or another, I was excited. Even though I appeared to be cool on the outside, the energy was just shooting every which way in my body. My mind was like a tape recorder, catching every word. I had always went to all the big shows, read the magazines, grown up on hip-hop. But I had never been on the inside. As I really thought about it, on the inside is where I needed to be. And if these people didn't know how to take advantage of an opportunity, it would be their loss because I didn't intend to miss a beat.

"What's so weird about them?" I tried to seem half interested.

"Now figure, that dude can get any girl he wants. He comes here a few times a week, talks to Souljah for hours. Two, three o'clock in the morning, you get up to go to the bathroom, them two is laughing, talking, and whatnot. He picks her up and takes her out. On her birthday he was in here cooking for her."

"You lying!" I blurted out.

"No, seriously. He'll do anything for her. *But . . .*" She stopped talking.

"But what?" I pushed, revealing my desire to know.

"She ain't fucked him. He's not even her man or nothing."

"You're killing me," I said.

"Killing you? It's killing me!"

"Well, what's the deal?" I asked.

Lauren said, "He's not gay. I know girls he fucked before. But check how his man liked Souljah. He caught beef with his man for liking her. But she ain't his girl, ain't giving him no pussy, nothing."

"Maybe she's lying to you about it," I told her.

"Nah, if there's one thing I know, it's my sister. She had a few bad relationships in the past. Now her legs is Krazy Glued shut. Funny thing is, she got more niggas coming and calling since she stopped fucking. Now you go figure."

One thing she said made my mind wander. It was the statement about past bad relationships. I wondered if Midnight was one of them. I wanted to ask, but I knew it was too soon to seem so interested. I figured I wouldn't have to be that nosy to put this puzzle together. The way her sister just volunteered information, it would only be a short time until I could see the whole picture. Me and Lauren just clicked. The way she was just cool like that I knew we would kick it together.

Back in a Benz. Things couldn't have been better. Doc drove us to go shopping. She was the first black female doctor I had ever seen up close. Everything she had was high quality. She looked young, acted young, and didn't even get snobby about being a brain surgeon.

When we'd go into a store, she whipped out her gold card. When her wallet flipped open, I peeped she had platinum cards, Diners Club, the works. She was picking clothes and accessories for herself out of the top-line designer sections of the store. There were items only a professional shopper like myself would have the eye to select. When I seen how she'd just run everything on the card, I thought to myself, *It's like she's not even paying money for it.* I needed one of those plastic cards so I could walk out of the store with bundles of stuff in my hands. I grabbed every credit application in sight.

While me and Doc shopped, Souljah would lean on anything and read her book. Her sister Lauren was playing me so close it was annoying. I could tell she was a sponge just trying to soak up my flavor. She watched what clothes I selected. Even stuff I just picked up, looked at, and placed back on the rack. When I put something down, she would pick it up. Her eyes would be bulging as she looked at the price tag. I never liked shopping with a couple thousand dollars to spend while your partner only had a hundred and fifty. The person just keeps giving you the "buy me something" look. And y'all know I ain't buying nobody shit. What was the icing on the cake was I bought a red leather Coach bag. It was a perfect match for the red Range Rover I seen last night. After following me around the whole afternoon without buying nothing, Lauren went and bought the *same exact* bag I purchased. Shit like that is unforgivable. But, I told myself, she's not a shopper. She's definitely no competition. So I checked what she did and let it go.

Before I knew it, my hands were heavy with packages, but the yellow envelope taped to the bottom of the pocketbook was light. I only had five hundred dollars left to my name. Doc had challenged me to floss. I couldn't let her go on a shopping spree for herself with me sitting back looking like the pauper. Plus if you have a Benz, you ought to be able to fill it with packages from Bloomingdale's, Saks Fifth Avenue, Nordstrom, and whatnot.

It all fit into my plan anyway. I would reverse last night's scene of embarrassment with the messy clothes and slippers. GS would never catch me off guard again. The next time he ran into me, he wouldn't even know I was the same girl who answered the door.

Dinner was crazy. Picture us all seated around the large table at

Doc's on the third floor. Boxes of Chinese food everywhere. Every-one's gettin' their grub on. Then the questions begin. First it was Doc. "So Sasha, where are you from?" Now they may think I'm dumb, but I remembered answering these same questions with Souljah yesterday so I was prepared.

"I'm from the United States," I responded. They all laughed.

"No," Doc said, smiling, "what city, state, borough."

"Oh, I'm from Long Island."

"Whereabouts?"

"Way out, almost the Hamptons."

"Oh, that's a nice area. I bought a house for my mother out there in Dix Hills. Souljah tells me your mom has cancer. I hope you don't mind me talking about it," she said, smiling innocently.

"Actually, I'd rather not talk about it. I was having a good day and I just don't like to think about it because it makes me sad." Then Soul-jah jumped in it.

"Oh no, it's just that Doc is excellent in medicine. There may be some way that she can help. A lot of times when people are sick, they keep going to the same doctor, getting the same diagnosis and reme-dies. Sometimes a second opinion could help." I just nodded my head, not wanting to encourage them to keep asking questions.

"If it's the money you're worried about, Doc can—" Now Doc cut Souljah off.

"If she's from the Hamptons I'm sure her family has a private physician and good care," she said.

"But Sasha's been living at the House of Success where Rashida stays so—" Then I cut Souljah off.

"So I don't live in Long Island anymore because my mom's medical bills got so expensive that the family went through a lot of changes. And, like I said, I really don't want to talk about it. You all don't have to worry about my mother. She has a doctor and a specialist."

Me and Lauren decorated our room after dinner. She was inspired by the jokes I made about how plain and boring the room was com-pared to Doc's place. Now, I let her lead on the designs 'cause I wasn't planning to stay. What we ended up with was three walls plastered with LL Cool J posters, him in every kind of hat ever made. Lauren had some kind of thing for LL, to say the least. She talked about him like she knew him personally. She admitted that she had never been introduced to him face to face, but was in the greenroom with him at one of her sister's concerts.

"Why didn't you go up to him?" I asked.

She said, "Are you kidding me, I couldn't even move. I was in a state of shock. I knew he would be there. But there's a difference between knowing it in your head and then actually seeing the person. You know what I mean?" she asked. I just shrugged my shoulders. "Come on!" she continued. "When you answered the door last night and seen GS, tell me you didn't freak out for a minute and just lose your cool?"

"Nope," I fronted.

"You're a liar, Sasha." She pushed me down and tickled me like I was five. We both started laughing as she kept rephrasing the questions. "Come on Sasha, you know you felt a little electricity in your pussy." I kept denying it. "I don't care if you don't admit it. 'Cause I know you felt the same thing I felt."

"Seriously, though," I asked her, "do you want to get with him like that?"

"Word up," Lauren said. "I'd do anything to jump that nigga's bones." We cracked up.

Lauren was crazy. We stayed up all night long talking. "Do you have a man?" I asked her.

"A man! I got a *bunch* of guys. Why, you wanna meet somebody?" she asked.

"Maybe," I told her.

"Well," she said, "it depends on what you like. Let me take out my catalog." She whipped out a red leather phone book with some of the pages falling out. "I'll start with the beginning," she said, opening her book to the first page. "What do you like most of all, like the most important thing?"

"Money," I answered quickly. We laughed again.

Lauren wrapped a towel around her head like she was a swami or gypsy or something. She turned a glass upside down like it was her crystal ball. I hollered, "You're nuts, you're nuts." She pushed a sheet of paper over toward me.

"Write down what you want in a man in the order of importance."

So I did. Money, car, clothes, jewelry, apartment, masculinity, big dick, clean, white teeth, nice body. I slid the paper back to her.

"Sshh," she said, holding her finger up to her lips, signaling for quiet. After a thirty-second pause, she said, "It seems as if we have a problem."

"What is it?" I asked.

"We have fifty guys with big dicks and nice bodies."

"Nothing wrong with that," I joked.

"Yeah, but they're all broke, on foot, living with their mommas." We cracked up.

Midafternoon, we woke up to Souljah's complaints. "Lauren, get up. You're not taking care of business, as usual. Just because we are sisters doesn't mean you should take advantage. The man at the church is waiting for the contract and the money. You were supposed to be there at eleven."

"Why didn't you wake me up?" Lauren asked.

"Because that's not my responsibility. I was out early taking care of what I'm supposed to take care of." Lauren sucked her teeth. Within minutes, she was tapping me.

"Hey, hey, get up. You can either come with me or stay here with Souljah, what's up?"

"That's not a choice," I said. "I'm coming with you."

Fifteen hundred dollars cash passed from Lauren's hand to the hands of the pastor. That's how much he was charging Souljah to rent the church. She was giving a benefit for an organization that worked with AIDS patients. When I asked Lauren why it cost so much she said, "You know the deal. It's business. Everybody wants something, even the church."

"What does Souljah get?" I slid in the question, since the opening was handed to me.

"Nothing," her sister said dryly.

"She has to get something," I pushed.

"You're right. She gets an audience. She gets to tell two thousand people what's on her mind, what her deepest thoughts are, and what they should be doing with their lives."

"What else?"

"That's it. That's what gets her off."

"But how does she pay her bills like that?" I pressed.

"Look," she said, becoming annoyed, "I hope you're not gonna be one of these people who takes up all my time to ask me about Souljah.

'Cause I hate that shit. How does she pay her bills? People just give her shit. She's supposed to pay Doc rent. She doesn't. She's just different. Don't try and figure her out. You'll only give yourself a headache." Within seconds Lauren was back to her joking self again.

Different had to be the word for it. Thursday night about thirty-something guys crammed into the large front of the apartment. There was some who seemed as young as sixteen. Some seemed as old as thirty. As promised, Lauren and I bounced as the last few filed through the door.

"Did you see that?" I asked Lauren. "Wall-to-wall niggas." It was like an ice-cream store up there. Mad, crazy, all the flavors. Big, small, tall, short. Bodies galore. I was bugging at the shock of it all. Lauren was blasé. "Wait a minute," I asked her, "are any of them in your red book?" She laughed.

"No, Souljah would kill me if I messed with her clients. Nah, her thing and my thing are separate."

I wanted to know what Souljah was doing up there in the apartment with all those men. I wanted to understand it. I wanted to hear what she was saying. What was making them listen to her? Did she tell Midnight the same thing she was telling them? What was the hustle, the technique? What could she tell a man as fine as Midnight that would keep him under her spell? Did she meet him at one of these meetings? I wanted to ask Lauren. But she warned me already. I didn't want to set her off. That might stop the flow of information completely. I'd wait awhile and figure how to get at it another way.

The men's meeting ended around ten. We were back in the house an hour later. I had a feeling GS was coming so I got ready. First I showered. Seated on the bed with a towel wrapped around my body and a towel wrapped around my hair, I twisted a paper towel. Carefully I rolled and weaved it in and out of each toe to prepare for the pedicure I was about to give myself.

"Going somewhere?" Lauren asked.

"Nah. This is just my routine. I like to keep myself nice. I hate the way old chipped nail polish looks on fingernails and toes." Lauren glanced at her own fingers. She quickly tried to cover her two fingers with the chipped nail polish. Who was she fooling? I had noticed her nails days ago. She sat on her bed and proceeded to watch me. As I blocked her out, my hands worked feverishly to perfect the French pedicure.

"Damn, your hands are steady," Lauren said. "If that would have been me I woulda never got the line straight." Then she did it. "Can you do my feet next?" Now, the long pause between her question and my response should have been enough of an answer. But this chick seriously expected me to touch, clean, and design her crusty toenails.

"Funny thing, I can do my own, but I can't seem to do anybody else's," I told her.

"Well, then, do my hands. I'm sure you can figure out how to do that," she said, being too pushy for my taste. So I did my toes, her hands, my hair. I shaved my underarms, trimmed my pussy hairs into a cute little design. Convincing Lauren that everything was regular, I tried on some of the outfits I purchased early this week. When all the stalling tactics were used up, I put on some short shorts and a baby tee with no bra. Flipping through Lauren's tape and CD collection, I picked out a mixed tape.

With each cut playing came a memory. Music just had that kind of power. I thought about all the fun I used to have in Brooklyn. I shivered just thinking about how all my friends just turned on me, one by one. And when DJ S and S slowed the beat down, the slow jams put me in a state. I started thinking about various sexual positions and how they made my body feel. Then the pressure came between my legs. It's crazy, I thought, how getting my hustle on had nearly wiped out my sex life. When Daddy was out . . . ah Daddy . . . Everything was smooth and safe. He took care of everything. All of my energy could just go to fun stuff. Now I was uptight, backed up, and definitely gonna get fucked, sucked, and licked real soon.

Lauren turned the music down. "Sasha, can you get the door." I rolled my eyes like it was a problem. I didn't bother to turn the light switch for the staircase on. In the dark, I stepped swiftly and softly down the five flights of stairs. Loosening my top button on my Daisy Dukes, I let the zipper come down.

The light wind that rushed through the door when I opened it made my nipples hard. They stuck out through my baby tee. My nipples might as well have been eyes 'cause when that door opened, that's what GS looked at first.

"Um, yeah, Souljah here?"

"Do you see me standing here?" I asked him in a pushy, but sexy way.

"Well damn, how could I say no to that question?" he asked, with a sexy smile and white teeth.

"Well, why don't you ask me my name?" I demanded.

He stood there, his eyes falling down to my Ralph Lauren panties, which were discreetly exposed under my shorts.

"Why don't you just tell me?" he said, with that masculine force that gets me hot every time.

"It's Sasha. When you come here next time, if there is a next time, you say 'what's up' to Sasha—then you can handle the rest of your business."

"Is that right?" he asked, looking like he didn't mind joking around at all. As he stepped through the door, he asked, "What's up with the lights?"

"I'll show you up," I said, gently taking his hand, using one finger to run across the inside of his palm 'cause I knew it would get him going. I walked in front of him, leading the way as if it was his first time in the house. When we got to the third floor, I pulled his hand and placed it on my waist. His fingers gripped the naked skin in between the top of my shorts and the bottom of my baby tee shirt.

On the last step I dropped him like a hot potato, turned around and said flatly, "I'll get Souljah for you, wait right here." She came out with a big smile on her face. Happy to see him, I guessed, she noticed nothing. I went right into my room, shut the door, and sat down.

Lauren looked at my titties and in a half of one second she said, "Yeah, I don't even have to ask who was at the door."

We were awakened early the next morning. As Souljah stood in between me and Lauren's beds, I thought to myself, *Damn, is this bitch a crackhead vampire? She stays up all night. In the morning you're looking at her like, did you ever go to sleep?*

"I want you to come with me, get dressed."

On the train the destination was revealed. We were on our way to Riker's Island women's prison.

"What for?" I asked.

"I have to speak to some young sisters behind bars."

"What are you going to tell them?" I asked, really wanting to know.

"I don't know," she said. "I move on a vibe. Whatever I feel when I see what I see is what I will say."

"Just like that?" I asked. She nodded yes. In what was probably a bold move in their eyes, I asked, "And how much does this speech pay?" Somewhat surprised, she responded.

"Nothing. When I speak at prisons, high schools and community places it don't cost anything."

"Well, then how do you make money?" I pushed.

"Different ways. I do projects. Also, when I speak at colleges they pay me well."

"How well?"

"Very well," she said.

"And all you gotta do is say what you feel? That sounds easy. How can I get down?"

"It's not that simple," she said. "You have to be talking about something that is important to people in their lives. You have to study, read, watch, work, and interact with people. When you master a particular field, then your words, knowledge, and insight become valuable. You know what I mean?"

I indicated yes. Inside, I'm like, *Yeah, I know what you mean. You're saying you can do it, but I can't. That's bullshit.* I know more about what goes on in the street than she does. I sure know more about a lot of shit than she does.

We didn't take the normal visitors route into Riker's. We went through the entrance the corrections officers use. We were searched. Beads of sweat began to gather as I placed my purse on the conveyer belt. One of the officers took my box cutter, saying politely that I couldn't bring it inside. He was taking it to protect me from the prisoners. "They cannot be trusted," he said. It was bugging me out to see how they treated Souljah and us, her guests, versus how they treated you when you came to visit the prisoners. The officer who was leading the way began to introduce Souljah to all of the other officers. They were smiling, shaking hands, giving her props, and all that fake shit.

The officer in charge said, "The women who you are going to speak to today are all HIV positive. They are in a separate wing of the prison." For the first time since I met her, Souljah's face appeared to be uncomfortable.

With her eyebrows screwed out of position, she questioned the officer, "Didn't you say I would be talking to adolescent women today?"

"Yes," he said, "I did, and I have to apologize to you. I didn't get the proper paperwork to my superior officer in time. He wouldn't give me clearance for you to speak to the adolescent women today. I can arrange it for some later date. But believe me sister, these women need to hear from you." Now, all of our eyeballs are bouncing around. I'm asking myself, Winter, what the fuck are you doing here involved in this mess?

Souljah asked the officer, "Can I use the ladies' room first?" The officer said, "Sure, right this way."

"Come on, y'all," she said, making it clear that we were to follow closely behind. In the bathroom, it was just us three. "Oh no," Souljah said, placing her two hands in her face. "I'm sorry y'all, I didn't know we were going to the HIV wing."

"Well, what's the matter?" Lauren asked. "Can we catch it or something?"

"They say that you cannot catch it except through the blood or bodily fluids. But I never trust what 'they say' anyway. I'm just surprised; I'm nervous." Souljah leaned against the sink, looking into the mirror.

"I thought you worked with the AIDS people," I said. "I thought you was giving a benefit for people with AIDS."

She smiled nervously and said, "Yes, I work with professional people who work with AIDS patients. And yes, I give money. But I never had to knowingly touch nobody with AIDS. I never had to be in a small room confined with them. I never had to see the effect of what the nasty disease does to a person's body. It's different, it's a different thing." Then she splashed water on her face, looked in the mirror and said, "I don't know what to say to them. This one will be left to God. I pray that I receive a message to give." She took a deep breath.

Now if you were one of those corrections officers you would never have guessed what went on in that bathroom. When we got back out into the hall, she stood confidently on her two feet as if she had never broken down in the toilet.

When we entered the doors to the wing, we were standing in the middle of a huge room. The beds were narrow, thin, and very close together. There had to be about a hundred beds. The first thought I had looking at these women was, *This is a waste of time.* These chicks are finished. Most of them were lying down on their beds doing nothing. Their bodies were thin and withered. Their faces were sunken in like many crackheads I had seen back in Brooklyn. Some of them had fresh bruises and stitches. Some of them had black eyes and blotches. Most of them had big ugly plaited braids, like dykes. They were in bad need of hygiene and a fashion rescue mission.

When they saw Souljah most of them had no reaction at all. In fact, it was the military voice of the man-built female c.o. that got them dragging their half-eaten bodies out of bed and into the room. Souljah stood, wringing her hands nervously and looking bewildered. I chuckled to myself, *go ahead smarty-pants, get yourself out of this one. Now you're on the front line.*

The women were quiet. Many of them looked disinterested. After all, they had no choice but to be there. They really were a "captive audience."

When Souljah didn't say anything, the c.o. in front of the room cleared her throat loudly and said, "Go ahead, they're all yours. Good luck." Souljah looked over their faces. For two whole minutes she said nothing. Then it came out.

"I can tell that all of you used to be very pretty women. I can look at your faces and see that you once were somebody's sweetheart, some- body's love, somebody's life. And I know when you were younger you thought being beautiful was the best thing in the world. But really we women don't have to do anything to be beautiful. It's a gift from God. The woman is.

"Somewhere along the line many of us as women are led to believe that being pretty is enough. And while we rely on that, we forget to strengthen our minds so that we can learn how to think, how to build. How to survive. We forget how to live our lives to protect our spirit, to be clean and decent. We forget that everything we do matters so much.

"Every right decision brings us blessings. Every wrong decision brings us pain. And then, when times get hard, our struggle and our pain shows on our faces and our bodies. When people see our pain and weakness in our face they say, 'She used to be fine, she used to be this, she used to be that.' When men feel our beauty has faded we become shocked at how well they ignore us and forget us. We'll do anything to get their attention, money, love. Can I suck your dick? Can I do anything, can I, can I?

"When we hate ourselves we destroy our bodies with alcohol, drugs, casual sex, and a bunch of stuff. Then we look at ourselves and hate ourselves even more. When I first came in here, I said, 'What will

I say to these women? They are all dying.' When I looked at your faces I thought to myself What have they done to themselves? But in spite of everything, your children love you. Your daughter needs you. Your sons miss you. We need you to live. We need you to want to live.

"What is a community without you, the mothers? What will a community of motherless children be like? Killers, haters, evil, negative, mad at the world, unable to love, hug, and live because they hate themselves, because they needed you to teach them how to feel, how to love, how to just be.

"So when you look in the mirror don't see death, see life. Don't see ugly, see beauty. It may not seem like it, but you are powerful. A change of mind, a change of spirit, and a change of actions can create a new you. You are needed. We need you to make the rest of your life mean something special. We need you to take good care of yourselves and each other, so those of us who love and need you, can still have you back in our homes, our communities. Yes, there is much to live for."

And when I looked up, everyone's eyes were filled with tears. Not mine. I hated her for making me think about my mother. I hated the way she thought she could get into everybody's personal business. I hated whatever it was in her that gave her the nerve to say out loud what everyone else thought, but had sense not to mention.

She hugged those women. When she forgot to hug one, they would ask for a hug. She gave it to them. She shook their sweaty hands and stood still while the ones with many missing teeth accidentally spit in her face while attempting to express themselves. She gave out pamphlets, book lists, advice, and too many autographs. After what was way too long of a wait, we three went straight home. One by one, we took long hot showers right away.

13

The same evening she called me into her bedroom. I had almost been staying here a week, yet I had never seen it. Now, the bedroom is a place where a girl gets to say who she is. Just by the arrangement of things you should be able to tell something about the girl that maybe you didn't know. Souljah's bed was round. It had a big, circular base and a circular mattress on top. The sheets, blankets, and pillows were expensive. I took her to be freaky, even though that's not how she seemed. But why else would she have a round bed? She had to go out of her way to get it. It must have been a sizable investment. I'm sure she had to go to a catalog or some custom designer to order proper linen and all that. Plus she took more pride in her bed than she did in her footwear.

On the wall there was a sketch of Souljah. It was accurate because you could tell right away that it was her. The eyes in the dark pencil sketch stood out because they looked even bigger than hers usually did. They were full of sadness. The artist even caught her earrings, big ones, like most ghetto girls rock.

"Do you like that picture?" she asked, after I guess I had been looking at it too long.

"Why do you look so sad?" I asked as if I cared.

"Well, I was in Paris when that picture was drawn. It was my twenty-first birthday. I was happy to be traveling, learning, studying there, but I missed my friends and family."

"You mean you missed your man?" I asked. She laughed a little.

"Yeah, him, too."

"How old are you now?" I pushed that question in.

"I'm twenty-five." *Damn*, I thought. She looked younger than that. Lined against the floor were three big black file cabinets. They were completely out of place. If you're tryna set a mood, get your groove on, why have a banging bed and set it near a set of file cabinets?

Next to the file cabinet was another bookcase filled with books and papers.

"What's with all the books?" I asked her.

"Well, the books in the living room are mostly the books I read in college. These books in here are the ones I have to read every day to keep up."

"Keep up with what?" I asked.

"With what's happening in our community, our world. You know."

"Seems to me if you live in your community you already know what's happening. You don't need no book to tell you. Hell, I could tell you that."

"Well, these books help you to understand *why* what is happening is happening. Usually in life the same things are happening over and over again, in cycles, you know? And if it's not a good cycle, you got to understand it in order to make it stop. But anyway," Souljah said, "I called you so we could talk about what's happening with your life. What's happening with your education?"

"I was in school but my family moved a couple of times and, you know, that was that."

"So what are your plans?" she asked.

"Plans, I don't know. Plans for what?"

"What would you like to become?" she asked.

"Rich," I said right away.

"How do you plan to get rich?"

"I don't know right now, but I'm working on it."

"I'm asking because I would like to help you do what you want to do. You're a pretty girl. I can tell you're very smart. You're quick on your feet. You seem very creative, maybe that's the direction you want to go in?"

"Creative?" I repeated.

"Yes. I saw how you did Lauren's nails. And your own are so beautiful. Your clothes are always so well-coordinated. Now that's a talent. Your hair looks as good if not better than I've seen any hairstylist around here do. That's a talent, too. So you just need to decide what you want to do and then get started. Otherwise, time will pass you by. You'll look up five to ten years later and you'll have nothing. So what do you think?" Souljah asked.

"Think about what?"

"When are you going to the hospital to see your mother?" she asked, changing the topic.

"Soon," I said, tryna keep it all brief.

"Well, if you need a ride or anything we can make a time and take you up there. What hospital is she in exactly?"

"Long Island College Hospital," I shot out quickly, "in Brooklyn. It's easy for me to take the train. It's no problem."

"Alright," she said, exhaling like the conversation wasn't going her way. "There's a book I have that you can take a look at." She sat on her bed pointing at the book lying on the file cabinet. It was a career guide.

"If you look through the book, you'll see fifteen hundred different careers. The good thing about it is the book has a lot of ideas, jobs, and business suggestions that the average person might not even think of. Maybe you'll see something that interests you."

"Thanks," I said, trying my best to seem like I was into what she was saying.

"I go to a lot of colleges to speak. I wouldn't mind taking you to see them. College isn't for everybody, but sometimes just taking a trip to one or two of the nice ones will change the way you look at education, yourself, and the world."

"Can I ask you a question?" I asked her. "Why do you have change all over your floor?" Souljah looked at the quarters, dimes, nickels, and pennies she had thrown all over her floor.

"I'm just sloppy and a little careless about some things." Well, sloppy was the right word. As I'm sizing everything up, I noticed she had more food in the bedroom than in the refrigerator. Half-eaten bags of barbecue chips and a can of onion dip with some of the dip stuck to the outside of the can. She had empty apple-juice bottles, and half-empty Evian waters. On top of that, she had an exercise bike in the room. Putting two and two together I figured she eats a family-size bag of barbecue chips with dip, feels guilty, jumps on the bike, and tries to burn it all off.

"And why do you have file cabinets in your bedroom?" I asked, laughing now.

"Oh, so maybe *you* need to be an interior decorator," she kidded me. "I'd hire you 'cause I have no sense of all that. Seriously though, I get letters from a lot of people. I keep files on some of the people I work with. I write a lot. I keep copies of *everything* I mail out. Now, my room might not be in order, but I know every book on my shelf and would know right away if one was missing. I know where every piece of paper in this house is located. It may not seem like it, but there is an organized system to it. I guess it's just a matter of different things being important to different people." I had gotten her on the defense and now was the perfect time to dip out of this boring little meeting.

"Here. Talk to Boom," Lauren was passing me the phone as soon as I got back in our room.

"Boom who?"

"You said you wanted to meet somebody."

"Are you ugly?" the deep voice on the phone asked.

"Are *you* ugly?" I shot back.

"Nah, I'm just saying, though. It don't make no sense for me to drive up there if you ugly. For all I know Lauren and Sarge could just be setting me up to give them a ride and I ain't playing taxi all night. So just let a nigga know what you look like?"

"What you pushing?" I asked.

"A Infiniti."

"Well, you come see for yourself," I challenged him.

"Alright, but if you ugly, I'm just pulling off."

"Whatever, nigga."

My arms were folded one into another. I stood on the stoop outside the house with much attitude waiting for Boom and Sarge to pick us up. Lauren was standing in the middle of the street. Lauren's nigga was called "Sarge" 'cause he was in the army. He jumped out the passenger seat all excited and grabbed and squeezed Lauren up. The notorious Boom had one foot in the car, one foot on the ground, as he stood up halfway out the car to check me out. He was light-skinned, with two big dimples in his cheeks and a cleft in his chin, a mad cutie with curly black hair. We smiled at the same time. "Ah shit," he said, throwing his hands in the air. "You fine. Come on, get in."

We checked an action flick. Don't ask me the title. We was mostly tonguing, feeling each other up, and giving each other shotguns with Sarge's bag of weed. When we got tired of buttered popcorn and the real munchies kicked in, Boom said, "What's it gonna be, McDonald's or Uno's?"

"Uno's is better," I said quickly.

"Uno's is pussy," Boom said. "So what's up, you gonna give me some pussy or are we going to McDonald's?" We all started laughing. A few mixed drinks, some pizza at Uno's, potato skins, and salad, we all was feeling good. I wasn't worried about shit.

Boom's basement was damp and dark. The little lamp he had in the small matchbox house located in Queens didn't even light up the entire room. But I could see the mattress he had on the floor with no sheets. The "room" Lauren and Sarge went into was only a room because it was divided by a blanket hanging on a string. Before I put my pocketbook down next to me on the side of the mattress, I could hear Lauren and Sarge ripping off their clothes. The sound of Sarge's belt buckle clicking, the zipper noise, and their heavy breathing got me good and ready.

Boom flicked off the dim light and it was pitch-black. I like lights on, but there was no time for complaining. When Boom found my titties, he started rubbing my nipples between his fingers. At first my body got excited, but he rubbed them so long that they were burning. I turned onto my right side. I moved his hands off my titties, saying, "Suck 'em, suck 'em." He sucked them, but it was like he thought they was popsicles he sucked them so hard. I pushed his head down further so he could eat my pussy. He licked all over my hairs before he could find the inside of me. I heard him tryna spit the pussy hairs caught in his teeth out. When he found the inside of me he was licking all the wrong places. He wasn't sucking my clitoris which would have sent me over the top. "Come on, baby, just fuck me," I said.

"That's right," he said, all gassed up on himself like he was doing something. A few pumps, maybe eight, and he was laid out all over my body, tired and finished.

"Nigga, what?" I said.

"Ah girl, you know what," he said all cocky like he had just busted me down.

"Was it in?"

"Don't even play yourself, girl," he said all calm.

"Was that it?" I crawled around the mattress looking for the little lamp. Finally I fumbled, then found it. I clicked that switch real fast and flipped the lamp over like a flashlight, shining it on his dick. "That little fucking worm. That's it? And you got the nerve to call yourself Boom!" I yelled at him.

"Ah baby, you missed it, shit was this big." He held his fingers for a ten-inch stretch. "It's just cold in here, so you know, after I busted a nut my shit just shriveled up." By this time Lauren and Sarge's naked bodies had rolled onto the floor. They laughed so hard that Sarge kicked his foot and the curtain wall fell down.

"Ah nigga, I knew there had to be something wrong with your ass. Good hair, dimples, all that, and you just a little dick nigga. Take us home," I screamed on him.

Lauren couldn't stop apologizing. But she couldn't stop laughing either. I decided I would choose all of my dates from here on. How I expected her to understand my desires, I don't know.

On Sunday, the pressure was on for many reasons. First off my stash was down to three hundred seventy-five dollars. It was the smallest amount of money I had in a long time. I was surrounded by a sense of panic. All I could think about was loot. Several times I caught myself pacing back and forth with various calculations racing through my head. As my pacing got faster and faster I grew more and more angry. Every plan I would start to cook up would hit a dead end for one reason or another.

With Souljah out of the house for the afternoon, and Lauren, who woke up mad late, in the shower, I began to walk all over the apartment. I looked at everything on the fifth floor. Believe it or not, there was nothing of value that I could see. Maybe the answer was on the second, third, or fourth floor. I pictured myself going to the pawnshop with an elephant tusk. I erased that thought. I knew Doc might have some jewelry down there in her apartment or maybe even a strongbox or safe. Now, the bottom line was I couldn't carry or crack a safe. It wasn't my line of work. But as my forehead broke out in a small sweat, I was willing to consider anything.

Second cause of my tension today was the womanhood meeting. I was itching to bounce. The reality that I had no place to go was pissing me off 'cause I'm not the dependent type. I would be forced to attend another boring event. Somehow I was hoping that I could make it work for me. The difficulty would be seeing Rashida again, who I was determined to avoid completely.

"Let's go see Doc," I told Lauren.

"Nah, you go. I gotta make some calls," she said. Perfect. I went down to strike up a conversation and to see what I could see. Doc was on the first floor. I heard her moving around behind the two wide wooden doors. I knocked softly. There was no response, so I knocked a little harder.

"How you doing, Sasha?" she said in a pleasant voice, but looking distracted.

"I was a little bored. Curiosity led me down here to see you."

"Oh really, what are we curious about?" she asked, like I was a pre-schooler.

"About what you do. I'm fascinated with the fact that you're a doctor," I said, speaking her language while gassing her up for my plan.

"I didn't know you were interested in medicine."

"Yeah, very." I looked past her figure into her office.

"Well, come on, let me show you around." Now all I had to say was I was interested in medicine. She showed me every slide under a microscope, every test tube, instrument, and even the tables her patients lie down on. She pointed out charts on the wall, breast self-examinations, pregnancy information. She even asked me, "When is the last time you had a checkup?"

"I don't remember," I responded.

"Well, that doesn't sound good," she said, looking as if she wanted to examine me or something. "Well you know once you become a young woman like yourself, you need to get regular exams and a pap smear every six months."

"Pap who?"

"Pap smear. It's part of a vaginal examination. We check for any sexually transmitted diseases, cervical cancer, everything. Since your mom has cancer you have to be extra careful." She pulled out a long steel tool. "It looks worse than it feels," she said. "This is a spectrum. It's used in a gynecological exam."

"Don't point that thing at me!" I joked, as if it were a gun.

"This is a serious matter, Sasha. Are you sexually active?" I knew the answer to that question would lead me into a trap so I said, "No, not yet." The doctor raised an eyebrow and twisted up her face. She didn't want to call me a liar, but I could tell she didn't believe me either. She walked away as if she was insulted. Opening a small drawer, she pulled out a gang of condoms.

"Alright, even though you're not sexually active," she said sarcastically, "take these just in case something unexpected pops up."

"And if I wanted an exam, how much would it cost?"

"Do you have coverage?" she asked.

"Not right now. What will it run me?"

"Well, usually it would be a hundred and fifty dollars, but since you're a houseguest, I'd be willing to examine you at no charge. You pay the lab fees."

"I'll think about it," I said.

"Don't wait too long," she said, with the serious concern I had grown to hate.

Talking to Doc for half an hour had gotten me more useful information than eight days with the upstairs duo. I had peeped the strongbox where I was sure Doc kept her money. I had figured even on a bad day she had at least two patients who each paid her a hundred and fifty dollars in cash. Depending upon what day she goes to the bank, and whether or not she goes every week, there could be a minimum of fifteen hundred weekly or three grand every two weeks in that locked box. I would watch her carefully, get to know her. I wouldn't be satisfied until I was able to see what kind of treasures she had on each floor of this castle. After all, she pushed the Benz. She paid the bills, so what was I wasting my time with the other two for?

Right away, I understood why Lauren said she went to the womanhood meetings for the laughs. As a gazillion chicks with an assortment of bad taste filed into the big room on a Sunday night, I bugged at the whole scene. Girls with turbans on like they were straight out of the desert. Girls with ashy feet and ashy elbows. A bunch of fake jewelry, cheap shoes, and bald heads. I couldn't believe that these girls couldn't understand that the real problem was they had no style. How you gonna be a female with a head full of unkept nappy hair or a fade like a man? Now they didn't all look the same, but they all looked busted. Some of them were young, like fifteen. Some of them seemed as old as thirty-five or forty. I'm thinking if you're forty years old getting advice from a twenty-five-year-old, you might as well hang it up.

A wave of young girls came in ten minutes later. They was regular block girls. What a combination. Everybody stood around, eating cheese and crackers, celery sticks, carrots, dip, and other types of rabbit food. When Souljah came out her room in the back, they all got quiet like she was Confucius or Kung Fu or something. When she sat down, they all sat down, like dummies. I spotted Rashida's pitiful ass and bounced my eyes in another direction. Determined to get my attention, she picked her chair up and moved it to where I was, squeezing herself into a small space.

"How's it going?" she asked, all overexcited. I held my finger to my mouth, *sshh,* I said like I was really interested in the meeting.

Souljah started talking. "Well, the purpose is for us as women, especially young women, to come together, learn from each other, and prepare for our future. If we plan well, we will be in control of our lives instead of being controlled for the rest of our lives. Hopefully, all of us can improve the way we think, and the things we do as a result of how we think." Then Souljah gave out a book list. "This is a list of the books we will be reading for this class."

I'd say that's when she lost me and about half of the girls in here. When we looked at the list of ten books to be read over a period of one year, we were like, "She's crazy." We didn't even have to say it to one another. It was a silent agreement.

One of the girls couldn't take the silence so she blurted out and said, "Well, it seems to me like the main issue is money. I came here to get with some other women like myself who wanna get paid. We can give parties, do bus rides, all that shit. Once everybody gets a little bit of money in their pockets, then all of us will feel a little better." Then Souljah moved to shut her down even though at least half of us could feel what that female was kicking.

"Money is important, no doubt," Souljah said. "But there is some business we need to take care of before money comes into the equation."

"Like what?" the girl with the ideas asked.

"Like, how are we gonna have a business together when we don't even like each other? How we gonna trust each other when we don't even know each other? Think about it. When you first came in this room and you looked at the other females in the room, what kinds of things were you thinking? I'm willing to bet the majority of females here had a bunch of negative thoughts about the other females in this room." Everybody let go a nervous chuckle. But the big girl with the ideas was not convinced.

She said, "Business is not personal. I could go on a bus ride with fifty people. I don't care if I like 'em or not if the price is right." Some girls nodded their approval.

"Yeah, you could do that," Souljah said. "But it wouldn't mean anything. The reason why I open my place for these meetings is so we can do something meaningful, something dramatically different from what goes on in our community from day to day. Everybody thinks it's all about the Benjamins, but if every black person in the ghetto received a thousand dollars cash in the mail tomorrow, what would happen?" Most people got excited at that thought. A bunch of side conversations about what people would do with their thousand jumped off.

"Exactly," Souljah said. "In one week, 90 percent of our people would be broke. The money would be spent on overpriced jewelry, clothes, liquor, food, and crack." Everybody started laughing.

"True," some of them said.

"Now if we could work on who we are, what we stand for, getting to know each other, and what we believe, then we can make better decisions. For example, if everybody in here received a thousand dollars each and we believed in unity, we could have fifty thousand to buy a piece of property or put a down payment on a house, or we could open up a business and all become shareholders. It would be hard work, but at the end of the day it would mean so much more." People got quiet as they thought about it. *She's slick,* I thought to myself. I watched as she turned everything around the way she wanted it to be.

The girls in the room got sucked into her hustle. Meanwhile, I'm thinking how all the girls in the room was basically broke. Most of them took the train to get here. Meanwhile, Souljah was chilling in this mansion with full access to the Benz. I was waiting for her to pass around the basket for everybody to make a donation to her personal treasury.

Then she had us go around in a circle. "Say your name, and state what you believe."

"My name is Tashay," the first girl said. "And what do you mean by what do I believe?"

"Do you believe in something, anything?" Souljah asked, but the girl's face was blank.

"Are you, say, a Christian, Muslim, Jewish, 5 percenter?" The girl didn't say nothing.

"Do you believe in God, for example?" Souljah asked.

"Everybody believes in God," the girl said.

The next girl said her name was Kim. She's a Christian.

"Do you believe in premarital sex?" Souljah quizzed her. The girl laughed.

"Well everybody has sex, nothing wrong with that, is it?"

"I'm not here to judge," Souljah said. "We're just listening to what you believe."

"My name is Phoenix," the next girl said. "I'm not tryna impress nobody, and I don't know what I believe."

"What do you live for?" Souljah asked.

"What do you mean?" Phoenix asked.

"What makes life for you worth living?" The girl looked uncomfortable and she didn't answer.

"Okay, what is so important to you that you would risk your life for it. Fight for it, die for it?"

"My daughter. I'll do anything for her. I'm a dancer. Sometimes people have a lot to say about that, but I don't care. I gotta feed my daughter."

"What kind of dancer are you?"

"In a club."

"What club?"

"The Silk Den."

"That's a strip club," another girl blurted out. Phoenix rolled her eyes at her.

"Yeah . . . and what, you got something to say? I bring home three to five hundred a night. How much you make?" The girl with the big mouth didn't say nothing.

"How old is your daughter?" Souljah asked.

"One."

"Do you need three hundred dollars a night to feed your one-year-old daughter?"

"Oh snap," the girl with the big mouth said. Phoenix didn't answer.

"I'm not tryna play you. I'm just asking that in introducing ourselves we be as honest as possible. If you strip because you like to strip, or because you like to have a lot of money in your pocket, or because you have a habit, then say that. I'm not here to tell you what to believe in. But I am here to say that if you don't know what you believe in, everything else in your life will be confused. Knowing what you believe lays a foundation for your life. Then you can have principles and ideas that you follow. Things that you are unwilling to compromise. If you're deciding what you believe every day and every day you believe something else, you have nothing to look forward to but chaos."

"I want to look nice," Phoenix said confidently, after a short pause. "Nothing wrong with that, is there?"

"It depends on what you're willing to do to look nice. Are you willing to let strangers feel you up at a bar? Are you willing to do a lap dance in a string? Are you willing to suck a dick for a new dress?"

"I don't do all that," Phoenix said.

"A lot of women do. Then they think the new dress is going to make them feel better. It won't. A new dress might make you look better, but that's it."

One by one she knocked them down like bowling pins. She had an answer for everyone about everything. I could tell she had sat and thought up these responses. She said she was doing it to help. Somehow people couldn't figure out whether she was helping or just getting off on herself. After a while it didn't matter. There was one girl left before my turn. Suddenly, I felt the need to pee. I tiptoed off down the corridor and stayed locked in the bathroom long enough to stick my head out the window to get some fresh air.

By midweek, I had successfully explored the entire house. For a surgeon, the doctor was not so hard to figure out. Just showing a little interest got her to spill her guts. At night, after hours, she was easy to talk to. At the time when any other woman would be chilling with their man, she would be on any of the four floors that were exclusively hers with all the finest stuff in the world, but no mate. It wasn't long before I put it all together. Four years in one college, four years in another college, two years working around the clock in the hospital with no pay, then back to college and certification for this and that. She was a medical doctor, a gynecologist, and a surgeon. By the time she looked up twelve to fifteen years later, everybody was all paired off. All she got was a bunch of degrees. She could fix people's bodies and brains, but she couldn't repair her personal life. I wasn't gonna make that mistake.

14

Lauren busted down the bedroom door holding party laminates in her hand. "This is it!" she said, throwing herself on the bed. "GS's birthday party is tomorrow. Every bad ass in the entertainment industry is gonna be in the jam. What's wrong with you, Sasha? Maybe you didn't hear me. GS's birthday jam is tomorrow at the Palladium. LX is giving him the party. That's like chocolate ice cream with chocolate syrup and nuts all over the place." My face was twisted 'cause all I had left was three hundred fifty dollars. I would have to buy something special. But there was no doubt that I was going.

Life is a crap game. Or, as Santiaga would put it, life's a poker game. So the next day I laid my three hundred on the counter at Saks Fifth Avenue. I walked out with a designer shopping bag with one Calvin Klein slip dress inside. I already had the banging shoes and a matching shoulder bag.

My nerves were on edge. I kept telling myself, *This is an investment. This is an investment.* In less than twenty-four hours I would emerge as the baddest bitch in the universe. Some trick in that party was gonna bankroll all of my fantasies one way or another. Just to keep it real, I had my eyes set on the big catch, GS. I knew if I could hook him, my problems would be over. Life would be all Range Rovers, rugs, chips, cheddar, and pleasure. He was wasting his time with Souljah. She was no trophy. That's why he picked her up at night. He left her before the sun came up. You can't sport no bitch like her. I am the girl you go to bed with and wake up with. The one you bring the dough home to and leave it on the counter so I can take care of the house. I'm the girl who gets other niggas to envy you, want to be like you, want to kill you. Me, it's all about me, and real niggas know that. Real niggas love drama. Otherwise life ain't no thrill. If there ain't no drama, what's the point? A live nigga needs a bitch who's so bad that other bitches know when they see her to just lay the fuck down. Now, the other chick might of got some dick from the nigga at some time or other, but in the presence of wifey she knew all she could do is shut the fuck up and be mad.

With only enough money in my bag to buy one last dinner, I stepped into the Benz with Souljah, Lauren, and Doc. I couldn't understand why Doc was coming to the party. Her time had already come and passed. But I wasn't sweating the small stuff, especially because Doc was the driver, and she was pushing my kind of whip.

The thick of things is putting it mildly. When we rolled up, there were scores of people outside the club, everybody dressed to kill. The November breeze was chilling thighs and giving gobs of goose pimples to girls with no nylons. With cars parked in all directions, traffic was jammed. Luxury vehicles were everywhere and only the music was pumping louder and faster than my heart. Doc swung into the thirty-dollar parking garage that others were avoiding, based, I guess, on the price alone. It was not even a second thought to her. Those platinum and gold credit cards erased her worry over that.

When we walked up Souljah signaled security and they parted the crowd in seconds. As we walked up the slim aisle to the special entrance all eyes were on us.

"That's Sister Souljah."

"Who's that?"

"That's Sister Souljah," they whispered. I felt like a movie star as our tight little foursome entered the building with no problem, leaving the little wannabees hanging on the outside only to imagine what was going on inside.

Inside, players were seated in booths, sipping Moët, Cristal, and Alizé. Some were talking to each other. Some were kicking it with females. One big, buffed bouncer type invited himself to our table.

"You ladies want drinks? The bar is open till 10 P.M., after that it's gonna cost you."

"Why is everybody outside? Let 'em in, let's get this party started," Lauren said.

"The bar is free until ten. We'll let them in after ten, get it?" He smiled at Lauren like he was interested in her. We all went and got drinks and left Souljah in the booth.

By ten-thirty, the party was shoulder to shoulder. The music was loud. More than that, the music was crisp. It was the difference between a car radio, a house radio, a stereo system, and a club. The club system took it up ten notches. It was like the music had hands that ripped off your clothes and made you naked and crazy on the dance floor. With only the liquor to slow me down, my whole body was hypersensitive and completely sexual. When someone accidentally rubbed up against me the sensation was magnified. Wet lips looked even more enticing, and the more the scene sucked me in the more I liked it. Me and Lauren stuck together. We were looking for the celebrities. We weren't sure where they were. But we knew they were here.

"Souljah and Doc disappeared," Lauren said to me at eleven.

"So," I said, "let's go have some fun."

"You don't get it," Lauren said, as she tried to shout over the music that nobody's voice could compete with. I turned my head so she could speak directly into my ear. "If Souljah's gone and we can't find any celebrities, that means all of them are somewhere in a separate section, the VIP room."

"Well, come on, let's go to the VIP room." The place was huge. We had to move slowly through the growing crowd to each side and corner of the club to find out where the celebrity section was. When we finally found it, Lauren whipped out her VIP laminates and flashed them at the security guards that had the secret entrance sealed off. Facing us was the same big security guard from earlier. He stopped us.

"Wait a minute, Shorty. You can't do nothing with those," he said to Lauren, flashing his smile.

"VIP," she said, like he didn't see them the first time.

"Check this out. You got the wrong color laminates. They was orange, but they switched them to blue." He flashed his blue laminate. "Now to get inside you need a blue laminate." Lauren leaned on him a little, brushed his chest with her titties, and asked, "How can I need a blue laminate when you have one?" He flirted with her and laughed and all that, but still didn't let her in.

She was talking so much she must have been telling him her life story. After a while I wasn't even listening no more. He was getting off on joking with her, didn't believe or didn't care that she was Souljah's sister and definitely didn't believe she knew GS personally like she said she did.

Seconds later, the celeb door opened and four guys came out. My eyes were searching their faces to see if they were anybody. If they was leaving, at least they could give up their laminates and let us use them.

As one particular face drew closer my mouth dropped open. Recognizing him shook me up a little.

"Winter," he said, with mad passion.

"Bullet?" I said, more like it was a question. He grabbed my two hands, pushed me back a step, and said, "Damn, you look like a million dollars."

"Ain't nothing change, nigga," I said, noticing how sexy he still was, but giving him much attitude. With his mouth open, playing with the toothpick between his teeth, it was like he was talking but no words were coming out.

"Damn," he said again. He pulled me close to him and picked me up with his strong arms like I didn't weigh nothing.

"Put me down. I ain't forget, nigga."

"Forget what? I ain't forget either. I been looking all over for you forever. Man, I asked Natalie, your girl Simone, Natasha, Reese, I even asked your mom where you was at."

"I ain't forget about the videotape. I heard how you let niggas disrespect me down at Moe's place," I told him, with thick attitude.

"Ah that shit wasn't nothing. That was Slick illing, not me. You know that kid is sick. I don't get down like that. I see you still got your shine," he said, looking at my diamond tennis necklace and matching bracelet. Watching him surveying my whole body with his eyes, my body temperature intensified. What I dug about Bullet was he was a real lover. He knows how to rock a woman's entire body. He's a guaranteed orgasm. "Come on, why don't you take a ride with me?" he asked. My eyes peeped his black baggy slacks, leather jacket and heavyweight gold link. I wanted to say yes, but I kept thinking about what Midnight said about Bullet being down with Santiaga's enemies. What I wanted was battling my loyalty to Santiaga. But I know loyalty comes first. So I resisted. I still asked the important shit though.

"What you pushing?" Then the nigga started fidgeting, mumbling something which amounted to the fact that he was a passenger in another nigga's car. That made it easy for me to tell him no.

"Come on, Winter. You sleeping on this nigga," he said, patting his chest with his heavy hand. "A nigga been stacking chips, I'm about to cop something lovely. I got a little business on the side making moves. I'm about to come into something real big soon." I turned him down not with words, but with my eyes. The bottom line was right now I had a chance at getting with GS. Why should I fold my hand to pick up some unknown cards? He sensed my rejection, and didn't want his boys to see me turning him down. But he was gonna go for it anyway. "Winter, straight up, this nigga got love for you."

Knowing how to be cool and not play him out, I leaned over, gave him a kiss on the cheek and whispered in his ear, "Maybe some other time. Not tonight." He smiled, with 100 percent confidence. It was this kind of certainty that made me want to undress.

"Let me get those digits," he pulled a pencil from behind his ear and flipped open a book of matches to write it down.

"No phone. I don't have no phone," I told him.

"C'mon, Winter, don't try to play me."

"I don't. I haven't been wanting no calls, that's why. I just been staying to myself."

"Where you staying at?"

"You asking too many questions," I told him.

"Well, how's a nigga gonna get up with you then?"

"You give me your number," I told him.

"Fuck that. Come here." He signaled over to his man, one of the three rolling with him that night.

"Give me your pager." His man looked confused.

"What?" he said, unwilling to give it up.

"You heard what I said. Give me your pager." He snatched the pager from his man's hand.

His man protested, "I just got it today."

"Here, take this." He handed me the pager. "You gonna see how serious a nigga is. Learn how to respect a man when he talks. I'll page you when I finish setting up. Seeing is believing. You'll see. My code is 000." He hugged me again. "You gonna be mines."

"What's the phone number for the pager," I asked.

"You don't need it. I'm the only one calling that number," he said strongly.

It was hard passing up good dick. It was easy to pass up a broke passenger nigga. Tonight my aim was much higher. As Bullet walked away, I tapped his arm and asked for his laminate. He laughed and said, "Nah. *Why would I feed you to the sharks?*"

Lauren had it all worked out, or so she said. By this time she knew Frankie the security guard personally. Frankie couldn't let her in, but he let her know that GS was having a private party out in his house in

Alpine, New Jersey, at 2 A.M. All we had to do is meet Frankie around the back of the club. The four black trucks in the back would be bringing the party to Jersey and . . . "All the finest honeys get a free ride with security."

Four trucks, sixty chicks, and a caravan of niggas following behind in Benzes, Lexuses, Rovers, Rangers, Acuras, you name it. Twenty girls left standing on the curb 'cause security said they were either too fat or too ugly.

What do you know about five chicks sitting in the seats and four chicks sitting in they laps in each row of the Suburban? Now I was sitting on some girl 'cause I definitely wasn't gonna let her sit on me. I wasn't gonna say a word 'cause I already decided it was better just to watch. Besides, I wanted to check out the competition. The first thing I realized was me and Lauren were younger than most of these girls. A whole bunch of them was in college. I heard them talking about a football game, Grambling U. versus somebody. Some of them was talking like they came from far away. They mentioned that they was up for the weekend or drove all the way up from Washington, Baltimore, and Virginia.

Four of the girls in the back sitting on laps and positioned right near my ear were wilding. Every song that came on was, "Ahh, that's my jam!" Then they would make a high-tone screeching voice—skee wee skee wee skee wee—every time. It bugged me out when they started bouncing to the beat while sitting on the girls who I'm sure had to have black and blue knees and legs by then.

We invaded this private first-class neighborhood like an infection. GS's mansion was accentuated by an array of colored lights, which lit it up like the Walt Disney palace. The driveway was more like a parking lot at the cineplex theater. Manicured bushes and evergreen trees gave the place the air of seclusion. Inside there were more rooms than you'd care to count, three floors with steps leading to the west wing and the north and south side of the house. Cristal, Moët, fine wines, cheeses, buffalo wings, pineapple turkey meatballs, shrimps, and crab cakes were plentiful finger foods available to all special guests.

It wasn't but half an hour before everybody started asking where's GS? Where's LX? Where's this celebrity or that celebrity? After a while, I started getting vexed with security 'cause I wasn't sure if they just wanted to keep all the women for themselves.

At 3 A.M., one of the security guys stood on top of the couch and shouted, "OK ladies, GS is ready for some pussy. Who wants to give up the pussy?" We all jumped up. "If you're not here to get your freak on, bounce now. Any virgins in the house bounce now.

"Now y'all know it's too many of y'all. GS told me to bring up the baddest female in the house." All the girls were screaming, raising hands, trying to get security's attention.

"Hold on now. Hold on. Here's what we gonna do. We gonna have a contest. Line up. Get up. Line up. If you too drunk to stand up, sit down. You're out. You're not in it. We gon' have a beauty contest." In the huge living room there were ten rows of six girls each in the contest.

"I'm the host," one of the other security guys said. He was supposed to be big and intimidating. As far as I was concerned he was just big and fat. He walked through each row of girls with his tall, fat, sloppy self, carrying a vodka tonic in his right hand. Then he started pointing. "You ugly, sit down. You ugly, sit down. You ugly, sit down." The three girls was mad, mumbling all kinds of insults to him. One of 'em said it loud enough for everybody to hear.

"You big fat bitch," she called him.

The second girl said, "I thought you left all the ugly girls at the club?" Fat ass sipped his drink and said, "It was dark, I missed you three. Now sit down and shut up."

"Alright now, hold out your hands." Each row of girls stuck their hands out. "Man hands sit down. Goddamn, what your mother do, burn you with cigarettes? Sit the fuck down." He was eliminating contestants.

Next the other security guard stood up. He walked up and down the aisle like he was a military drill sergeant. For seconds he didn't say nothing. Then he started pointing, "Cheap shoes, sit down. Cheap shoes, sit down. Cheap shoes, sit down." I looked behind me and one of the girls he told to sit down was Lauren. She caught my eye. I just raised my eyebrows at her as if to say I'm sorry. I knew them cheap shoes would be her downfall.

Next thing I know the same dude was asking us to take our shoes off. A lot of girls didn't like that and they were complaining and suckin' their teeth. I wasn't affected, I had pretty feet. I even did my pedicure over especially for tonight. Dude started pointing out girls, "Hammertime sit down, Hammertime sit down, Hammertime sit down. Goddamn, sit down!" There was only like forty girls left.

"Alright ladies, this is a big one. Everyone with a weave sit your bald asses down." Twenty-five girls were out on that one call. My shit was straight and real.

With fifteen girls left, I was planning on winning. Then the next security guy got up and said, "Pull up your shirts. I'm checking for them nasty worms." Everybody was confused. We just stood there asking him and each other, "What? What worms?"

"Stretch marks. A lot of you slick bitches got nice figures and ugly stretch marks. You know you got four kids. Your ass shouldn't even be here. GS do not wanna be your baby's daddy!" All the guards started laughing. Five girls with worms were eliminated.

The security guard called over to the DJ, "Throw on some Biggie Smalls. Let me see you hoes dance. You gotta have rhythm. If you can't dance, you probably can't fuck. Sit down, you off beat. Sit down, you're whack. Sit down, your butt fell off." Seven girls left. Everybody was like alright, OK, alright already, just pick one. "OK, one of y'all step up, the other six sit down." Everybody stepped up. "OK now we gon' see who got some sense upstairs in the head. If you give the wrong answer to the television trivia question sit down.

"Contestant number one: Who shot J.J. Evans?"

"Who?"

"J.J. Evans, in *Good Times.*"

"I don't know."

"Sit down. It was Mad Dog. Contestant number two: What was Janet Jackson's name on *Good Times?*"

"I know, it was Penny," the contestant answered.

"You're right. Contestant number three: What was Alice's, the maid in *The Brady Bunch,* boyfriend's name, and what job did he do?"

"Oh, I don't know."

The security guards was laughing so hard they was bent over. The one who fell on the floor yelled, "You're out, it's Sam, the Butcher."

"Contestant number four: What was Fred Sanford's favorite drink?"

"Come on, that one's too hard. Hers was easy," she said, pointing to number two.

"Sit down. Fred drank Ripple. Contestant number five: What was Samantha Stevens's mother's name on *Bewitched?*"

"Umm, um, Sabrina."

"No, it was Endora."

"How was I supposed to know, I didn't watch that shit. I don't have cable."

"Sit down. Contestant number six (that was me): "What was the name of the dog on *The Jetsons,* the dog on *The Flintstones,* and the dog on *The Brady Bunch?*"

"Astro, Dino, and Tiger," I said swiftly.

"Ah shit. That's right, that's right."

Security laughed. The buffed one was like, "Yo, that bitch is smart." Contestant number seven was disqualified 'cause she didn't know who beat Rerun in the dance contest on *What's Happening.* But I saw that episode at least ten times; it was Danny Disco Dynamite.

"Now we're down to two contestants. Who's it gonna be? Let me see." Then one of them security guards jumped up and said, "What size is your bra?"

The girl said "36D."

I said "34D."

"Pretty close," he said. "But who has on clean panties with no holes and no loose strings? Open your legs." He got down on all fours and looked under her skirt. Then he crawled over and looked under my dress. When he saw my nicely trimmed, bare, hairy pussy he said, "That's it! You're the winner!" All I could think was, *Thank God I didn't wear no panties.*

It seemed like we would never make it up to the top of the wide, steep, and curvaceous staircase. Every step closer I got to the bedroom on the west wing of the mansion, the more excited I became. I wish I could have a Polaroid snapshot of the look on GS's face when I walk into the room.

As we got closer to the door the fat security guard who escorted me said, "Me and you could dip into any one of these rooms right now. If it's me you really want just give me the word." I wouldn't even respond to him. A few steps before the entrance to GS's bedroom the fat guy turned around and walked away.

I could hear the music in the room pumping real loud. Standing outside of the door I checked my clothes and touched my hair with my fingers. I turned the knob to let myself in. Surprisingly, the room was dark. The only light was coming from the television where the image from the PlayStation street fighter game was stuck on pause.

I ran my hands along the wall trying to guide myself to the light switch. Accidentally I tripped over what I guessed was a Timberland boot tossed on the floor. Now I was glad the lights were off. I didn't want GS to see me in an uncool position. When I stood up I walked a couple of steps before feeling the night table with my fingers. As my hands were extended in front of me to keep from crashing into anything else, I almost toppled over a Cristal bottle. I knew that's what it was from the shape of it as I held it in my hands. It was empty. Oh shit. I knew GS was wasted, probably crashed out on the bed. It was either that or he's a sexy motherfucker who likes to play games in the dark. I could get with that. With a few more steps I found my feet tangled in his pants that were tossed on the floor. Now I was getting real excited.

Finally, I found the sound system, but I couldn't read the buttons so I just started turning and pushing them one by one. There was static, then shit just started going crazy for a minute. I pushed the buttons faster until, luckily, one shut the sound off.

"GS," I called out softly, not really knowing why I was whispering now that it was so absolutely quiet. I heard him groan a few times and moved into the direction his voice was coming from. Soon as I bumped into the bed I started undressing.

"Who that?" he asked, sounding disoriented.

"It's me, Sasha. I came to give you what we both been waiting for." He laughed slow and sexy. Butt naked, I slid my silky legs in, then the rest of my body. Taking total control, I threw my legs over him, then mounted him like I was the jockey and he was the thoroughbred. I was determined I was gonna revive the million-dollar star. I was gonna make love to him so he would remember my name and come back sniffin' round my door tomorrow. Laying my titties on his chest and my hairs against his now erect, big thick thank God dick, I began to suck his neck, lick his shoulder blades, and suck his chin.

Only seconds passed before his lips came alive and gave way to my sweet passion. We was tonguing. His strong arms grabbed my hips and lifted me up slightly, positioning to penetrate. I pulled myself to the side, resisting him, so I could suck it first to keep it hard longer. As it went into my mouth and halfway down my throat, I moved my lips slowly back and forth. GS let out a groan that let me know I had him in the palm of my hands. Tonight it would be all about him. Once I turned him out, it would be all about me.

When I felt the pressure mount in him I withdrew my tongue and lips. He grabbed my head wanting me to keep going. Instead, I mounted him then, pushed him inside of me. I put everything I had on him, double-jointed hips, and my flexible body moves. He wouldn't never call me a lazy lover. As my pussy muscles held him in a lobster grip, I vibrated all over him. I heard him scream in ecstasy like he was my bitch. The sound of his surrender caused me to lose my head and my orgasm caused my whole body to shake uncontrollably. He responded by busting a nut, a big fucking walnut, inside of me. We both collapsed into sleep. I don't know about him but I went out with a smile.

In the morning, I tidied up after our houseguests. I was dressed in GS's shirt. Downstairs I tried to bring together some breakfast for us; I had music playing at a low volume. The sun was filling up the entire house the way it does in classy neighborhoods where architects design houses with the position of the sun, moon, and water in mind. As I walked up the long wide staircase, I felt a pain in my side . . .

"Excuse me, sweetie. Hey, hey. You got to get up and get out of here. I don't know what you're doing in here. But don't respond. I'm afraid of the answer." Everything was a blur. I attempted to focus. My head was pulsating the way it does after a night of a wild mixture of drinks.

The harmless-looking thirty-something woman was poking me in the side with a long black antenna, on which I assume was a walkie-talkie. When I sat up my eyes confirmed the images that were jetting through my mind. I was in GS's mansion. It was not a dream. The untidy room of last night was now spotless except for my naked body. Like a zoom lens, my eyes scanned the floor for my clothes, which I recalled dropping on the floor on my side of the bed. I spotted them laid neatly across a chair.

I grabbed my neck with my hands. My diamond necklace and my bracelet were still on so I could rule out robbery from this bizarre situation. As I collected myself and began dressing, the woman watched me as if I was acting in a scene she was directing. Clutching my bag, I asked her, "Where's GS?"

"He's not due on the set until two this afternoon. It's 9 A.M. right now. But you will have to go."

"Think about it, lady. If I'm here in his room I must be a welcomed guest in GS's home."

"Oh really," she said, doubtfully. "I'm sure he wouldn't mind if *his girl* waited downstairs for him."

"This house is big enough for everybody."

"Listen, sweetie. I'm sure you're GS's girl. However, this is not GS's house. Now, we have it rented for a video shoot until twelve midnight. I've got to get every shot finished by then. So I'll have to ask you to leave in the interest of GS's *money.* Overtime is an ass-kicker in this neighborhood." She tossed my clothes at me.

I flung the door open, turned left, then right to figure which direction to head in. As I moved down the marble staircase I suddenly noted how beautiful, yet empty, the house seemed. I was mad at the sarcastic woman upstairs. But I wasn't worried. I was certain that what I put on GS last night would stick. I wouldn't have to go looking for him, he would find me.

When I exited from the multithousand-dollar crafted doors, it reminded me of my old house on Long Island. Just acres of perfect landscape and trimmed trees. Finding the bus stop would be like looking for a lost contact lens. Once I walked past the evergreens, I saw the black trucks that we all rode over here in.

The huge security guys who were the phantom comedians of last night were now looking very sober and serious about guarding this house. As soon as one of them spotted me, he called out, "Where you headed, lovely?" Slowly walking toward him I weighed my options.

"I'm tryna get back to the city."

"You can ride with me if you can wait until eleven. That's when I get off."

"Were you here last night?" I asked him. "I don't remember your face."

"Why would you?" he said casually.

We putt-putted in his Datsun. The deteriorating jalopy was so slow it added forty minutes onto what should have been a quick trip. Maybe it was because his speedometer wouldn't break forty-five miles per hour. As I crawled out of his car, I ask, "So were the black trucks rented just like the house?"

"Yep. Just for the video shoot," he said nonchalantly. "Listen, I'll see you around," he said, while looking like he wondered if he had a chance with me.

I muttered back, "No you won't see me," and I slammed the door.

Souljah was aggravated when I got upstairs in the house. As she munched on some barbecue chips, more out of habit than hunger, she asked, "Have you seen Lauren?"

"Not since last night," I responded, walking straight back to my bedroom. Hmmm. She knew better than to try to get in my business. As I relaxed on the comfortable bed I thought about everything. My only regret was not getting a photograph, autograph, or a piece of GS's personal belongings. Nobody would ever believe me if I told them me and him got down together. But I soothed myself with the idea that there was still time. As the minutes slipped away, sixty seconds at a time, I waited patiently for Lauren. Hell, she was there last night. She was a witness. Me and her would have one up on Souljah. While she strutted around all proud, Lauren and I would know that she didn't really have it all as tight as she thought she did. After all, she let me slide that ace right out of her hand.

Stuffing envelopes and answering phones was not my line of work. But Lauren didn't come home in two days. She didn't even call. Souljah was more worried than anything. Somewhere along the line I guess she decided to substitute me for her sister 'cause here I was doing all the goddamn work. I wanted Lauren to come back just as much as she did. It was as if I was left alone in the apartment with a set of gigantic eyes watching me. Souljah had a way of looking at people that I didn't like. She was very slick about using every minute that she's around a person to ask certain questions which led her to knowing more than she needed to know or more than a person wanted to give up.

"I never heard you mention your father. Is he alive?" she would ask in an innocent voice, as if she didn't know that it's disrespectful to ask niggas about they daddy.

"Yeah, he's alive," I answered, with the mind-your-fucking-business tone.

Each time the phone rang I was hoping that it was Midnight. Above everything else, I always pictured him as the man who could rescue me. I wondered what kind of game Souljah was playing. Or if she even really knew him at all. If she knew him well, why didn't she have his phone number or address? A lot of people don't have phones, but everybody got an address.

While filling in for Lauren I got to watch Souljah more closely. Every now and then she would ask me to file some papers away in the file cabinets in her bedroom. She had everything neatly arranged in alphabetical order. I checked under my name just to be sure she wasn't piling up no file on me. I even checked under "M" for Midnight to see if she was holding out information I needed to have in my hands. No luck. No file on me or him.

"So how did you meet my cousin?" I asked her. I was learning how to hit her with the questions before she could start hitting me. She stopped writing in her notebook, dropped her pen on the paper, and leaned back in the chair. She looked like she was recalling images in her mind.

The loud doorbell broke her mood and deaded my question. Without her even asking me to get the door, I zipped down the stairs. Lauren was standing there with a big smile on her face.

"Why didn't you use your key?" I asked.

"I wanted you to come down so you could tell me what's going on up there before I step in the fire and get burnt."

"Your sister's mad. But she's more worried. If you just limp in, act like you hurt or like somebody mugged you or something things will turn out better." We laughed.

"But get your ass upstairs, I'm tired of doing your work."

"Ooooh girl, what happened with GS? I want to know everything." Lauren was excited.

"*Shhh.* I'll tell you when we get to our room. Stay cool, your sister's right in the living room," I warned her.

One second after giggling with me Lauren was standing in the middle of the living room with tears spilling down her face, looking sorrowful. I only heard the beginning of her story. The voice that came out of her mouth wasn't her usual voice. She was talking like she was seven years old instead of seventeen.

"I was mad at you, Souljah. What happened? You disappeared at the club. I tried to use the passes you gave me. They wouldn't let me in the VIP room. I didn't get to cash the check you gave me so I was broke. I didn't have no money for a ride so I called Fever." Blah blah blah, and Lauren had reversed it on her sister. Now Souljah was standing there, explaining where she went that night and what happened with the passes. I checked it all out. When Souljah noticed me watching the two of them like a tennis match, she took Lauren into her bedroom and their voices faded behind the closed door.

15

The Jamaican spot around the corner got to break my last twenty. Two patties, ginger beer, and two blunts. The speed of my thoughts increased, then doubled. I had to make a move soon. According to my calculations, GS should be coming around any day now. It was unlike him to let four days go by without showing up. Even though I had about five plans brewing, I felt real uneasy. Staying at their house had me out of my element. Like a true Santiaga I could figure something out when my back was against the wall, but this living arrangement didn't leave me a lot of options.

First off, I was never left alone. Second, I had no one to feed off of. What I needed was a connection. It was like it was right there in front of my face, but I couldn't hook up the main line. Careful thoughts led me to conclude that Souljah was cock-blocking. She was interrupting my connection to Midnight and GS. She was clogging up my flow.

When I stepped back into the crib, I knocked on Doc's office door. She came to answer the door, opening it up only slightly. "My secretary quit. It's real hectic in here. We can't talk now." She closed the door in a hurry.

As I turned the knob to Souljah's apartment, I wished that I had not. I walked right into one of those womanhood meetings. I tried to shut the door swiftly hoping no one saw me, but Lauren pulled the knob from her side and said sarcastically, "Sasha, come on in. I saved a chair just for you." As I saw all of the girls seated in a circle Lauren locked eyes with me. She kept making funny faces and gestures 'cause she had busted me trying to get out of a meeting both of us hated.

"How many of you have figured out the answer to the question, 'What do I believe?' Who knows the answer to the question, 'What do I live for?' Who thought about the question, 'What would I sacrifice my life for?' "

"I'd sacrifice my life for my family," one girl said.

"In what way?"

"If somebody was messing with my sister I'd kick they ass. If somebody killed my brother I'd try my best to kill them, even if it killed me."

"Oh, are you and your sister tight?" Souljah asked, setting the girl up for the kill.

"We alright," the girl responded. After a small pause, the girl continued, "It doesn't matter if me and my sister are tight. The fact is that she's my sister and if anybody puts their hands on her then we gon' be thumping."

"How about for a cause? Would you fight for a cause?" Souljah asked.

"What kind of cause?" the girl asked cautiously.

"Say, for instance, the school in your neighborhood didn't have the right books for the children to learn. Or, say, they needed computers, or even healthier food in the cafeteria?"

The girl seemed to sense that this might be a trap so she thought before she answered, then blurted out, "No, I'm not getting involved in all of that. That's different. If somebody's beating my sister up or cheating her out of money, that's different 'cause that's like an emergency."

"What about you?" Souljah asked the next girl.

"If my sister was in the school, then maybe I'd do something," the girl said.

"But why would your sister have to be in school for you to fight for the school?"

" 'Cause my sister's in my family, *my family.* I don't know those other kids," she said, with attitude.

"But the school is in your community. Even if your sister isn't in that school, your sister still has to live in the neighborhood. She will be affected by whatever happens to those other children. If they don't get a proper education maybe one of them will bust a cap in your sister's ass. Then what?" Silence fell for three seconds.

Then the girl said, "Then I'll bust a cap in they ass." Everybody laughed. Souljah pulled out a blackboard and started gibbering about how we all a family.

"We are all connected. We have to look out for one another in our schools and neighborhoods. We have to make anybody who makes money in our neighborhoods accountable to us who live here."

As far as I was concerned this whole topic was a waste of time. The girl was right. If somebody touch family, then family touches them back. If somebody fucks with the money in my pocket then it's grounds for war. How are we all connected when all of us live in separate places? I bet none of these chicks lived in an apartment as laced as Souljah's. When you get a bill in the mail it ain't a "we" thing. When I buy clothes they ain't for "we" they for me. I live for me. I die for me.

Luckily Doc interrupted the meeting. She pulled Lauren out into the hall and I followed. "Listen Lauren," she said, "I need a big favor. Can you fill in tomorrow until I hire a new secretary?" Lauren didn't look enthusiastic.

"But I work up here," Lauren said.

"Souljah won't mind if I borrow you. My office is swamped. I'll talk to her, she'll understand." Doc put the pressure on her.

"Alright then," Lauren agreed.

Back inside Souljah was still grilling the girls.

"How will we as women get along with one another in our communities if we can't agree on the rules?" she asked.

"What rules?" one of the girls questioned.

"How should we treat each other? How should we speak to one another, and about each other? What about our men? How should we treat them? How should we require them to treat us? What could we change about our own actions to cause them to treat all of us better? Will we continue to sleep with each other's men and fight and lie about it? What do we believe? How will we raise our children? What will we tell them?"

Souljah was shooting those questions like rapid-fire. It was clear to me that she wanted to control everything and everybody. That's it. She was a definite control freak.

Late that night when GS rang the bell, I beat my record time getting down the stairs.

"What up, Sash?" he said like I had him trained to say.

"You know what's up, nigga," I responded, in my playful sexy way. "I knew you'd come around looking for me. Slide me your number so we can talk. You know, just me and you." I smiled wide and stuck my tongue out a little on my teeth.

"You crazy," he said, laughing. "Souljah here?" Steamed, my smile turned to tight lips.

"Stop playing, GS. You know what's up. We don't have to do this here. But we definitely got to do this." GS brushed past me, pushing me to the side. As he headed up the stairs I ran close behind him and grabbed his shoulder. He jerked his shoulder back, shoving me off. At the top landing of the first flight of stairs I pushed him. He pushed me back.

"Look, girl. You want to get fucked, I'll fuck you. But don't trip in her house. I ain't checkin' for that." In the dark shadows of the stairs Souljah appeared. With her eyes cutting through the darkness like a cat, she asked, "Is everything straight?" looking at GS.

"Everything's cool," he said in a raspy low voice.

"Peace, Sasha," Souljah said as they left. But in them two words a lot more was hidden.

Upstairs Lauren was waiting. I was so vexed. I didn't feel like swapping stories with her now.

"What's wrong?" she asked. "Was that GS? What did he say?"

"The motherfucker didn't say nothing. He acted like I was whylin out, like he didn't know what's up."

"Well what do you expect him to do with Souljah right here in the house? What you got to do is get him one on one."

"I already did that," I said, calm, but angry.

"Did you get his number?"

"No."

"How about the beeper?"

"Nope, nothing."

"Damn, you fucked up. How did that happen? You didn't get nothing? What the hell were you doing up there in his room?"

"I guess we were too busy to talk," I laughed half-heartedly. "Where did you go?" I asked her.

"I was with Frankie till about five. Then he said he had to pick up GS, so I told him to drop me off."

"He didn't drop you here 'cause you weren't here when I got here."

"Yeah, he dropped me off at Cameron's house."

"Who's Cameron?"

"This other dude I know."

"What did Frankie say about that?"

"What could he say? He don't know me. I told him it was my mother's apartment." We laughed again. "Frankie won't see me no more no how. Once he told me he was GS's personal bodyguard I decided to cut his ass off. I don't need my business getting back to my sister."

While Lauren slept I sat up all night. When I heard Souljah coming up the stairs it was about 4 A.M. I only heard one set of footsteps. I decided to confront her in the darkened hallway with my nightgown on.

"So is GS your man?" I questioned her.

"No, we're just friends," she said with no hostility.

"So how come the two of you are always together?"

"We like each other, but we both know it wouldn't work out. Besides, he's leaving on tour tomorrow." She checked the time and said, "I mean today. We were just saying goodbye. Why do you ask?" I guess I didn't answer quick enough because she started talking again. "I thought you had something for him," she said, like she was pleased with herself for knowing things before they happen.

"But if I did it wouldn't matter to you, would it?" I asked.

"It would because I have feelings for him. But I wouldn't try to stop the two of you 'cause he's not my man. Come on in?" We walked into her bedroom. "Sit down," she said. "GS is an entertainer. I told myself there's two kind of men I would never marry, a performer or a preacher."

"Why?" I asked, thinking, *Damn, who said anything about marriage anyway?*

"Because you have to know yourself as a woman. You have to know what you want out of love and what you don't want. You have to know what you expect and what you're unwilling to accept or compromise. Now a million women are in love with GS or at least think they are. Whatever girl eventually 'gets him' can never be happy. Her man will be hunted and desired by so many other women. Everyone will see her as the person who's in the way, the person they need to get rid of.

"A man like GS would have to work overtime to convince the woman he chooses that he really loves her, that he really will be faithful. For the most part, he'll probably try. He'll say no to a thousand girls. Then there will be just that one. Someone with a beautiful face like yours, Sasha, a perfect figure and pretty toes, and he'll say yes to her. Or let's say he's faithful. Half the time he'll be on the road. You would have to be the kind of woman who doesn't mind being left alone half of the time. That's not me. That's not what I want. Then, with the performers you never know anyway." Her voice lowered to a whisper like this was top secret information.

"Never know what?"

"A lot of them are bisexual. They look like men, dress like men, talk like men, are surrounded by women, but they sleep with men also."

"Not GS," I blurted out.

"You never know," she said. "That's why you gotta watch for a long time before you jump into bed with someone. It's not what they say that gives them away, it's what they do and how they do it. I watch closely. Most things are not what they seem to be in this life. Most people are not what they seem to be in this life. Most people find it extremely hard to tell the truth about themselves. Living has taught me that." Souljah was undressing as she spoke. It was as if I wasn't even standing there.

"So who is good enough to be your man?"

"I don't really think of it that way. I look at it as when I meet the man for me I'll know it; I'll feel it and he will too. But even when I feel it and know it, I'll wait and watch for a good while. But if you like GS, give it your best shot if that's what you really want."

As she sat down on the round bed in her bra and panties under the dim light, my mind raced to figure out the riddles she was speaking in. She was like the kid around the block who you'd get all pumped up to fight. You'd take off your earrings, necklace, pull back your hair, and Vaseline your face. You'd give her your best punch, then she wouldn't hit you back. It just took the fun out of everything.

"So what's up with the digits?" I asked, on my way out of her bedroom door.

"What digits?"

"Oh, I thought maybe you'd hook a girlfriend up with GS's phone number?"

"Come on now. I'm nice, but I'm not stupid. If you want to hook up with GS you'll have to work it out on your own, between the two of you."

The next afternoon I worked on Lauren. I needed her to get in touch with Frankie. He would know how to hook me up with GS. I had thought about it and the idea of going on tour with him was getting me all worked up. I mean, I'm realistic. The nigga don't have to marry me straight off. We could just travel, spend his money, and enjoy our fame. The other chicks didn't matter as long as I controlled his pockets. Once I got on the road I would be unstoppable. I'd be out of this prison, have access to the dough, and I'd be meeting real, not broke down ghetto girls or chicks in turbans, or philosophers or wannabees. I would learn the game, whatever the game was, 'cause I was a fast learner. Right about now I was giving GS the benefit of the doubt. OK, I shouldn't have played up to him in this house where he couldn't act natural. I should've waited, set the scene and the mood. But I was gonna give him a second chance to make the smartest move of his life.

"I don't want to talk to Frankie. I already told you that." That was Lauren's response to my pushing her.

"C'mon. Just do me a solid. Girl, you know I would do it for you." I sensed that maybe she was reluctant to get GS's phone number from Frankie because of her sister. I tried to put Lauren at ease.

"Look, Souljah told me to go for mine with GS."

"No she didn't," she said with disbelief.

"Yes she did. Last night we was up talking."

"When? *She never told me to go for mine with GS.*" Lauren's words were laced with jealousy.

"Whatever, Lauren. Look, are you gonna do this or not?"

"What makes you think Frankie's gonna give me GS's number anyway?" she asked me.

"If he's GS's bodyguard, he should be right there with him. He could just pass him the phone. All I need is five minutes. Five minutes and I know I could persuade GS of some things."

"Alright, but Frankie is an asshole. He's on his own dick too hard. But I'll do it. Go in Souljah's room and pick up her phone. I'll call him on this phone. You listen and write down the number if we can get him to give it to us."

Lauren got Frankie on the phone.

"Frankie! What's up, baby?"

"Who dis?"

"Dis Lauren."

"Lauren from New York or Lauren from Philly?"

"Lauren with the chinky eyes and the sweet New York pussy!"

"Ah shit. I know that's right. Damn, you miss a nigga already, huh?"

"Well, you know how it be."

"What you got on right now?"

"Nothing but a black leather belt around my waist to spank your bad ass with."

"Yeah, this my freak. Like to tie a nigga up and all that."

"So where you headed?" Lauren asked.

"North Carolina. We got a show there tonight. You should've called me yesterday. I'da brought your ass with me."

"Where GS at?"

"What you asking for that nigga for."

"I'm not asking for him."

"Sounds like you was asking for him to me."

"Nah." She denied it.

"We on the tour bus. That nigga's in the plane riding first class."

"Oh. Well where are y'all staying at down in Cackalacki?"

"Some of us will be at the Hyatt Regency. Others of us will be at the fucking Best Western, ain't that right, dogs." Everybody started laughing. I could hear male voices in the background through the phone.

"Well which hotel are you stayin' at?"

"Why? You coming to see me? Don't surprise a brother, let me know."

"Maybe. Are you staying with GS?" I asked him.

"There you go again. Tony, tell this little freak how much we hate bitches using us to get to GS."

"Yo, this is Tony. Why you tryna play my man?"

"Put Frankie back on the phone," Lauren said in an aggravated tone.

"Well, who do you want to talk to, Frankie or GS?" Tony teased.

"I want to talk to Frankie."

"Are you sure?" Frankie asked, back on the phone. "Make that little noise you was making the other night."

Lauren started moaning on the phone. She sounded like a cross between a snake and an owl. But Frankie loved it.

"*Now* you remember who you wit?" Frankie asked.

"I was asking for a friend," Lauren said.

"Oh, dogs, she's asking about GS for *her friend.*" They all started laughing wild. We could hear them loud and clear.

"Oh, so your friend want to get stretched out by GS? She got any friends? If we hook her up with 'G,' she gotta serve the rest of us too . . . or bring some freaks with her."

I ran back into the bedroom to coach Lauren on what to say. "Tell him to set up the meeting. We'll meet them down there," I told her.

"In North Carolina?" Lauren asked me, whispering.

"Why not?" I asked, rushing her to set it up.

"You got money to go to North Carolina?" Lauren asked sarcastically.

"No, but I can get some. I'm going to see my mother today. She got some money for me," I lied.

"Yo, Lauren, is Shorty there with you?" Frankie asked.

"Yeah, it's Sasha. You know from the party the other night at GS's house?"

"The one who won the pageant?" Frankie guessed.

"What is he saying, what is he saying?" I asked Lauren. She didn't answer, so I ran back to Souljah's room and picked up the other phone.

"Lauren, between you and me, if she's fiending for the dick, it's Tony she should be talking to. He's the one who fucked her. Ain't that right, dog?"

"Who that?" Tony's voice asked from the distance.

"You remember that little freak we played switch with the other night out at the Alpine video shoot?"

"Do I remember? Tell that bitch I love her." Lauren dropped the phone. Within a second she was standing in Souljah's room looking in my face, feeling sorry for me. I held the phone to my ear, frozen in position. "Yeah, baby, this is Tony. I know you thought I was GS. But the good news is now I don't have to explain to you what good dick you would've been missing. Fuck that nigga 'G,' what you need to do is come get with me." They all laughed at his cheap rhyme.

You lying motherfucker!" I screamed on him.

"Alright then. When you came in the room I was on the bed waiting in the dark. You couldn't even find the light. You started knocking shit over. You tried to suck a sip out of my Cristal bottle but I had already drank it all. But here's the hook. You got long pretty legs, big titties like cantaloupes, a small tight waist, and you love to go horseback riding!" They all started cracking up. "I love you! I love you, girl! Let's do it again."

Vendetta is the word, except it isn't strong enough.

That afternoon, while Lauren worked in Doc's office, I sat and talked with her. That conversation cost her three hundred dollars, because that's how much I lifted from Doc's strongbox without Lauren even knowing it. Seems like everybody around here got something to prove. But these bitches were not going to outsmart Winter Santiaga.

The next day was the AIDS benefit. I had forgotten all about that bullshit. My nerves were shot. I promised myself I wouldn't sit through one more meeting or speech, nada! But the pressure was on. Souljah was bossing everyone around, rehearsing Lauren about how to place the volunteers, security, etcetera.

Dressed in red and white, the colors for all workers from the womanhood class, me, Lauren, and Souljah were on our way out the door. Doc's voice stopped us. "Souljah, I'm sorry. I can't make it to the benefit. Not having a secretary has left me in a bad position." Souljah looked disappointed. "But here's a check for a thousand dollars to support the wonderful work that you're doing." Souljah gave her a hug and kiss. I'm thinking, see, it ain't no sweat for her to just throw away a thousand dollars.

"One more thing," Doc said, "I need Lauren's help today. I know how much you need her, but right now I don't have anybody else." Now after Doc gave a thousand dollars what could Souljah say? Lauren turned on the heels of her cheap shoes and went back into the house.

"Well, you been around for months," Souljah said to me. "You know how important this benefit is to me. I'll need your help today. Do you think you can handle it?"

At the church Souljah went into the back with the important people. At 5 P.M., hundreds of ticket-buyers started to file in one by one. By six, the crowd was so big they had to open the second balcony. Girls from the womanhood class in red skirts and white blouses stood against the wall every couple of feet. They were ushers and security. More girls lined the wall on the now packed balcony.

Up on stage, Souljah was seated at a long table with doctors, dignitaries, and other stuffed shirts. And among all of this bulging crowd, in their haste, they somehow left me at one of the three doors to collect money!

I was amazed at this crowd of people I had never seen. Ladies with big church hats, men in suits with brims, Volvos, and Benzes. Even the young people had on suits and dresses. No sneakers to be found, not even a pair of baggy jeans. And definitely no hats—there was an old man who stood at the entrance and reminded each boy to remove his hat. More surprising, however, was the flow of twenty-dollar bills piling up in my basket as I sat behind the table collecting on one side and two other girls, one of whom was Rashida, sat behind the table on the other side. I began to separate the ones, fives, tens, and twenties, and turned all the dollar bills in the right direction the way Daddy showed me to do.

When the preacher said, "Let us bow our heads and pray," everyone bowed. I gently grabbed a stack of twenties, tens, and fives. I was not greedy. I left at least half in the basket. It was only a two-step motion dropping the bills into my red Coach bag, the one I had purchased to match GS's jeep. When heads raised from prayer I was my calm, courteous self. I resumed taking funds from the latecomers and stragglers.

Setting myself up for a flawless getaway, I told Rashida, who was always ripe for the sucker role, that I had a terrible stomachache. To gain her complete trust I asked her to hold my money basket while I went to the bathroom.

The bathroom was situated in the back of the church by the stage. I walked slowly and confidently to the back, checking on the ushers like I was the manager or something. It was so easy to give them orders and watch them follow. Just a little bit of authority in my voice and I had them all jumping. In the bathroom overly helpful ladies chatted with each other.

"What a lovely church."

"Oh, are you a member?"

"No."

"I am. Yes, our pastor is the best. How do you like our stained glass windows, aren't they beautiful?"

"This place is huge, isn't it?"

"Sure, it seats at least fifteen hundred people."

The "fifteen hundred people" sounded the loudest in my ear as I stood behind the door counting my new riches. Fifteen dollars a person times fifteen hundred people? Without paper I calculated twenty-two and a half thousand dollars. Seven thousand of them were in my bag. My heart started to beat fast. The small space in the toilet seemed to get even smaller. My scalp busted a sweat. A couple of deep breaths and I was OK. Hell, aren't the benefits to raise money for those who need it? Why did people with AIDS need the money when they were just going to die anyway? I rolled the money up and placed it in rubber bands that I usually use for my hair.

In my boldness, I walked to the front of the elevated stage. As soon as Souljah spotted me she leaned over and asked, "What's the matter? Are you OK?"

In the baby voice, the one I had watched Lauren use so effectively, I said, "My stomach's going crazy. I just threw up in the bathroom. My mouth tastes so nasty. I'm so sorry."

With a face full of concern, she responded, "You've done a lot to help out. I have a check for you for all the work you've done for me when Lauren wasn't around." Just then a young, suited man was at the podium introducing Souljah.

"Go to the house," she said. "I have some baking soda, Kaopectate, and Pepto-Bismol upstairs in the medicine cabinet. Whichever you prefer. Lay down for a while. You'll feel better soon." In an unusual move she planted a kiss on my cheek. As I looked up at her in surprise, she smiled and said, "In all the commotion I forgot to tell you that I spoke to Bilal this morning."

"Who?"

"Bilal. Midnight!" she repeated. "Your cousin."

Gagging for air and holding my stomach, I said, "Oh, Midnight."

"We'll talk," she shouted over the crowd's applause. She gestured goodbye with her hand, then stepped to the podium.

A track star couldn't have been faster than me. My legs were carrying my body swiftly toward the house that was a little more than a few blocks away.

I rang the bell. It took about five minutes for Lauren to answer the door. Even though I had my poker face on, my forehead was sweating too much for a winter afternoon.

"What's wrong?" she asked. "How did it go? It can't be over so soon?"

"No, it just got started."

"Then what are you doing here?"

"I got some serious stomach pains out of nowhere."

"Did you tell Souljah you were leaving the church?"

"Yeah we talked. She sent me home to get some medicine. She said I should get it from upstairs in the medicine cabinet."

"Do you want to see Doc?"

"No, I'm just going to take some of the Kaopectate and head back to the church to help out."

"Oh," she said suspiciously.

Upstairs I ran into Souljah's bedroom. I took the key off of her jewelry box which was right on top of her cluttered dresser. I opened the file cabinet and flipped feverishly through the files. I had to check each one for the first name Bilal. I didn't know his last name. Finally I got to "Bilal Odé." I grabbed the folder. I snatched the *New York Times* off of Souljah's bed and placed the folder and all of its contents in between the pages to conceal it.

In Lauren's room I grabbed my empty Nike luggage bag and placed inside it everything that absolutely could not be left here. I surveyed Lauren's dresser for my belongings, saw my beeper, and threw it in the Nike bag. Out of nervousness I checked my red Coach bag again. No problem. My money was still there. I grabbed a roll of twenties, peeled off two of them, and slid them into my red leather jacket pocket for easy access. I opened the small drawer on the bureau and collected my diamond necklace, my bracelet, and my earrings. I put them into my red bag. My lipstick, hair comb, brush, and, of course, my box cutter were the last to go in. I double-checked everything. With my hands full, I stepped lightly down the five flights of stairs; I was so excited to be leaving this place forever.

Panic racked my body when I hit the landing approaching the last flight of stairs. I was staring down at Lauren, who was standing at the front door, paying what appeared to be a delivery man. There must've been twenty medium-sized boxes covering the foyer floor.

"Are you going somewhere?" Lauren asked.

"Yeah, back to the church." Without saying anything Lauren's eyes dropped down to my Nike bag. "Oh yeah, I didn't get a chance to see my mother yesterday. She was pretty upset so I'm going to see her right after the benefit finishes."

"Oh," she said suspiciously. "Well, can you help me out with these boxes before you leave? They're Doc's medical supplies."

With my hands full I looked at all twenty or so boxes. I was hoping when Lauren saw in my face that I really didn't want to do it she would say never mind. But she didn't. I was leery about acting different than normal. So I agreed to help.

"Come on. Put all that stuff down. Four hands will be better than two." I kept checking the clock as we moved the boxes the short distance from the foyer through the big wooden doors into the office. The final destination was the supply closet. No matter what, I kept sweating. Even my palms were sweating now. My heart was pounding so fast I swore Lauren could hear it. I reassured myself I was being ridiculous.

As soon as we finished I picked up all my stuff. As casually as I could I said, "Alright Lauren. I'll see you either late tonight or tomorrow morning."

"Sure, thanks," she said. "See you."

Outside, the cabdriver asked, "Where are you headed to?"

For seconds, nothing would come out of my mouth. I did not know. "To a hotel," I finally said.

"What hotel?"

"The Marriott in New Jersey, right over the bridge and off the highway."

"In Jersey?" he repeated. "That's gonna cost you thirty-five dollars."

"No problem." But he still didn't move the cab. I reached into my pocket and gave him one of my twenties to get him to start driving. As I looked to my right I saw Lauren's face disappear as the window curtain being held by her hand dropped back into place. We pulled off.

When I opened the file tucked inside the *New York Times,* the first thing that fell out were old newspaper clippings. The first article I picked up had a picture of my father and our house in Long Island. The second paragraph mentioned me by name as well as my mother. "Fucking bitch Souljah," I mumbled. She knew who I was all along. But the fact of the matter is I got the last laugh. She would never be able to prove I took that money. She had too many people collecting it and no system to account for who had what. As I checked further into the file, there were letters in opened envelopes and loose papers. Some letters were from Midnight to Souljah. The papers were copies of letters from Souljah to Midnight. There would be no more secrets. I was going to look through everything and read every word. Most importantly, I would soon discover, I hoped, where Midnight lays his head at night.

"We need a major credit card to secure your registration, ma'am," the lady at the desk said.

"You don't take cash?"

"Yes, if you would like to pay cash that will be fine. It'll be two hundred dollars for the room and a twenty-dollar refundable deposit for the phone."

Happy to shut the snotty receptionist up, I unzipped my Coach bag and reached in for my roll of twenties. Instead, I pulled out two bottles of Wet'n'Wild lip gloss and a half-eaten chocolate chip cookie. I stood staring at my own hand as if I had six fingers. The picture frame froze. Everything in front of my eyes stuck in the same motionless position. Lauren, described by her sister as "the trickster," had switched her red leather Coach bag with mine.

As I squatted down to check the bag, not because I had hopes that it was mine, but out of disbelief, I flipped it over and emptied its contents onto the hotel carpet. There was nothing of value in the bag. The inside stunk from the odor of two bottles of rubbing alcohol she had in there. She must of thrown these in at the last moment so I wouldn't notice the weight change. As every muscle in my body collapsed from the sheer stress of the situation, my butt hit the floor. The voice of the hotel woman was flying over the counter and dropping down onto my ears.

"Excuse me miss, do you want the room?"

"I'll be back," I called to her. I used my hands to sweep all the junk, except the crumbs, back into the bag. I walked away in slow motion, lifting my Nike bag off the bellhop's trolley.

16

I found myself seated in the hotel bar. I didn't have no thoughts 'cause my brain was shut down or frozen or something. I didn't even know what city I was in. I was able to hold off the waiter who at first was pressuring me to buy a drink. I told him I was waiting for my boyfriend who had a room in the hotel but was running late. After one hour, that excuse was exhausted so I gathered my bags and walked out the front door of the hotel.

The hotel was situated right off the highway. I could hear the cars passing behind the wooded area that separated the hotel from everything else. As I stepped out into the street I looked to my left and saw nothing but trees. About a half-mile up there was a traffic light. Complete silence. To my right there were more woods, no stores, pay phones, no sign that people even lived there.

As the winter chill cut through my light red leather jacket I clapped my hands together to keep them from stiffening. When you have someplace to live you don't think about the weather too much. Facing the reality that I had nowhere to go I realized that it was me versus nature tonight. As I thought of every person I had ever known, my list of who could help me out added up to almost nothing. I had a brainstorm and ran back inside the hotel. I sat in the telephone booth and tried desperately to remember Sterling's phone number. *Calm down, don't panic,* I told myself. *You know what Daddy says.* But it was useless.

When I relaxed enough to recall the number, I dialed it and got the stinking operator's voice. "This number has been changed to a nonpublished number." In a rage I kicked the folding telephone booth door and injured my own toe.

In the hotel bathroom I removed my red skirt, white shirt, and stockings. Pulling my jeans, Polo shirt, and Clarks out of the Nike bag, I got dressed to be more comfortable for the unknown. Leaning against the mirror I realized that not only was my diamond jewelry that

Daddy gave me and all my money gone, but so was my box cutter. I felt naked without a weapon. I was taught that a girl should always have a razor, switchblade, box cutter, needle, mace, or a burner for her defense. Remembering a Brooklyn specialty, I pulled out a pair of socks from my Nike bag and headed out the door.

Across the street where the woods lined the outside of the highway, I filled my extra pair of socks with big, sharp rocks. Squatting down, digging in the dirt separating the rocks, the voice in my head said, *This is it*. Packing the socks in my pocketbook I headed back to the hotel bar. There was no plan. Everything was spontaneous. I didn't know what to do now, but I would know when the time was right.

In all the movies I had ever seen, the bartender is always the one with all the information. So I ordered a ginger ale to purchase the right to sit on the bar stool and talk to him.

"Do you live here?" I asked him.

"Sure do."

"It seems like a small place, I'm from the city."

"It's a great town, Teaneck. We're part of Bergen County, the third richest county in the country."

"Is that right?" I acted casual, unimpressed.

"We've got great shopping malls just a short way down the highway. That's where all the restaurants are, too. You like dancing? There's a few clubs out here, but mostly people party at the bar scenes."

"Do you have homeless people?" I asked him.

"What?" he responded, a little puzzled.

"Ordinary question for a New Yorker," I smiled.

"Our homeless live better than I do, and I work! When you live in a town where people have money there's a lot of charity. Practically any church could point ya in the right direction. Hey! You're the most glamorous homeless person I ever saw," the baby-faced white boy said.

We laughed. He was just passing the time, but I was taking in everything that surrounded me. Every customer was important. I watched the opening and closing of the cash register, and the woman playing the jukebox. There was an elderly woman who entered the bar forty-five minutes later. She caught my interest. She was wearing a Versace blouse, ugly, but expensive earrings, and some fine slacks. As she sat down at the bar and ordered a Bloody Mary she fumbled with her wallet and accidentally dropped some loose twenty-dollar bills on the bar top. When she gathered them up to put them back inside, I saw about seven different credit cards. Her hands kept moving like she had that shaking disease. It only took seconds to catch the pile of diamonds on her wedding finger. The slim driving shoes by Gucci with the leather patch at the heel were being wasted on her old feet. I tried to guess what she had in the Nordstrom's shopping bag underneath the tissue paper.

"I guess your boyfriend's a real jerk," the waiter said to me. "It's either that, or he's some kind of NBA player. You know they stay here sometimes. What kind of guy other than a superstar could leave a beautiful girl like you in the bar alone?"

"Alright, alright, don't tell everyone," I teased him, gathering my stuff and waving goodbye.

It was only twenty minutes later that the old lady came out into the parking lot. When she saw me emerge from behind the side wall she was startled and placed her wrinkled hand over her heart.

"I'm sorry," I said in my most pleasant voice. "It's just me, from the bar."

"Oh not to worry," she chuckled nervously. As she clutched her bag, zigzagging in between this car and that car, I walked behind her. She was chatting about the cold weather and how she always misplaces her car when she parks.

"I do that, too," I told her.

"But a young girl like you shouldn't have a memory problem."

When she reached the Jaguar parked right beside the shrubbery, I laughed.

"What a coincidence, that's my car right beside yours." We both turned our back to one another. Me to get my keys out, her to place the keys which were already in her hand, in the lock. In a split second she didn't know what hit her. It was my stone-filled sock up against her head. She withered like a flower and fell to the ground. I had two hundred in cash, one credit card—the American Express gold card—two diamond rings, and those Gucci shoes. I was on my way. Lucky for me I was smart enough to leave her car and that Nordstrom bag right there. I didn't run or nothing. I just walked up the pathway alongside the woods. The bartender had told me how to get to the bus.

On the highway route, I discharged at the Holiday Inn. It was sixty dollars for the night, which was more reasonable for me at this time. After a long, hot shower I sat on the bed with the pillows behind me. For some reason I couldn't settle. I could not sleep. I pulled out those letters. I would read them all. I would find out Midnight's address. Maybe I would go wherever he was. He was the only link to my past. The only free person I could trust right now.

May 1993

Dear Bilal,

When I first saw you in the library at Columbia University I assumed you were a student. I'm sure you didn't notice me. There were many reasons why I noticed you. One, you were reading Hadith. Secondly, you just had a powerful presence. Now this may sound odd but I watch everything and everybody very closely. It's my way of learning to understand life and people. Most of the brothers at the Columbia campus have no presence at all. In fact, it's as if they made a conscious effort to reduce themselves so no one would find them offensive, too black or too strong. Even the brothers who are not introverted are not like men. They are like children or caricatures. They play games they should have left behind many years ago, and find it extremely difficult to focus on anything that is not of a required academic nature. So there you were, mature, black, and yes, beautiful.

I didn't disturb you because you seemed perfect as you were, uninterrupted. I knew if I did not stop to say what's up or to introduce myself, I might not ever see you again. After all, I am not a Columbia student and am only on the campus once a week. But still, I let it go.

After not seeing you for a couple of weeks, I was surprised to notice you heading toward me with Phil, the Columbia student and volunteer in the children's program where I teach. When finally he introduced us, it seemed that we barely said peace to one another, yet we looked into each other's eyes, forgetting to drop hands from our initial shake.

I'd be lying if I said I was surprised when Phil asked me if he could pass you my phone number. Before giving it to him I asked him your age. He said you were twenty-two. He volunteered that you were not a student, just a friend of his from Brooklyn. When I asked him what you do he fumbled around for a few seconds, then said that you were a mechanic.

If I came off cool when you called, my voice hid my real feelings. Inside I felt everything shift. On a usual day I am so unimpressed with everything and everybody. It seems every word shared between a man and a woman has already been said and nothing could be done that I didn't already see. And nobody means what they say anyway. So it didn't really matter. Yet as we talked, I felt my breathing intensify, a sign that I'm still alive and capable of feeling.

I felt you watching as I taught my students on the day we agreed to go out after class and you arrived early. At the cafe, after debating with you about whether there is hope for a new uprising among today's youth, the thing that stood out most in my mind were your hands. On one side they were dark and strong, long and thick. On the other side they were soft with deep colored lines. Your nails were clean, I'd even go so far as to say they were manicured as I noticed their dull shine.

When I asked you one on one what you do for a living, you responded with the same silence that Phil had. Seconds later you said you were a businessman. When I pressed, you said you owned a car service in Brooklyn. It probably was the way that you walked, like you owned all of Manhattan, or the way that you talk in a masculine slow yet steady way, or maybe it's the way you place your hand in the middle of my back as I'm walking through a door that you're holding. So I figured an auto mechanic and a businessman with a car service were not so far apart. Besides, you even gave me your business card.

Because we are both busy, I treasured the time we had after class once a week. I held onto things I wanted to discuss in politics concerning the progress of our people. I knew you would always introduce an interesting angle or unexplored response. Besides every now and then I get sick of staring into the blank faces of students who could care less about world events, politics, or even people they are not directly related to.

So you got inside of me, not physically, but in more intimate ways. You got inside my mind, my thoughts, my spirit. When a girlfriend of one of the sisters on campus said your name was Midnight, I told her she must be thinking and talking about the wrong guy. But she described you so well, knew the car you drive, and said she heard you were involved in "questionable activities."

Sitting in my bedroom one night, I pulled out your business card. It listed the name of your company, B-K Car Service. But nowhere on the card did it say your name, Bilal Jones. The phone number on the card was the same as your home number. When I called information neither your name or the name of your car service was listed. I confess that I went to the address on your business card. There was no car service. It was a mailbox place. So here I am, reviewing everything in my mind, knowing in my subconscious that a man with such a sensual level of confidence about everything, a trait which has been erased from so many black men, had to have some kind of tragic irony to him.

I flipped through the scenes of our two and a half month emerging friendship. Despite my sweet addiction I have decided to end it. I'm writing to you because it's easy for me this way. I cannot be deceived or seduced by the passion and strength of your voice. I cannot be persuaded by the power of your reasoning. I will not call you. I ask that you don't call me either. As this class ends this week, you will not see me anymore. I see no reason to know you, to continue if you are involved in what I suspect. In fact, it makes you so typical and undesirable to me.

SS

May 1993

Sister Souljah,

All a man has is his business. Without it he has nothing. Women are confused. The same things you love are the same things you hate. Have you ever seen an aggressive, confident man with broke pockets and no business? If you did you would not remember him. If you remembered him you would not respect him. You could have just bounced and not said nothing, no goodbyes. You said something, so what we have between us must not really be over. If I don't see you now, I'll see you later. But I will see you.

Bilal

July 1993

Peace Souljah,

You are always on my mind. Even when I try to push you out, you're on my radio or on somebody's television. So you're holding out on me. I'm surprised, I just knew I would hear from you. I even bet myself it would be a week to ten days after I dropped you a line, but nothing since. So the strong girl thing isn't an illusion.

You were right about one thing. Everything being said by the women I date has already been said. Everything being done, I already did. As you put it one time when we was chillin', "What's the sense in fucking an empty-headed girl? It's like fucking a hole in the wall." I know I bugged you when you said it. I didn't even consider it seriously. But now that it's been brought

*to my attention, I find myself tripping over the words we shared, the thoughts
we exchanged and your pretty smile. I miss you. Give a man a break.*

Missing You,
Bilal

September 1993

Peace,

*I reread your letter. You said you like to watch people, that's how you
get your understanding of life. Well I live in these streets. That's how I get
my understanding of life. The hard way. The real way. A man's way. I
heard you talking about black unity the other night on the radio. Look
Souljah, I dig you, but you're fooling yourself. Niggas ain't never going to
be unified. You put all your time into organizing niggas yet you lock out
the nigga who's real with you, me.*

*What do you want from me? Can I live? Are you better than the niggas
you supposed to be helping? You put yourself in a position to judge. Only
God can do that. I want to see you. I know your Columbia classes start up
again next week. I'm coming to check you.*

Peace,
Midnight

September 1993

Dear Bilal,

*It's funny how the same thing a man loves, is the same thing that he
hates. What makes me stand out as a woman is that I have nonnegotiable
principles, strength, and faith in my people. From the time that we shared
you seemed to love that, admire it, even. Now you hate it because my ways
have isolated you. The truth is, you've isolated yourself.*

*I move on a vibe, a combination of what I see, think, learn, and feel.
If I was to move strictly on feeling I'd get myself into a whole lot of trouble.
I already did that when I was eighteen, nineteen, and twenty. Now I'm
twenty-four. I've learned a lot 'cause that's what we're all supposed to do.
Only a complete asshole would keep repeating the same old mistakes and*

blaming it on something else. Hell, we have all had it hard. It may not seem
like it, but I grew up in the projects. I lived in poverty. I didn't have no
father in my house. I'm not asking for sympathy. Every black face has a story,
many times a gruesome story. But we have to get over it no matter how bad
it might be. We have to re-create our families and build our communities
again. It may seem hopeless. Many times I get depressed but I move on
because I have to. God requires this from me.

I do know something. Where there are drugs, there can be no love. There
can be no family. Drugs rob every person, man, woman, and child of their
beauty. Drugs turn people into animals who can only respond to instincts.
Drugs are so powerful they eradicate the God in both the taker and the giver.

I have worked with prisoners incarcerated in New York, New Jersey,
and North Carolina. Hundreds, thousands, and millions of drug-related
convictions. The contradiction, maybe I'll find out after death, is that
behind those walls seem to be the majority of black men, and increasingly
women. The tall, the dark, the beautiful. But how do we get men and
women before they are hunted like foxes and trapped like rats and treated
like ants to understand the concept of unity, working, building, living
together? It seems the Black National Anthem is If it's broke, don't fix it.

What do I want from you? The best that you have to offer instead of the
least and the easy. Do I think I'm better than you? No. I know in many ways
you're brilliant. That was my first real attraction, the power of your mind. But
you lack the understanding of life that every man should have. I can assume
this because you have not denied being involved with drugs. Therefore . . . In
life we make choices, conscious decisions to move left or right. We reap the
rewards and/or disasters of the choices we make. I do feel you. I feel you all the
time. However, I won't see you. Don't bother to check me.

SS

September 1993

Yeah,

You want it raw dog, here it is. I tried to hold back because of my
respect for you. You won't see me so at this point I have nothing to lose. Men
and women will never think the same. They live different lives, separate
realities. Women want love, peace, unity, and shit like that. Men are tribal.
I ain't tryna save the world. I'm just tryna get my piece for my crew, that's all.

That's all it's about and that's the most you can ask for. What you know about that?

You want to know who I am and what I'm about and how I'm living? You want the truth? My name is Bilal Odé. My mother and father and I were born in the Sudan. They raised me to understand love, honor, respect, loyalty, and family. Then my father was killed by tribalism in a war for what men want, power, control, land. Just so you be clear, my father was killed by black men, African men. Me and my pregnant mother came to this country when I was 7. From the minute I arrived I had to fight. Niggas disrespecting my name, disrespecting my accent, disrespecting my clothes. While holding my ground I got rid of my accent, my clothes, and even my name. I found out quick what brought respect and I schemed to get it. In the hood I been fucked up by black cops and white cops. Why? For no reason. Except the cops is a tribe and they fighting for a piece of the action as well. I got into my body, working out, judo, tai kwon do, all of that. I learned everything I needed to know about burners, all kinds.

One afternoon I'm walking down the staircase to get my little sister from the baby-sitter's house. I was late. The elevator was broke as usual. Now this big nigga around my way named Lance, a dude three times my size who had banged me up more than a couple of times, had my eight-year-old sister pinned against the wall with her panties down and his dick in his hands. I'm wondering what this motherfucker is doing 'cause she ain't got titties, curves, nothing yet. When I called out his name he turned around and charged at me. He had the same face on that he did the last time he almost broke my jaw. So I shot him, right between the eyes.

At fourteen years old, I was convicted of manslaughter and incarcerated. I didn't read about it. I didn't go to jail to give a speech. I was a prisoner.

The whole time that this was going on, my mother was praying, crying, being emotional, and going back and forth to work, ten hours a day. You know what she wanted? The same thing you wanted, peace, unity, happiness. But that's not what was happening on the streets.

Inside I was stomping with the big dogs, imprisoned with grown men due to "prison overcrowding." What was going down? Tribalism, war over anything, the toilet, the phone, cigarettes, space to breathe. Niggas vs. niggas. Niggas vs. Ricans. Decepticons vs. Bloods. Niggas vs. Aryans, The Latin Kings, whatever. Everybody had a crew. My moms came more than once a week, kept my commissary stacked. Anything I asked for she brought it, sneakers, gear, whatever. All she did was work and save. Point-blank she would have done anything for me.

It was 7 P.M. when they came for me. Six big grown ass men (some of those dark, beautiful motherfuckers you wrote about). I fought like a warrior, but they still left my ass ripped open, twenty stitches to repair. For six months, in addition to the pain of shitting, I'm wondering does this mean I'm a homosexual? My cellmate said "Don't worry about it, it's just an initiation, that's what they crew do. You fought back, you held it down. Now they'll look at you like a man." Easy for him to say, he was getting out in one more year. I did five and a half years.

On my second year locked down, my mother disappeared. No more letters, no more visits, no more commissary. I called home but never got an answer. Soon the number was disconnected. After hassling one of the c.o.'s who knew I was a good kid who got caught out there and killed a nigga the neighbors and even the cops wanted dead, he revealed the truth to me. My mother was arrested. In a state of panic I cried like a bitch and laughed like a madman 'cause I knew my mother, a devout Moslem, the type who kept her head wrapped, walked with a prayer cloth and even stopped to pray at work, would never have violated any law. Upon further investigation I found out her conviction was for transporting drugs. No matter what kind of rumors I heard about the incident I refused to believe them.

Four years later when I was released, the lady next door to our old apartment told me my mother was out of prison and in the hospital. I went straight to her.

"Son," she told me, "I'm sorry. An inmate from your prison told me if I didn't bring him some drugs to the prison on my next visit to see you they were gonna hurt you again. They said when you come home I would no longer have a son, I'd have a daughter. I didn't know what else to do. They told me if I told anyone I'd be attending your funeral. I just needed to see your face before I die. Don't cry for me son. Allah has a place for me. I cannot live here, these are not my people." My mother died trying to tell me about my sister. As she lost her life, the words just wouldn't come out. It took me four weeks to find my sister. She had been adopted by a white family. The agency told me I could not see her. I could not think about getting her back until she's eighteen. Then only if she wants to come to me.

My mother left a will. In her six years of work in the U.S., combined with the inheritance left by my father, she had managed to save a good piece of money. Even from prison she was able to keep up her life insurance payments somehow. I couldn't collect any money according to her will until my sister turned eighteen. It was placed in a trust under my sister Efe's name.

After my release I searched for work for six months. The one line they gave me on every job application to explain—"Have you ever been convicted of a felony? If so, please explain"—didn't work out. How do you explain murder? It just runs people and employers away.

The man who took me in when I was jobless and homeless has been like a father to me. For that he has my eternal loyalty. In my youth I was taught that if someone saves your life, you owe them your life.

With steady work, good money in my pocket, a roof over my head, and all the things a man needs to be more than invisible in this world, I stand firm on my two feet. You cannot teach me to be a man. You may know a lot, but you know nothing about that.

I'm drawn to you Souljah. I hope you know how to take this. You remind me of my mother. There is something so pure about you, so beautiful. I respect your mind, your body, the whole package. If I could possess you I know my mother would smile down on me. But could you think about me and you instead of the whole world? Could you think about me?

Bilal Odé

October 1993

Midnight,

I'm sorry about your momma. During the months that we spent together I noticed how sometimes you would be so alive and talkative. Then suddenly you'd fall into a strange silence. I figured there was a very personal story behind that silence. In time I told myself you might confide in me.

It just so happens that time is not on your side. It seems you want me to care about your feelings and your family. Yet and still, in your line of work you don't care about anyone's feelings or family. What makes your momma so important when you would sell crack to someone else's momma?

If I dared to love you, my momma, my family, my life would be in jeopardy. It is only a matter of time before you will pay for your wrongdoings. To every action there is a reaction. When it comes back to you, the depth of your tragedy will be even greater than the wrongs you perpetrated. How do I know? It is the law of nature. It applies to every human being. Because I love myself, my family, and have worked very hard to do the right thing in my life, I don't want to be standing next to you when the walls come tumbling down. And they will tumble.

It's ironic that a young male who had so much more than some young blacks in America, a father, a country, a culture, would end up in the same low-life business that killed his mother, with the same attitude that murdered his father. So you say it's about your survival huh? If that were true, you would of quit after you accumulated some loot. Maybe started a little legit business, rescued your sister. But no. The money is in your blood. The money is your God. It's all about the Benjamins. So call it what it is. In life people make choices. We pay for every little choice we make. You traded everyone else's life for yours. I traded my life for everyone else's. We don't belong together.

Drugs is a government game, Bilal. A way to rob us of our best black men, our army. Everyone who plays the game loses. Then they get you right back where we started, in slavery! Then they get to say "This time you did it to yourself." I won't play that game.

SS

February 1994

Souljah,

It's been a long time. Every man moves at his own pace. I'm free to call you now, on your terms. Now there is no reason you shouldn't accept my calls.

Midnight

The Holiday Inn maid woke me up. It was not her knocking at the door. It was her knocking and me not hearing her. Then she used her key to let herself in. My body was stretched across the bed, with envelopes and papers everywhere. When my eyes opened they attempted to adjust. Before I could get a clear reading on everything she asked in a Chinese accent, "You checky out now or stay one more night?"

"Damn, what time is it?"

"Twelve. Check-out time," she used as few words as possible. I got up, walked to the dresser, and picked up the DO NOT DISTURB sign. Placing it on the outside knob, I glanced over at her. Without speaking she got my point: Get the fuck out.

Right now the daylight was my friend. I needed to use every

minute constructively. Not wanting to sleep in the same place twice, I showered, packed my stuff up and bounced.

The bus system was easy. It stopped right in front of the Holiday Inn. It was weird riding a bus that had stops on the freeway but it was also convenient. The mall was only a four-mile ride.

Seated in the food court I put my plan together piece by piece like a puzzle. After arranging all the letters by dates, I realized the most recent one Midnight mailed to Souljah was postmarked from Silver Spring, Maryland. All the other letters he sent her were mailed from either Brooklyn or Manhattan.

After purchasing a phone card, I asked the operator how I could call information in Silver Spring. "Can I have the number for Bilal Odé," I asked.

"How are you spelling that? We have no such listing, ma'am. Are you sure about the spelling?" I slammed the phone down.

Passing the American Airlines ticket counter located right inside the mall, I asked the woman behind the table the price for a ticket to Silver Spring, Maryland.

"The closest airport to Silver Spring is Baltimore. When would you like to fly, ma'am?" The question was so simple, yet so crazy. I had never flown anywhere in my life.

"Now," I blurted out. The airline lady laughed.

"You would be leaving out of Newark Airport I presume?"

"How far is that from here?"

"You can take public transportation from this mall to the airport. It should take about an hour, calculating the stops and all. The earliest flight I could get you on would be leaving today at 5:15 P.M., arriving in Baltimore, Maryland, at 7 P.M. this evening. Is this round trip?" she asked.

"No, one way."

"With one day's notice, one way will be three hundred twenty dollars and ninety-seven cents, tax included."

"I'll be back," I mumbled.

I figured the bus had to be cheaper. All I had was a hundred thirty dollars and change. I would also need money once I arrived. The bottom line is I would need much more money, regardless. I would need money to stay and money to go. If I traveled to Maryland it would probably take me a few days to track Midnight down. From the sound of Silver Spring, it was a small town. I'd check the obvious places that no one could avoid; the supermarket, the barber, the mall. I'd even go to the post office, the party spots, and ask around. I was sure Midnight had an apartment by now. Some place that was laced with all the finer things in life.

He would allow me to stay there with him. I had no doubt in my mind about that. Circumstances were different now. When he left I had places to stay or so he believed. Now I had no one to turn to but him. Santiaga needed him. Like Midnight said in his letters, "A man has his loyalty."

After a short shuttle bus ride, I arrived at the Greyhound ticket counter. I was given a schedule for travel to Maryland. The woman quoted a price of sixty-five dollars one way, which was only eight dollars cheaper than the round-trip bus ticket. Don't ask me to figure it out. Next to the Greyhound counter was a bus line called Peter Pan. A little Mexican guy handing out coupons called my attention to the place. "Twenty-five dollars round trip," the old lady with the I-smoked-too-many-cigarettes deep voice stated.

"I'll take it," I responded with no hesitation.

"Let me tell you now, sweetie, this ticket is a special rate. It's non-refundable."

"I said I'll take it."

I didn't know what Maryland had in store for me. I did know that in exactly one hour, I'd be out of town. I cut across to the deli and grabbed a seltzer and ordered a sandwich for the road trip. The woman said it was almost a five-hour ride with the stops included. At the magazine stand I picked up one fashion magazine, *Cosmopolitan,* and a pack of butterscotch Life Savers. I don't know whether my stomach was rumbling from hunger or from the excitement of knowing I was gonna see Midnight.

I was falling in love all over again after reading Midnight's letters. He was right to make it clear that a man has to make his own choices, handle his business and whatnot. She was trying to take a good man and turn him into a broke punk, some type of poetic philosopher who's of no use to anyone. I'm sure that by the time he got his finger on the pulse of what was going down in Maryland, he had set up his operation and was watching it grow. I approximated about almost a year had been gone. I bet his connections were ripe.

The bus rolled in fifteen minutes early. I grabbed all my stuff to board. The driver swung open the doors. As I lifted my foot to get on the driver said, "We're not leaving until the scheduled departure time." Aggravated, I stood outside in the cold wind rather than drag all my stuff back into the heated station.

The noise was little. Then it got a little bit bigger. I looked left, then right. No one else was close by so it had to be me. Unzipping my Nike bag I pushed clothes every which way. Hidden on the inside of a pair of my lingerie was a beeper. Oh shit. Oh shit! It's Bullet. Damn, what does he want? With five minutes left to boarding time I debated. Call him now? Call him later? I gathered my bags and rushed into the station only to find that all three pay phones were occupied. Peeping a businessman with a cheap suit holding a cell phone I rushed over to him. "Excuse me, mister. Can I use your phone? It's an emergency." He was reluctant but I gave him the little girl help-me look, nervously licking my lips. Still no answer from him so I repeated myself. "Please, sir. That's my bus right there. It leaves in five minutes. I just need to make one call." He handed the cell phone to me. My eyes bounded from the beeper to the phone buttons punching out the phone number. I pressed SEND and took a long deep breath. When Bullet got on the line I had to be cool, not pressed.

"What's up, baby?" I asked softly, immediately noting the aggravation in the businessman's face.

"Winter. Happy Birthday, girl. You official now?" Bullet was hyper and happy.

Oh shit, I forgot it was my birthday. That's a first. "Thanks," I said, still playing it cool.

"I'm coming to get you. Where you at?"

"I'm in Jersey."

"What you doing all the way over there?" he asked.

"I just came out here to do a little shopping. You know how I do it."

"Well, get something sexy. Last year this time it was all about you driving me. This year your man got everything under control. We done elevated. What you know about a birthday in Key West."

The owner of the cell phone said, "Miss, I need my phone back."

"Who that? Who the fuck is that? I know you ain't with no nigga. Oh, a nigga taking you shopping. That ain't nothing. Whatever he got I could double it. Shit, I could triple it. I'm caked up, Winter. Stop fucking with those small-timers. Who is that?"

"He ain't nobody," I said coolly.

"You damn right he ain't nobody. Tell that nigga to bounce. Tell him." Bullet was all the way gone with anger so I decided to play him. The phone owner's face grew red with anger as well.

"Bounce, nigga," I said to the white man.

"What?" He questioned me with his veins popping out of his neck. "Give me my phone." The owner grabbed for his cell phone.

Jumping back from his reach I told Bullet, "I told him to bounce. Did you hear me?"

"Good," Bullet said. But the man was demanding his phone back. "Oh, what? Is he beefing? Is the nigga beefing? Tell that nigga he better be gone by the time I get there or he's a dead man."

"If you know what's good for you, you'll bounce before my man gets here," I told the white guy.

The confused phone owner warned me, "I'm gonna get security. I'm gonna call the police."

"Pick me up at Nordstrom on Route 4 in Jersey, right over the GW Bridge. I'll be on the northside entrance."

"Don't worry, baby, I'm on the way."

"Bullet, one more thing. Where's Key West?"

"That's Florida baby. Don't worry about it."

I followed quickly behind the irate man. I handed him his phone before he could alert the authorities, who were nowhere to be found in this little bus station. Thanks was all I said to the man, with a polite half-smile.

Quickly I jetted out of the bus station. I jumped on the mall shuttle, jumped out at Victoria's Secret and dropped my last yard on some sexy lingerie. I jetted to the north entrance of Nordstrom and waited.

Standing with only one hundred dollars' worth of Victoria's Secret goodies, my Nike bag, and the red leather Coach bag, my mouth hung open. Then I checked myself as Bullet rolled around in a cream-colored Lexus coupe. All my juices everywhere in my body leaked out with excitement.

It took great concentration for me not to just jump out of my skin and go buck, dance naked on the hood of the car or something. The warmth in the car made the winter cold seem like a crude prank. I checked out every inch of the interior. Yet I knew I had to chill like I ride in one of these whips every day. My father had a car like this. But this was the new model. As my ass fit into the soft grooves of the leather seat, Bullet leaned over two inches from my face. "Where that nigga at?"

"He's been gone," I told him, going right along with it. Bullet threw the car into reverse and raced backward to the corner of the building. He peered out the tinted windows down the sidewalk lining Nordstrom. Then he shifted into drive and raced to the opposite corner, checking down the street. My imaginary lover was nowhere to be found.

"You know you mine's now," he said, like I was a trophy or an expensive piece of jewelry. His lips were wet, teeth white, and haircut fresh like his barber trimmed it on the drive over here. It had been a year since I took a real good look at him. I don't know if it was his Armani leather coat or if his body was even more buffed than when I saw him last. This nigga Bullet thought he had to fight to make me his girl. I'd let him believe it, too. Little did he know, I was his when he pulled the whip around the bend.

Bullet made me throw my Nike bag and all of its contents in the garbage. He said he didn't want me wearing nothing no other nigga bought. He could take care of his girl with no problem. I didn't have no arguments. After a twenty-five minute drive, we parked the coupe in the airport parking lot and boarded American Airlines. We sat in the first-class section with the executives. Sipping champagne and listening to hits on his CD Walkman, we felt good all the way to Key West.

17

Sunshine, heat, and palm trees, a dramatic departure from my life twelve hours ago. To say I was gassed would not be enough. It wasn't so much the scenery, although I seen a hundred types of trees I never seen before! It was the balls of the whole thing. This is the type of life I saw myself having, leaving town with no permission, warning, or limitations. This whole matter was what made Bullet so damn sexy to me at that moment. He was making the rules, maybe even breaking the rules. He was the shot-caller. A man who can only react to life could never have me. A man with excuses about why he couldn't make anything happen his way could only win pity, but never respect.

The airport limo delivered us to our Key West, Florida, villa. The beach was a short walk away. The most noticeable thing about the villa was that everything inside was white and clean. No dingy color, not eggshell, not cream-colored, but a crisp white, seemingly freshly painted place with ceramic tiled floors. We only explored the villa once over for about ten minutes. Next thing I know a driver was taking us shopping.

Now Bullet was obviously the one with the money. But he didn't push hard. He asked me where I wanted to shop. He walked patiently behind me as I led the way through the most fashionable departments. When I tried things on, he sat inside the dressing room despite the store attendant's objections and commented on every piece of clothing I modeled. The crazy thing is he never had nothing bad to say about anything I selected.

"That's it right there."

"That's the bomb, baby."

"You're wearing that dress."

"Look at those sweet thighs."

"Ten perfect toes—now when have anybody seen that before."

So I stretched things a little, was aware of how I stood, was stylish about undressing and did seductive things to keep him in the palm of my hand where he appeared to be.

We ate dinner in a little Cuban restaurant. It wasn't an expensive-looking place. In fact, it was more like a huge kitchen in someone's house. It didn't have a vibe like a business. But the food was mad good. I was surrounded by young Cuban waiters who served me hand and foot. More than two of them waiters was giving Bullet props for having a fine woman. "La Morena," they called me.

One of the guys started talking Cuban to me, or Spanish, or whatever it was. He apologized when he realized I couldn't speak it and explained to Bullet that I looked Cuban because of my skin, dark eyes and hair. Unlike the jealous rage I expected to see in Bullet, he smiled, pretty teeth all exposed, like the proud holder of a fifty-million-dollar Lotto ticket. Now, I don't know what they put in that food besides a half a pound of garlic, but they must of done some kind of voodoo on me 'cause it made me all warm inside and real horny. Even my chest was warm and my titties felt bigger than normal and extra sensitive. When the feeling of my own titties rubbing against the cloth of my own shirt turned me on I knew it was time to get back to the villa.

We didn't have to say much. We understood each other. After bags were put away he handed me a glass of champagne. We got nice. As the CD player pumped R. Kelley, Bullet began to tongue me slow and sensuously. I ain't no punk so I tongued him back, sucking his lips and chin. He kissed me with his eyes open and kept the lights on the way that I prefer it. He unfastened my hair tie and my hair fell down. He put his hands all through my hair like he was tossing a salad.

"This is all you," he commented, 'cause I didn't have no weave. The way he was all up in my head, if my hair would have been fake his fingers would've been all jammed in the strings, glue, or whatever. As he licked my collarbone, both hands exploring my shoulders and breasts, he said in a low sexual voice, "You have the softest skin I ever touched." It was live to see my roughneck turn into a house cat.

Easing me out of my blouse and unstrapping my bra, he laid my back on the cold ceramic tile and my nipples puffed up and out. Undressing me totally, the cold floor sent a sensation all over my body. "Your pussy smells good," he said as he buried his face in it and allowed two butterscotch Life Savers he had gotten from me to go inside of me while his tongue searched for them and sucked them out. By the time he found and got control of the melted candy I had come twice. I couldn't control my shouting. Getting eaten out always made me crazy. My moaning had him harder than U.S. Steel so I wrestled him over and mounted him. I tried to ride him like a prize jockey but he wanted to dominate. Seconds later I was butt up, facedown and we doggy-styled until my whole butt was filled with warm semen. In the air-conditioned villa we sweated. Our black bodies were pressed against the white tile.

As the CD played itself over again I thought about how it couldn't be any better than this. A man, a solid man, with loot and a luscious big dick, a champion pussy-eater and he was dedicated to my desire. I waited for someone to wake me up. But no one ever did.

In the morning we went straight to the beach. My new bikini was killing every onlooker. However, there was only a sprinkle of people out this early. Bullet was tryna teach me how to swim in the warm, clear ocean water. As I fumbled he patiently corrected me. He tried to teach me to do the easy stuff first, like what he called the doggy paddle. He even attempted to show me how to float on my back. As my body would tense up, it would sink to the bottom. He would pull me up. Holding my wet body against his chest, we were face-to-face as he said, "You see, the reason why you can't float is because you're not relaxed in the water. The reason why you're not relaxed is because you don't trust me. You gotta trust me. I'm not gonna let you down. I would never hurt you." He laid me back down and talked me into a state of relaxation. After an hour or so I could float and dog paddle, but still I was no swimmer.

"Don't worry, Sexy, you'll get the hang of it after a while. I'll teach you all the tricks. You won't be able to say I didn't teach you something your father didn't already teach you."

Now he might as well have hit me in the head with a brick. My body tensed up. Trying to run out of the water I felt as though my body was going in slow motion. He caught me on the sand a couple of feet from the water.

"Winter, yo, yo. Winter, what's up? What's the matter? Why you flipping?"

My anger took a jump on me and my mouth just started going.

"Midnight told me you was my father's enemy. That makes you my enemy. Don't even fucking mention my father. You keep his name out of your mouth." My chest was heaving in and out. My titties were easing out of my bikini top against my permission.

"I thought you understood business, Winter. I ain't got nothing against your father. I got mad respect for your pops. Your pops is my motherfucking hero. I'm tryna be part of the world he built."

"I know you was a part of the takeover. You think I'm stupid? I know what happened."

"How you know what happened when you wasn't even there? I didn't see you for months. I was there. Hell your pops wasn't even there half the time I was in the thick of it from the beginning to the end. A true soldier. What happened was business. It was bigger than your pops. If your pops wasn't who he is, it still would of happened. That's how big it was. Winter, I want you and me to have an understanding. I got mad love for you. You know how much money a nigga is losing just being out here with you for three days? Mad money! Now I got cats moving shit for me but everybody know the money ain't gon' be all the way straight unless you there, right on top of it watching it. I brought you out here 'cause I know you a classy woman, top-of-the-line. I know you is used to the best 'cause I seen how Santiaga treated you. I knew I couldn't just throw you a pair of 10-karat gold earrings or take you up to the played-out Poconos. I had to let you see that I know you're special. This ain't about ass. I can get plenty of ass. I got bitches lined up around the corner. It's about quality and style. It'd take forty of them bitches to make one of you. They all glued together, fake hair, fake nails, fake clothes, high mileage. They ain't been raised right so they always running they mouths too much, exposing a nigga's business, bringing a nigga down. Now you, on the other hand, you know how to act. You know how to keep your mouth shut and hold a nigga down. You proved and tested. On a bad day you still gonna be the finest bitch in the world. You know what to wear and when to wear it. You came up in the first family. You got training. That's what I'm talking about. I'm a family man. I have to be able to concentrate. I learned that watching Santiaga. Too many bitches coming in and out, next thing you know your whole shit is falling apart. You dig what I'm saying?"

"Yeah, I check for that," I said coolly. Inside I'm like, *Hell yeah!* He gave me enough compliments to last me six months. But I was still curious, so I asked. "So what really happened?"

Shaking his head from left to right he said, "Man . . . it's a complicated story . . ."

"Are you saying you don't think I can follow the story? Or are you saying you want me to trust you but you don't want me to know what's happening around me?"

"See, that's what I like. You got mad smarts."

Bullet picked up a stick that washed in with the tide. Not only was he going to tell me the story, he was drawing a picture in the moist sand.

"This is me," he said pointing to a small stick figure. "No mother, no father. They was both killed. My father was killed by the police when I was four. My mother was killed by her boyfriend when I was six. I got two relatives. My half-brother Bryce who lived in D.C. with foster parents, and Granny. I was raised by Granny from seven years old up, right there in them Brooklyn projects. You seen Granny around our way. She's a good woman but she got a little gambling problem. She was collecting welfare for me and blowing it all at the Lotto machine. After a while she elevated to every weekend, bus trips to Atlantic City. A nigga didn't have nothing, no food, forget clothes— you saw me, you and your little girlfriends chitchattin'.

"At eight years old, I started earning my own dough. I was a look-out for Rings. Now Rings had me watching the block. All I had to do is sit on the bench and clock everything and everybody. I had a Mickey Mouse watch Rings gave me. I knew when everybody left and came, who worked, who didn't. I knew when people got checks, new furniture, whatever. Back when the building had buzzers. All I had to do was stand by the wall and press the buzzer to let Rings know when someone was coming up into an apartment he was in. Or I'd press the buzzer to let him know 5.0. was on they way up. Man, a lot of people had no love for Rings, including your father. Everybody considered him a thief. He was a thief. But I thank him to this day, may he rest in peace, because nobody took the time to teach me nothing. Rings did. He taught me patience. You had to have patience to sit there hour after hour, day after day. That's how I peeped you. Watching you everyday from the bench. You always stood out like a diamond. But Santiaga protected you, like a diamond. I'd sit right there in my fucked-up clothes, snot running down my nose, unable to run upstairs to get a tissue, scared to miss a beat. I said to myself I'm gonna get her. She's gonna be mine.

"I knew to get into your world, I'd have to work like a dog, scheme like a motherfucker. Hell, nobody was gonna just let me get down, just like that. I was already an outcast because I worked for

Rings. I didn't have no family, no connections. So I started to watch Santiaga. He was my hero. He had the respect. There was something so smooth about that nigga. Even before he became boss. He was like a politician, all dressed up like every day was an occasion. Everybody liked his way of talking. I always thought he was able to connect with the big-up whites 'cause he's light-skinned with that good hair. Them same cops he had on the payroll doing business with him was the ones that would beat a brown nigga like me with no mercy.

"Now, when Santiaga connected with Captain Chulla at the precinct, it pulled the heat off a lot of niggas around our way. They loved him for that. I watched the block so close, so long, I knew all the police routines. I knew when a patrol car was coming around; which cop would be riding in it, when the shifts changed, everything. I could almost read the badge numbers I watched them so close. I knew who was getting payoffs, who wasn't. I mean there may have been more cops on the payroll than I knew about, but a lot of them dudes I watched knew how it was going down.

"Santiaga made use of most niggas in the 'hood. He knew how to make everybody feel good. He gave every man a purpose, some money for their pockets, money for their families. But some niggas he shut down. Like Rings, who he had no respect for and a few of the independent dealers, and Stack and 'em, the stick-up kids. There wasn't nothing they could do about it though 'cause he had it all hemmed up. He was making it possible for so many cats to get paid that any bad talk against him was not only bad for that person's business, it was bad for they health. Next thing you know you might turn up disappeared.

"About a year and a half ago, right before your family left the area, there was a crew of Young Heads, thirteen- to sixteen-year-olds. In a surprise attack they stuck up one of your pop's spots, got away with mad cheese. Word went out on the streets that Santiaga got stuck up by some kids. At the same time, Captain Chulla retired. It was unexpected, but that old fuck caught a stroke. Rudolph became D.A. He started up some campaign about cleaning up the drugs in the 'hood and busting crooked cops. On the streets the D.A.'s office started recruiting informants. Any available two-buck nigga signed on as a snitch with Rudolph. Meanwhile the crooked cops panicked, tried to cover up they tracks. They started supplying protection, guns, and ammunition to the Young Heads even though they were still cops on Santiaga's payroll. They made it appear to the D.A. that there was a war between the Young Heads and Santiaga. But without police backing, the Young Heads couldn't have gone head up in a war with Santiaga.

"Your pops got paranoid and started strong-arming niggas. He was even twisting arms of niggas who was loyal to him, niggas who would've killed for him. Niggas who would've died for him. Without Captain Chulla at the helm coordinating the cops on the inside, it was hard for Santiaga to know who was who. Plus, in the shake-up there was just too many new faces. The cops started busting more of Santiaga's men but they went easy on the Young Heads. When Santiaga moved your family out there to Long Island, there was no way for him to see how the pieces were moving. The pieces were moving too fast. Some of Santiaga's men who got busted wasn't cool with him moving out of the 'hood. They looked at him like he jumped ship. With Chulla out and Rudolph in, some of Santiaga's other connections dried up. Even money couldn't get none of his men out of the pen. But I could dig it. Santiaga had to move. Them Young Heads was ruthless. They was hitting whole families, players and nonplayers. They even eighty-sixed KK and Butter."

"Miss Sonya's babies?"

"Yeah, her man got in the way so they sent him a message. Two corpses: heads off. One three-year-old, one four-year-old, dead. But I gotta give Santiaga credit. He held it down for a long time. But with the police behind the Young Heads it was only a matter of time before they wiped Santiaga out. When the cops working with the D.A. applied pressure on niggas in Santiaga's crew, they started telling on each other. Once one or two started talking, there was a chorus of singers. Everybody was tryna cut a deal with the police, save they own tails."

"What about my mother? Who shot her?"

"She caught a bad one. But the niggas who did that is dead. They said that was one trigger Santiaga pulled himself."

"So what's up now?"

"The same fucking cops get a bigger cut of the business now than they did when Santiaga ran shit. They got the Young Heads working on a seventy-thirty split, their favor. That shit is crazy. Plus they got their hands in even more areas than they had before. So the top dudes in the Young Heads is now tryna squeeze out the small niggas in the

Young Heads, the ones who did the bloody work, the dicing, the slicing, the soldiers. So niggas is breaking off tryna do their own thing. Little businesses springing up here and there. You know."

"And what about you? Where do you fit in the story? The Young Heads, that's not the name of your crew is it? Captain Chulla, that's not his real name either, is it?"

Bullet smiled, "Damn you smart."

"It was easy to figure. Why would you tell me all this? I am *Santiaga's daughter*. I could tell him everything you said."

Bullet hung his head between his legs and mumbled, "It wouldn't matter. Santiaga's finished. He's a legend, but he's out of business. He's charged with everything. He even killed two niggas in the pen. He'll get life four times over."

"He hasn't been convicted of nothing yet." I defended him. "So what do you want from me?" I asked Bullet, with tears for Daddy in my eyes.

"I just want to put you back where you belong, on top. I just wanna be your man, from when I was broke on the bench." He smiled a seductive smile, almost as if he was popping the question.

"One more thing, the Young Heads, that's the fake name for you, Slick Kid and them, ain't it?"

"Who me?" he smiled. "I'm just a lookout. Seriously, I got me a little side hustle that turned mad big for me. I hook up all the hip-hop stars with what they need. Like a private doctor who's on call. I got a couple of other businesses brewing. I'm 'bout to close out business with the Young Heads. Niggas is too shady. They always talking about 'we.' They call us 'the family.' But the dividends don't spread around the family like they should. They don't want to bless the real soldiers. So I'm about to relocate."

"Oh, and bounce on me." My attitude reignited.

"Never that. When we get home you just let me know where you want to rest at. We'll get an apartment. However you want it. But I got to be able to trust you, that's the main thing. I almost killed that bitch Saria. I could've lost everything I have now killing some lunatic bitch who lied about being pregnant with my kid. I don't want to chase behind no chick playing detective. You understand me?"

"I check for that," I reassured him.

The next two days or so in Key West, Florida, was more than cool. Bullet concentrated on learning me, my likes and dislikes. He said he wasn't gonna ask me about my past 'cause he expects every woman to lie about what she done no matter how small it is. He made it clear over and over that everything between us starts now, today, and "you belong to me from here on in." The penalty for betrayal is death, he said, with the seriousness of the cancer disease. "If I catch you lying to me about anything, no matter how small, the penalty is pain."

I don't know what he was so uptight about. His dick was good and his dollars were long. I had no reason to complain, leave, or cheat. There was only one thing that wasn't open and straight with him. I told him I needed to find out where my father was locked up at. He got quiet for awhile as if he knew the spot, then promised with as few words as possible to help me locate him.

"It can't be that hard, he's locked down." Now I thought about it a minute and decided maybe Bullet thought my father would be against us being together. I wasn't planning to tell Pops about me and Bullet. I just needed to see Pops to make sure he was straight, stack up his commissary, and let him know I'm still his number one and he's still mine.

I didn't push it with Bullet. As far as me finding my father goes, it was nonnegotiable. Hell, Pops had put 17 years of loving and taking care of Winter. That's 16 years and 361 days more than Bullet put in.

As we lay on the bed in our undies, kicking our feet up, munching popcorn, and watching old movies on the rented VCR, *Cooley High* brought back memories of our kiddiehood in Brooklyn. It was odd that me and Bullet grew up in the same place yet had different childhoods. He was telling me grungy survival stories. My stories was mostly funny.

An icy cold fell over me in the villa on our last night when our reminiscing revealed what was happening now in the place I used to love, Brooklyn, but wouldn't be caught alive in anymore.

It was Bullet who brought Simone's name up. "Yeah, that crazy bitch got pregnant. She got big as a house. She went into the hospital to have her baby and came back home empty-handed. Nobody wanted to ask her mean ass what happened." As Bullet continued talking I didn't ask him no follow-up questions on the Simone issue. It was clear that he had no idea that me and her had beef.

"I don't want to get an apartment in Brooklyn," I told Bullet calmly.

"Oh, you too big up for Brooklyn now?"

"Nah, nothing like that. I just ain't cool with a lot of them chicks and I don't need no static."

"You ain't gonna have no problems, I'm holding you down now."

"I was thinking lower Manhattan by the water," I told him.

"That dirty-ass water," he said. I cut my eyes at him. "It's cool if that's what you want. I could use a little hideaway with an exclusive parking space with my name on it. Yeah, and a doorman. Maybe a butler, some shit like that," he said, and we both laughed.

Driving in from the airport Bullet headed straight to Brooklyn. As the wheels turned silently, because I couldn't feel no bumps, I became angry and nervous. I told his ass I didn't want to stay in Brooklyn. When we got so close to my old spot that it was indisputable where we were going, I asked softly, suppressing my emotion, "What are we doing here?"

"I want you to see where I rest at."

Getting loud, I said anxiously, "I already know where you rest at."

Bullet smiled and said, "Look, Sexy, it's been a long time. I'm not in the same spot. I'm one flight up from Granny. I couldn't have her making bets with my money." He peeped my reluctance. "Look, tomorrow after I handle my business we can bounce to find the crib you wanted. Ain't nothing open tonight no-how." I didn't move out of the car. "Oh," he laughed. "Them bitches got you shook. Couldn't be, not Winter Santiaga."

"Nah, I ain't shook. I just don't like being caught off guard." Bullet pushed a button in between the driver's seat and the emergency brake. The brown, hard covering on the island separating the driver's chair from the passenger chair opened.

"You tell me what you need. Whatever it is, I got it." As I peered down into the hidden well I saw a Glock, a 9 millimeter, a .22 and a 4-pound staring me dead in my eye. Bullet said, "Now, if this nigga can't make you feel safe, you choose what you need. I told you, times change."

Stepping out of his Lexus coupe I figured if I ever wanted to come back to Brooklyn, this is the way it should be, in style. It was evening time. For some reason everything in the neighborhood looked smaller than I remembered it being, and maybe even a little dirtier. I saw some familiar faces. Or maybe I should say, they saw me. But I didn't see Natalie, Simone, none of my girls or my aunts. I wasn't surprised not to see them. People have the tendency to stay inside during the winter. Now, if it was summertime there would be more people than roaches. Crackheads were running up begging to wash Bullet's whip that had collected dust in the airport lot. Bullet's man popped up like he was fucking valet parking. Bullet dropped the keys in his hands and he jetted off around back.

His apartment was definitely a man's place. It had the necessities, a big-screen TV, PlayStation, CD player, sneakers, magazines, beer cans, weed, reefer roaches in the ashtrays, a dirty bathroom, no toilet paper, and nothing in the refrigerator. But, it was secure. Like Santiaga, Bullet had a double security door, with a crack slot in the outside door about two inches wide and four inches long. A thick metal sheet could lock the slot or it could be slid open from the inside. On the table where dinner should be eaten there was Bullet's little chemistry laboratory. I made a note of that 'cause Santiaga would've never had it there in the open like that, even with the two metal security doors. But Bullet was a bachelor.

We wasn't in the crib thirty minutes before Bullet had to step out. All hyper-like, he said he couldn't wait until tomorrow to collect his shit. It was the time of the month where dumb niggas was about to be low on dough. He had to round up his boys. He tossed me the .22 and said, "Here. Hold this. I'll be right back. Don't answer the door no matter what. Don't even fuck with the phone." When I twisted my lips at him he responded, "It's business. They can all wait till I come back, till then nobody's home."

Within minutes I heard knocking at the door. They would come. Then they would go away. To drown out the sound of the knocking I flipped on the radio, then the TV. When I remembered nobody was supposed to be home I turned them both off. I started checking everything Bullet had. Don't ask me why. I just figured I had a right to. I was looking under the beds, in the closets, in drawers. Any pieces of paper I found laying around I read. In a matter of minutes I found five Timberland boxes filled with cash. One was filled with one-dollar bills, one with tens, one with twenties, one with fifties, one with hundreds. I put everything back the exact way I remembered finding it. I didn't lift one bill.

Tapping my nails on the table, I had only been in here one hour and I was being tortured by boredom.

Another knock at the door. The knock soon turned into a scratch.

The scratch turned into a screech. Disobeying orders, 'cause I was never one to follow, I opened the first door and stood in the darkness between the two. Placing my ear on the cold metal door I listened for a voice. I heard what sounded like moaning. "Come on, come on, I'm sorry. Where you been. I need something now." The words were coming out like a whining child. The screeching was louder now, too. I slid the heavy metal slot back an inch to see where the screeching was coming from.

The thin lady was hunched over scratching the door with two keys. Hearing the slot open slightly, the lady raised on her tiptoes and stuck her face to the slot. She was so close up I could only see her one bloodshot, tired eye. I don't know if she was rocking on her toes or what, but small sections of her face, the left eye, the right eye, her nose, a piece of her hairline would fall into my one-inch view and out again. When she stuck her two-tooth mouth in the slot, I saw the scar, the twisted position. The ninety-pound crackhead at the door was my mother.

"Give me something. Give me something. I got this." She tried to stick a fake gold chain into the slot. With my finger I pushed it out and slammed the metal slide. With my back now against the door I slid down to my knees, then doubled over.

"What you doing up here? What the fuck you doing up here? I told you to stop coming to my crib," I heard Bullet yelling in the hallway.

"Where you been? I been looking for you," her voice said.

"You got no more credit with me," he said in a lowered voice. "Now get out of here." Quickly I opened the next door, closed it gently then turned the lock. I heard her begging, but it turned into silence when I closed the last door.

Bullet stuck the key in the first door, then the second. He looked at me sitting coolly in the chair. I erased all traces from my facial expression of what I had seen. "You didn't open the door did you?"

"Nah," I said, with no emotion at all. He went in the kitchen, opened a cabinet, pulled out the cookie jar, and took out a vial of crack.

"You with me?" he asked, testing my loyalty for the umpteenth time. I nodded yes. "Here, slide this out and pass it off so I can get this crackhead off my dick." So I did.

18

The next day I was perched in the window at Bullet's sixth-floor apartment. It was as though I was sitting on top of the 'hood. I could see everyone as I peeked through the blanket he used for curtains. But no one could see me. Bullet got out early that morning. He left me the keys for the house but I don't know why he bothered, I wasn't going anywhere until he got back.

Bullet shot through the door when darkness fell. I was so vexed there was no reason to speak. Not to mention that with nothing in his refrigerator, I was starving. Ignoring my attitude, he glided across the floor, slapped me on my ass, and said, "Hey, I got something for you." When I didn't respond he threw the money on the bed. Wrapped in rubber bands there were three stacks of bills. Two of the thickest stacks were all hundreds. One of the stacks was all fifties. Picking up each stack individually, and flicking them from the top bill down to the bottom bill, I arrived at an estimate the way Daddy taught me to do. I figured there was about twenty thousand dollars here.

"Where the fuck did you get this?" I asked, knowing full well that no crackheads were walking around with large bills.

"I'm a businessman, baby! I told you I make moves. Leather sofas and color TVs cost money." He smiled so sweet I forgave him instantly. Sensing he broke through my wall of anger, he jumped on top of me and started kissing me all over my face. "Yeah, I know how to make it hot for you," his rough conceited ass said. And I loved it. After I got all excited about the loot, I noticed he packed it all away as if he had never thrown it at me.

First thing the next morning his man pulled Bullet's Lex around the corner. Handing Bullet his keys, he was so busy staring at me, in my fine winter wool Benetton minidress and matching jacket, that he missed Bullet's hand and dropped his keys in the street. As he bent down to get the keys, Bullet slapped him in the head on the way up.

The next man, Bones, who was in the passenger seat, laughed that he got chumped. But Bones was staring at me, too. I peeped that.

We rode into the city in bumper-to-bumper traffic. I convinced Bullet that it would be easier for him to let me get the newspapers from the stand, and travel to the apartments for rent by train. He paused before he agreed, and looked into my eyes like he expected to find something. He handed me a stack of dough, then snatched it back before my fingers closed. "Just beep me when you find something. I'll meet you with the money."

"Yeah," I said dryly. This nigga just can't relax.

It was almost 6 P.M., when I found a place. Instead of overlooking the river, it overlooked the FDR highway that was beside the river. It was located on the East Side, in the thirties block. There was a doorman, but no butler. The place was spacious, with large windows. I knew I could freak the layout with all kinds of designs. The important factor was that the greedy man renting the apartment was easy to work with. He was the first landlord I met who understood to mind his business. He wanted cash. I wanted the keys. I figured he needed the loot to feed a nasty cocaine habit. He sniffed all the way through the twelve-minute interview. Besides, the tip of his nostril was eaten away from the drug. I had seen that effect before. Now, when he started babbling about how I could pick up the keys next week, he had to have the apartment cleaned, I threw him another three hundred dollars to get the keys on the spot. He grimaced when I told him I needed one hour for my boyfriend to bring me all the dough. I don't know if he was mad that he had to wait sixty minutes or mad that I had a man.

Magazines were spread out all over the living room floor in the big empty apartment. I took my time reviewing each magazine design ad. Selecting an item from each ad I admired, I pieced together a collage of a one-bedroom apartment that was perfect for me. Bullet, who was out concentrating on what he described as the biggest move of his lifetime, had agreed that whatever I wanted was good for him. His only request was for me to leave the huge walk-in closet for his private use.

Initially, I was cool with the amount of time he spent away from home. Decorating was taking up all of my energy anyhow. But, Bullet was slowing down my decorating with his lack of trust. Every time I wanted to purchase something I had to wait for him to have free time to go with me to each store so he could pay the cashier directly.

It was clear to me that he wasn't gonna let my hands feel no dough. Half the time I had to go to each individual store to locate whatever item I wanted. I'd keep the items on a shopping list. At the miraculous moment when Bullet had a few hours available, we'd pick up each thing I wanted one by one. I tried having pieces of furniture delivered. I even had to schedule that around Bullet, who didn't want "no delivery man sliding around my crib while I'm not home." He even conveniently struck up a relationship with the doorman, passing him twenties and fifties for whatever favor he needed. After a while, I started to think one of the doorman's assignments was to watch me come and go. I figured it would only be a matter of time before Bullet would see that I was down for whatever. Not only could I decorate the joint and order up delicious dinners for two, but I'm a businesswoman who should easily be at least half of the team.

But I was swift. Daddy taught me how to think my way through and work around certain people to achieve the same results. The first thing I did was lease the apartment in my name. He handed the money to the designated person in each transaction, but I signed off every time. As soon as we moved in, I filled out all my credit card applications and mailed them away. One day soon I'd get one or two cards in the mail and use them to walk out the store with whatever I selected. If Bullet took too long to include me in his business plans or left me at home with too much time to think, I could easily see myself cooking up my own little hustle.

He must have been reading my mind. More than a month had passed. I completed my decorating project and had the place looking picture perfect. No one could front. Our spot was phatter than the designs in the magazine ads. Not only was everything top quality, it was elegant, a smart use of the space, and had flavor and attitude. I was just sitting on the white leather sofa listening to a little Mary J. Blige when his key slid in the front door earlier than usual. Busting in with speed and urgency he picked me up and spun me around.

"What got you all gassed up?" I quipped.

"I'm almost there. Everything is good. Trust me."

With my face close to his face, I responded, "Should I trust you like you trust me?" He busted a smile.

"Ha. Smart tongue. Get dressed, we going to a party." He flung open my closet and said, "It's a triple date. You got to look your best. Here." He flung a box onto the sofa. Excited like I used to be when I was just a little girl, I ripped open the wrapping paper and pulled out a brand new diamond bezel Lady Rolex. I started jumping up and down until I pounced right on top of him. "Thank you, Daddy!"

"What did you call me?" he asked, looking at me with surprise.

"I said thanks baby. This is the shit right here."

The dinner spot was the meet-up point. After all, we agreed not to bring anybody from the old neighborhood to our new apartment. That meant nobody would know where we rest, which is how it should be. The spot was called Houston's. Dimly lit, it was a restaurant on the down-low. As we sat parked outside of the place, a black Benz pulled up behind us and a blue Lamborghini jeep behind that. As I watched through the rearview mirror, I asked Bullet, "Are their girlfriends anybody I know?"

"I doubt it," he responded. "You know what to do. Don't talk too much."

"Is this business or pleasure?" I asked, sensing something.

"For you, it's all pleasure."

They were already seated when we stepped up. We slid into the big semicircle booth and Bullet introduced everyone. Right away a bottle of Cristal was brought to the table. I was kind of happy to meet Tiffany and Iris. It had been a long time since I kicked it with any female friends. I wasn't under the illusion that we was gurlz or anything. But it was important to me to hang with females who had they own loot so I wouldn't have to deal with no jealousy and funny business. It was obvious that at least for tonight they were rolling with two fat cats as well.

After the order was placed, all three of the men politely excused themselves and left the table. We were left looking at each other. It seemed like nobody wanted to say nothing. *So I'm the party-starter,* I thought to myself.

"So where are y'all from?"

"I'm from D.C.," Tiffany said.

"Me, I'm from Virginia," Iris said. The way Iris hesitated I assumed she was lying.

"How about you?" Tiffany asked me.

"I'm from Long Island." Lifting the bottle I said, "Well, we might as well drink this. They bought it for us." We sat there and drank the whole bottle together. Then everything loosened up.

"I like that dress, girl. Where did you get it? That shit is banging,"

Iris said to me. I knew for sure she was from out of town 'cause if she was from Brooklyn she would have never gave the compliment. Moreover, she definitely wouldn't of played herself by asking where did I get it from.

"Thanks."

"How many pieces you got in your head?"

"What?" I asked.

"Your hair."

"Oh, this is all me," I said, gesturing by pulling my hair. They both started laughing.

"Yeah, we all use that same line. It looks nice though."

"Which one of y'all was riding in that Lamborghini?" I asked.

"Me," Tiffany said.

"Is that shit comfortable?"

"It's a lot of space in there to do whatever you want to do. It's like an army truck. Roland told me if someone was shooting at us, the bullets couldn't even get inside."

"That's bullshit," Iris said.

When the food came, Iris pushed her plate away. "I already ate. I'm not hungry."

Tiffany dipped two fries in the ketchup and said, "That's it for me." Searching through her oversized MCM pocketbook, she finally found her lipstick. "Let's go to the bathroom." I moved to let them out. Then I continued to sit there. Tiffany called to me and gestured, c'mon. I looked around the restaurant. I saw Bullet standing in between the bar and the window, talking. He saw me looking but didn't say nothing. *I guess it will be alright,* I thought. So I got up and went with them.

"Iris, your titties is coming out of that bra." Tiffany helped her to adjust the straps. Everybody was touching up their hair, looking in the bathroom mirror. Iris was smoking a cigarette.

Then Tiffany picked up my pocketbook. I noticed she left her bag on the sink. "Tiffany, you got the wrong bag," I told her. But she kept walking toward the door.

"That's your bag right there," Iris said to me pointing to the MCM bag.

"What the fuck?" I rushed Tiffany, grabbing my bag by the strap. Iris pulled out a nine and pointed it directly at me. Both the wind and the words left my mouth. I couldn't talk.

"Take that bag. It's for your man. Don't blow it. Somebody should've put you up on it in advance." They bounced.

In the bag I found several guns and a small bag of coke. I'm not dumb, so I caught on. I tore a small hole in the bag and tasted it. It was the real thing. I closed it up and stepped out. When I walked out, Bullet, Bryce, and Roland were seated at the table laughing and talking like they were best friends. They had started to eat their food, each of them. Tiffany and Iris had slid themselves back in the booth. Bryce asked, "Ladies, is everything OK?" My eyes shot over to Bullet. Our eyes locked into one another. He nodded slightly.

"It's all good, baby. Sit down." Now I'm thinking, *No it's not all good. This fucking bag don't match my dress. Nobody in Brooklyn rocks MCM anymore.* Somebody needed to tell these down South hoes that. I wanted to be in on the business. But I didn't like being the only one who didn't know what the fuck was going on.

We continued to sit casually for five more minutes. Money on the table, a tip to the waiter, phony hugs and kisses, and we were out. When we got outside in the cool, crisp air I thought I seen the feds milling about across the street. I recognized their whole style from the takeover of my house. Now that I understood what was going on, I could view the entire scenario clearly. With his arm draped around me, Bullet kissed my cheek and whispered in my ear. "Drive the car home. Put the bag in my closet." He gave me a deep tongue kiss, like natural, while passing his keys into my hand. I walked to the car with no sign of strangeness. I started it up and pulled out slowly. When I waved goodbye, Bullet was standing talking to Bryce and Roland. The feds were focused on the men. I slipped right by.

An hour later Bullet walked in all smiles with his arms extended wide. "Sexy, you did it."

Without raising up from the couch where I was seated, fully dressed with my shoes kicked off in front of me, I said, "I thought we were going to a party." He picked up his keys. By now he was inside the walk-in closet, checking behind me as usual. Three minutes later he came out with work tools in his hands. He talked to me while he put a new lock on the walk-in closet door.

"We *are* going to a party. Give me five minutes."

"Oh, you ain't gonna say nothing, nigga?"

"Nothing about what?"

"That little scene an hour ago."

"You said you wanted to be in. Now you're in."

"Why didn't you put me up on what was going down?"

" 'Cause the key to success is to be natural. Everything was easy. Nobody acting strange or unusual. Them fucking feds can smell you when you're nervous."

He didn't want to talk about it in the crib. He didn't want to talk about it in the car either. We picked up his man and another dude named Moose. We rode to the club with the music blasting. "Real Love. I'm searching for a real love." Mary J. Blige. I love that old record.

We pulled around the back of the club. His man switched into the driver's seat, and me, Bullet, and Moose walked through the back door straight into the VIP section.

"Whose party is this?" I asked. But I was drowned out by the music, noise, and excitement that surrounded us.

Everybody in the place knew Bullet. It wasn't like cats was excited to see him. It was like a respect thing. They acknowledged him quietly, said a few words in low tones, gave him pounds and hugs. But nobody got in his way, asked him for the VIP passes or identification or shit like that. Moose had Bullet's back so close, you'd think them niggas was joined at the hip. When Bullet wasn't giving somebody a pound, his hand could be found right on my waist, resting lightly on the top of my ass.

We found a small table in the corner in the dark. After ordering drinks, Bullet relaxed a little and began to talk to me the way he felt comfortable—in a crowded room, with the music at the high point, and Moose with his back to him facing the crowd like a gigantic black stop sign.

"Winter, you did good. I knew you could. I been checking your flow, I like the way you think. The way you move."

"So what does that mean?"

"What do you mean what does that mean? I'm giving you a fucking compliment."

"How much was it worth?"

"How much was what worth?"

"The guns and the powder. What? A quarter of a million, a half?"

"You see, you getting ahead of yourself now. I did the setup tonight *for you*. To get *you* accustomed to shit. *I could've pulled it off without you.* I have plenty of times. You think you could just walk into this cold? You can't. They'll see you coming like a neon purple

lightbulb. You gotta work your way into this shit slowly. You gotta
feel everybody you dealing with. You gotta feel yourself. It could be
the littlest shit that gives you away. A itch on your nose, or tapping
your feet and fingers too much, or the way your eyes move. If you do
this shit enough then you can give the appearance of being comfortable, at ease. Then you're natural at it, instead of looking, smelling,
and walking like a suspect."

"I ain't new to this, Bullet," I said with mad attitude.

"You wasn't a player on your father's team, Winter. You think
street smarts is inherited," he laughed. Just when I opened my mouth
to say something back, Moose turned and tapped Bullet. His attention
was drawn away. Now I was waiting for him to finish talking to some
dude. I was thinking at the same time that I just wanted to get my
hands on some loot. Not for no specific reason except I didn't like him
keeping me with no more than twenty dollars in my pocket and a few
train tokens. I wasn't asking for a cut of his product or profit, just a
few hundred dollars, maybe a thousand in my pocket so I could feel
good.

"Alright, Bullet. I'm willing to work my way in. I ain't no slouch
or nothing," I reassured him.

"Oh, for a minute I thought you was unhappy. Don't your man
get you everything you need? Don't I keep your hands heavy?" he
asked, pointing out my new Rolex. "Don't I keep the roof of your
choice over your head? Name one thing you wanted that I didn't get
for you."

"My father's address," I said softly.

"Damn, Winter. What you need. What the fuck you need *that I
didn't get for you?* What do you want. I'll get it for you!"

It was that second I wised up. I would never mention Santiaga to
Bullet again. For some reason that I wasn't getting, it was like asking
about Daddy was an insult to him. Now I would get to my father on
my own. I wasn't trading my own smarts for Bullet's. I could find my
pops and stay on point with Bullet. I'd watched for an opening to pull
it off. But this was exactly why I needed some cash flow.

The whackest thing about celebrity parties is you're locked in the
VIP section where nobody dances. The live party goes on outside of
the VIP room. But Bullet had business in here. I should've known this
wasn't no fucking date we were on. By the time we was leaving I felt
stressed. Usually when I'm partying I ain't feeling no pain.

It was going out the back door that shit went crazy. I was walking close but slightly in front of Bullet. Bullet was directly in front of Moose, who had his back. Some fool came walking up to me. Within seconds, I recognized him as the bodyguard who drove me home from GS's mansion.

"What's up, Sasha?" He was directly in front of me so I stopped walking. Besides, he was about six-foot-two, much taller than me, and built.

"Do I know you?" I said in a cold, flat voice. I played it off. Bullet, who was only six feet tall, put his hand on the cat and pushed him out of my path.

"You got the wrong girl, nigga. Move on," Bullet threatened.

"Sasha," he said again, feeling himself and testing Bullet. "You don't remember me from GS's?"

"My fucking name ain't Sasha," I tried to cut him with my words.

"Money, I told you move on," Bullet said with death in his eyes. Bullet's leather jacket swung open, revealing his arsenal.

Moose stepped in and said, "Here, let me talk to you a minute," pulling the bodyguard to the side. Meanwhile, Bullet's man pulled up. Me and Bullet got in the car. Bullet gave his man the order. He parked on the opposite curb of the back entrance.

I asked, "What are we waiting for?" Bullet, still heated, didn't answer. Bullet got out the car and signaled somebody. Next thing I know he's outside talking to GS. Through the tinted window, I'm watching. Bullet's back was to me. I could see directly into GS's face. It didn't look like an argument. It looked like a friendly, casual conversation. Then Bullet's knuckles was knocking on the window. I pushed the button. The window came down.

"Winter!" Slowly I stuck my head out the window. "I want you to meet my man GS."

Without smiling or nothing, I said, "Nice to meet you," and pulled my head back inside.

I heard Bullet say, "Yeah, that's my girl. You never seen her before, have you?"

"Nah, never, man," GS replied. I sighed relief. I don't know why GS covered for me. Or maybe he was just protecting his own ass. There was no way he had forgotten me. I knew then that Bullet was the man. He wasn't taking no shorts and I got to dig him for that.

Moose never got back in the car that night. We dropped Bullet's man and went home.

Focusing on food was never my thing. As I listened to my stomach growl the next morning, I felt a desire to eat. As I held the refrigerator door open, I couldn't decide on what I wanted. My hunger turned to nausea. My nausea turned to vomit. After hurling in the toilet, I laid on the bed staring at the ceiling with a nasty taste in my mouth. Seven minutes of silence, then panic settled in.

Immediately I began pacing the bedroom floor. I ran into the kitchen to pull out the calendar the Chinese take-out guy slid under the door. Frantically, I tried to remember the date of my last period. The problem was the numbers on the calendar didn't mean nothing to me. I couldn't even match certain incidents with corresponding dates. When I actually thought about it harder, I tried to remember the last time I bought Tampons. Lashay's face popped in my head. I remembered charging her two dollars for one back at the House of Success! But I had blacked all that bullshit out.

In jeans, with a pajama top on under my jacket, I walked to the closest pharmacy and purchased a pregnancy test. Back in the bathroom, I zoomed through the directions. Placing the small cup underneath myself, I pissed on my fingers while trying to hold it. Then I pissed on the toilet. Then I pissed on the floor. Therefore, my little cup only had a droplet of piss in it. I turned on the water faucet to make myself able to pee again. I waited a half an hour and finally was able to deliver a half a cup. While I waited for the little plus or minus sign to show up, I smoked a joint to calm my nerves. Three minutes to doomsday . . .

It turned out positive. I was pregnant. The only thing to do now was get rid of it. After a short while, I remembered hearing an abortion jingle on the radio. I couldn't recall exactly how the commercial went, but I knew if I tuned in, within minutes the ad would come on.

When I called, they gave me the location of the nearest clinic. A quick shower, I was dressed and on my way.

It was a cloudy morning. Girls were jammed like sardines into the clinic. As I surveyed the room it wasn't hard to figure the girls whose stomachs were not poking out yet were sure to abort after looking at the obviously pregnant idiots who decided to keep their babies. One big, pregnant girl had dark, purple circles underneath her eyes. I saw stretch marks on knees, arms, titty tops, and even on her elbow. Some girls were balding from their condition. I even saw swollen hands, noses, and feet. One girl's ankles were so fat it looked like elephantitus. She had her big tree-trunk legs propped up on not one but two chairs. Meanwhile, others didn't even have nowhere to sit. Now I'm steady counting who came in first, next and next, and so on. I wanted to get this over with before Bullet came home that night.

The girl seated next to me leaned over to ask, "Are you nervous?"

"Nah!" I said, keeping it brief, not wanting to invite her into conversation.

"Then why are you shaking your foot like dat and bumping against my chair?" As I checked myself I realized I was tapping my foot. I got control of it immediately.

"I was nervous the first time I got an abortion. It turned out it didn't hurt, though. It was like one, two, three, over." The girl was still talking. I didn't say nothing in response to her. But I was glad to hear, once again, that having an abortion doesn't hurt. Back in the day, my girls told me the same thing.

"Yep," I couldn't believe this girl was gonna keep on going in the conversation, without any participation from me. "This is my fifth one. I really can't get into creams, that shit makes me itch. Them pills make me sick. Can't feel shit with a condom. It's easier this way. It works pretty good, too. I only get knocked about once a year."

"Yeah, but it must be expensive," I said, allowing her to pull me in.

"Girl," she went into her pocket and pulled out a Medicaid card. "I got an abortion credit card!"

In the examination room, the doctor grilled me.

"Do you have a private physician?"

"No."

"When is the last time you had a gynecological exam?"

"This is my first time. Why, do you have a problem with that?" I asked the doctor.

"I'm asking the questions, young lady," the Indian doctor with the dot said, like I was a lowly soldier in her army. "When was your last period?"

"I don't remember."

"Try to remember."

"I can't remember."

When it was all said and done I was three months pregnant, or more.

"What do you want to do?" she asked with a sickening look of concern.

"I want to get rid of it right now. Give me the abortion."

Pulling the rubber gloves off her hands, one finger at a time, she said, "Not so fast. Have you given this any thought, there are options to consider."

"Look, on your commercials you said, 'It's a lady's choice.' You do abortions? Now get it out."

The doctor got up from the chair with the wheels on it. She went to the counter with her back toward me. I'm like, *This bitch is crazy. She acts like this is personal.*

"See the nurse on the way out. She'll give you an appointment for your termination. If you wait too long this can get real messy."

"What's wrong with now?" I asked her.

"There's another doctor who performs the procedure. You'll have to schedule it with the nurse now." I went right away to the nurse. It only took me two minutes of talking to convince her that I needed to be scheduled to abort tomorrow. "You wouldn't want to be responsible for pushing me over the three-month line, now, would you?" I challenged her.

Back at the apartment I was seated at the kitchen table. Rapid picture frames flashed through my head. I traced the baby back to Boom. It was either him or GS's asshole bodyguard. I wished it was Bullet's. I knew it wasn't because I was too far along. I remember the first time me and him fucked 'cause it was on my birthday. Images merged as I made comparisons in my mind. Boom had silky hair. Bullet has naps in a Caesar cut. Boom was yellow, Bullet is brown. Boom has hazel eyes. Bullet has brown eyes. If it was Bullet's baby he would marry me, give me the whole world, the whole nine yards. But it's Boom's or the other guy's. There was no way to be sure. I couldn't front it off. So I'd get it scraped out first thing tomorrow.

"What you been doing all day?" Bullet's suspicious ass asked.

"Nothing."

"Did you go out?"

"No."

"How come you didn't pick up the phone when I called?"

"I was probably at the incinerator emptying the garbage. Why you didn't page me? You usually page me," I turned it around on him.

"I did page you," he said, staring dead in my eyes.

"I didn't get no beep!"

"Then you must of been on the subway. That's the only way you didn't get my beep."

I got up, pulled my pager off my side and said, "Oh damn, I need a new battery."

Bullet spent the rest of the night in the walk-in closet, with the door closed and locked.

The 11 A.M. train to the clinic was packed. I'd be lying if I said I wasn't thinking about what was about to happen. I mean, Bullet didn't come to bed before I went to sleep. Even though this gave me the opportunity to clip three hundred from his coat, which he left draped over the chair, I was nervous. He didn't kiss me before he left. I didn't even hear him make a sound before he bounced. Would I be able to conceal the abortion without leaving a clue?

These thoughts converted into new thoughts when my eyes caught the front page of the New York *Daily News*. The man in the trench coat sitting right across from me was reading the paper. He had it held up with both hands in front of his face. It wasn't the headline or the big picture in front. It was a bold line typed across the top of the paper. Rap Star Bodyguard Found Dead. My eyes locked in on the sentence. I read it over and over again. Immediately I got up. I started walking slowly through the moving, packed train car, looking left to right. I knew someone would have left a *Daily News* on the train after being done with it. When the train paused for a stop, some people got out. That's when I got my hands on the paper.

As I suspected, there was the face of the asshole from the other night, Tony, GS's bodyguard. It was a picture I guessed came from his high school days. He looked younger, with a big doofy smile. His full name was written underneath the photo. I never knew his last name was Creighton.

Rap star GS lost friend and bodyguard, Tony Creighton, 22, who was gunned down with three bullets to the head. Police don't yet know the time of the incident. The body was discovered yesterday afternoon in a vacant lot located on . . .

Then they had the mother of the bodyguard saying he was such a good boy. He volunteered to feed the homeless on the holidays, blah, blah, blah. People were always talking shit like that after somebody dies. Everybody gets together and starts lying about how a mother-fucker was all this or that. He wasn't no saint when his ass was laying up in that bed pretending to be GS that night, fuck him.

I was only concerned about one thing, myself. This abortion shit had to go smooth. I didn't want Bullet coming after me. I could get this behind me. It wasn't like I cheated on Bullet or nothing. This happened before me and him hooked up. But it didn't matter. I knew that. I just needed to get rid of it and give him no reason to suspect me of nothing. I mean me and Bullet just clicked together. We were thick like that, business and lovers.

As soon as I got to the clinic the nurse started asking me stupid questions.

"Did you come here alone?"

"Yeah, why you got a problem with that?"

"Did you drive or take public transportation?"

"Why?"

"Answer the questions please, miss."

"I took the train."

"Okay. You'll need to take this pill." She handed me a big pill with one of those small white paper cups. The kind that are only good for one drink before they crumble. "Once the procedure is completed, you'll probably feel disoriented. You cannot drive a car. You should really have a companion with you in case you don't feel well and need assistance getting home. Is there anyone you can call to pick you up?"

"Yeah. I have a ride coming for me," I lied.

She would read my chart, then look back at me. "Good, you're eighteen. You'll need to sign these papers." After they got my promise not to sue if they accidentally killed me on the operating table, I gave them the three hundred dollars.

The doctor came in. It was a man. He held my hand while some-one else gave me an injection. "You may taste a salty solution in your mouth, it's OK." Then the machine roared. It sounded like a vacuum cleaner. What seemed like only minutes later, the machine stopped. In my head, I heard the voice of the girl from the waiting room yesterday, "one, two, three, over."

First everyone left the room. The nurse came in and began stuffing big pads in my middle. The kind I would never choose to wear, like diapers or something.

"This is to absorb the bleeding. If the heavy bleeding doesn't stop by tomorrow evening, call us immediately. But you should continue to have bloody spots." She handed me another pill and a paper cup.

"This is to help stop infection." She handed me a small white envelope with six more pills in it. "Take these three times a day for two days. Do not bathe. Do not engage in sexual activity for the next four weeks to avoid infection. You need time to heal." She left me alone in the small room. I was fine until I got down from the table to stand up. The stuff in the room was moving around like I was in space. It was hard for me to stand straight. I looked at my Rolex and the numbers started to float off the face. The nurse busted back into the room as I was crouched over, trying to pull my pants up.

"Let me help you. Do you feel dizzy?"

"Yes."

"This happens to some people. You don't need to worry. You will need to lie down. Has someone arrived to pick you up?"

"No."

"Just as I thought."

She escorted me to a different small room with a small basic bed. She helped me to lie down. Without notice, I slept. About two hours later I felt a hand on my shoulder.

"You can go now. It should be OK. We need to use this bed for another patient right now." I felt much better. Everything was steady. I headed home.

At the apartment, I ate, then slept. When I woke up, I left out to go to the drugstore. I purchased some pads for heavy-duty flow.

I cleaned everything up. I checked and rechecked to make sure the apartment had no trace of nothing that happened today or yesterday. As I sat at the kitchen table, I felt down-low. I didn't know why. It was like something was pulling me down, making me feel deep depression. It was something I couldn't control.

The lower I felt, the more I thought of Daddy. The more I thought of Daddy, the lower I felt. Tears started running down my face. I picked up the telephone.

"Excuse me. Can I have the number for Riker's Island . . . Thank you . . . Prisoner information please. Yes, my father, Ricky Santiaga, was incarcerated at your facility almost a year ago. I came to visit him and was told he was shipped out. Is there any way I can find out where they sent him? No, I don't remember his prison number. Yes, I'll hold on . . . He's on Riker's Island? But the corrections officer told me they moved him out. Oh, they moved him to another building? Twenty-three-hour lockup? Can he have visitors? Noncontact twice a week for one hour only. Tomorrow."

I couldn't believe it. My pops was at Riker's all along. The fucking fake cop lied to me. Bullet knew. I knew he knew. The problem is, he didn't want me to know. I said I would find out myself. I will visit Daddy tomorrow. Nothing and nobody would stop me.

Bullet came through the door quietly that night. I was up. "How you doing, baby?" I greeted him with a hug.

"Joey said you went out yesterday for three hours."

"Joey who?"

"Downstairs, the doorman."

"You know his name? Why is he all in my business?"

"Where were you?" Bullet asked, looking dead into my eyes.

"I went shopping."

"What did you buy?"

"I didn't see nothing I liked."

"Are you lying to me? I told you never to lie to *me.*"

"I went window-shopping. It wasn't nothing. I was gonna ask you for some money. I just went to look at a few things."

"Why did you say you didn't go out?" he asked.

"I don't know, it was stupid. I don't know. It won't happen again." I couldn't arrange my words fast enough. Bullet had me all off guard.

"What won't happen again? You won't go out again?"

"No, I'm saying I'll let you know if I'm going out and where I'm going."

A dick-suck cures everything. So I unfastened Bullet's belt, dropped down to my knees and went to work. I centered myself so he could see my lips sucking and pulling. So he could see my tongue.

He needed to know he was the boss. I had no problem with that. When I saw his mouth open wide, a look of pain covered his face, but I knew it was just the ecstasy of him busting in my mouth. He got down on the floor with me and we talked.

"Baby, you're fucking up my head," he said in a soft tone, the anger removed from his voice. "When you fuck up my head, you fuck up my business. I can't let nobody fuck up my business."

"I ain't doing nothing, Bullet. I swear it's all about you and me, that's it. You think I'm leaving this good dick alone, you crazy." He smiled.

"This dick is good, ain't it?"

"It's the best."

"Would you die for me?" he asked.

"Baby, I'd lie for you, ride for you, die for you. But if I die for you, I couldn't have no more of this good dick." I laughed, feeding his ego. I needed to shift him off of thinking I did something I didn't do.

He rolled on his side with another hard-on. He began to undo my pants.

"I'm on my period," I said, trying not to panic. I bent over to lick his balls again.

He pulled my head up and said, "A nigga wants pussy. This is my pussy, right?" he questioned. I answered with a nod. "A little blood ain't gonna hurt this big dick." He was all up in me. How can I describe the feeling? It wasn't pleasure. It wasn't pain. It was noth-

ing, like a dick plunging into an ocean. But still, I conjured up some
moans for him.

I grabbed the tech nine out of the small drawer in the dresser next
to the bed. It was early morning. There were crazy noises coming out
of the living room. If somebody besides Bullet was in there, they was
about to catch a bad one. As I yanked open the bedroom door, standing behind it with the tech, I heard growling. Not human noises, but
like an animal. Walking backwards, I stepped away from the door. I
heard running, barking, then howling. Then I heard chains buckling.
Motherfucking Bullet had two rottweilers in our NO PETS ALLOWED
building. Vicious-looking, no-nonsense killer dogs with a chain that
allowed them to roam the entire length of the living room and kitchen
and two feet into our bedroom.

"Bullet! Bullet!" I yelled out to him. "Are you home? What the
hell's going on?" But he wasn't here. I sat on the bed with the tech,
debating. Them fucking dogs sat and stared as if all they needed was
one miracle to pop the chain and eat my ass alive. I used the bedroom phone to page Bullet. Minutes later he called back.

"What's up baby, talk fast . . ."

"What's up with these fucking dogs?"

"My bitches?"

"Yeah, your bitches!"

"Them some loyal bitches. They do whatever I tell them to do. I
tell them to sit, they sit. I tell them to stay, they stay. Are you loyal,
Winter?"

"You goddamn right I'm loyal and I'm ready to blast your bitches
to pieces."

"That would be dumb. You would draw attention to yourself,
cops, neighbors, the whole nine."

"The barking dogs is gonna draw attention." I tried to reason
with him.

"If you don't bother them, they won't bark. Just close the bedroom
door and stay put."

"You crazy," I told him, without hostility.

"Yeah, your pussy smelled funny yesterday." Click. He hung up.

I was vexed that I couldn't get out to see Pops. If I missed the
one-hour visit today, I won't be able to visit again for another four
days. By evening time, that was the least of my worries. I couldn't

leave the bedroom, so I couldn't eat. All I had was a bag of Lorna Doone cookies that Bullet had been eating in our bedroom last night. The hungrier I got, the hungrier the dogs got. By midnight, they were growling and so was I. My stomach was roaring and the pills that the nurse had given me was wrecking me on a damn near empty belly. That night, Bullet never came in. In the morning, I paged him but he didn't call back. My mouth was so dry from the Lorna Doone cookies, I started drinking tap water out of the bathroom in our bedroom.

For two nights and three mornings, I was held hostage by the dogs.

Finally Bullet came in with somebody else. I could hear them talking. I listened as he fed the dogs before feeding me. He didn't even open the bedroom door to look in on me first. I wasn't gonna open the bedroom door. I was too mad and too weak.

A half-hour later, the bedroom door opened. He stood in the entrance with a big smile. The same smile that I found so seductive.

"Where are those dogs?" was the first question I asked.

"I sent Joey to walk them."

"What was Joey doing up here?"

"Someone had to clean up the dog shit."

"I'm hungry," I mumbled.

"Oh, so you remember who feeds you?"

"I never forgot."

"Good." Bullet carried me off the bed and into the kitchen. He had two big breakfast take-out orders ready for me and a large container of orange juice. I ate without a word.

"Get dressed. Take a walk with me," Bullet demanded. As I was learning not to resist him, I followed his instructions. When we reached the lobby, Bullet untied the killer rottweilers from the outside black gate where the frightened but greedy doorman, Joey, watched from a distance. We walked with the dogs, who, in Bullet's presence, somehow turned friendly—two-faced bitches.

"I gotta make a run. I'm taking you with me." I smiled 'cause I like to travel. But then I thought about my father and how it's been too long since I've seen him.

"That's right. If I leave you here, I don't know what you'll get into. I know if I was the next nigga I'd be willing to die tryna talk to your fine ass. Now, I could leave you with the dogs," he said, petting them like they were pups. "But I get the feeling you don't like them. You know I got a kennel full of these babies. They sell for eight hundred fifty dollars each. I train 'em in the basement in Brooklyn. They sell like crack; they just cost more."

"I thought you was gonna bounce from Brooklyn," I reminded him.

"I am. But I'm gonna flow from there real natural. No one will notice. I'll just get in my car one day and pull away from the curb and never come back. No moving trucks, nothing. No one will know the difference for a while."

"I'm sure they'll be some hoes left crying at the curb when you leave," I teased.

"I don't fuck with them low-class bitches. They all ran through. All your girls is all fucked up, fucked in, fucked out," he laughed. "Brooklyn got new hoes coming up. Now all the old bitches are fighting them."

"Whatever. So where we traveling to?" I asked.

"Baltimore. What you know about that?" he said, peering into my eyes again.

"Not a damn thing."

"Then why you had a bus ticket to Maryland in your coat pocket when I first picked you up."

"Damn, I forgot all about that I had that ticket. As you can see, I never went."

"Where was you going?" he questioned me further.

"I don't know, nowhere," I lied.

"Why you be lying so much, Winter?"

"What?" I stalled to arrange my defense in my own head.

"You was probably gonna check that nigga Midnight from Santiaga's crew." He was talking casually, and exploding bombs all at the same time.

"How you figure that?" I played it off.

"Don't play dumb. I never forget a face. It could cost me my life. I never liked that cat. He was too quiet. Never knew what he was thinking. I watched how he moved. When Santiaga's empire started crumbling, that cat just started scaling his shit down. I know some cats who ran up in his spot. They said that nigga didn't have nothing.

Just a mattress on the floor, a sheet, toothbrush, and a fucking candle. I mean, no jewels in the place, no money, nothing. Dude didn't even have a phone. It was like he knew they was coming. In the whole team, he was the only one who walks away free and standing. Cats said he was clean, not a fed, snitch, nothing. He had to put all that dough he stacked somewhere. Anyway, my niggas down in the Baltimore area keep an eye on him for me. But ain't nothing popping with him. He ain't pushing no weight."

"Why you telling me this?" I asked, as if I didn't care.

"In case you got any ideas about the trip. That man don't have what it takes to keep you," he warned.

"I don't want him."

"Yeah, whatever. So check this out. Let me tell you how we gonna do this. A lot of cats roll south in Benzes, Lexes, and BMWs. They got the tint, rims, music blasting, car full of niggas. They getting pulled over by the cops. Point blank. Police search the car. They end up doing ten, fifteen, twenty years. We gonna think smart. First, we gonna rent a car. You'll get it with your credit card."

"I don't have no credit card."

"Yeah, it came in the mail for you the other day. I was holding it for you. We'll play the part. I'll dress up, slacks, shoes, dress shirt. You'll rock a conservative dress. We'll play something on the radio, like light FM."

"What difference does it make what station plays?"

"I could swear the fucking police got some kind of nigga radar. If they hear you pumping hip-hop, you get pulled over. If we get pulled over, we'll both tell the same story. We're in the church. We're on our way to a revival; we sing in the choir."

"You're fucking crazy." I cracked up.

"I'm dead serious. You gotta rehearse the small stuff. They'll catch you on a technicality. I got a bunch of close call stories. I know how this shit works. Are you scared?"

"I'm not afraid of nothing." I told him the truth.

"Good. Keep it natural."

At the apartment, Bullet made a few calls and finalized arrangements. He came out of his walk-in closet with three teddy bears.

In the bedroom, he told me what to wear. I changed. He got did up like a Sunday school teacher in a suit. Me, him, the dogs, and the teddy bears, headed to the car rental spot in his car.

At the spot, he pointed out a lady standing in front with a big, pink sweater on. He told me to go in, use my credit card and her driver's license. She's the driver, you're the payee.

"But who the hell is she and where did she come from?"

"She's just a chick from around the way who doesn't mind doing a favor for me."

I looked at him, then looked back at her. She was homely, so I said OK. He told me to ask for an infant car seat. We rented a Buick LeSabre family car. The Rent-A-Wreck people were just so happy to have a customer! After awhile, I understood why Bullet had involved this chick. She was twenty-six years old. They had all kinds of discounts for people over twenty-five. It seemed he had thought of everything. She drove the rental out of the place. I hopped back in the Lex. She followed us.

"Now where are we going?"

"Brooklyn. I gotta give the Lex to my man for safekeeping. She's going home. She'll drive the rental to Brooklyn. Me and you, we gotta drop the dogs. Then we hop in the rental and be out." Bullet saw how skeptical I looked at going to Brooklyn. "You want to hold the burner?" he asked.

"When we get there," I told him.

Something wasn't right. You know how you just get that feeling? As we turned onto our old Brooklyn neighborhood block that midday afternoon, it was crowded with fire trucks and emergency vehicles.

"Maybe we ought to turn around and come back when the commotion dies down," I mentioned to Bullet.

"It's a four-hour drive to Baltimore. We gotta make good time," he said. We pulled up to a parking space. Donna, the chick with the pink sweater, pulled up and parked the rental behind us. She got out and knocked on the driver's side of the car, and handed Bullet the rental keys. She stood crouched over at the window like she was expecting something. He stepped out of the car. I was watching that bitch like a hawk. I saw him slide her a yard. Then she bounced. Bullet reached back in the car and grabbed the dogs. "I'll be right back." He was going to drop the dogs off.

"Aren't you forgetting something?" I asked him, looking dead in his eyes.

"What?" His face was blank. "Oh, yeah." He leaned into the car, opened the special compartment, and passed me the .22. "Keep the doors locked," he ordered.

Ten seconds after he left a white guy in a car pulled up alongside us.

"Fire Marshal. You'll have to move this car." I smiled pleasantly and agreed. Yet my stomach was like a butterfly cage. I threw the gun under the driver's seat. Then I opened the door, walked around to the driver's side, used the key in the ignition, and started the car. On exactly the opposite side of the curb, I parked. Through the tinted window I sat and watched as the courtyard filled up with people filing out of the building. The way everything was positioned on an angle, I couldn't get a full view of what was happening, but I saw the smoke. I saw the long water hoses running from the fire truck through the courtyard and toward the building. Now my eye is like a zoom lens. I'm trying to check faces in the crowd so I could be on the offense instead of the defense.

Shame and disgust are the only things that could describe my state of mind when I spotted Momma in the crowd. She was wearing purple hot pants in the winter, a red T-shirt, runover Reeboks, and carrying a dirty yellow crochet bag. She was bumping into people in the crowd, pushing them out the way the whole time, staring at the ground, looking for loose change or a vial, the way crackheads do.

Oh no, I hope she don't come over here, I thought to myself. But she did. When she saw Bullet's Lex she scuttled right on over. She knocked on the window. When she didn't get no response, she started mashing her face against the window to see if anyone was inside. By now, I'm curled up like a snail trying to get as close to the floor as possible. When she got to the window on the passenger side and pressed her face against the window, she saw me.

"My baby, Winter . . . Is that you? Come out here, girl." When I didn't move, she demanded, like she was in charge, "Winter Santiaga, this is your mother speaking, get out the car."

With my legs tired of being jammed, I crawled back into the seat but wouldn't open the door.

"Oh, I know . . . I got something for you." She started digging in the dirty yellow bag. I'm thinking, there ain't shit in that bag that I want. Just then I saw Bullet walking back toward the car. His stride was rhythmic, like a leopard. He looked real important in his suit.

He was moving swift, but trying to keep it natural, as he would say. When he recognized my mother, he yelled from a distance.

"Hey! Move away from the car!"

Just then, my mother pulled some dirty envelopes out of her bag. She had a big smile on her face, like she was very pleased with herself. "Winter, these are letters to you from your father. I been holding them for you. I didn't know if I would ever see you again."

I felt a shock wave shoot through my body. At that split second, those letters became the most important thing in my life. Just as Bullet arrived at the door, I jumped out to get the letters.

"She don't want that shit," he swatted my mother to the side like she was a fly.

"I want those letters, Bullet. My father wrote those letters to me and you can't keep me from having them." He saw the fire in my eyes.

"Bullet, what you got for me? What you got for me?" My mother hopped around like a three-year-old waiting on a lollipop.

"I don't got nothing for you," he growled at her, while steadily looking in my eyes.

"Come on Bullet, we friends, we friends. Tell Winter we friends," Momma said.

"Give me the letters." I stepped up and extended my hand to my mother. She pulled her arm, securing the letters behind her back, teasing me. "You want the letters. She wants the letters. What y'all got for me? You look good, Winter. You look like you got *a whole lotta money*. Do you owe me some money? What you got for me?" my mother sang.

I lunged at her. She fell on the ground. I fell on top of her. I grabbed the envelopes out of her weak fingers, clenched into a fist. Bullet lifted my body off the ground and into the air, "Go get in the rental." From the look on his face I knew to follow his instructions. I didn't care 'cause I had the letters. He threw a ten-dollar bill on the ground and told Momma go get what you need somewhere else. She picked it up and disappeared as fast as she came. Bullet placed the teddy bears in the backseat of the rental, next to the infant car seat.

"Don't fucking move," he threatened me. I saw him signal to his man who was standing on a car watching the firefighters put out the fire. His man got in the driver's side of the Lex. Bullet leaned in the passenger door. He put all his guns from the compartment in a carry bag. He walked back and threw the bag in the trunk of the rental.

As he returned to the driver's side of the rental, I asked him, "Did you get the .22? It's under the driver's seat in your car." His man was pulling off. Bullet trotted in his church suit behind the car to catch up with him.

"Yo, hold up. Hold up, man."

I didn't even have time to turn my head a little bit. A brick came crashing through the window of the passenger side of the rental.

"You stupid fucking bitch. You had the nerve to bring your ass back around here." The car door swung open, Simone charged in. With her heavy hands around my neck, her weight was holding me down on the front seat. I started throwing mad punches, swinging at her face, punching her in the eyes to get her off balance. The car was rocking. People started gathering around the car, cheering. I could hear people walking on top of the car roof, the whole nine. Me and Simone was still thumping. I bit her. She tore open the top of my dress.

Next thing I know, we both fell out of the car into the street. We was wrestling. I was using my knee to kick her in the belly. Laid out on the ground she reached her big arm toward the gutter and grabbed a dirty bottle. I tried to shake it out of her hand, but she was a big buffalo. She broke the bottle. I caught flashes of the faces in the crowd that now had us pinned in. I saw nasty, little Natalie standing there, egging Simone on. "Cut the bitch, cut her," she called out. Simone kept coming at me. I was lighter on my feet, so I ducked and dodged. For a second, I looked up 'cause I saw Bullet coming through the crowd with the gun in his hand. Just seeing him got me feeling pumped. Now I had super powers. But Simone took advantage of that split second when I looked away. Her big arm came swinging down, slicing a seven-inch gash on the left side of my face. I felt my face open up, I grabbed my head and blood was all over my fingers. My face felt hot, like it was surrounded with heat. Bullet shot the gun in the air, everybody started running. Even Simone bounced. Some bold people stood right there and kept watching.

"Ah baby," Bullet said when he saw my face and the blood. He led me to the rental. He sat me down in the car. For seconds, he just kept saying, damn, damn, damn. Then whoop, whoop, police sirens. I could see the red lights bouncing in the rearview mirror as the police cars ripped down the street. Bullet closed the passenger door and ran around to drive the car. Suckers in the crowd pointed our car out to the police.

That wasn't as shocking as me watching Bullet walk, pass the driver's side, pass the car, onto the sidewalk, and down the street like he had nothing to do with it. I opened the door on my side and tried to get out, but the cops was up on me.

20

Twenty-five hundred and fifty-five days later, I checked the calendar on my wall. I had twenty-nine hundred and twenty days left to serve on a mandatory fifteen-year prison sentence.

But this particular day was special. What made this day special was simply that it would be different than the rest. In fifteen minutes, I would be walking out of this cell, down the corridor, and out the doors to attend my mother's funeral. She had died suddenly. Whatever that means, 'cause she was dying all along. Some type of blood clot to the brain. And since mothers are so important, I was about to enjoy the only legitimate method of leaving this institution before a prisoner's time is served. Of course, I would be chained at the feet and at the wrists. I would be escorted around like a preschooler. I would be returned to this cell within hours. Then the routine would resume. But at the age of twenty-five, in the twenty-first century, a small trip to the graveyard was about as much excitement as I was gonna get.

Because I was gonna get a few hours outside of these walls, I was like a superstar. Everybody in here wanted me to be sure to tell them everything and everybody I saw outside as soon as I returned. Other than people's relatives, there was no real way for us to know what was going on outside. Even relatives were hard to come by. Who really wants to take an almost eight-hour trek out to this joint, which damn near sits in Canada? In my seven years served, I never received one visit.

I had to work several hustles to keep my commissary in livable condition. Then, of course, there were always the suckers who could be shook down if things got too bleak. Fighting didn't mean nothing to me now. There was no nervousness or nothing. I just did whatever was necessary.

There ain't no special clothes or fashion in here. When I first came, I tried to make myself stand out the way I always did. But after while, you'd figure, what the fuck for? You can't get no dick. I don't want no pussy. There's no one to impress here except those broke-down broads. Every now and then, I do hair for cigarettes or stamps or cookies. Most of the time, I keep my own hair braided. It's so long that bitches get jealous. I have to braid it, then roll it up and tuck the ends under just not to have extra beef.

But me, Natalie, Zakia, Chanté, and a bunch of Brooklyn girls got a crew up in here. We got a little name for ourselves. Even Simone's tryna be down with us for her own protection. She finally stopped blaming me for the death of her daughter. Or at least she puts up a good front. But that's how it goes in here. There's all kinds of strange alliances.

Everybody got drug-related charges stemming from their own lit-tle situations. But we wasn't nothing but the girlfriends to niggas mov-ing weight. Sometimes when we be playing cards and listening to the radio, it's almost like we at home. I got enough family and friends on the inside. That's why I don't get no visits. Everybody's already here.

As far as mail goes, I get letters from Santiaga, that's it. We just always gonna be close like that. I still got the letters from that wild day in Brooklyn. That day plays over and over in my head. I calculated about 263 what-ifs. *What if I had done this? What if I had done that?*

What really blew my mind was finally reading Santiaga's letters while I was in the holding cell the night of my arrest. He admitted killing two dudes in prison. Both of them was my mother's brothers, who used to work for him. But he broke it down so I could under-stand it. He just had a justifiable hatred for weak men, said there is nothing worse than a snitch. He told me he knew he was never com-ing home. He was right. It turned out he got two consecutive life sentences, with no chance of parole. The crazy shit was he gave me Dulce Tristemente's phone number in those letters. He told me to call her because he didn't want any more money wasted on his trial. He instructed her that I would be calling. She was to meet me and hand over fifty thousand dollars. There was only one condition. I had to get my mother and place her in a rehab, he even gave me the name of the place. That's what he had wanted Midnight to take care of. After collecting the money, I had to promise to take care of my moms after she came out of the rehab. But, I wasn't supposed to mention to Dulce what I was going to do with the cash. I called that bitch Dulce collect from the jailhouse. Once she found out I was incarcerated, she changed her phone number and never passed off the money. That hoe was living lovely. If she was supposed to give me fifty thousand, imagine how much she had stashed for herself.

That's neither here or there. I don't even think of getting out. I take one day at a time the eight years I have left. I cross out each day as I survive it. I know I'm not guaranteed to see the next day or the outside ever again. It's not like I miss anybody other than Daddy, anyway.

Two guards came to get me. "Santiaga, let's go. Keep it moving." I walked on the right side of the corridor, on the inside of the white line the way we were trained to do. They took me into a room I had been in hundreds of times before. I stripped naked. Naked wasn't nothing to me. I done seen thousands of breasts and hundreds of asses by this time. It was almost the same as seeing somebody fully clothed. In the beginning, I would try to cover myself up. But surprise searches in the middle of the night would have sixty chicks standing side by side, butt-naked, then squatting for a rectal inspection. We are naked in the wall-less shower. Naked in the bing, naked, naked, naked. It meant nothing.

Dressed in a jail jumpsuit and an army jacket, with an officer in front of me and an officer in back of me, I proceeded down the hallway and out of a series of automated doors. My prison number was checked and rechecked at each checkpoint as if they didn't know who I was already. Hell, I'm here every day. Once outside of the building, I was placed in a van with bars in the windows and driven across the facility field where snipers and officers were stationed every couple of yards, twenty-four hours a day.

When we passed the last checkpoint, my way of breathing changed. It might be hard to believe, but the air in prison is different. There's like one thousand people sucking on the one little piece of fresh air until it turns stale. Then all you suck in is recycled oxygen and bad breath. In the van I could feel the breeze. I could even smell the trees, the sap, and the flowers in the spring air as we drove down the road, headed to the airport.

I stuck my face up against the window bars. The sun in my face was a luxury. Because of the way my cell was situated in the building, I rarely got any sunlight.

The airplane offered more magazine selections than we were

entitled to inside. The officers, who pretty much know my style, were relaxed. They had no reason not to be. I was chained to my airline seat. I peeped people tryna glance over at me. It wasn't easy for them to get a good view because I was seated in the middle chair, in between two guards. I looked right back at them though. I was checking out shoes, watches, jewelry, dresses, just so I could tell the girls on the inside what was up. When food time came, I got filled up on the aroma alone. Three choices of food were offered. That's two more choices than I'm used to having. My nose was so keen now I knew what they were serving before the stewardess read off the selections.

When we got to the city, I was placed in a prison vehicle. New York street sounds brought back memories of so many things. Mostly memories of freedom. Being able to go to the store or the movies. Getting fucked in a parked car by the river or in the grass or on the back stairs. My eyes checked the cars, the updated series and models. I noticed new hairdos, new buildings that weren't there before.

As I rode in the back of one of those prison vehicles, the car with the metal gate separating the officers from the convicts, I saw people looking. It seemed like they were wondering what I did. I wanted to tell them nothing. I didn't do shit. I'm doing fifteen years for having a bad attitude. That's what it boils down to. Sure, I rented a car that was being used to transport guns and cocaine. But they wasn't my drugs. They wasn't my guns. But since I was sitting in the car I rented, with the stuff concealed inside the teddy bears in the backseat, they considered me guilty. I'm a conspirator for renting the apartment me and Bullet lived in. I'm a conspirator 'cause guns discovered had bodies on them, people I didn't kill. Some of them I didn't even know. Now, you tell me how can I be involved in a conspiracy when nobody else involved in the conspiracy was convicted of nothing? They wanted Bullet, but I wouldn't help them. The name is Santiaga. We don't snitch. Besides, even if I was a rat it wouldn't matter. That nigga Bullet had it all figured out. His name wasn't on nothing. He wasn't caught doing nothing. Joey the doorman disappeared before the cops could get to him. There was nobody to testify against him about shit.

When Natalie got sent up here one year after me, for just riding in a car with a nigga with contraband, she told me the deal with Bullet. Now he has a bootleg tape business. He got all the rappers shook, be stealing they music and selling it on the streets before the record companies could. He's got a legit record store that he sells the tapes out of, and he's paid out the ass.

The graveyard was located in Queens. When we pulled up, all I could see were the backs of about four men. As we came into closer range, I saw that three of the men were armed and wearing bulletproof vests. The two officers with me greeted the three officers with Santiaga, my father, who I had not laid eyes on in eight years. As soon as he turned to greet me, the tears came gushing out of my eyes, after so many years with no tears at all. I couldn't stop them from falling. Santiaga gestured slightly like he wanted to hug me but his hands were chained, and so were mine.

"What's up, baby girl?" he asked in a low tone. There was no privacy. Any emotion shared here was a group thing. We were being watched like a motion picture.

"Hey Daddy," I whispered, admiring how handsome he still looked, his tall frame still sturdy, filled out and masculine.

"You're beautiful," he said, looking into my face in a concentrated way. I cried more because I knew how hideous the scar on my face was. I had stopped bothering with the mirror about five years ago. "Even with the scar," he added, as if he could read my thoughts. "You're still the prettiest girl in the world."

The old white priest cleared his throat. All six of us, me, Daddy, the guards, stepped up to the open casket to take the last look of Momma we would ever have. When Santiaga looked in, he broke down. He broke down so bad, he fell to his knees. "Who is that? Who is that in the box? That's not my wife." The guards prodded him to stand back up. Both Daddy and me tried to collect ourselves.

Seconds later, some more people wandered over to where we were. We didn't know them. We assumed they were looking for another plot. As two of the guards moved to inquire, words were exchanged and they allowed them to pass on to our way.

For the first time in many years, I became self-conscious. I felt ugly. I wanted to fix myself. I wanted to rip off these clothes and tear out these braids, comb my hair or something. It was Midnight. He was tall, black, and regal. He looked more amazing than I remembered him being. Instantly, I felt jealous of the women with him. It was a piece of me that was dead, that was somehow coming to life again. My eyes locked in on their faces for an immediate comparison. It's funny. The girls' faces were familiar, but I could not place them. Then an alarm went off within me. Lexy and Mercedes, the twins, my sisters. They had to be at least fifteen years old now. They were so soft and delicate and different. Their eyes were different.

Midnight approached Santiaga first. He hugged him, which the guards allowed. Then he presented Lexy and Mercedes, like they were strangers in an initial meeting. They talked to Daddy in a formal way, not like daughters. They spoke to me with sympathy and distance in their voices. Everything that needed to be said was not being said. Midnight did most of the talking. Like old times, he reported to Santiaga on the status of things. It was about Santiaga's daughters. I turned away from them. I didn't want Midnight looking at me.

Just as the priest started going through the motions, a big, black 600 series Mercedes Benz with black-tinted windows pulled up on the pavement. It had been moving at a high speed so it stopped with an abrupt jerk, alarming the guards who had already assumed the shooting position. They called out for the person to identify himself. But the music coming from the vehicle was so loud, I was sure the people inside could not hear anything else. As the door opened, a model type of girl, straight out of the pages of a high-fashion magazine, stepped out of the car. Dressed in a white Versace slinky dress—odd color for a funeral—and white Dolce & Gabbana leather stilettos. She was obviously paid out the ass. I still couldn't see her face behind the sunglasses. Stepping carefully on the new, soft spring grass, she came right over to me.

"What's up, Winter?" She smiled wide and pulled off her sunglasses. It was Porsche, my sister. She came alone, pushing a whip it would take the U.S. president's salary to pay for. She hugged me. She kissed Daddy. She waved at Midnight, Lexy, Mercedes, and the two women with him. She stepped up and looked in my mother's coffin for all of three seconds.

She stepped back, grabbed my arm, and leaned inward to talk privately with me. The guard signaled for her to back up. "Damn!" she screamed on the guard. "Can't I talk to my own sister without you being all up my ass!" So they let her talk. I couldn't believe how she chumped them.

"I wanted to come and check you, girl," she said, chomping on some bubble gum. "But you was just too far away. Tell me what you need. Whatever it is, I can get it for you."

"Whose fucking whip is that?" I asked, amazed.

"Buster's," she responded.

I raised my eyebrows, like *Who dat?*

"It's a long story," she said, waving her hand in the air like it wasn't nothing.

"What's up with Lexy and Mercedes?" I asked her, almost at a whisper.

"Midnight adopted them. They all religious and whatnot. They be wanting to tell somebody how to live they own motherfucking life. That's his wife right there. She ain't all that. I look better than she do."

"Who's the other girl?" I asked.

"She's his sister. They live out in Maryland. Midnight owns a barbershop, can you believe it?" she said chuckling.

"So what do you do? Where do you live now?" I asked her, cautiously.

"Oh, I do a little bit of this, a little bit of that. We stay over there by Central Park in Manhattan," she said casually.

"We who?" I asked.

"Me and Buster." She said it like I should've known already.

"Oh." Now I took a good look at Porsche. She was perfect. Her hair was perfect. Her legs were perfect. Her clothes were perfect. But I wanted to warn her about certain things in life. Usually I'm not at a loss for words. But I didn't feel good enough to tell her what I really thought. I knew what she would think: Winter, you're just saying that 'cause you're in jail. Winter, you're just saying that because you're old. Winter, you're just saying that because you're ugly. Winter, you're just saying that because you're jealous. So instead of saying what I had learned, what was on the tip of my tongue, I said nothing at all. Hell, I'm not into meddling in other people's business. I definitely don't be making no speeches. Fuck it. She'll learn for herself. That's just the way it is.

THE COLDEST WINTER EVER

SISTER SOULJAH

Special Collector's Edition Reader's Guide

THE TOP TEN QUESTIONS

1. Why did you choose to focus on and write about drugs in your first novel?

I have always been in love with the human soul. In every person, I see some beauty, and most of all, a lot of potential. As a very young child I remember watching everyone very intensely, as if I were a visitor in my own home. At first, I believed all human beings shared the same feelings and ideas. I assumed that all mothers and fathers were similar. In a short period of time I was proven wrong. I would sit and wonder why a person would do a certain mean, strange, or destructive thing. I was always searching for an understanding of what was going on in someone else's mind. In the slim corridors of my Bronx, New York, project building, my brown eyes captured a lot.

Each night when I would lie down to sleep, it would be difficult for me to ease into it. I would think about what caused one of my "good friends" to suddenly turn against me that day. I would be obsessed with words my mother had spoken to me earlier, and would lie on my back wondering about them. After all, I depended upon her to explain every little detail I observed and experienced. Fighting sleep, my mind would still be reviewing, dissecting, and questioning.

This condition of wondering and searching for answers led people to refer to me as "deep." I did not know at the time what "deep" meant. I did know, however, that being seen as deep separated me from everyone else who surrounded me—my people, family members, friends, and other ghetto dwellers.

Within my immediate family I became separate. If something tragic happened, my mother and her boyfriend of the moment would tell my older brother and younger sister not to tell me about it because, if I would have known, I would not only question it for a long time, I would feel it in my heart. It would echo in my mind and live there forever.

When a man in my building was murdered by his girlfriend, my family hid it from me. I would see this man fixing his broken down car outside of our building almost every day. When he disappeared I kept asking why he wasn't outside anymore. It was a very small detail missing from my everyday snapshot of my little ghetto world. After about a week, my brother finally confided in me late at night, when I was having trouble drifting to sleep, that the man had been killed by his girlfriend inside the apartment upstairs from us.

My mother was right. Maybe he should not have told me the truth. Because every day for a long time I wondered what happened right before he was murdered. What did he say or do to his girlfriend that made her feel it was all right to rip his chest open with a knife and spill his blood onto the floor, stealing his breath and life and presence? I wondered how he felt while being stabbed. I wondered how she felt while stabbing him. I wondered how she got out of jail so quickly, in weeks even. I wondered how she could still be walking around smiling and dating like nothing ever happened. I wondered about her soul and his too.

My mind had the power to relive incidents as if I had been there, even though I hadn't. I could feel what I believed others felt, whether it was terror, depression, or joy. I could easily place myself in someone else's shoes and this added to my sense of humanity. I became both more compassionate toward the pain of others, and more furious with wicked people and unjust circumstances. I would soon learn that I had the gift of imagination, complicated by the gift of powerful spirit.

It was my extremism that caused my mother to introduce me to books. She felt she did not have the answers to all of the questions that I bombarded her with. She would read to me and my siblings at night. She got me my public library card at age five. My efforts to understand my family and the people who surrounded me by reading and studying books began then.

Although many of the books I read were fascinating, they were not really about the world that I lived in. None of the children's books described my day in my hood, the people, places, or familiar things.

In fact, when my mother held my four-year-old hand and walked me around my project building, describing everything around me so that I could learn to be strong and unafraid of walking to the store alone in the ghetto now that I was about to be the big five years old, the things she showed me were not in any children's picture book.

Momi pointed to young men with needles in their pocket, heroin addicts. She pointed out men standing on the corner. They were so drugged and so high that they looked like tightrope walkers inching their way across a thin line elevated 500 feet in the air, while attempting simply to stand up.

Momi pointed out what route to take and which ones to avoid. How to walk foward and watch behind you at the same time. She told me never to eat or drink from anyone else's house or hand, not even a so-called friend. She told me to never go into anyone's house without her permission no matter what. She told me if she granted her permission for me to visit a friend, I was never to go into their bedroom. I was never to allow anyone to take me into a room alone and close the door. She told me not to talk to strangers, especially men with their drugs, teenagers with their tricks, or fast little girls or women. At the end of this lesson in bravery, my greatest fears were born.

I was afraid of drugs, needles, smoking, the people who used them, the people who sold them. I was afraid of the way the drugs caused the people to act. I was afraid of the way drugs caused the drug taker to look. I was afraid of what the drugs "made" people do. I was afraid of the drug dealers too. I did not fear the boogey man or monsters. There was no evil green or red guy with horns under my bed. There was only the men who were described as "the pushers," who might slip something into the punch bowl at the block party and make the minds and hearts of all of us children and adults change forever.

In my deepest thoughts, drugs were responsible for changing love to "I don't give a fuck." They were responsible for turning beautiful girls into ugly old hoes in a matter of weeks. They were responsible for turning good men—fathers, brothers, and sons—into enemies to be feared and despised. I was afraid of a thing so powerful it could make a child not love her own mother. Or a father not love his sons and daughters.

So I buried myself in books. I separated myself from people who I deemed were not in their right minds. I even slept on top of my arms at night, so no one could inject them with heroin while I slept. I did not eat or drink from others. I did not accept even the gas mask at the dentist's office, for fear the gas would make me high, ignorant, broke down, and most of all out of control of my mind, and separated from my true feelings, the ones God gave me at birth.

So I guess it's not so suprising that as a grown woman, I would write about the effects and impact of drugs, the topic that troubled, frightened, and disturbed me so much as a child.

2. Is *The Coldest Winter Ever* a true story?

No. My novel is not based on a true story. However, it is based on real events that happen every day. That's why it feels so real. After all, drugs are real. Drug dealers are real. Drug wars are real. The ghetto is real. Jail is real. The state is real. The consequences of drugs are the most real; the shootings, disappearances, kidnappings, murders, the slow death, the quick spurts of wealth, shopping sprees, then shocking downfalls into poverty. All of that is real.

So many people have felt *The Coldest Winter Ever* so deeply. They believe that it is their own story. The incredible thing to me is the idea that anyone thinks a drug tale can be their own private or personal story when everyone in the drug "game," thousands and thousands of people, have all experienced the same exact thing: material wealth, spiritual poverty, shootings, killings, fear, pain, loss, incarceration, and devastated families and friends.

I felt that in weaving this tale in an attractive and dynamic way, I was bringing forth a gift that would free thousands of youth and families who believed these horrible and crazy things were only happening to them. I believed I could place into the minds of the young certain universal truths about drugs, growing up, family, sex, and life. I was certain that it was needed.

The focus of the modern drug tales needed to switch, I thought. So many writers had taken time to write books and screenplays about the rise of drug kingpins and their empires. I thought the effect of *The Godfather, Scarface, Goodfellas,* and *New Jack City,* had been to cause poor young black and Latino boys and men to identify heavily with the real poverty and truly emasculating conditions that created the drug dealer in the first place. Of course, they then accepted that the drug dealing business was a justifiable, suitable, and acceptable way to rise out of poverty. It would elevate them from the underclass, not into the working class, but into tremendous wealth and power. They loved the way the characters in these books and films went from being boldly disrespected to being respected, served, and feared. They loved the way the characters beat the system, the same one that had them trapped. These books and films became the *Black Boys' Guide to Business.* In the ghetto, barrios, and favelas, the actor Al Pacino, star of *Scarface,* the movie, became more well-known, impactful, and heroic than Jesse Jackson, Muhammad Ali, and Bob Johnson.

The effect of these books and movies was swift. It swept through our community like an airborne infection. The message was loud and clear. Only the men who were willing to become killers and enemies to their own people could make it to the top. Only the men willing to become ruthless would become respected. Only the men with real money could become substantial providers and receive the admiration of their women and children.

But who was going to tell the story that focused on the fall of a drug kingpin, and of how he descends back into poverty and slavery? How the state places him back in chains naked and pinned in, chained to another slave just like him? How he loses everything he ever loved? How he murdered his own friends and family? How the world pimps his unprotected daughters and dwarfs then devours his sons? I wanted to suck the romanticism out of those blockbuster books and films, all of which I had read and seen, like most ghetto youth.

My decision to tell my tale through the voice of a teenage ghetto female quenched another desire I had for a long time, the desire to write and show an authentic version of black girls, teens, and women. I felt that Hollywood had completely missed the real story of black girls and women. They had created female images that for me were simply figments of their imagination. They were not authentic. The sound of their voices, the depth of their thoughts, their manner of speech, their style of dress, the gravity of their hearts, the varying levels of love, the challenges they faced, and their attitudes had been all wrong. Writing *The Coldest Winter Ever* for me was to set it straight, to capture an array of black female personalities, to explore the many psychoses, the real strengths and weaknesses. To allow female characters to speak free from cultural domination or projections of how others thought we are. To get it right, finally.

It was also an opportunity for me to set a new blueprint and criteria for depicting accurate ghetto girls, teens, and women. Hopefully this one book will help to free black actors from having to fit themselves into the strangely written roles and characters that have been misrepresenting them for years, yet may have paid the bills. Additionally, I hope it will help girls living in and outside the hood to understand that there are many women who you may model yourself after, as you attempt to come into your womanhood. You can be Winter or you can be Sister Souljah. You can be Mrs. Santiaga, or you could be Doc, the medical doctor who owned the building in which Sister Souljah lived. You could become Natalie, famous for blow jobs, or you could become Rashida, who took the help from concerned others and healed herself. I wanted to show all of these different girls and women and the consequences of their choices. This way a young female can pick up the book and decide which one she really wants to be. *Which reality and consequence can she really handle?*

After I wrote the novel and it became popular, I was invited to speak at Danbury Federal Prison. I was invited by Kemba Smith, a young lady who was incarcerated for being the girlfriend of a drug dealer. I was amazed as I stood in the room with about three hundred young female inmates. First of all, they looked familiar, although I did not know any of them personally. They rocked the same hairstyles, had the same bodies and faces you would see anywhere in our hood. The group was made up of hundreds of mostly black and Latino women who had all been convicted and locked down for long periods of time because they were in love with a drug dealer, letting him bag up and cook up in their apartment, carrying a package from one location to another, or doing something simple like answering his phone calls, standing beside him at the wrong moment, riding in his car, or receiving and spending his money.

I thought about how incredibly important my novel was at that moment. I thought about how *The Coldest Winter Ever* could become responsible for thousands of teenagers, women and men, staying out of prison because they read the book and now understood the truth of the drug deathstyle, the truth that had been for so many years either shrouded in secrecy or glamorized by Hollywood. I became proud of myself, standing there. I became hopeful that I was on the right path in fulfilling my purpose in this short life. I thought about how this was only one women's prison in America. There were several more. I had already made the rounds as an activist and speaker in various male prisons. I knew those were stuffed to the breaking point with our boys and men, fathers, brothers, and sons.

I had already been to a women's prison where the incarcerated thirty- to forty-five-year-old women who were HIV positive were secluded in one particular wing. But at Danbury, the young females looked strong and healthy. You could be walking down the street or taking a class seated right beside them and not tell the difference between them and anyone else. They did not appear to be drug addicted, sick, or crazy. They appeared to have been ignorant of their reality, the consequences and losses that the "drug game" would create. They were unaware of the specific laws of the United States of America. They were unfamiliar with the intricacies of a conspiracy charge, what it meant and the long extreme punishment it would carry. They had never thought that the men whom they loved and held down (some of them) would receive lesser sentences or none at all. They had never thought that during their incarceration in an unbreakable female prison, their man, or baby's daddy, would never even write them a letter, pay into their commissary, give them a visit, or take care of his children whom the newly imprisoned mother left out in the world.

I imagined that most of them had seen or personally experienced the majority of things I had written about in my book. I knew that they knew, that Sister Souljah had not been a street girl and had not participated in the drug game. I understood then why they felt they owned the story, that it was them and theirs, that they were Winter Santiaga. I now accept that the novel that I wrote has a life of its own beyond me, the author.

3. How did you write the story so authentically when you said that since your early childhood, you separated yourself from people who used and/or sold drugs?

Yes, great question. As a child, I was engulfed by fear. As I grew, I made a point to learn. I came into knowledge. Knowledge frees you from fear. It brings about complete understanding. It offers each of us the opportunity to explain and develop solutions to the problems we once ran away from.

At age ten my mother moved us out of the New York projects. We were now officially homeless. We moved in with my grandmother who lived in a small house in the half black, half white suburbs of Northern New Jersey. She accepted us, but we were not welcomed. True, I was out of the ghetto, but my ghetto upbringing was within me. People say "Hey, Souljah, you only did six years in the projects," from age four through ten. I say so what? How many years do you have to be in Vietnam, or Korea, or Iraq, or Afghanistan to know your ass is at war, or at least under attack? Can those ghetto feelings, observations, the intensity of them, can that ever leave you? Impossible.

Besides, the black suburbs had problems too. There were still drugs, drug dealers, cultural confusion, and even murders. There was no peace in the souls of the humans who surrounded me. Yet everything looked better, was dressed up and nicely secured behind closed doors framed by manicured lawns. The coverup was much more orchestrated.

I was a hard worker on every aspect of my life. I worked hard at my studies. I worked hard at maintaining and improving my body. I worked hard at balancing my emotional self. I worked hard at praying, staying sincere in word and deed, and remaining spiritually connected. I worked hard to combat my poverty and the suffering of my family members. I came to be someone who respected work intensely. I never ran away from it.

I emerged from high school, therefore, a quiet but well-known young lady with a reputation for having a sharp mind, quick wit, and for being a fierce debater. I was the president of my freshman and sophomore classes. I was a thespian, lead actress in all of the school plays. I ran track, played volleyball and basketball. I was captain of the high school rifle team. I played the clarinet. I wrote for the school newspaper, *The Oracle*. I wrote for the literary magazine, *The Eagle*. I was the student liaison to the Board of Education. I had lunch with the principals, the mayor, and the head of the Board of Education. I won several oratorical contests on the U.S. Constitution. At sixteen years old, I went to Washington, D.C., as a legislative intern. I wrote a book of poetry and recited a few pieces on a New York–based television show. I attended Cornell University as preparatory, earning six college credits while still a high school student. Still I worked at McDonald's, delivered the town newspaper to local homes on foot, and worked telemarketing jobs. I was the girl who had never smoked weed. I never did a drug. I never took an alcoholic drink. I was still in love with the human soul. I was still in love with black people, our unique experience, challenges, and lives. I was still in love with love. Yes, I was separate, urgent, intense and "deep."

Upon entering Rutgers University, I learned concisely and precisely the history of the United States. I was introduced to books, facts, and ideas that were never accessible to me in my local library or in public school. I read *The Mis-education of the Negro, The Autobiography of Malcolm X, Angela Davis: An Autobiography, Assata, Institutional Racism in America, A People's History of the United States, One Hundred Years of Lynching, When and Where I Enter, The Soledad Brother, Blood in My Eye, The Wretched of the Earth, Before the Mayflower, The Choice, Native Son,* and *American Hunger,* among a host of other books. Reading became my way of having the conversations that desperately needed to happen between people but were not. Reading kept me more than well informed. Reading became my means of mind travel.

My education at Cornell University and Rutgers University, partnered with my own observations and experiences, gave me a solid understanding of not just my ghetto, but ghettos worldwide. I understood how and why they were set up. I understood how they were maintained. I also understood who profited from the arrangement, and who suffered. This knowledge made it possible for me to love still, but now to understand and defend my people. I wanted to have a hand in rebuilding our men, women, and children, our institutions, our culture, our lives. I believed in what many thought was impossible. I believed I could be part of changing the direction of the world.

How I became an activist, traveling the world from America to Europe to Russia, to Africa, speaking before student audiences, organizing events, fighting for rights causes, making television appearances, all before the age of twenty-one is another story. I'll tell it at some later time. Suffice it to say, when I returned to New York City, which was inevitable, I returned with my brown eyes, sharp mind, and my heart open, ready to work.

I arrived in Harlem to live at age twenty-one. I had a new Madison Avenue job, which paid 200 dollars per week. I got an apartment on 119th Street between Malcolm X Boulevard and Fifth Avenue. I split the 600-dollar rent with a roomate. Working at a civil rights firm, I received information from all around the world about injustices, biased legislation, and racism. The issue that I connected with most, however, was the homeless families and their children living right there in midtown Manhattan next to my job. (For greater detail see my first book, nonfiction, *No Disrespect.*) I struck up a relationship with one of the young homeless girls, which led to a relationship with all of them. I got a firsthand glimpse at the miserable way they were surviving. Because of the love I carried within, the knowledge I gained in life, I felt responsible for them.

These homeless children gave me a great gift. They were young, honest, and raw. They were the truth. They brought me down to the earth after having been in educational orbit. I thought to myself, Soul-jah, if you've been to so many places, read so many books, and know so much, fix this. By interacting with them and their families, I was back in the middle of the same world I feared as a child—the world of drugs, drug dealers, and drug users. The world of poverty. Not the poverty sheltered by grandmothers, scholarships, or college dorms, the real world of the have-nots, lower than the world of project poverty, welfare, section eight, and Medicaid that I grew up in. This was the world of no place to lay your head at night besides a welfare hotel. So at seven years old, these kids worked the streets at all hours, stopping cars and begging for money, or selling whatever they could find or steal. They had nice hiding spots for the little monies they earned, which was necessary to keep their crackhead relatives from smoking it. They would only sleep for a couple of hours during the day, the time it was least likely that they would be molested or raped.

I met these young homeless girls and boys, their older brothers and sisters, boyfriends, mothers, and mommas' boyfriends. I came into this world through an eleven-year-old girl, the first homeless child I met. I was not afraid of the people I encountered from know-ing her. I met young cats I knew hustled drugs because the children told me. They were not the scary drug dealers of my childhood. Phys-ically in fact they were beautiful, pretty brown to awesome black skins, crafted physiques, clean, even, perfect teeth, alluring.

In their homeless state (living in a one-room "welfare hotel" with maybe five to eight other family members, one bathroom, no cooking, no kitchen, no privacy, no amenities), these young black males had high confidence and a great sense of masculinity, much more mas-culinity and confidence than most college men whom I had met throughout the world. As drug dealers, they were not rich or even close to it. They were lookouts, workers, and hand-to-hand dealers who were just getting by. Their sums earned equaled enough to pay for food for the family of eight, "basic living" expenses, with some left over to style so that they never appeared to be homeless to other friends, girlfriends, and associates whose opinion definitely mattered.

If a college degree does not make you a problem solver, you might as well take it back and demand a refund. So I started to educate the homeless children, the five through eleven year olds. Over time it became clear that I needed a separate space to give the full impact that was needed to change their lives, for real.

After conducting careful conversations and research (see *No Disrespect*), I developed a curriculum for an academic, cultural, and recreational summer sleepaway camp. I knew for certain, after traveling throughout the city with a gang of little kids, to the movies, the museums, conferences, libraries, and restaurants, that I needed to offer them more than educational outings, my measly paycheck, and used clothing and shoes. I needed to offer them what I had; peace of mind, safe surroundings, the tools to think, information, intelligence, and the strength to bring about a new reality in a life that had started out all wrong. Returning them every day to the same crazy, state-controlled, drug-infested, prostitution-funded environment was not going to make the lessons stick.

The number one thing that held these kids together was hip-hop music. It was the only thing that they could agree on. It was the only device that made them go from combative hotheads to a cool calmness. It was the only popular thing through which their lives and struggles were recognized and celebrated. It was the only thing that they would listen to, and really hear. Hip-hop artists were rhyming the only words these kids would memorize. They were the only ones discussing the jacked-up conditions, so they were the only black leaders in the minds of these children. There was no Malcolm X or Marcus Garvey. Who were they anyway? "Who cares," they would say. We want Eric B. & Rakim, Big Daddy Kane, and Salt-N-Pepa.

There was no sense, I believed, in fighting the hip-hop celebrities for one of the leadership positions in the ears, hearts, and minds of ghetto youth. I was open to seeing hip-hop as a vehicle, a means to an end. I realized also, if I could make a way into hip-hop, we could save not only these children, we could rock youth worldwide into a new way of living, thinking, and producing.

I knew hip-hop music too, personally. I had grown up right beside it. Whether you were from the ghetto or the 'burbs, there was no way to miss the Sugarhill Gang's "Rapper's Delight" in 1979. The entire country received "The Message" from Grandmaster Flash and the Furious Five in 1981. My brother would play driving hip-hop beats in his room huddled together with his all-male crew. Hot beats, break beats were valuable, shared in secret by the young like a bottle of hypnotic. The walls in my bedroom would buckle when those beats came through his speakers. In junior high and high school, I was never allowed to go out to party the way he was. Usually I was studying something somewhere, probably far away. It would not have mattered much even if I was home. I was never a party girl. I stayed away from parties on purpose. They seemed like obvious places to have fun while making the biggest mistakes a pretty young girl could make. Everybody jammed into a small space, body to body. Parents absent on purpose. The lights out, the music real loud. The beats infectious and sexual. The breasts and thighs sucked into a vacuum of desire. Plenty of young heads ready to satisfy a girl's need. One altercation or wrong glance leading to a casual shooting. It was more than I knew I could handle.

After careful thought, however, I now realized that twenty-one-year-old Souljah needed to get involved in the hip-hop. Not the party, the business. I needed to flip some money into a huge amount that would be enough to send a hundred or more homeless kids away for a safe, educational, cultural, and positive experience for the summer months.

Big ideas came to mind. I needed to let the world know about these kids, who I thought were pure gold. I used the talk radio shows to tell the metropolitan area what was going on in the middle of the financial capital of the world, New York City. This was in the late 80s when radio was open to working with the community instead of against it. Many youth, adults, and even elders from the broader black community became aware and supportive. Precious pennies and small amounts of money were donated in drips. We were grateful. Students from Rutgers, Columbia University, and City College began to help through a student organization that I created along with a handful of friends, The National African Youth Student Alliance.

The hard, cold reality was that I needed more than the popularity of the welfare hotel, homeless kids issue. We needed money, big money to hire buses, rent the camp facility, pay the counselors, purchase the supplies, and a bunch of other important things.

A popular nighttime talk radio personality, Bob Law, introduced me to Bill Stephney, then the vice president of Def Jam Recordings. After a couple of meetings with him, we struck an agreement for him to allow his artists, LL Cool J, Run-D.M.C., and a host of others, to perform at the world famous Apollo Theater. They would donate their performances. I would control the ticket prices. I would pay the cost of renting the theater, the limos, the backstage amenities, security, and the upgraded sound system.

Truthfully, I had no idea what I was doing. I had never done this before. I had never even attended a real music concert before. But everybody had seen me in the five buroughs of New York with these kids who loved me because I was there every day, putting real heart, mind, and time in. People had seen me and the children together on the trains, in the parks, theaters, and museums. The realness made them want to help. Maybe also, the fact that I was willing to do what no one else was willing to do, with the population that no one in power wanted to acknowledge, address, or stand beside.

After learning incredible lessons, small but important details, business practices and requirements, I arrived at the week of the actual concert. The buzz on this event was unbelievable. So many popular artists had signed on to appear. LL Cool J was the headliner. Run-D.M.C. and Salt-N-Pepa dropped out, but Big Daddy Kane, KRS-One and Boogie Down Productions, Queen Latifah, and Rob Base had signed on. All together there were about ten major artists performing, the biggest hip-hop show ever in the history of the Apollo. I was able to raise the ticket prices to an unprecedented amount because of the demand, and because it was a charity event. I was amazed as the artists battled for more onstage performance minutes, when no one was being paid a cent.

On a security walk-through, I learned more than anyone could learn from a book. This was becoming both my business training ground and my street boot camp. I was instructed by the security team on how to deal with hustlers. That's right. I was told that the drug dealers would be out in full force to my show. I was shown where they would sit, how they would act, and what they would require. I was told that they were friends and not enemies. Many of them were buying up entire rows. The box seats had sold at triple the regular price. It was important that certain ones be seen. It was important that I had a popular and appealing show host. It was important the dealers and their crew be acknowledged and respected. Quietly, I was shocked that the elderly man in charge of the security detail, as well as the appointed police officers, were in full awareness of and cooperation with the dealers.

I was told that the dealers were good for business. After all, they would buy the jewels for their girls from the merchants whose shops were located on 125th Street. They would buy their own gold and diamonds out of the 47th Street diamond district. Their dentists would mold new gold fronts and gap fillers. They would have their outfits custom made at Dapper Dan's, a famous African tailor who had a shop on 125th Street. Everybody would purchase new kicks, fresh designer clothing. All of the beauty salons would be packed with girls needing fabulous same-day styles. There would be limos ordered, cars rented, upgraded, and exchanged. There would be new cars, pimped out and rimmed up. Even some Harlem crackheads who had formed an impromptu car-wash business would profit. The drug dealers clearly were big business for the shops owned by whites, blacks, Jews, and Asians. The money makers could not be any happier. The dealers were insiders. "Rabble rousers," community organizers, and activists like myself, who challenged the system and who worked with the poor and powerless, were less acceptable to these businessmen, and made to feel much more uncomfortable than those who supplied the neighborhoods with the illegal drugs that had destroyed so many of us.

Preparing for the show, I learned bits and pieces of what to expect from Harlem, where I lived, versus what to expect from Brooklyn youth or the Bronx or Queens or Staten Island. After breaking through the initial shock that a twenty-one-year-old female was the promoter of the biggest hip-hop show ever, the regular street people, show people, and record industry insiders were toughening me up.

I had to own up to the idea that most of the political and conscious blacks knew me, but the street blacks and middlemen business types did not. The political ones knew me from my activism on behalf of our community. They had seen me on the political television shows and heard me on the political radio shows. They knew my intellectual toughness, cultural commitment, work ethic, and sharp tongue. The streets were just getting to know me. The middlemen in business were in awe and envy. They saw me as incoming competition that must either be coopted or crushed. It became clear that I needed to consider making some kind of alliance.

I hired the Fruit of Islam to do security for me. As far as I was concerned, at that time they were running things. They were an army of big, beautiful, strong black men respected by and respectful of the black community. The artists, the businessmen, the youth, and even the dealers would yield to them. They were under the direction of Farrakhan, leader of the Nation of Islam, who was on fire in the '80s, and I knew that they respected me as well and would hold me down, making sure that everything was at peace, and everybody played their part correctly.

On the night of the show, no one was more excited than me. I had never seen so many beautiful young girls, decorated and adorned so perfectly. Their styles were so original, carefully crafted and alluring. They had outdone Hollywood, Fifth Avenue, and Paris. They stopped me in my tracks as I watched with my jaw dropped open. The cats were correct also. They had leathers and suedes, Gucci and Louis Vuitton prints, all arranged differently than how they were offered and sold in the department stores. The tailor had hooked it up just right. They looked better. They complemented the black physique and style superbly. They strolled into the theater slowly, mindful of being admired. Their heads were held high. They were surrounded by entourages, they were at least as famous as the rap stars on the stage.

When the curtain opened and the first act appeared the crowd went wild. I watched from backstage. I could see the audience head on. No one could have accurately described the love, enthusiasm, dedication, and complete obedience the artists received from this crowd unless they were actually there. I watched a thousand youth and young adults get up and recite every rhyme. They danced, screamed, cheered for whatever building, block, or borough they hailed from. They acknowledged the hustlers in the crowd and box seats. It was incredible.

That night we had two shows. We made all the money for the buses, the kids, the camp, the staff, and all the related fees. The homeless children were backstage in disbelief that the same artists whom they worshipped had paused to give something back to them. I was mindful that it was incredible that the hip-hop stars were all between the ages of fifteen and twenty-four. I was twenty-one; the youth we were working with and for were six through sixteen. We had made a complete unified leap forward and we were all barely adults.

I never got swept away by the entertainment world. I remain, even today, close to the earth. I still run an annual summer camp for our youth. Now it is financed by Sean P. Diddy Combs. I don't have to go out and make the money myself anymore. Over time, I have seen the young come under my guidance and direction and go from crack families to become chemical engineers, social workers, teachers, and doctors.

On the writer's side, I developed a careful eye. I learned the difference between the young teenage male selling drugs hand to hand for basic survival and the men who had the box seats, the cars, trucks, jewels, homes, and riches. I learned the difference between one-hit wonders and huge hip-hop stars that go on to create empires. I know the difference in the way a man feels when he can earn and when he can't. I know the difference between street girls and college girls and professional black women. I know the difference between friends and enemies, the used and the users. I know the difference between love and sex, between life and death, between incarceration and freedom. Every writer needs to know the difference between one thing and another. It is critical to creating, developing, and shaping characters who are so natural and so authentic that people read your work then go looking for them as if they really exist.

I went on to promote similar hip-hop events over a seven-year period. I went from drawing audiences of 1,000 to audiences of 30,000. I went from promoting shows with LL Cool J, Doug E. Fresh, Slick Rick, and Public Enemy, to promoting shows with Notorious B.I.G. and Lauryn Hill and the Fugees. They were all community shows with a conscious purpose. Many of the artists became aquaintances and friends. One business led to another. I became a real part of the black community on every level. I was no longer just an intellectual who could only read and speak about it and not be about it. I was now respected as someone who criticizes constructively, but also builds institutions, and organizations. I became known as someone who gathered alot and shared alot. I became known as a woman who was respected for her mind, thoughts, words, and actions, whose physical appearance was nice but not all up in your face.

The authenticity in *The Coldest Winter Ever,* the story line and characters, comes from having lived a real, full life. The richness comes from having walked and worked among and beside all kinds of people from the poorest, who may in fact have been the most colorful, to the mediocre and wealthy. There is a difference between writers who are impatient and writers who are patient. There is a difference between writers who live in front of a television or inside a movie theater and writers who live by doing, working, participating, talking, and observing. There is a difference between writers who live on one particular block, or in one particular place, and those who move all around the globe. There is a difference between writers who have read and studied the great writings of powerful writers who came before them, and those who have not. There is a difference between writers who have had the discipline to at some point sit still and study the craft of writing and those who have not. I would say to all up-and-coming writers that you need to first be willing to learn, to be observant and patient. You must also live life, build something, do something, develop something. It is the only way to sit down and create an authentic work with vivid descriptions and compelling characters. Capturing the truth of the human soul and experience and weaving it together like a fine tapestry is creating characters, voices, and scenes that will live forever.

4. Why did you decide to include yourself as a character in the novel *The Coldest Winter Ever?*

As an author, the first task you have is to make the reader care about your story. If you can create an emotion in the reader in the first paragraph, you can be certain that you got 'em. If you fail to create an emotion right away, you lose the reader.

At the time that I penned *The Coldest Winter Ever,* I knew I was both loved and hated by hundreds and thousands of people. When the main character in the story, Winter Santiaga, stated up front that she hated Sister Souljah, she created an instant emotion in the readers who knew and loved me. They would naturally be curious and defensive. They would feel something that would drag them right into the tale.

For the people who hated me, there would be a feeling of solidarity with Winter, and the great expectation that yes! Sister Souljah is about to be challenged and exposed. As a result, they would also be dragged into the story.

Besides, females competing and fighting is cheered on in American society. Many people love to read about it, witness it, and choose sides. For African women it is outright expected that we hate each other. It is known but not discussed that we have many conscious and subconscious problems with image, complexion, identity, culture, finance, love, community, and family.

Also, as a literary technique, I thought it was clever to have the protagonist, Winter Santiaga, and the antagonist, Sister Souljah, in reverse positions. After all, the protagonist is supposed to be not only the principle character, the protagonist is supposed to be the leader of a cause, the one whom the reader cheers for. The fact that the reader ends up cheering resoundingly for Winter, the drug dealer's daughter, who uses, abuses, and manipulates people, is revealing and refreshing to me. Because, in America, it happens in real life. Those who are doing what we have traditionally accepted as being wrong, get the most attention. They are seen as the most cool, sensual, sexual, and acceptable. As the reader cheers for Winter no matter how deadly her behavior becomes in the story, I am hoping that the reader will pause and ask, What do I believe? What kind of person am I? What is right? What is wrong? What kind of woman would I like to be and/or become? Or, What kind of woman would I like to love? Or, What kind of daughter would I like to raise?

In the meantime, I am hopeful that as Sister Souljah the character, who attempts to do right in the world, becomes more and more of a nuisance in the story, it will cause readers to ask themselves why is it so common to reject and even hate the people who are helping in a real way to reverse the tide of evil? What do helpful/activist types of people really make you think and feel? Are their lives and their work a complete waste of time? Should they stop completely and get a "real" job? Or, is there some value in what they have dedicated themselves to? Is the actual truth that helpers and activists can only be loved after they're dead? Or should the community consider their continuous contributions while they're living, conscious, and available to be appreciated?

Overall, I knew by including myself in the story, I was giving readers a compass to find their way. I would have been wrong and guilt ridden to simply throw readers into Winter's world without a way to navigate themselves toward what I perceive to be the truth. To do so would've been to create another piece that glorifies greed, and excuses violence, and leads young males and females astray.

5. When and where were you when you first started writing *The Coldest Winter Ever?*

Writing is a process. No one just sits down and lets it rip. In 1993 I started breastfeeding my son. The whole adventure of getting married, then giving birth to my child was the richest and most peaceful period of time in my life. It was also the most emotional time in my life. It was the most sensitive I had ever been. My thoughts became even deeper. It was the most isolated and secluded I have ever been, personally by choice, politically by design. Knowing that I had released into this world a new life made me feel even more responsible for improving cultural, economic, and social conditions. In other words, it was the best time to get writing. I felt if the twenty year olds didn't write of love, work, life, war, and death, then the teens would not know about or be prepared to make better choices. If the thirty year olds did not write, then the twenty year olds would not know. If the forty year olds did not write, then the thirty year olds wouldn't know what to expect and build toward, and so on. I started by scribbling notes on odd pieces of paper. While out buying things for our baby, I would pick up random notepads and jot down thoughts and ideas, then tuck them into my private library. I knew I wanted to be a part of stopping the cycle of stupidity in our community. I knew that to do so, I had to write something that kids and adults could take home and devour, learn from, and share, and pass on.

It's funny. When you find peace in your personal life the word goes out. The simple discovery of it brings people from miles around to come take a look. They want to know is it possible? Is it real? Can it last? Can it happen in more than this one case? Two youths who came seeking my counsel in 1993 were the perfect examples of absolute black beauty, grace, and talent. Yet they were the examples also of social, cultural, and spiritual chaos. I was not able to be a mother to them. I was not old enough. However, I could be their older sister. I knew that sharing my experiences, observations, philosophies, and beliefs would help them at least to know what their options could and would be and what the consequences of their choices would feel and be like. I started to think about how I had received thousands of letters from youth wanting guidance, none of them famous like Lauryn Hill and Tupac Shakur. Yet they all deserved it. Young people deserve hearing the truth from any wise and balanced adult. I knew that it was essential that I continue to create life-altering writings, fiction and nonfiction.

The bulk of *The Coldest Winter Ever* was written in Jamaica in 1995. I was still breast-feeding. (I did so for the first three years of my son's life.) After successfully producing a concert for Lauryn and the Fugees, which 30,000 young black and Latino New Yorkers attended to watch the most famous artist in hip-hop worldwide perform and speak in a free outdoor concert in Harlem, N.Y., we flew to Jamaica. Because everyone on my producing team had worked so hard, I thought it would be cool to share the production fee and bring them. On what was my first trip to Jamaica, me, my husband, and son were accompanied by ten others.

The Waterhouse section of Kingston, Jamaica, is a straight up ghetto. My Jamaican-Panamanian husband had always made jokes about me being a Yankee girl from the projects. I was shocked standing in the huts his people called home. With very little food, and "no water at the moment," his relatives who insisted that we stay with them and not in a hotel, escorted us to the bed where all ten of us were supposed to sleep. I looked around in complete amazement. My eyes shot toward my husband, the five female workers, the five male workers, and then fell onto my son. My husband smiled. We bounced to a resort.

After a comfortable sleep each night, I'd roam into the Jamaican streets and ghettoes. I watched grown men and women walking around outside wearing no shoes, while hungry goats mill about. I became sad. Despite having run around the world, I had never been to the islands. Over the years, however, I had met plenty of youth and famous music artists from Jamaica. They were all ten times more proud than anyone else. They were always the ones careful to big up the African culture. They were always the ones to encourage the natural, cherish the family. Bob Marley was their undisputed king.

But clearly there was so much unfinished business in Jamaica. There was massive poverty. Yet there was a new generation who refused to love the land and grow foods. They felt farming was beneath them. There was an ocean, yet there was not enough fish for everyone to eat at mealtime. There were black workers anxious to accommodate white tourists but visibly and verbally hostile to the black tourist. There were girls everywhere, naked with foul attitudes and a miseducation.

It was the Jamaican ghetto climate that encouraged me to finish *The Coldest Winter Ever,* an exploration of not only ghetto life, but ghetto psychology and the set-up that people in hoods everywhere face. While there I also completed four songs (unreleased). Once again I was shook into producing something that I hoped would resurrect the human soul, and save the women and men from an obvious and evil cycle of destruction.

6. Which character did you create first?

Winter Santiaga was the first character I created. I wanted to write the most accurate depiction of the characteristics I felt were becoming popular in the teen female population. I felt if I could use all of my powers of imagination to capture that crazy, selfish attitude, along with that uncontainable spirit, all packaged inside the typically beautiful black ghetto girl body, I would have the most powerful and accurate urban female character ever written up until this time.

The second character I created was Midnight. I felt like a sculptor with a chisel. I loved the process of breathing life into him. Santiaga was next because I knew I needed to show what Midnight would become if he did not make a dramatic change in his lifestyle. Then there were Bullet and Natalie. Mrs. Santiaga came afterward. I knew she would be a mother who basically talked a lot of foolishness and rah rah, while basically standing by and letting things that should not be happening, happen.

7. How did you write the novel, what method?

I saw the novel as a movie in my head. As the pictures connected one by one in my mind's eye, I wrote down the words that described exactly what I saw. I knew I had to choose the right words. I wanted you, the reader, to see what I saw, exactly as I saw it in my mind. I tried to make each character be the kind of character who wanted to get the reader onto his or her side. In order for each character to struggle for a space in the mind and heart of the reader, I had to let them argue their position, which was to convince you that they are real. There are no small characters in *The Coldest Winter Ever*. Even the characters who did the most subtle things or appeared the least, wanted to be real. The bodyguards of GS, the girl in the abortion clinic who kept having all of the abortions, the girls in the bathroom who gave Winter the bag with the guns and drugs, the old lady in the hotel parking lot whom Winter clobbered. I imagined that they all wanted to convince you that they existed.

I write every word out in longhand with a regular pen and paper, not a computer. Usually I write surrounded by people in motion, for example in a library or bookstore, or at a family wedding!

8. Are Winter Santiaga and the Santiaga family black?

Yes, they are a black family. I was surprised by how many people asked this question in letters and emails. However, I do understand where the questions are coming from. The name Santiaga is a Latino-sounding name. Therefore, many are assuming that the family is Spanish, and that if they are Spanish, they are not black. The confusion on these type of issues stems from not understanding African history, geography, and culture. Black people were the first humans to inhabit this Earth. We were navigators, merchants, and travelers throughout the globe. Therefore we may be found living and or born anywhere on the globe, speaking any of over 1,000 languages. There were even black people living in what we now know as America, before the coming of Christopher Columbus and Amerigo Vespucci. (See Dr. Ivan Van Sertima's book *They Came Before Columbus*.)

For most students of every race, because of the inaccurate American public school curriculum, the study of the black presence and contribution to the world begins at slavery. It's as if blacks did not exist, prosper, and build before becoming slaves.

However, through slavery, black Africans were captured, transported, and dispersed as unpaid laborers throughout the globe. As a result you will find large numbers of blacks living everywhere, speaking every language. Because the blacks were considered property, and were then owned by the English, Spanish, French, Italian, Irish and Portuguese, they were forced to abandon their original African names. The new names that blacks were assigned were European names. This is why millions of blacks today have Spanish, French, Italian, German, Dutch, Swedish, Portuguese, and English–sounding names even though they are not Europeans. This is also why you cannot determine whether a person is black or white by simply knowing their name.

When I was a college student, I learned all of these truths. When I traveled outside of the country, they were reiterated. When I was in Russia, everyone kept asking me if I was from Cuba. I thought that was completely strange. Then finally I met a Russian college student who had traveled to Cuba. He explained that most of the people in Cuba are black like me!

My husband, who is black, has a Latino-sounding last name. Now so do I. I am amazed by his many friends who come from Jamaica, Panama, Belize, Costa Rica, Guyana, Antigua, Barbados, Grenada, and Puerto Rico. They are all black-skinned people speaking English as well as other languages.

9. What were you trying to achieve with the novel *The Coldest Winter Ever?*

First, I wanted to write a great piece of literature. I wanted it to have wonderful characters, accurate language use, vivid but not over-done descriptions, intricate foreshadowing, powerful themes, multi-leveled plots, and an ending that created a craving for more. I wanted to write something so great that even if you hate me, you still would be willing to truthfully say "that was the best novel I ever read in my lifetime!"

More specifically, I wanted so much good to come out of the novel. I don't know if to this day, what I wanted is what was achieved. I know the book is extremely popular. But here is what I was going for.

a. **To put drug use out of style.** I thought by creating characters like Mrs. Santiaga and showing step by step how she went from Halle Berry or Angela Basset type of beauty to a crazy, crumbling crackhead, I would let all youth know that drugs make you not only unhealthy, but mentally unstable and ugly.

b. **To put drug dealing out of style.** I thought by showing the decline of Ricky Santiaga, how he went from being at the top of his game to becoming a slave, I would teach the youth that drug dealing is not a smart or viable business option. Especially now when so many businesses have opened up to the youth through the success of hip hop. Now you can become paid, happy, and successful doing so many other things. You can go into photography, graphics, clothing design, styling, real estate, film directing, video directing, game design, shoe companies, vending, or writing. Nowadays, if you're smart, it's about creativity, patience, and aggression, teamwork, and profitable legal business practices.

c. **To get youth to recognize their talents and convert them into business.** I thought that Winter Santiaga was so incredibly talented. I see so many ghetto youth like her in that way, every day. If she would have recognized that all of her talents were gifts that could have been shaped into successful and legal business, she would never have had to chase after dudes with money, rappers, or the drug game. I see girls in the ghetto every day who may not give a damn about school, but who are so creative. They can zig-zag a thousand braids on your head in unbelievably perfect, neat designs. That is both a talent and a business. It's part of the beauty industry. In New York you can charge professional women one hundred dollars or more for those type of styles. Two or three heads a day, you could be straight. Instead of walking down the jail corridor in a straight line.

d. **To get the youth to use their time wisely.** Natalie was a good example of someone who wasted a lot of time. She would have her radio on, her television on, and be gossiping on the telephone at the same time. She was in everybody's business. But she did not have any real business of her own. The reason why she did not have her own money was because she wasted so much time doing things that added up to zero. All the while, she believed she was doing big things! I think every kid should realize that this is America. America is made up of businesses. You are either the owner or the owned. So use your time to figure out what kind of product you are going to create and sell. Make it legal. Do a good job and make it of good quality. Your career could start off as something simple. Maybe you'll become a world-famous photographer who started off with an instant throwaway camera from the corner store. Maybe you'll begin by photographing your friends, your hood. Maybe you'll tell your story to the world in pictures.

e. **To recapture the black male identity.** I felt that too many people had too great an influence over who our fathers, brothers, and sons have become and are becoming. When it becomes normal for our sons to name themselves after reputed murderers, gangsters, drug dealers, and pimps, we can be sure they have decided they have no one else worth looking up to, no one else's life who they would like to imitate. We can be certain they have no clear understanding of what manhood is, as well as no black man who they feel represents all of the characteristics, dimensions, and power of what black manhood is supposed to be. Currently our sons are naming and imaging themselves after Noriega, Escobar, Gotti, Alpo, Don Corleone, Gambino, Bishop Don Juan, Pretty Tony, and a host of other destroyers.

I believe there are some real examples of black masculinity and manhood. However they have not been popularized, marketed, written about, filmed, and commercialized. I am trying, as one woman, to bring back and magnify the true and accurate essence of black manhood. Writing the character of Midnight was one way in which I am trying to accomplish it. Perhaps when he is brought to film, one of my goals will be achieved.

f. **To redesign the black female identity.** I wanted to shake up the backward notions of womanhood pushed by the American money machine. It seems that they are pushing images of women that are only one- or two-dimensional. For example, you are either cute and stupid, or ugly and smart, or scientific and reclusive, or business-minded and morally bankrupt, or sexy and whoreish, or athletic and masculine, or political and boring. Most women, I believe, are not only two things. They are so much more. We also would like to raise our daughters to be so much more. In marketing Sister Souljah as a character, I hoped to show that the possibility exists that you can be from the projects, drug free, paid, political, popular, cultural, pretty, productive, married, motherly, powerful, feminine, intelligent, beautiful, and loved.

g. **To put the black family back together again.** Through the Santiagas I knew people would be impressed with the idea of family. I knew daughters would fall in love with the idea of having a father. I knew wives would fall in love with the idea of being married to a sexy provider. I knew single women would fall in love with the idea of having a husband. It's sad that family has become an "idea" as opposed to a reality. I wanted to have readers fall in love with the idea of family. I wanted people to repeat Santiaga's famous line, "Family sticks together." It is my hope, however, that the story successfully translates that family must stick together around a positive, life-giving, meaningful plan. Because when family is united around negative leadership, and a wrong plan, they don't end up together. They end up separate.

h. **To expose how the American economy is fueled by drug dealing and drug money.** I thought it was important to show that it is not a coincidence that there are so many drugs in poor black and Latino neighborhoods. I wanted to highlight how the government made it possible for these hoods to be flooded with drugs, so that the poor would remain doped up and powerless, unable to focus, concentrate, organize, protest, or build. I wanted to show how some police officers, police precincts, and politicians participate in drug dealing. I wanted to show how prisons, which are huge money-making ventures, can actually be filled up with entire neighborhoods of people who were simply trying to enjoy life and ease the pain of poverty.

I also wanted to show how those who have the potential to provide the leadership in a poor ghetto community end up turning on that same community by becoming drug dealers. Instead of adopting the philosophy that we can work together to save, to heal, to build legal business in, and to control the politics of our hood, a few go for the quick dollars and sacrifice the souls they could have saved.

Lastly, I wanted to show through the character Bullet how the state will finance and protect a drug dealer like Santiaga, as long as he pays off the right people. However, when they decide to take him down, they still have another crew to replace him. Because there is a need for the powerful to keep the drugs available in our communities, to keep our kids either dealing or incarcerated for dealing. To keep our families using or either rehabing from using. To keep the probation officers checking our urine. To keep the corrections officers locking our cells. To keep us fighting one another. To keep the police policing us. To keep us in a constant state of aggravation, disunity, powerlessness, poverty, and slavery.

10. Will there be a movie of *The Coldest Winter Ever,* Part I?

Yes, however it will not be quick. Sister Souljah in Hollywood, feels like a lion in the middle of an ocean.

CHARACTER ANALYSIS:

WINTER SANTIAGA

The voice of Winter Santiaga is strong and decisive. Her boldness is the everyday style of millions of ghetto girls worldwide who wear attitude like battle armor. This is why she is the thirteen-year-old, undisputed protagonist of the novel *The Coldest Winter Ever*.

A five-year-old ghetto girl is as grown as any twelve-year-old girl living anywhere else. Her experiences are multiplied and accelerated, as she lives out her life right beside, on top of, and below hundreds of men, women, and children, all project dwellers.

In the projects, space is tight. Too many times it is dangerous, sometimes dirty. A five-year-old ghetto girl may be in charge of an apartment that is mostly motherless. She may be responsible for the care of an infant child, to cook, to guard the door keys, to lie to the curious welfare workers, children's service agents, probation officers, and other controlling onlookers. She "holds it down" while Mommy works for metro money, chicken, and 150-dollar sneakers.

She can stare you dead in your eye without blinking. Deceive you without smiling. Put you in your place when you cross well-drawn lines and boundaries. She knows when someone is looking at her funny, drinking too much, or about to do something shiesty. If you fight her, she'll fight you back, even if you're bigger. If she thinks you want to fight her, she'll punch you in your face first, just to get the jump on you. If you help her, she'll take what you've got but never trust you. She'll use it but won't depend on it happening twice.

Ghetto girls are hell-bent on survival. They don't think they might be attacked. They're sure they will. This ain't poetry or music. She's trying to grow up without people stealing all her stuff; her pocketbook or her pussy, her shoes or her sanity, her money or her man, her rights or her reputation. The victorious are the ghetto girls who are able to, through hook or crook, gain the most and lose the least.

This is why the fearless Winter Santiaga, an alluring teen in a ripe body, is liked, lusted after, and loved in ghettos from Brooklyn to Jamaica, Johannesburg to Brixton, Brazil, and back. Winter pushes to remain the taker and not the tooken.

Imagine the mixture of fight and fortitude the ghetto breeds, with the arrogance of affluence, a human Molotov. The result—little Miss Winter Santiaga. Born in 1977, in Brooklyn, New York, Winter is the daughter of Mr. and Mrs. Ricky Santiaga. Her younger sisters are named Porsche, Mercedes, and Lexus Santiaga. Their family gained wealth through her father's carefully constructed illegal drug dealing empire.

The drug money and all of the expensive material possessions it can buy place Winter in the position of being an upper-middle-class girl, living in an underclass ghetto. Her father's henchmen, a network of uncles, aunts, and cousins, all of whom earn from her father's business, protect and insulate Winter from the hatred and jealousy that is unavoidable when one clique in the hood is eating and earning while the majority of people starve and scrape to get by.

Winter, in turn, decorates herself in jewels and authentic designer wear. The amount of beautiful things she has stands out, because it is not one or two items from time to time. It's an unrelenting daily fashion onslaught of the best of everything from small to large, accessories included. Under normal standards, living where she lived, she would've been challenged and robbed, maybe even raped, definitely harassed. Instead, it was this "unreality" that framed her mentality. She had these things, she believed, because she was supposed to. She was a princess, the other girls were not. Her father was the king, the other men were not. Her mother was the queen, the other mothers were not. It was a ghetto hierarchy that moved from the top, King Santiaga, to the bottom, the defeated crackheads. Winter's attitude was, "Hey . . . bow down to the family who puts food on the table for you and yours."

Winter's ghetto love was rooted in things remaining exactly how she experienced them as a member of the reigning family. The fact of the matter is, for sixteen years she never had the authentic ghetto experience. Or at least we can say, she never had the same feelings, fears, realities, and hard times that girls her age had living in the same exact building.

For example, Winter does not have to deal with poverty of any kind. The other girls do. She does not have to answer to or prepare for welfare workers, probation officers, or intruders. The other girls do. She doesn't fear the police like many poor people who have been unfairly brutalized or murdered for being black while standing, running, driving, or putting their hands in their pockets. "They work for Poppa . . . ," she says of the police. She does not have to deal with unwanted sexual advances by boys or men. The other girls do. Just a glance at Winter by a peeping locksmith leaves the worker trying to hold his face together after having it slashed open by Santiaga's knife as punishment. Not to mention the fact that she has a biological and present father, unlike the overwhelming majority of her friends.

The fact of the matter is, there is no threatening authority in the life of Winter Santiaga prior to her father's downfall. She does not even have to respond to teachers, guidance counselors, or school administrators. Winter says:

> I wasn't gonna report to school everyday like it was some type of job when they weren't even paying me for it. School was like a hustle. Teachers wanted me to come . . . so they could get paid to control me . . . I just wasn't having it.

Everyone is beneath Winter, beholden to her and her family, or irrelevant and nonexistent. This permanently alters her ability to experience healthy friendships. When one person has money and her friends don't, the bond that supposedly holds them together can be either flimsy or completely artificial. When the money holder speaks they all listen. When the one with the money is wrong, no one corrects her. Instead they fear being cut out of the benefits that hanging out with the money girl brings. Even a spunky friend like Natalie can be impacted by a simple reminder that she's wearing one of Winter's old dresses. And, in every situation where there is a good thing and an excellent thing, the friend without the money is expected to settle for a good thing while of course the friend with the money takes and deserves the excellent thing. When it's time to fight, a brawl with some chicks, Winter does not have to fight. Just the sight of Winter's face, a reminder that "Santiaga runs things," causes would-be bullies to stop dead in their tracks and fall back.

Winter grew addicted to this arrangement. She fed off of the attention. After all, the entire neighborhood had watched her grow up, experiencing life as none of them had. The neighbors saw Winter and her family floss, ride expensive cars and limos, throw big parties, spend money, gather gifts, and parade privileges. Earline's Beauty Salon was a stage for Winter and her mom to flex their power. All business stopped and was redirected toward them when they entered the already packed facility.

When the Santiaga family, under the leadership of the father, picks up and moves to a Long Island mansion, Winter does not see this as advancement as most people would. She prefers the projects to the palace. She prefers the cement to the grass. She prefers the commotion to the peace. She needed to be in the projects with hundreds of people beneath her. She needed her friends to need her and to depend on and sweat her stuff. She needed her captive audience, and jealous schoolmates. She needed to be surrounded by familiar but subordinate things. It was her position in the hierarchy that drove her personality. In the suburbs no one knew her position or cared who she was, or worshipped and feared her father. Out there, she met her worse fear. She just blended in.

The Daughter-Father Relationship

From birth Winter was handed some twisted traditions. Her father sent a limo to pick her mother and the infant up from the hospital. He gave her a 24-karat-gold diamond ring on the third day of her life. He obviously thought that this was special, as she was told this story as soon as she was able to understand. The moral of the story he told Winter was "It was important for me to know I deserved the best, no slum jewelry, cheap shoes, or knock-off designer stuff, only the real thing." So what's wrong with this picture?

Stories of early childhood clue children in on who their parents really are, what really happened, and who they will ultimately grow up to be. The story of the limo and the ring is not about how a loving father slept in the hospital room right beside the mother in anticipation of the birth of his first child. In fact, Santiaga was not even there, hence the limo. The story that Winter holds up as told by her father is not about the smile on his face or the fear on his face as he witnessed a baby coming through the birth canal. It's not about something she saw her father do that stuck in her mind forever. It's about material possessions being given to define and/or express a father's connection to his daughter. The story reveals the depth of the connection of the father and daughter, and the lack of depth at the same time.

Fathers set their daughters' standard of manhood. Winter grew to see her father as a proud provider. One of his greatest values to her was his consistency in giving her stuff—diamond rings, necklaces and tennis bracelets, clothes, shoes, coats, pocketbooks, hairstyles, and of course cash. She consequently began to look at men as being worth what they could give her. A man who could not buy her, was less of a man. He deserved nothing more than to be used, sexually or otherwise, like Sterling.

Santiaga taught Winter that she deserved the best, but not because she worked for it, or accomplished anything in her life. She deserved it because he said so. She deserved it because she was royalty.

When a child is given things of great material worth, through no effort of her own, she loses the awareness of its value. No matter how much it cost, or what it took for the parent to acquire it, the child does not get the actual life experience of earning. The child has no scale on which to weigh or appreciate its value. Whether a child is rich or poor, by not requiring a child to prove herself worthy of gifts, valuables, and excess, the parent corrupts the child's understanding of capital in capitalist America.

The child who is flooded with things, grows to expect them, needs them even. As time moves on, it will take more and more things to excite and delight the child, coming at a faster pace. Those items, although they increase in monetary cost, become less and less impressive to the child. However, they remain very impressive to the child's friends who have never enjoyed even one hundreth of that lifestyle. The delight therefore then comes from the child showing off her stuff to her friends and getting a charge out of the envy and excitement the onlookers display. Winter Santiaga was so addicted in this way, she clearly stated that she would go to school only "If I had a new outfit to show off or some new jewels I knew I'd get sweated for. . . ."

In the process of giving Winter too much, Santiaga was also taking something away. All the years he spends "over providing and protecting" her from the real world, is time lost helping her to develop a skill of her own. Time is lost that she could've spent charting an independent course where she would have challenged herself to answer the question: What will I do when I grow up and am on my own? What is my personal plan and purpose on this Earth?

Another twisted tradition was the decision not to send Winter to school with regularity. In the novel, she never discusses any academic course or extra-curricular activities. Now, we all know that education can happen in many ways. It is not always necessary to attend the public school that is offered up to American youth. But, no private school, no home instruction, no family library or bookstore outings, no outside reading or information coming in, is a guarantee that your child will be naive and ignorant.

For many decades, many blacks in America have been confusing looking good with doing well. Mothers have taken two jobs to "make their children look right, and keep up," when, in fact, no matter how well dressed, manicured, and heeled your child is, if she does not have any knowledge, any skill, if she has not mastered anything, she is not doing well. Winter Santiaga looked great. Winter Santiaga could read, write, and count. Yet, Winter Santiaga was ignorant.

In the ghetto if you are born into the painful reality of having a criminal parent, an addict parent, an alcoholic parent, or an uneducated parent, the other adults in your extended family—the grandmother or grandfather, the aunts and uncles and cousins—become your opportunity to see beyond the limitations of your parents' choices and circumstances. Any one of them may provide the alternative model or blueprint for you to pattern yourself after. Winter Santiaga's extended family, the ones who lived close to her, were all involved in, or hostage to, or beneficiaries of criminal activity. Criminal activity was her norm.

When Winter is in a tight spot, after the takedown of her father, she cannot, or does not, think constructively about how to make money, employ herself, or reignite her education. Even though her skills as a cosmetologist, manicurist, beautician, decorator, and designer were impeccable and apparent to the reader, they were not considered viable options to Winter. They were, she figured, just something she would use to raise money to invest in and get herself set up in the drug world. The drug world, because of her father's and family's example, seemed the obvious choice. It was almost as if the legitimate options she had available, she considered beneath her and temporary. The illegal options she considered a step up and in.

Ricky Santiaga did talk to his daughter. His words were lessons in street survival. For example, he taught her how to be the daughter of a drug kingpin. He taught her to keep the family business quiet. He taught her how to profile and stunt, to look the part. He taught her not to go out with men who were not sharp and aggressive, not to go out with men who can't give her, again, what she deserves. He gave her little stories about how he set up his drug business and why.

Yet he never trained her to survive in the real world, the legitimate realm. There was no talk of managing savings and bank accounts. There was no talk of life insurance or trust funds. There was no talk of a cash reserve, property ownership, deed transfers, equity, godparents, a plan B, a plan C. He never prepared Winter for the legitimate business world. He knew that his "profession" was susceptible to collapse and seizure. Still, when he was incarcerated, in the absence of access to his team, he attempted to use an unprepared Winter to conduct business with his lawyer or at least to serve as his messenger girl.

I never got the sense that Santiaga knew that what he was not saying was so much more heavy than what he was saying. The everyday example he set was so loud. His style was so overwhelming. The words he shared with Winter could not counteract his actions. His words did not steer her away from wanting his lifestyle. In fact his everyday presence seduced her. It made everything else in the world look miniscule and unsuccessful. Him telling Winter, therefore, to forget about marrying someone like himself or Midnight, fell on deaf ears. In his last moments of freedom he tried to urge Winter toward " . . . one of these big-headed doctors, lawyers, engineer boys . . ." instead of desiring a man in the drug game. But, her definition, image, and understanding of manhood had already been cemented by the example his life choices had already set.

There is no sense in labeling Souljah the hater. The flimsiness of the foundation Santiaga built for his daughter was made obvious by Winter herself. When she dates Bullet and Midnight reveals to her that Bullet is from the other team—"While your daddy was being raided you were having drinks butt naked with the enemy"—Winter does not side with her father and refuse to have anything to do with the man who brought about her father's downfall, according to his top lieutenant. We are not discussing here Winter's words or her emotions. We are discussing her actual actions. She speaks of loving her father, being loyal to her father. When it comes right down to the bottom line, how deep is her love?

Love is a demonstrative word. *Webster's* lists love as a noun. I believe it is a verb, an action word. Love is supposed to make you do something. It is supposed to make you feel something deep and compelling that leads you to be unselfish, loyal, and protective. When someone violates the person you love, the least you can do is refuse to acknowledge, interact with, and support the enemy.

The fact of the matter is that Santiaga raised a daughter who was a hustler. A hustler's first law is to get him or herself into a lucrative and sweet position. A hustler will trade anything for success, even people. A hustler will say anything, do anything, hurt anybody who stands in the way. Additionally, Winter's criteria for choosing a man was based on what a man can do for her. Santiaga was down. Bullet was up. Therefore Winter chose Bullet, conveniently forgetting to support her father and ignoring the fact that Bullet was from the other team. "Family sticks together."

The Mother-Daughter Relationship

"Momma didn't work 'cause beauty, she said, was a full-time occupation."

This is Winter's description of her mother. All of the additional words and scenarios Winter spoke of were some version of the above quote. Winter's mom gave Winter the tradition of women as physical, sexual beings, one-dimensional creatures. She taught Winter how to reach visual perfection. It was because of the mom that Winter knew how to dress and take care of her hair, skin, and nails. Her mom taught her what to be—"a bad bitch." A bad bitch, according to the mother, is a woman who outshines every other woman. She is so alluring that she attracts the big fish, the man who is supposed to take care of her for the rest of her life. Winter's mom taught Winter that "beautiful women are supposed to be taken care of." They are supposed to shop, spend, and shop some more 'cause "like mom says, you can never have too much." Although physical beauty and sexuality is one aspect of feminine power, what happened to the other 358 degrees of wisdom and understanding that should have transferred from mother to daughter? The absence of this information created a Winter Santiaga who was an emotional, mental, spiritual, and intellectual midget.

Moreover, the absence of a mother whose presence teaches love, compassion, intelligence, consideration, and consciousness leads to the creation of daughters and sons who cannot love anyone in a wholesome way themselves. Consequently, the mother's shortcomings become the daughter's shortcomings.

Once Winter's mother is shot in her face, her visual perfection is shattered. Since Winter was taught that this physical beauty was the essence of womanhood, and is in fact what makes you a "bad bitch," the crooked face meant that her mother went from being a queen to becoming an irrelevant peasant.

We witnessed Winter's lack of capacity for emotion in the treatment of her mom. When her mother returns from the hospital, she plots to gain control of her mother's new red Mercedes Benz instead of having a genuine commitment to her mother's healing. She's thinking, well, I'm still beautiful, why waste too much time worrying about anything or anyone else?

After the takedown of her father and the seizure of his material possessions, Winter is forced to ride the New York City subway. She mentions being embarassed by her mom's appearance. She turns her body away from her mother to pretend the two of them are not really sitting and riding together on the train.

Throughout the hard times Winter never sees her mother as an asset. The idea that two or three heads is better than one when attempting to solve a problem never crosses her mind. She does not respect her mother's ability to think or hustle. Moreover, because her mother is now "ugly," she looks at and treats her as if she's useless.

Winter, as an emotional dwarf, lacks the awareness and intelligence to help her mom fight the mental illness and drug addiction that is quickly approaching. She thinks only of how her mother's downfall will effect her friends' image of herself.

In fact, after her Long Island home was raided, and all of the material possessions seized, Winter takes her mother's last 700 dollars and selfishly hogs it to adorn herself with new clothes in the middle of a crisis situation. We could only wish that this was the worse of it. However, Winter Santiaga moves on to establish a life separate from her mother's ruined life. She never once checks on her mother while she is living in the group home called The House of Success. Even after she gets the passes to go outside and move about freely. She never checks on her mother while living with Sister Souljah. In fact she uses her mother as a pawn in her game. She pretends that her mom is a cancer patient nearing death to manipulate the sympathy she knew would come from Souljah and Doc. Despite the fact that after the fall of Santiaga thousands of dollars passed through the hands of Winter Santiaga at different time periods, she never gave, sent, or set aside money for her mother. Moreover, she never even intended to.

The only thing that Winter did ultimately give her mother was crack. She took it from the cookie jar in Bullet's apartment and dropped it through the sliding slot in the door. She secretly watched as her mother groveled for it. She even listened as Bullet humiliated her mom, treating her like a common crackhead worthy of no kind of respect.

These attitudes and actions are what makes Winter the coldest Winter ever.

Winter and Her Sisters

While the Santiaga family is on top, Winter does the normal babysitting chores that an older sister would do in any family rich or poor. She takes Porsche to her dance lessons, the children to the mall. Winter's all decked out in a T-shirt that reads, "These are not my fucking kids." She is so perfect at always distinguishing herself as separate from and mostly above everyone else of any age. However, we never get a sense that the word *sister* has any deeper meaning in her mind and heart. We never hear her speak of them as more than an obligation, intrusion, or nuisance. In fact, in the presence of Midnight she views her sister Porsche as up and coming competition.

> My eight-year-old sister wanted to fight me for the front seat of Midnight's Acura. I told her to take her little ass in the back with the twins. I wondered what would make her think she could ride in the front seat with my man . . . Little girls start getting horny at a younger age every year.

While *Webster's* dictionary offers a limited definition of the word sister, "a female having one or both parents in common with another individual," I believe the word embodies so much more. As an older sister, Winter should have been her sister's second most important teacher, after the mother. Whether a sister embraces the responsibility or not, the younger siblings, especially the girls, are using her everyday example and choices as a destination point. Most younger sisters aim to emulate their older sister whether or not she is a positive model.

They will be in a constant battle to seek the older sister's attention, acknowledgment, and more importantly, approval.

When the Bureau of Child Welfare removes Winter's sisters from her home, Winter has the appropriate outburst of anger at her house-keeper, Magdalena. However, if she actually loved her sisters is never made clear. Again, love is an action word. It's supposed to make you feel something, do something compelling. It's supposed to make you determined and powerful. Winter visits her sister Porsche once, along with the mother. At no point in the remaining months of her freedom does she pick up the phone to inquire about her three sisters. She does not send them a letter, card, clothes, toys, food, or cash. She does not ask anyone to check on them and report back or look after them for her. Nor does she ever visit them to offer a simple glance of solidarity and concern before her eventual incarceration.

Even in the novel's final chapter Winter does not mention her sisters. It takes the jolt of her mother's funeral for them to come into focus for her. We can assume they do, only because she can see them walking up to the gravesite. But couldn't she feel them while they were gone? Why didn't she wonder or care or cry or fight over them?

Winter, Friends, and Acquaintances

Winter romanticizes her friendships in the beginning of the novel. She believes that she and they are tight. However, the bond between Winter and anyone is only valid if Winter is in the higher and envied position. If her friends ever showed even a desire to reach for the place where Winter stands, she finds a way to cut them off, knock them down, put them in what she believed should be their perma-nent low position.

Winter betrays her best and lifelong friend Natalie. When Winter is forced to move back into her old Brooklyn neighborhood, she senses that Natalie has emerged as the new leader of her clique. When mutual friend Simone informs Winter that Natalie has a new man, a drug dealing hustler, Winter is not happy that Natalie has what she wants for herself. Instead, Winter becomes consumed by jealousy. The envy escalates as Winter feels challenged by the new clothes that Will has purchased for Natalie, which she wears to the concert. The idea that Natalie is seated in the box seats with her man Will, above the head of Winter who is seated below, is unacceptable to Winter. Upon entering Junior's Restaurant in Brooklyn after the show, Winter seethes as Natalie has all of their friends gathered at a table where she and her man Will are picking up the bill.

Innocently and conveniently Winter excuses herself and heads for the ladies room. Will follows under the guise of using a pay phone, despite the fact that he's carrying his cell phone. In the hidden corridor he comes on to Winter, offering to drop Natalie and take good care of her. He feeds Winter's ego, reminding her that she's better than Natalie. Winter rejects him once, then yields to his charms and compliments. With her nipples fully erect, she gives Will her phone number and agrees to meet him later on that same night. The complete betrayal of her best friend of sixteen years takes less than sixteen minutes.

In business Winter betrays Lashay, the group home girl who served as the "middleman" in Winter's clothing and hair business. The fact that LaShay helped Winter when she was confined in the group home did not make Winter treat her loyally. As soon as Winter received permission to come and go in the group home as she pleased, she dropped Lashay. She decided that the small piece of money she paid Lashay in a very profitable business, was better kept inside her own pocket.

When Winter receives a call from Simone, who got arrested while boosting clothes for Winter, she hangs up on her and refuses to use any of her personal money to get nine-months pregnant Simone out of the cold jail. Ultimately Simone, Winter's girl from her Brooklyn block, and Lashay team up and attempt to attack Winter. In the pursuit of Winter, Simone falls, killing her unborn baby girl. At no point does Winter express regret, remorse, or even sympathy for Simone's loss of her first child. Even in the final chapter of the novel Winter's words concerning Simone are freezing; "She finally stopped blaming me for the death of her daughter. Or at least she puts up a good front."

Winter moves on to betray Rashida, who was very helpful in Winter's escape from the newly planned second group home attack. Rashida is also the girl who introduces Winter to Souljah. Rashida sets it up so Winter can safely reside at Souljah's house, locate Midnight, and recover from the group home experience. Obviously Rashida had not done enough for Winter, who spoke against Rashida, assuring Souljah that she and Rashida were never even friends. Winter stops communicating with Rashida, isolates her and focuses on robbing Doc and Sister Souljah, the two women who allowed her to stay in their New York home. Weeks later, Winter is successful in robbing both a church and an AIDS charity spearheaded by Sister Souljah.

Winter and Her Community

The most overlooked fact in *The Coldest Winter Ever* teaches us a lot about the character Winter and the readers who love her. In three years of touring after the publishing of *The Coldest Winter Ever*, no one has ever asked me about Chapter 16, where Winter fills a sock full of rocks then beats a female senior citizen with them. In describing her attack on the old lady, Winter says:

> Across the street where the woods lined the outside of the high-way, I filled my extra pair of socks with big sharp rocks . . . In a split second she didn't know what hit her. It was my stone-filled sock up against her head. She withered like a flower and fell to the ground. I had two hundred in cash, one credit card . . . two diamond rings and those Gucci shoes."

The fact that no book club member, audience member, or inquisitive independent reader has ever asked about the female senior citizen demonstrates the temperature in our community—below freezing. It reveals the disconnection from our culture that years ago protected, revered, and honored the elderly. The idea that this crime remains unimportant, unresolved, and undiscussed exposes how our community now accepts the mentality echoed in a famous hip-hop song, "Players Anthem" by the Notorius B.I.G., "That's okay, she was old anyway." It bluntly admits that the murder of the old means nothing, they're just going to die anyway. This was certainly Winter's mentality. She never even questioned whether or not she had actually murdered the old woman. Why would she? After all, she felt comfortable peeling the unconscious woman's Gucci shoes right off her feet as she lay silent between two cars in the dark parking lot in the middle of the night.

Of the thousands and thousands of letters I receive about this novel, ninety percent of them are from girls and women ages eleven through forty, all who swear in ink, "Sister Souljah, I am Winter Santiaga." For so many women—the majority identifying themselves as black and/or

Latina—to identify this way supports my long-time belief that there is a state of emergency in ghettos worldwide.

When a young girl or grown ass woman says to me, "I am Winter Santiaga," she is saying to me, "I feel trapped. I don't have the answers. I'm a ruthless fighter. I feel desperate. I'll do anything. I'll rob you if I have to. I'll kill you if I have to. I'll get rich, or we'll all die while I'm trying."

Are we saying that Winter Santiaga's attitude is beautiful? Or is it that beautiful-looking girls and women should be excused and able to get away with absolutely anything? Are her choices cool and acceptable? Is this what we want for our daughters? Is this what we want for ourselves? Is this what we expect and accept for our communities worldwide?

MIDNIGHT

Midnight is the heart of *The Coldest Winter Ever.* Through him is delivered the strongest and most relevant message to black men ever delivered in the form of literature. He is alive in the most important place, the minds of both men and women. For men he is a goal and a standard. For women he is a dream and destination. In every instance he is a permanent Midnight. Without a man like him in each and every home, there is an absence so deep it stains the face of our women, steals the chastity of our daughters, and ensures an early burial for our sons.

In *The Coldest Winter Ever,* Midnight symbolizes the black man's return to manhood and culture.

Physically speaking, Midnight is blackskinned because black is the most beautiful. Black is the most dominant and alluring, and somehow threatening. Midnight is tall, because in so many ways he towers over most men. His body is lean because even his personality is devoid of "fat." Midnight's skin is described as being "smooth and perfect, laid on top of his bone structure tight like Saran Wrap."

I wanted his beauty to carry the precision and power of the ancient African cities, the height of architecture. They were the first cities to be created in human history. They have been admired, imitated, but never properly duplicated. Despite thousands and thousands of years of being hated, raided, and robbed, they still stand as the most unexplained, envied phenomenon. Physically speaking this is Midnight, tough and tightly constructed like a pyramid, visible and explored and desired by everyone. Damaged but still superior, a handcrafted carving, the symbol of the black man.

Most female readers think they are in love with Midnight because of his looks. I think, however, Midnight's spirit is the most compelling thing about him. He represents a departure from the characteristics typically assigned to and associated with young black ghetto males.

Whereas young everyday males, as well as famous entertainers and athletes, are usually bragging about themselves, their possesions, appearance, jewels, clothing, cars, women, and skills, Midnight is humble. He is not arrogant. He is comfortable and confident. Everything he has you could see. But he would not point it out, brag, or front.

Many men today lack the beauty of humility. That is why they appear in the eyes of women as boys, and not men. If they have beautiful jewels, they lift them up, talk about them, rhyme about them, shove them into the camera and show them off. But the beauty of jewels, like the beauty of men, shines without assistance. Like diamonds, when they are authentic and clean, they sparkle and capture the seeing eye.

When Midnight plays basketball, it is a metaphor for life. He wears quality possessions, yet he enters quietly and thoughtfully. Still, everyone notices. He plays with skill, drowning out the voices of trash talkers in his mind. He focuses on the goal, getting the basketball into the hoop. He wins the game, but doesn't shove it in anyone's face. He leaves in the same manner in which he came. Humility, in fact, became one of the keys to how Midnight ended up being a rare survivor in the deadly drug game.

Most men need too much attention. Like small female children, they will do anything to get it. That is why today's everyday black male is constantly showing off. Moreover, he shows off his woman and not necessarily because he is proud of her. He shows her off to bring attention to himself. To make himself seem like more of a man. This is why rappers strip their women and parade them around. They are insecure. They need to parade these women so that people will view them as big men who control lots of women, thus the constant reference to themselves as pimps. Even everyday men in the streets pimp their women. Male youth brag about the women they've got, how they manipulate them, and sometimes even destroy them. They brag about how they fuck them, make them cry, make them work, get money from them. They detail how they use and then dump them.

Midnight does the opposite. In the novel, when he is rumored to be having a relationship with Tasia, the rumor can never be confirmed. As a man he knows not to discuss with other males or females what he does with his woman. He understands that this is their private business. He does not need to destroy Tasia or her reputation in order to build or big himself up as a man. Winter attempts to ask Midnight about his relationship with Tasia. He refuses her conversation.

When Midnight is, at the request of Santiaga, traveling with Winter and her little sisters on the low, he takes Winter shopping. As Winter reaches for the sexiest and most revealing clothing, he guides her to something stylish, high quality but more conservative. He does not need to walk beside a nearly naked woman to feel good about her or to feel good about himself. Besides, he acknowledges that his primary responsibility to a woman is to protect her. Part of providing that protection, is to not complicate any situation with her public near-nudity. Many battles have been fought, boys and men locked up or lost lives, because of young men's belief that women who are nearly naked in public are extending an open invitation to be looked at, approached, conversed with inappropriately, and unfortunately, even touched. Therefore, any man who walks beside a nearly naked woman in today's troubling times, in today's streets, escalates the possibility of conflict.

If a man cannot be humble, it is likely that he cannot be still. To be still is to be silent, without motion. Every man needs to have or develop the ability to be still at some point in each day. It is the time where he can stop and hear his own thoughts. It is the time when he can consider or reconsider his past actions. It is the time when he can think or pray. It is the time when he can allow his conscience to do its job, which is to remind and lead him to know and choose between what is right and what is wrong concerning his own actions and choices. Any man who is constantly talking, constantly moving, constantly high, or afraid of being silent and or alone, is a lost and misguided man. He will never be able to correct himself, a serious flaw that will cause him to die a thousand spiritual deaths, repeating the same mistakes over and over again, a cyclical hell.

Midnight was able to be still. In the novel he prayed, thought, considered, and reconsidered. Moreover, he studied. In fact, when the character Sister Souljah first saw Midnight, he was seated in the Columbia University library reading. There are many grown men today who never even consider going to a library or bookstore, or opening a book to read and actually think about and consider its content. Their lack of humility convinces them that there is no need to read. Their arrogance reminds them that they already know everything. As a result, they can never grow or change.

When Winter was in the hotel room with Midnight, she pointed out the books he chose to carry with him, *The Art of War* and *The Wretched of the Earth* to name two. He was reading them before they became the popular books for men to read. We can therefore conclude that he was in a voluntary and constant state of reading, thinking, and learning, of evaluating the world and his position in it. This state of reevaluating created an opportunity for him to become a better man who makes better choices in his life.

The message is clear. To rely solely on your own unimproved state of mind, your own limited thoughts without reading, learning, and debating the thoughts of others, conversing meaningfully and studying from time to time, causes a man to become small minded, closed in and trapped. Careful study increases both your awareness, understanding, and options. A man without study is a hostage to his own faults.

In business and in his personal life, Midnight was loyal. To be loyal means "to be constant," to be consistent. In plain language, to be loyal is to know who you are, to know what you're doing, to know what you agreed to, and to follow through. Word is bond.

Santiaga gave Midnight an occupation, a job. For hundreds of thousands of youth/men who have been incarcerated in the past, this is an opportunity that is extremely hard to come by. Therefore Midnight was loyal to Santiaga. Many men today cannot do business together successfully because their minds cannot grasp the simple concept of loyalty. When a man puts you on and creates an opportunity for you that you otherwise would not have had, the laws of nature dictate that you be grateful and loyal to him for the agreed amount of time of service. Now remember, you had a choice. You were presented with an opportunity. You had time to consider the terms of the agreement and the details. You accepted and agreed to it. You did not have to agree to it. You could have altered or negotiated the terms from the beginning. Once you put your word on it, this is supposed to seal you into the deal, specifically as you agreed to it. A loyal man sticks to his agreements. He does not make excuses for why he cannot do the job correctly. Each time, and every day he should present the same man that he presented in the beginning. Even if he changes his thoughts, or his mind in the process of the agreement, he does not grow angry with the giver, or betray and change the agreement. If he feels strongly that he must alter his behavior midstream, he requests a face to face and respectfully explains his position requesting a change, also known as an "amendment" to the agreement. However, a loyal man should be prepared and understand that the giver has the right to decline his request and hold him to the agreement he made in the first place. If the giver does enforce the original agreement, a loyal man should be ready to continue as agreed without hatred or revenge. As a man he is obligated to handle and take responsibility for his agreements. There should be no transferring of blame.

A man who is humble, confident, and intelligent thinks ahead and thinks carefully. Then he has no cause to be disloyal. A man who makes choices swiftly, signs contracts without reading them, or does business while high or drunk, without careful thought to the work ahead, is a fool. He will betray you every time.

Midnight understood and accepted his agreements. He was loyal. He did not get mad that Santiaga had his own business and made more money than him. He did not compete with Santiaga as a man, or use Santiaga's contacts and business associates against him. He did not do half the job then quit in the middle. After he learned the job, he did not cut Santiaga out and open his version of the same business. He didn't dime Santiaga out. He did not use Santiaga's personal weaknesses or confidances against him. He remembered the order of things. He remembered that Santiaga was the boss. He appreciated that Santiaga created, then extended the opportunity to him. Even when Midnight's job was over and his obligations dissolved, Midnight demonstrated the depth of his understanding that appreciation means a whole lot more than simply speaking the words "thank you." Midnight embraced the responsibility of demonstrating his appreciation by adopting and securing Santiaga's two daughters, Mercedes and Lexy.

Midnight is emotional, as every man should be. Emotions and the ability to really feel should never be a contradiction to masculinity. America advances the image of the unfeeling man's man, who can act without emotion. America promotes emotion in a man as a weakness. However, this is not an African belief or trait. While young misguided black boys follow the American mis-lead, many of them are in the process of depressing their mothers, avenging their fathers, and attacking their own kind. In fact, in America, when a male youth displays emotion, the misguided majority labels him "soft." In order for young men to prove that they are not momma's boys, they don't listen to or heed their mother's good guidance and advice. In an effort to prove to their fathers, whom many never do meet, that they don't miss, need, or love them, they grow a hatred, lack of respect for, and suspicion of all males. This hatred makes murder possible, then easy. In an effort to prove that they are America's version of "strong," black male youth say, "I don't love them hoes." Then the process of labeling and diminishing all of their women begins.

Midnight, on the other hand, has a clear respect for and love of his mother. He admires how she chose to live her life. She mattered, her words and his memory of her. He looked for the qualities of his mother in the women he chose to spend his time with. He explains in the novel that Souljah reminded him of some of the qualities of his mother in many ways, one of his points of attraction to her. He does not regard women as whores to be taught a lesson. He was able to love and appreciate a good woman, an art that is becoming shamefully rare. Midnight's respect for and emotion toward women is what led him to murder a youth who attempted to rape his biological sister in a dark stairwell of a building. After serving five years in prison, and in honor of his mother's wishes, he took responsibility for his sister, who was lost in the adoption system after their mother's death.

Throughout the novel Midnight is protecting and saving women. His ability to listen to a woman when she speaks (not obey, but listen), is what actually allows him to hear, consider, and feel what Sister Souljah says and writes to him in their letters. Many men may have thought that it is "soft" for a man to be guided by a woman. However, in the ancient African tradition women are the sacred key to life. They carry, then push all life into existence. They are a metaphor for wisdom.

Midnight's ability to have emotions, yet not allow his emotions to emasculate or master him, is the kind of mental wellness all women wish for their husbands, fathers, brothers, and sons. It is this careful balance that allows Midnight to feel, then adjust and change. Many hustlers who have a positive change of mind, spirit, and heart may feel they're turning soft or lowering themselves when they move from an illegal business like drugs, where money is fast, long, and strong, to a legal business like barbering, plumbing, or construction, where money comes at a slow and steady pace. However, a man who is in charge of his own thoughts and feelings will soon realize that if you love anyone at all, and wish to continue to do so, the change from hustling drugs is necessary. A former hustler who makes the change in business has great potential to be productive and profitable if he goes at his new business with equal emotion and passion. If he's too damn slick for himself, and tries to deal drugs behind the scenes while fronting a legal business, he will fail miserably, mostly without the possibility of freedom and recovery for himself and those he loves.

Questions concerning Midnight's relationship with Winter pour in steadily. Both males and females have been perplexed as to why Midnight consistently rejected Winter's friendship and sexual advances. Many readers argued that Midnight and Winter were a perfect match. This is a common mistake in analysis and assessment. Readers should instead label it a "perfect-looking match." There is a tendency for males to believe they need a perfect-looking woman. Likewise, women form a picture of what their perfect prince is supposed to look like. In actuality, the only thing that Midnight and Winter have in common is the fact that both of their lives are immersed in the drug world. She is sixteen. He is twenty-one. He is quiet and reserved. She is talkative and wild. He loves books. Winter never read a whole book, or anything else for that matter, including the New York *Daily News* when it was right there in her face. Midnight loves intelligent conversation. Winter loves gossip. In effect they would've had very little to talk about. While he craved modesty in a woman, Winter wanted to be the top showpiece.

It has been difficult for American males and females to understand how to choose a mate. Certainly it has been even more difficult for them to stay together, build something, and appreciate one another. There is no agreement on what American rules and parameters for dating are. Commonly, American women enter relationships backward, when compared to non-Western women. American girls have sex with handsome strangers, then they attempt to get to know them afterward. The shy American girl will forgo sexual intercourse in the first one or two dates. She'll opt to give the stranger a blow job to demonstrate her interest in him as well as her modesty!

On the other hand, a non-American, non-European, non-Western girl or woman must go through a process to even meet a man. Her family guides her encounter. They get to know one another amongst their families and relatives. The couple gets to converse with and consider one another. Both sides assess their intentions, compatibility, and combined possibilities. It would be difficult for Winter Santiaga and even most readers to understand that more than sexual attraction matters between a man and a woman. It will be difficult for them to understand that many men from other cultures actually like and wish to honor their own culture. They enjoy the process it involves to find and then win the hand of a good woman.

Moreover, when a girl is easy, sometimes she's undesirable. Real men enjoy working to earn a woman's attention and admiration. Some men enjoy unraveling the mystery of a particular woman and journeying to see and feel the various prizes and delicacies that are in store. Midnight was born in the Sudan, a country located on the continent named Africa. His view of women was shaped in that land. He carried those views from Africa to America.

Also involved in Midnight's relationship with Winter was his self-discipline. Unlike many men who take all that they can get, Midnight chose to evaluate, then step away from women who he thought subtracted something from his essence and success. In a moment of frustration within the story, he said these words to Winter:

> Can't you read? . . . That's what I'm talking about—dumb women! You don't even know what's going on around you. If it ain't on the front page, you don't know it.

Midnight's anger toward Winter may have been his view that she was both arousing and pretty, while being completely useless. His attempt to discipline himself in regard to Winter became that much easier.

Loyalty factored in as well. Midnight knew that to have sex with Santiaga's daughter was foul, a breech of confidance. When a man allows you into the inner circle of his life, the unspoken agreement is that you don't abuse the proximity. It would have been wrong for Midnight to simply satisfy his sexual desires with Winter, then dump her as he knew he would have to, since she was not relationship material, nor was she worthy of ever becoming his wife. Instead he chose to discipline himself. He kept a purposeful distance from her to make sure it all worked out at as it should. In her moment of loss of her mother and father to incarceration, he knew not to take her to Maryland with him. Yet he still showed his humanity and compassion by giving her $3,500 dollars of his own money, despite feeling skeptical about how she would use it. Midnight, in the African tradition, gave Winter Sister Souljah's business card. He felt an older woman was better suited to help Winter Santiaga improve herself and that a man placing himself in a position to teach a young girl was more likely to mess it up.

Midnight's encounter with Sister Souljah sparked the opposite emotions within him. When Souljah first saw him he was reading in the Columbia University library. When he first saw Souljah, she was teaching a class at Columbia University. It was a powerful first impression. It was completely different than a dude saying "Hey, I saw you bending over in the park the day you was rocking a miniskirt."

As Midnight and Souljah began to explore one another, they both entered through the mind first. For people who are thinkers, this is very important. Even the pimps admit that "the mind is the most powerful sexual organ." Souljah and Midnight's conversation were mutually enticing and intriguing. This does not mean that there was no basic raw sexual pull shared between them. After all, they are both human. They both have deep feelings. However, they did not let the sexual energy lead them. They were led by their thoughts and considerations.

At a certain point Sister Souljah decided that Midnight was not good enough for her because of his involvement with drugs. By challenging Midnight, Sister Souljah revealed characteristics and qualities that many women, rich or poor, simply do not have: self-reliance, self-assurance, and contentment.

Many single women are desperate. When they give into their desperation and loneliness their standards collapse. On the other hand, Sister Souljah's action of separating herself from Midnight said and proved; "Yes, I admire you. Yes, I see you. You're beautiful and I desire you. However, because you can't meet my spiritual, cultural, and moral standards, then I cut you off. Because I am certain of and satisfied with myself. I'm sure I will be rewarded in the long run. And no! I am not your ride-or-die bitch who's willing to trade my life and freedom for yours!"

Because Souljah happened to be a historian and teacher, she stepped away from Midnight even as she offered up the sentiment, words, and truths that would stick in his mind forever, and raise his standard of manhood. Now Midnight had the choice, to do what a real man loves to do. He had to work to get to where Souljah was at. He had to meet the challenge to make himself a better man.

Had Sister Souljah been like most women, she would have broken down, bended her rules. She would have allowed him to have sex with her a couple of times in the heat of the moment, in the dark of night. He would have then bought her a nice gift and eventually she would've given in and accepted him, broken, in a dead-end occupation and lifestyle. However, Souljah's clean break from Midnight forced him to have to choose. She realized she was not the only woman in the world and that she might by having the standard set so high, lose him. However, she figured that winning a broken man, one set up for a possible second then third incarceration, slavery, or an early death, was an option she was completely unwilling to accept. To accept this would've been to contaminate herself spiritually and to dramatically alter the outcome of her life as well.

Midnight did the manly thing. He changed. Ultimately he did not change because of Sister Souljah. He changed because he already knew that what he was involved in was wrong. He changed because he had a conscience. He changed because he always had a religion. He changed because he had a culture to which to return. Sister Souljah, therefore, was simply the character who brought about Midnight's epiphany. She did what no one else in his world would do. She leaned on him to recognize and acknowledge his true self, his purpose. She was the inspiration, that revealed to him that nothing else was more important than his purpose, not his business, money, pretty women, or his justifiable anger.

Not every man could have latched on to these simple truths, even after meeting a positive and powerful woman who has the patience to break it down for him. Some would simply fall short. A man has to have what is called the "will" to rescue his own soul. Perhaps the most meaningful example of a man rescuing his own soul occurred when Midnight was incarcerated. In his letters to Souljah he admitted that he was raped by some men who physically overpowered him in prison. He admitted that he suffered as doctors placed twenty-two stitches in his behind to initiate the process of the physical healing. He admitted that after the trauma he questioned his own sexuality and how the rape detracted from his sexual identity.

This is a huge dilemma not only for Midnight, the character, but for black men worldwide. Living in a perpetual state of war, poverty, powerlessness, confusion, and crime creates an immense pressure on the psychology, personality, spirit, and soul of a man. So many men, in a subconscious response to the various and continual pressures of American rule, capitalism, and racism, have lost control over their sexual and gender identity. Some men, in an attempt to adapt and avoid the pressures, become other than their natural selves.

Midnight, like many boys and men who are victims of either father-lessness, foster care, adoption, incarceration, molestation, rape, abuse, poverty, powerlessness, indoctrination, and misdirection, could've sur-rendered. He would not have had to wave a white flag. He simply would have to lose his internal will to fight back. To give into the pressure that threatens to redefine who each and every one of us are and were born to be as were our mothers and fathers before us.

Midnight, however, reaches in and reaches back to his under-standing of himself, his father, his culture, his God. He uses this ancient foundation to sort through the confusion, to resist the pres-sure, to rescue his soul. Ultimately he did not allow anyone to cloud what his parents and those before him made clear, that he is a man, the original black man made to love, protect, and provide for women and children. He did not allow any human to soar higher than God and alter his original purpose.

Midnight therefore represents for all black men, a return to your original purpose. A return to your original culture. A return to your original conscience. A return to being builders instead of destroyers, protectors instead of predators, leaders instead of sheep. He was by no means a perfect man. The fact that he was ever involved in drugs was a critical and undeniable flaw.

The message of his character is multi-dimensional. In his change for the better, he did not double-cross the individuals from his former life. He fulfilled and completed his obligations. He then isolated, worked, and rebuilt himself. He healed and went back to get every-body else.

In the end, what Midnight did made him majestic. He demon-strated the ability to make a complete and comprehensive positive change. His ability to learn, understand, grow, and adjust left him wearing the crown that many thought had been reserved for Santiaga.

MRS. SANTIAGA

Mrs. Santiaga is the only character in *The Coldest Winter Ever* who does not have a name. She is a symbol of incompletion. She represents all of the women who stop learning and growing in this life, the ones who turn into beautiful Barbie dolls.

You shower most dolls, especially your favorite one, with lots of attention in the beginning. You dress them up in the finest matching doll outfits and accessories. One afternoon you happen to lay her down. Then somehow, she becomes uninteresting, unimportant, and dispensable.

Years later you notice her, dirty, tattered, and broken, underneath your bed. At that point you may have a quick flash of memory. You smile at having loved her once. But mostly, you just pity her now.

When a woman has not established her own personal identity, she does not deserve to have a name. A personal identity tells and shows family and friends who you really are on the inside. It comprises what you feel, what you think, what you believe, what you are interested in, what gifts you have, what you dislike, what you spend the majority of your time doing, and what you're working toward.

Every woman's personal identity is influenced by others, such as her mother and father, her grandparents, sisters and brothers, and closest friends. However, she must shape finally who she actually is, which will end up being slightly different than who they are.

When a woman meets a man of interest, she should already be somebody. She should not just be a sitting duck or dandelion waiting to be plucked. She should not be waiting for his ring to turn her into a woman. She should not be waiting for his money, promises, adornments, or lifestyle to turn her into a woman. In fact, if she is clear and whole, her agreement to join her world to his should add something to the equation, instead of her just being absorbed, then blending in.

Not naming female characters who have not evolved or blossomed into whole women is a literary technique I developed when I wrote my first book, *No Disrespect*. In that book, which is about the young relationships of Sister Souljah, I never once named myself. Nor did I ever use the Sister Souljah title. I knew that as a young woman, from a teen through twenty-two years old, I did not deserve it. I hadn't finished the work I needed to do on me. I was not yet a woman.

What happens when a woman is old enough in age, let's say twenty-five, twenty-eight, or thirty-three and she still has not blossomed into a whole woman? She has the hips and tits. She has the flirtatious eyes and immaculate hairstyles. She has the manicure and pedicure. She has the Louis Vuitton handbag and the diamond bracelet. She has the husband and the children. But she has the mind of a twelve year old.

Her limitations, her lack of growth will transfer to her daughters. It will cast her sons out in the world to seek new but maybe less concerned teachers. It will either bore, limit, or run her husband away.

A whole woman is a natural magnet. She draws so much to herself, that sometimes she has to fight for time for herself and space to breathe. A whole woman creates an intelligent environment, where others can also grow and become something significant. A whole woman commands the respect of her husband. In fear of losing her respect he honors her boundaries. A whole woman's mind and voice are so entertaining that she keeps a permanent audience. She provides her children with an arsenal of common sense, pertinent information, and worldly wisdom, so that they might do more than survive. So that they might triumph.

Mrs. Santiaga gave birth to Winter when she was fourteen years old. When a teenager becomes pregnant at such a young age it is not a tragedy. However, it will take careful planning and teamwork in order for her to still be able to continue to learn and grow. The new life in her belly is of course the priority. In a good case, her parents and/or grandparents will pitch in. Her school will introduce her to a program with other young ladies needing the same kind of support. However, when this does not happen, or if she is the type of teen who doesn't make it happen, the formal education is jeopardized and usually not replaced by anything else.

In the novel we never hear Mrs. Santiaga speak of her own mother and father, or of having grandparents. We can assume that either they were dead or, more likely, that they did not have a powerfully positive impact on her. If this is true, the picture is beginning to come into focus. We now have a character whose education stopped on or before ninth grade, who also has a disconnection from her parents and past.

Apparently Mrs. Santiaga was with Ricky Santiaga since the age of thirteen since she became pregnant at fourteen. When a young girl who is disinterested in, or running from, her parents meets a boy who she likes, usually he becomes the world to her. Ricky Santiaga was Mrs. Santiaga's world. From what we know as readers, she did not have any other interest than him. She had no high school education. She had no high school degree. She had no occupation. Her main interest was getting beautiful, and remaining beautiful to keep his focus on her.

When a girl grows up on the block, finds love on the block, has babies on the block, and doesn't leave the block, how much can we expect her to contribute to her husband, children, and community? A small mind breeds bacteria. A pretty little empty-headed thing sits around and finds things to talk about. Gossip becomes the appetizer, a jealous competition with the other sitters becomes the meal. Mrs. Santiaga, trapped in a small mind, spent a lot of time comparing herself to others and making sure she was winning. After she had it all (as she knew it), she spent the rest of her time decorating her daughters and making sure they were winning. But winning against whom? Better compared to what? Is it really that hard to be rich in a poor neighborhood and be the best-dressed chick? Is it really hard to be rich in a poor neighborhood and be living a better lifestyle than the others?

These were the simple goals she set for herself. They were the small and useless goals of a woman who had stopped thinking long ago.

Through Mrs. Santiaga's words, "I'm a bad bitch," and her living example, Winter learns to understand her own womanhood, and how to exist in their small world. Winter is led to believe that the essence of womanhood is visual. As long as a woman is looking, dressing, and smelling the best, she is the best. As long as a woman is a fierce competitor in a ghetto beauty pageant, as long as she knows how to push the other women down to the floor and keep them there, then that's what really matters.

Winter was led to believe that womanhood was synonomous with vanity. *Webster's* dictionary defines vanity as "useless."

The shooting of Mrs. Santiaga represented the assassination of vanity and the assassination of useless and incomplete women. As an author, my hope was to drive home the point so incredibly clearly that no girl anywhere will ever think or believe that it is cute to be stupid, uneducated, small-minded and unproductive. My mission was to piss off every little stagnant ghetto girl, to stir up every little silly suburban until they get off their asses and become something great.

The twisted mouth of Mrs. Santiaga symbolized the twisted life she led. She felt so powerful yet could not influence her husband to become a better man. She used her imagined power to get diamonds, furs, money, and drugs. But she could not win over his mind. She could not help change his actions. She could not after all, even, command his loyalty.

A whole woman has resilience. Resilience is the ability to recover, to bounce back from a setback or horrible fall. When Mrs. Santiaga experienced the first crack in her imaginary perfect life, it was the beginning of her permanent fall. When her husband failed to buy her Mercedes Benz on her birthday, the way she imagined it should go, she triggered a series of events that would lead her into a perpetual unrecovery.

After unexpectedly meeting Dulce Tristemente, the other woman in her husband's life, Mrs. Santiaga's recreational drug use turned habitual. Whereas a whole woman searches for the strength to move on in the eyes of her children, and for the benefit of her children, Mrs. Santiaga falls to pieces. She loses not only herself. She loses her children as well. Where was her will to fight back? Where did it go? One visit to Porsche at the state facility, then no more mommy.

Her impact withered away so immediately, and so completely. Even her own daughters, the twins, Mercedes and Lexy, did not shed a tear or say a word over her unrecognizable body twisted in the casket. What mother wants her children and family gathered around at her funeral out of obligation instead of love?

Mrs. Santiaga's life symbolized incompletion. Her shooting symbolized the assasination of vanity. Her death symbolized the death of motherhood in our community. Drugs destroy the taker and the giver.

RICKY SANTIAGA

When a man makes a choice to take a wife, he no longer belongs only to himself. He is in effect now promising to share himself completely. He is sharing not only his thoughts and moods, but his words and secrets, his challenges and struggles, his actions, reactions, and consequences, his finances and debts, his blessings and his sins. This is a very serious move indeed.

A man must then, if not before, begin to build a foundation for himself, his new wife, and his children to come. The kind of foundation he is able to build will depend heavily upon his understanding of himself, his father before him, and the God he does or does not serve. If a man does not understand himself, his father before him or his beliefs, the foundation he lays for his family will rest in quicksand.

In judging a man, most women are very easily misled by his style and rhythm. They look at his face, teeth, hands, and for some, his shoes. They check out his clothes, his watch, his car, and his willingness to spend. His lovemaking. However, if a man is 100 percent in all of the above mentioned categories, and a zero in his understanding of himself, his father and God, then he will still be worthless in the long run.

Question: What makes a man worthless to a woman? Answer: If he cannot decide if he is good or evil. If he does not understand the universal spiritual laws of nature. If he cannot tell the truth about himself, his deeds and actions. If he carelessly places himself in danger. If he maintains control by feeding low self-esteem to and arousing jealousy and uneasiness in, his wife. If he is absent and unable to impact the shape and depth of the marriage, or present and setting a poor example for his sons and daughters to base their lives on. If he does not work hard he is short-sighted and incapable of securing the interests of his family in the event of his demise.

A lot of women cling to worthless men. They lie and cover up his wrongful actions. They make excuses for his condition. They create an environment at home that allows his backwardness to thrive and spread. It may take these women more than a decade to figure out that everyone knows what's really happening, that she's an actress in a tragic theatrical performance, fooling only herself. That even her youngest child recognizes her shame.

Question: What happens when a man is a good-looking, tall, sweet-smelling, gun-toting, fine-dressing, money-having, sexy, worthless man? Answer: The same damn thing!

A man who wants to build a drug empire must now and forever acknowledge that he should remain unattached. Or, he must accept that whomever he loves, his wife and his children, are fair game, living life at high risk, inevitable human targets.

Ricky Santiaga built a foundation for his family that rested on top of quicksand. His house was destined to sink. It never even had a chance. As a drug dealer he was by choice participating in the world of evil. Yet at home he attempted to build a house of love. When a man makes a conscious decision to do evil, he steps outside of the grace of God and loses his spiritual protection. In forfeiting his spiritual protection, it does not mean that the man will lose his life immediately. It means that as that man goes out into the world to live, struggle, earn, and do battle, he has no spiritual armor.

Spiritual armor protects a man beyond the limited physical and logical protection that he can provide for himself. When a man opts to do evil, he does so along with a multitude of other men who are also evil. The laws of God, the common boundaries of love, life, loyalty, respect, mercy, and compassion do not operate within the evil realm.

God's grace can only be earned by the man who acknowledges his wrongdoings, prays for forgiveness and strength to overcome them, then stops his evil doings. When he stops performing evil actions, the possibility then exists for him to earn back God's grace. However, his conversation with God is not a negotiation. Fast talking and quick hands won't get him more than he's worth. An ayat from the Holy Quran says, "Allah is swift in all accounts." This means that God is omniscient, sees everything, and is well aware of what your intentions and actions were and are. We will all be held accountable for each of our actions as God sees proper.

Many men who consciously do evil believe that they are smarter than God. They craft careful but fruitless plans to win back the grace of God while still purposely doing evil actions and activities. They go to church or mosque while doing evil, which will not save them. They make contributions to and form relationships with the pastor or imam while doing evil, which will not save them. They wear a crucifix while doing evil, which will not help or save them. They pray for prosperity and victory while doing evil, which will not save them. They offer money to charities, which will not save them, their spirit, or their soul. Spiritual armor is one thing that can never be sold or bought for any amount of money. While any man can purchase security or a body-guard, no man can purchase God's grace.

Some men don't bother acknowledging the existence of God in word or deed. They see those who do acknowledge God as weak. Their fate will be the same as the fate of those who pretend to honor God. They will be prisoners of their own dark minds. Ricky Santiaga attempted to outmaneuver God, whom he never acknowledged. He built a drug empire in the world. He built a house of love at home. In not understanding or accepting the universal spiritual laws of nature, he believed he could sell drugs, oversee crackheads, exact punishments, order beatings and even murders, then return home leaving the evil outside the double doors of his apartment and away from his wife and daughters.

However, when you invite the spirit of evil in through your conscious actions, that evil spirit lives within you. It will travel wherever you go, creating an evil energy. It places the ones whom you love the most in the most jeopardy. The Holy Bible says, "The sins of the father shall be inherited by the sons." This means that the spiritual deeds and misdeeds of our parents shall rain down on our heads. We shall then become responsible for carrying or correcting them, coming back into God's grace.

So it was inevitable that Santiaga's family would suffer, his roof cave in. At his wife's funeral we witnessed the grave impact that never acknowledging God or changing the spiritual path that he traveled had on Santiaga. It was not simply that his wife was dead that impacted him so heavily. It was her spiritual death etched across her lifeless face, that twisted her appearance and ate her body, that ran the knife through Santiaga's soul. At her gravesite, Santiaga's longing for freedom, longing to simply know his now grown children, longing for his wife as she was when he originally chose her, his guilt in knowing that his living was the cause of her downfall, brought Santiaga to his knees, finally.

In the physical world Santiaga tried to compensate for the danger his "occupation" placed his family in. He installed the double doors in his apartment inside of a project building. No doubt this took great expense, reputation, and intimidation to achieve. After all, every project building has a housing authority and perpetual police presence. Normally they regulate every detail of a resident's living arrangement. Each family must adhere to a plain and basic structure, but not Santiaga. Despite the accomplishment of having his expensively furnished apartment specially renovated for increased security, he soon, out of fear or intuition, moved his family out of the projects. Their new location was what he called a Long Island, New York, "safe house." However, without spiritual armor, even while living in the Long Island lap of luxury, they still were not safe.

Santiaga was present in his family's life enough for his wife and daughters to feel secure. But what did his presence teach his wife and children? We know it taught Winter that drug dealing was a preferred business opportunity, and her preferred lifestyle. It taught her that the drug dealer was the better man, at the top of the food chain. It became the criteria by which she judged all of her family and friends. Therefore, despite the love she said she had for her father, and the love he said he had for her, his presence set an example that was not a viable, life giving, life sustaining example for his children. His example led to Winter's eventual loss of freedom. For his other three remaining daughters his example led to being split up under the administration of the state's motherless-child protection system.

Santiaga, though good looking, proud, and smooth, was short sighted. "Smart" enough to design and manage a well-manned illegal drug business, he could not see his way clearly enough to construct a master plan, a plan B, an escape route for his immediate family. Where was his underground hidden treasure? Where were the bonds he purchased on behalf of his children? Where were the educational funds, life insurance policies, trust funds, or off-shore accounts? Where was the money set aside for his children in some name other than his own? In fact, all of Santiaga's money was either in his safe at home in Long Island, tied up in crack spots in Brooklyn, or surveilled, frozen, and out of reach in Manhattan bank accounts. By not planning ahead, Santiaga was in effect saying, "When I fall, we all fall." Or worse, he was believing, "I will never fall." A man's love is supposed to make him do something. It's supposed to make him think ahead to provide protection and security. It's supposed to make him insure and deliver the longevity and future of his family.

What about Dulce Tristemente? When a man is paid and good looking, women have a tendency to believe and expect that he is entitled to have more than one woman. However, if a man marries one woman and gives her the impression that she is his only woman, bringing a new woman into their life violates the trust he established in the beginning. Once a man does not tell the truth about his own deeds and actions, he calls into question all of his words ever spoken, his promises made, and actions taken. As the wife and Winter attempt to figure out how many times Santiaga must have lied to be able to carve out a separate life with another family, their trust diminishes. He has sprayed his family with the poison of doubt. When a wife and children doubt the husband and father, it corrodes the family and weakens the father's leadership capabilities within the family. It also now infects the family with the notion that "If he's not living right, why should we?" It loosens everybody's idea of morality and responsibility. How much did Santiaga's relationship with Dulce Tristemente, the other woman who birthed his only son (that we know of), spark the complete psychological downfall of Mrs. Santiaga? How wrenching was it for Momma Santiaga? How long did she blame and abuse herself for never having given birth to a boy? How much did his actions affect Winter's attitude toward visiting and sacrificing for and helping her father during his trial and incarceration?

Overall, Santiaga provided his wife and children with a home, clothes, food, jewels, and all of the trappings of American-style prosperity. Yet in his role as husband and father he was unsuccessful due to his lack of understanding of himself, his father, and God.

The Coldest Winter Ever
CHARACTER LIST

All of the characters' names appear in alphabetical order

Alvin Winter's uncle by marriage. He was married to Aunt B.

Aunt B Winter's aunt. Winter moved in with her after the Santiagas' Long Island mansion was raided and seized. This is the same woman who Winter believes set her up to be siezed by the Bureau of Child Welfare.

Aunt Laurie Winter's aunt. Winter's mother moved in with her after the house was siezed.

Bianca Winter's cousin and the daughter of Aunt B. Winter shared a room with this cousin after her home was seized.

Big Moe Operator of the local bar and dance set where Winter partied. This club was also one of Santiaga's business meeting spots.

Bilal Odé The birth name of Midnight, who was born in the Sudan, Africa.

Bob Goldstein Santiaga's lawyer.

Boom The little dick, bad sex guy whom Winter dates while hanging with Souljah's sister Lauren.

Bryce The half-brother of Bullet who lived in Washington, D.C. He was one of Bullet's drug-dealing, gun-running contacts.

Bubbles The locksmith who came to Winter's Brooklyn apartment to install a safe for Santiaga. Santiaga caught him gazing at Winter. He cut his face open with a knife to teach him a lesson.

Butter The four-year-old boy who was murdered and beheaded along with his sister KK by the Young Heads, a ruthless up-and-coming drug-dealing squad.

Cameron One of Lauren's boyfriends. Lauren stayed a couple of nights with him after the infamous after party for GS. Winter had to fill in as Souljah's office help during Lauren's absence.

Captain Chulla The Brooklyn police captain who was on Santiaga's payroll. He kept the officers "looking the other way while Santiaga ran his drugs through the hood."

Chanté The Brooklyn neighborhood girl who taught the young Winter and her female friends all of the sexual positions. She also let Winter and her girls watch while she had sex with boys and men.

Claudette The girl in the House of Success group home who, according to Winter, needed the most help with improving her appearance and overall style. She was Winter's guinea pig and first customer in her clothing and makeover business at The House of Success group home.

Doc A Brooklyn resident and war veteran with limited medical experience. Santiaga used him to give medical services to people whom he couldn't risk sending to the hospital, tipping off the police and causing the authorities to raise questions. Doc was not a real doctor.

Doc The medical doctor and surgeon who was Souljah's landlord. She owned and resided on the first two floors of her Harlem brownstone. Souljah lived on the top floor.

Driguez One of Santiaga's men.

Dulce Tristemente Santiaga's other woman. She gave birth to Santiaga's first and only son that we know of. She visited Santiaga in jail on the same day and time as Mrs. Santiaga, causing Mrs. Santiaga's emotional and psychological downfall.

Earline The operator and owner of the beauty salon where Winter and her mom got preferential treatment when getting their hair done.

Frankie The rap star GS's bodyguard. He's the one who invited Winter and Lauren to the celebrity after-party held in Alpine, New Jersey.

Granny Bullet's grandmother. She was a compulsiver gambler.

Ms. Griswaldi The Bureau of Child Welfare worker who arrived at Aunt's B's apartment with the sheriff. They picked Winter up by force and placed her into the House of Success group home.

Iris One of the girls who swapped guns, drugs, and money with Winter in the ladies bathroom at Houston's restaurant in New York City. She took Winter's pocketbook and gave Winter hers. She was working for Bryce. Winter was working for Bullet. However, Winter didn't realize what was going on.

Izzy The Macy's department store security guard who sexually molested Winter in the back office of the store after accusing her of being suspicious.

Jacob The first boy Natalie ever had sex with. He was a twin. Winter lost her virginity to his brother.

Jamal The first boy Winter had sex with at age twelve. He was a twin. Natalie had sex with his brother at the same time.

Judy Sterling's overweight girlfriend. She packed Winter's clothes and moved her out of his house. Winter was sleeping with Sterling, while posing as his cousin.

Kathy Johnson The psychologist at The House of Success who attempted to help Winter Santiaga.

Kim One of the young ladies who attended Souljah's womanhood courses.

KK The little three-year-old girl, who Bullet mentioned was beheaded by the Young Heads in the takeover of Santiaga's Brooklyn drug business.

Lance The bully who attempted to rape Midnight's little sister. Midnight murdered him and was incarcerated for five years for manslaughter.

Lashay The "middleman" in Winter's clothing and makeover enterprise at The House of Success. She picked up the stolen goods for Winter to resell to the group home girls. Winter used her while she was on restriction at the House of Success and forbidden to go outside.

Lauren Sister Souljah's sister. She lived in the brownstone with Souljah. She became "friends" with Winter.

Lexus Known as Lexy, she's Winter's baby sister. She is a twin.

Little Biz Simone's baby's daddy. They broke up, and the unborn baby died during Simone's attack on Winter at the group home.

Little Nickel Tasia's boyfriend after Midnight, according to Natalie.

LX A celebrated rapper who gave the party along with GS at the Palladium. Winter went to the party and the after-party with Lauren. She ended up competing in a "beauty pageant."

Magdalena The Santiaga family's housekeeper in Long Island.

Mercedes Winter's baby sister, Lexus' twin.

Midnight Winter's fantasy man and Santiaga's lieutenant in the drug empire. He secured Santiaga's daughters at different points throughout the novel. He also had a friendly relationship with Sister Souljah, which inspired him to evolve as a man.

Monique One of Winter's childhood girlfriends in Brooklyn. She was there when the girls slicked up their faces, braided down their hair, and went to fight some other girls in the neighborhood.

Moose One of Bullet's soldiers.

Natalie Winter's best friend. She lived in Brooklyn in the building directly across from Winter. She was the main girl that Winter kept up with after the family moved out of Brooklyn.

Nique Winter's childhood friend in Brooklyn who was being raped by her own mother's boyfriend. The mother pushed Nique off the roof, killing her.

Noni One of the group home girls at the House of Success. She was the defiant cigarette smoker with the curtain around her bed.

Patches The father of the baby Bullet thought was his own. He was famous for a mole on his face, as well as for giving girls stimulating oral sex.

Phoenix The stripper who spoke up for herself at Souljah's womanhood class.

Pizzaz One of Santiaga's men.

Rashida The group-home girl who genuinely cared about Winter. She protected Winter when she was attacked, by letting her know what was happening on the inside of the House of Success. She also introduced Winter to Souljah so that Winter would have a place to live temporarily.

Reese One of Winter's Brooklyn girlfriends.

Ricky Jr. The infant son of Ricky Santiaga and Dulce Tristemente.

Ricky Santiaga The father of Winter, Porsche, Mercedes, Lexus, and Ricky Jr. He built a drug-dealing empire in a Brooklyn neighborhood.

Sarge One of Lauren's men. He was in the army. He went on a double date with Winter, Boom, and Lauren.

Saria Bullet's ex-girlfriend whom he loved and cared for. She betrayed him, and led him to believe he was the father of her child. Bullet bankrolled her and bought a lot of baby gifts, only to be shocked at the real paternity of the newborn.

Sasha This is the name Winter made up for herself. She told Souljah that her true friends called her Sasha. While living with Souljah, everyone knew Winter as Sasha and called her by that name.

Simone One of Winter's girlfriends in Brooklyn. She became a clothing booster. Winter went into business with her while she was held at The House of Success group home. Simone was incarcerated while stealing clothes for Winter, and called Winter for help. Winter hung up on her. A pregnant Simone plus some friends attacked Winter at the group home, and Simone lost her unborn baby during the attack.

Slick Kid A friend of Bullet's. Slick Kid made the videotape of Winter, Natalie, and Bullet naked in the hot tub at the Marriott Hotel. He then showed the tape at Santiaga's spot, Big Moe's, and was beaten by Midnight.

Sonya The mother of KK and Butter, the three- and four-year-olds from Brooklyn who were murdered and beheaded by the Young Heads.

Souljah The Harlem-based activist who graduated from college and returns to the community to assist in the development, progress, and empowerment of the black community. Rashida brought Winter to live at Souljah's house after Winter was attacked at the group home. Throughout the novel, Souljah is fighting what appears to be a losing battle to bring cultural knowledge and positive lifestyles to the ghetto youth, men, and women.

Tashay One of the young ladies who spoke up in Souljah's womanhood course.

Tasia The Brooklyn girl who moved into the neighborhood after Winter moved out. She was rumored to have been dating Midnight.

Tiffany One of the two girls who swapped guns, drugs, and money with Winter in the ladies bathroom at Houston's restaurant in New York City. She was working for Bryce. Winter was working for Bullet but did not realize it.

Tony One of GS's bodyguards. He pretended to be GS one night in a rented mansion and had sex with Winter Santiaga, who believed he was the superstar. He was later murdered by one of Bullet's soldiers.

Toshi One of Winter's Brooklyn girlfriends. She was the cause of the big fight that Winter and her crew ended up avoiding because the neighborhood girls were afraid to fight Santiaga's daughter.

Vanessa The name of Winter's imaginary Long Island–based college girlfriend. Winter pretended to go to a sorority party with Vanessa at Hofstra University. She was actually out with Natalie, Slick Kid, and Bullet.

Vega One of Santiaga's men.

Will Natalie's drug-dealer boyfriend who triggered a dangerous beef between Winter and Natalie. Winter wanted to use him to get into the drug game.

Winter Santiaga The protagonist of *The Coldest Winter Ever.* She is a Brooklyn ghetto girl who shares her story from ages thirteen through twenty-five.

Young Heads The up-and-coming drug gang. They are very young and ruthless. Their feud with Santiaga for control over drug territory is financed by the police.

YOU CAN GET IN TOUCH WITH SISTER SOULJAH:

E-mail: souljahworkshard@gmail.com

Mailing address: Sister Souljah
Souljah Story Inc.
208 East 51st Street, Suite 2270
New York, New York 10022

Turn the page
to enjoy an excerpt
from Sister Souljah's novel
LIFE AFTER DEATH:
Winter Santiaga is back.

After a nasty breakup of any couple, the war begins. I knew bitches who keyed their ex's ride, or punctured his tires, or banged in his rims with a hammer. I knew bitches who beat the new bitch's ass, who her man had replaced her with. Or even stalked her, then choked her, stabbed her, shot her, or mercked her. I knew even live-er bitches who, instead of killing his new bitch, killed him. I knew bitches who ran up his credit cards, crashed his car, cut up his clothes, pawned his jewels, and even burned down his house. But when a man or woman who used to be lovers, living together, working together, eating together, showering and fucking together, and one betrays the other, betrayal makes the matter more meaner than murder. 'Cause you can just kill someone if you want to, no matter who you are. No matter who they are or where they hide. They bound to resurface eventually. Let down their guard eventually, and that's precisely when they can get got. But ex-lovers, who more than just creeping and fucking other niggas or bitches, where one betrayed the other, told a life-changing secret tat he or she had confided with, sold him or her out to his or her sworn enemy, called the cops on him or her for any damn reason, flipped on 'em in a court of law or was way-worser, like working as an undercover police, a bitch-ass informant, spying and telling on his or her lover, murder ain't enough get-back. A betrayed nigga or bitch wants to be the one who delivers the hurt over an extended period of time. Not a quick stabbing or gunning down. A betrayed lover wants to witness his or her traitor in severe loss of either: wealth, status, or something or someone he cherished. A betrayed lover wants to see the traitor in actual excruciating pain. He or she wants to taunt and torture first and then deliver the last blow that leads to the traitor's complete and final downfall.

I know. Bullet was the main one who betrayed me. He's at the top of my payback list. He was my nigga for many months before I got arrested. Yeah, he was a hustler. I fucking loved that. His fuck game was strong. I loved that too. Once he and I first hooked up, I never fucked around with no other nigga but him. I'm a loyal bitch. Loyalty runs through the Santiaga blood. But he never fully acknowledged my loyalty to him. He never gave his loyalty to me. It wasn't about me thinking, expecting, or believing that he was out fucking some random bitches while we was together. He didn't cause me to feel or think that he was. It was that he . . . I don't know. He loved me with his mind and body but never gave me his heart. He treated me like a suspect, who was bound to turn on him or turn him in. I wasn't. I'm the one bitch that wouldn't . . . ever, Santiagas are born snitch-free.

Bullet put our Manhattan condo in my name, and every purchase he made for both of us in my name. Back then, at the time, I thought that meant he loved me. Of course I did, he provided. In turn, I covered for him here and there. Held his coke, concealed his weapons, and carried his cash here and there quietly whenever he told me to. I was trying to earn my way up and also in, to his heart. I thought we should be on some Bonnie-and-Clyde shit. But fuck Bonnie and Clyde. We should be on some Winter-and-Bullet shit, stacking our chips and styling and fucking and eating and chilling and staying together.

Turned out, he put everything in my name not for love or for providing for a top bitch and daughter of legendary hustler and entrepreneur Ricky Santiaga. Instead Bullet was on some Brooklyn scheming. He made it so that if everything or anything went wrong, he could drop all the legalities and blame onto me without losing any street credibility because it wasn't like he snitched on me. He simply left a paper trail and documentation all in my name that told the fictitious story of me being the hustler and him being blameless, unarrestable, and scot-free. On the day of my arrest that led to my conviction as a drug dealer sentenced to serve fifteen years on a mandatory minimum, which at the time I had never even heard of, my nigga Bullet had a car rented with a credit card in my name. In the rental car was me and the product, I was 'bout to ride round trip to Virginia on a run with him, a big and necessary business move.

Simone, who for some reason can't get the fuck out of my mind or life or death story, saw me sitting there on our Brooklyn block in the rental waiting on Bullet. I didn't see her, though. Simone had bullshit beef with me that she swore was real. So, soon as she saw me that day, it was on. Bitch threw a brick through the rental window. Bitch dragged me out the car swinging. We thumped. My nigga Bullet saw the rah-rah from the distance. He started rushing over. He fired one shot in the air to cause the commotion to break. Seeing him boosted my confidence, but the gunshot distracted me from keeping my eyes on her. Simone took advantage and sliced my face. Bullet held my bleeding face in his hands. He sat me back in the rental car. He tossed the gun beneath the seat. He walked around to the driver's side. I was relieved that he had rescued me. But the furious fight and the gunshot drew out the cops.

The cops swooped in and Bullet, instead of jumping into the rental car and speeding away, walked off calmly as if he never was with me. Never even knew me and never intended to get in the car with me at all. I was arrested in the rental car that was in my name, with the weight stuffed inside teddy bears, and the weapon tossed beneath the seat. They cuffed, fingerprinted, mug-shotted, jailed, grilled, and investigated me. They asked me for names or just one big name. I gave them nothing. I rejected their bullshit tricks and game. The name is Santiaga, royalty not rats. I wasn't mad at Bullet for being a hustler, obviously. I wasn't mad at him for renting me the condo or even for taking me on his big business run to Virginia. I was down for him. I wanted to go. I didn't like being left out of the business or the action. It's that that nigga Bullet didn't come for me. He didn't add a dime to my legal defense. He didn't send one of his men to make sure I had all that I needed. He didn't put one cent on my commissary. He didn't write me one letter, slip me one kite from his peoples on lock. He didn't check for me and to me that meant he never loved me. That's why he's on my payback list. He betrayed me. I never betrayed him, not even once.

Now Momma was dead center in my mental line of vision. In that freeze-frame she was Brooklyn Momma, before the move to our luxurious Long Island mansion. Before some nigga who was jelly shot her in her face and permanently altered her perfect look. But most importantly, the picture of Momma in my mind was before she ever toked a hit of that crack pipe. I knew, after having fifteen years on lock to just sit and think about it, that for me to accept my mother, aka Momma, aka Lana Santiaga, aka the Baddest Bitch on the Planet, after her crack breakdown would be the same as rejecting myself. No! It would be the same as destroying myself. Brooklyn Momma was the voice in my head. She was the image in my eyes, my pattern, my fabric, my fashion. She was all of the ingredients mixed together that made me, *me*.

Momma was the most. She was the beautifulest, the livest, the baddest, the funniest, the finest, everything. *I didn't need no books.* Momma was all show-and-tell. She told me and showed me while she was telling me all that a bitch needs to know.

"Ooh now, that's not cool," she would say when I shitted in my diaper at age two. That's how way back my earliest memory of Momma goes. It is my first and earliest memory of anyone or anything, including myself. After Momma said that, she taught me how to pee and poop, where to pee and poop, and how to clean myself thoroughly and smell like a lady always should smell. "Come in the bathroom," she would wave me in. "Always close the door while you do your private business. And remember your private business and your business-business both ain't nobody else's business!" She would talk to me like I was an adult, and then laugh at herself. But I knew she meant it and I understood her perfectly. "No potty," she would say, kicking the baby toilet into a corner. "Sit on the real seat like I do," she would say, pointing. I would be trying my best to balance my little body on the adult toilet with the humongous hole. "Now tinkle!" she would say, like it was a magical thing, not just pissing in the bowl. While I tinkled, Momma would turn away and look at herself in the bathroom mirror while singing a song, which relaxed me. Momma had the dopest music collection of original singles and albums. She knew every song ever made from the oldest to the newest. In my first memory, she was singing "All I Need," an old joint that she loved. She was doing Marvin Gaye's part and Tammi Terrell's twisting and turning her body while fixed on her own reflection. She was singing so passionately I wondered. *Is she singing to Poppa? Or, is she singing to me? Or is she singing to herself?* After that first memory, I remember Momma singing "Everybody Is a Star" to me in the scented bubble bath as we bathed at the same time in the same tub. Momma was musical and Poppa had the whole house wired with speakers in every room, including the kitchen and the bathroom, so that Momma could be happy at home.

All fresh and clean, Momma is carrying me wrapped in the thickest, softest white terry-cloth towel to her bedroom. Both of us sitting on her king-sized bed, Momma would oil and powder and dress me. She'd comb through my silky hair like each strand was a thread of pure gold. "All good!" She would leap up and rush into her clothing closet, to the top shelf where she kept her collection of eye-catchers, showstoppers, high-fashion hats. She would carefully select one and put it on my little head, drowning me in it. "Tilt it like this! Lay it to the side!" she would cheer, as my little fingers attempted to adjust the hat to the style that was the only way a fashionable supastar like Momma would approve. Soon as I caught the right angle, Momma would be clicking her Kodak, or pressing out Polaroids of me that would end up on her wall of photos of everything Momma *loved the most.* That was us, *family.*

By the time I was six, Momma would play-dress me in her real clothes, with real bitch accessories, so that I could walk down the runway that Momma made in the apartment corridor which she lit up with colorful lamps and lights. I'd be killing the red carpet while the overhead speakers would be pouring out the sounds of Rod Stewart's "Da Ya Think I'm Sexy." I worked the runway to all Momma's music picks, which could be anything 'cause she knew everything musical. Donna Summer's "Hot Stuff," Grace Jones's "La Vie en Rose" or "Slave to the Rhythm." Momma loved Grace Jones. Momma loved anyone and everything that she loved to the fullest. She was the loyalest woman on Earth to anything or anyone who she chose. Momma marked time and her favorite memories through music. She loved to tell me her coming-up stories. When she would be narrating them to me it seemed she was more excited hearing the stories she was telling, even though she knew them all already, and had told them to me or Poppa more than once before. She never sat still when she was saying her stories. She was all movement, demonstrating, gesturing, and re-enacting. She told me I was born a product of two songs, Betty Wright's "Tonight Is the Night." She wouldn't sing the whole song, just certain lines to highlight and prove that this song was her story. Momma said Betty Wright's song was the soundtrack to her fourteen-years-young first love, first intimacy, first sexual experience with the one and only Poppa. She'd be acting like she could feel herself giving up her virginity right while she was telling the story. She squeezed her eyes tight in anticipation, clamped her legs together like she was really nervous, and even had sound effects like *ooooh* and *wooo* and *oh yeah!* The other record that made me happen, according to Momma, was Rod Stewart's "Tonight's the Night," 'cause he was cool, sexy, and smooth, and only Santiaga was sexier, smoother, and cooler than Rod without having to sing one note.

Momma had more style, got more looks, and had more wigs than the Supremes. She could rock it long and silky to the back of her thighs, or wear blunt cuts, short beautiful bobs, or her own hair in swirls of finger waves. She threw me big birthday parties, which could not be called just "parties" cause they were major events that niggas from Bk to Bx fought to get invited to. Many of the people who showed up I did not even know, even though the celebration was for me! After the huge crowd went home, when only family remained gathered in the ballroom, Momma would emerge dressed up on some karaoke-type vibe. She'd be Tina Turner and somehow lured Poppa into dressing like he was Ike. He didn't sing though, he just laid back and let Momma mesmerize him with her high energy and vibrant personality. No matter how she freaked it, Momma was larger than life and glowed more than any worldwide superstar.

That's right. Momma taught me how to talk, by always talking to me and singing to me. Come to think of it, hip-hop was Momma remixed, sampled, looped, slowed down and sped up with a dope-ass beat beneath it. Momma is the reason why I love hip-hop, memorized it like I memorized Momma, and moved my hips to it, up until this day, dead or alive.

Momma taught me how to walk, whether it was on her homemade runway, up and down the project steps, or on the stoops, cement streets, or curbs. Momma taught me how to stand, style, and strike a pose. Momma taught me body and style language. How to talk without ever saying a word. How to capture and wear the prettiest, most stylish meanest fashions, so I would never have to tell a next bitch anything. She would just stay the fuck back or back the fuck off because she knew beside me is not where she belonged. Momma taught me how to choose friends, and be so badass that they would choose to bow down to my look without me asking or having to be snobby or shitty about it. What to share and not share. What to give away and never accept back. What to keep and never allow anyone to touch, beg for, or borrow.